Four Great
Restoration Comedies

DOVER · **GIANT THRIFT** · EDITIONS

Four Great
Restoration Comedies

THE COUNTRY WIFE *by William Wycherley*
THE MAN OF MODE *by Sir George Etherege*
THE ROVER *by Aphra Behn*
THE RELAPSE *by Sir John Vanbrugh*

DOVER PUBLICATIONS, INC.
Mineola, New York

DOVER GIANT THRIFT EDITIONS

GENERAL EDITOR: MARY CAROLYN WALDREP
EDITOR OF THIS VOLUME: JANET BAINE KOPITO

Bibliographical Note

This Dover edition, first published in 2005, contains the unabridged texts from standard editions of *The Country Wife* by William Wycherley; *The Man of Mode* by Sir George Etherege; *The Rover* by Aphra Behn; and *The Relapse* by Sir John Vanbrugh. An Introductory Note has been specially prepared for the present edition.

Library of Congress Cataloging-in-Publication Data

Four great Restoration comedies / William Wycherley and others.
    p. cm. — (Dover giant thrift editions)
  ISBN 0-486-44570-4 (pbk.)
    1. English drama—Restoration, 1660–1700. 2. English drama (Comedy) I. Dover Publications, Inc. II. Series.

PR1266.F673 2005
822'.052308—dc22

2005050091

Manufactured in the United States of America
Dover Publications, Inc., 31 East 2nd Street, Mineola, N.Y. 11501

Note

In 1660, the Protectorate, the ruling power in England, gave way to the Restoration, during which Charles II was called back from his lengthy European exile and the monarchy was restored (Charles had departed England after Oliver Cromwell, the dictatorial Lord Protector, had defeated him in 1651, the close of the English Civil War). Amid tensions regarding the role of religion in English society and the governing power of Parliament, London was also exposed to the hardships of the Great Plague of 1665 and the Great Fire of London (1666).

Nevertheless, the latter part of the seventeenth century was an extremely fertile period for English literature. Fiction, journalism, and especially drama flourished during this time. Charles II, an enthusiastic theatergoer, encouraged drama productions in London, leading to a proliferation of new plays, as well as the reopening of the theaters themselves after a ban instituted under the Puritans. Notable Restoration dramatists include William Wycherley, Sir George Etherege, Aphra Behn, and Sir John Vanbrugh, all represented by their finest achievements in this collection. To a great extent, the concerns of the plays reflected those of the court and of the upper classes—Charles's social milieu and an important component of the theatergoing public.

The comedy of manners, as perfected by the preeminent French playwright Molière (1622–1673), was an important influence on the work of the Restoration dramatists. The English writers featured bawdy, risqué plot devices, witty dialogue, and double entendres aplenty in their comic treatments of the relations between the sexes and the behavior of the upper crust of society. The artifice of courtly behavior provided many opportunities for witty repartee as well.

A common element of numerous Restoration comedies was the rake—a stylish gentleman whose contempt for society's conventions provided opportunities for farce and cruel game-playing. In *The Country Wife*, by William Wycherley (ca. 1640–1716), a predatory rake attempts (and succeeds) in seducing the wives of a number of gullible husbands. His pursuits take an unexpected turn after his encounter with a supposedly ingenuous country wife, whose jealous, abusive husband proclaims, "If we do not cheat women, they'll cheat us." The notion that marriage is anything but sacrosanct among the privileged classes is frequently played upon—in fact, most of the characters in *The Country Wife* are willing participants in cheating of one sort or another. *The Man of Mode*, by Sir George Etherege (1635–1692), displays the influence of Molière in its satirical treatment of the upper classes. As London and its social whirl are the center of all things desirable, a reference is made to a woman who is supposed to be an "awkward, ill-fashioned country toad" (not the case at all). Another common element in Restoration comedy was the fop, whose slavish adherence to style is presented by Etherege in the character of Sir Fopling Flutter.

Women were beginning to achieve success as professional playwrights in England during the late seventeenth century, and Aphra Behn (1640–1689) is an outstanding example with her play *The Rover.* Inspired by earlier plays, including Sir Thomas Killigrew's *Thomaso, or the Wanderer* (1654), Behn presents to the audience a rake bent on seduction; however, unlike Wycherley, Behn delves beneath the witticisms to provide more weighty interactions; in addition, she portrays women as pursuers rather than prey.

The final play in the quartet presented here is *The Relapse,* by Sir John Vanbrugh (1664–1726). Vanbrugh wrote this work as a sequel to Colley Cibber's *Love's Last Shift* (1696). The supposedly repentant rake in the earlier play is examined more closely by the doubting Vanbrugh for a "relapse" from his good intentions. English dramatists delighted in using descriptive names to identify certain characters, and Cibber's/Vanbrugh's rake's name is Loveless; other comedic examples in this play are Mr. Smirk (a parson), Coupler (a matchmaker), and Sir Novelty Fashion.

The scrutiny to which the manners and mores of the English leisure class and court was subjected during the Restoration eventually diminished as the theatrical audiences expanded to include more of the middle class. By the close of the seventeenth century, calls for reform of the stage were being voiced—Jeremy Collier, a clergyman, published his *Short View of the Immorality and Profaneness of the English Stage* (1698), an indication that tolerance for the notoriously bawdy goings-on of Restoration comedy was on the wane.

The dates of the plays' first performances are as follows: *The Country Wife,* 1675; *The Man of Mode,* 1676; *The Rover,* 1677; *The Relapse,* 1696.

Contents

The Country Wife

William Wycherley

Dramatis Personae

MR. HORNER
MR. HARCOURT
MR. DORILANT
MR. PINCHWIFE
MR. SPARKISH
SIR JASPER FIDGET
MRS. MARGERY PINCHWIFE
MRS. ALITHEA
LADY FIDGET
MRS. DAINTY FIDGET
MRS. SQUEAMISH
OLD LADY SQUEAMISH
LUCY, *Alithea's Maid*
A Boy
A Quack
Waiters, Servants, and Attendants

SCENE—*London*

Indignior quicquam reprehendi, non quia crassè
Compositum illepideve putetur, sed quia nuper:
Nec veniam Antiquis, sed honorem & præmia posci.
HORAT.[1]

PROLOGUE

Spoken by MR. HORNER

Poets, like cudgell'd bullies, never do
At first or second blow submit to you;
But will provoke you still, and ne'er have done,
Till you are weary first with laying on.
The late so baffled scribbler of this day,
Though he stands trembling, bids me boldly say,
What we before most plays are us'd to do,
For poets out of fear first draw on you;
In a fierce prologue the still pit defy,
And, ere you speak, like Castril give the lie.
But though our Bayes's battles oft I've fought,
And with bruis'd knuckles their dear conquests bought;
Nay, never yet fear'd odds upon the stage,
In prologue dare not hector with the age,
But would take quarter from your saving hands,
Though Bayes within all yielding countermands,
Says you confed'rate wits no quarter give,
Therefore his play shan't ask your leave to live.
Well, let the vain rash fop, by huffing so,
Think to obtain the better terms of you;
But we, the actors, humbly will submit,

---

[1] I hate to see something criticized not on the grounds that it is clumsy and inelegant, but simply because it is modern. I hate to see people demand not merely indulgence for the older writers, but the actual prerogative of idolatry.—Horace, *Epistles,* 1,1, 76–78.

Now, and at any time, to a full pit;
Nay, often we anticipate your rage,
And murder poets for you on our stage:
We set no guards upon our tiring-room,
But when with flying colours there you come,
We patiently, you see, give up to you
Our poets, virgins, nay, our matrons too.

ACT I

Enter HORNER, *and* QUACK *following him at a distance*

HORN. [*aside*]   A quack is as fit for a pimp as a midwife for a bawd; they are still but in their way, both helpers of nature.—— [*aloud*] Well, my dear Doctor, hast thou done what I desired?

QUACK.   I have undone you for ever with the women, and reported you throughout the whole town as bad as an eunuch, with as much trouble as if I had made you one in earnest.

HORN.   But have you told all the midwives you know, the orange wenches at the playhouses, the city husbands, and old fumbling keepers of this end of the town, for they'll be the readiest to report it?

QUACK.   I have told all the chambermaids, waiting-women, tire-women, and old women of my acquaintance; nay, and whispered it as a secret to 'em, and to the whisperers of Whitehall; so that you need not doubt 'twill spread, and you will be as odious to the handsome young women as——

HORN.   As the small-pox. Well——

QUACK.   And to the married women of this end of the town, as——

HORN.   As the great ones; nay, as their own husbands.

QUACK.   And to the city dames, as aniseed Robin, of filthy and contemptible memory; and they will frighten their children with your name, especially their females.

HORN.   And cry, Horner's coming to carry you away. I am only afraid 'twill not be believed. You told 'em 'twas by an English-French disaster, and an English-French chirurgeon, who has given me at once not only a cure, but an antidote for the future against that damned malady, and that worse distemper, love, and all other women's evils?

QUACK.   Your late journey into France has made it the more credible, and your being here a fortnight before you appeared in public looks as if you apprehended the shame, which I wonder you do not. Well, I have been hired by young gallants to belie 'em t'other way, but you are the first would be thought a man unfit for women.

HORN. Dear Mr. Doctor, let vain rogues be contented only to be thought abler men than they are; generally 'tis all the pleasure they have, but mine lies another way.

QUACK. You take, methinks, a very preposterous way to it, and as ridiculous as if we operators in physic should put forth bills to disparage our medicaments, with hopes to gain customers.

HORN. Doctor, there are quacks in love as well as physic, who get but the fewer and worse patients for their boasting; a good name is seldom got by giving it one's self; and women no more than honour are compassed by bragging. Come, come, Doctor, the wisest lawyer never discovers the merits of his cause till the trial; the wealthiest man conceals his riches, and the cunning gamester his play. Shy husbands and keepers, like old rooks, are not to be cheated but by a new unpractised trick: false friendship will pass now no more than false dice upon 'em; no, not in the city.

Enter Boy

BOY. There are two ladies and a gentleman coming up.   [*exit*]

HORN. A pox! some unbelieving sisters of my former acquaintance, who, I am afraid, expect their sense should be satisfied of the falsity of the report. No—this formal fool and women!

Enter SIR JASPER FIDGET, LADY FIDGET, *and* MRS. DAINTY FIDGET

QUACK. His wife and sister.

SIR JASP. My coach breaking just now before your door, Sir, I look upon as an occasional reprimand to me, Sir, for not kissing your hands, Sir, since your coming out of France, Sir; and so my disaster, Sir, has been my good fortune, Sir; and this is my wife and sister, Sir.

HORN. What then, Sir?

SIR JASP. My lady, and sister, Sir.—Wife, this is Master Horner.

LADY FID. Master Horner, husband!

SIR JASP. My lady, my Lady Fidget, Sir.

HORN. So, Sir.

SIR JASP. Won't you be acquainted with her, Sir?—[*aside*] So, the report is true, I find, by his coldness or aversion to the sex; but I'll play the wag with him.—Pray salute my wife, my lady, Sir.

HORN. I will kiss no man's wife, Sir, for him, Sir; I have taken my eternal leave, Sir, of the sex already, Sir.

SIR JASP. [*aside*] Ha! ha! ha! I'll plague him yet.——Not know my wife, Sir?

HORN. I do not know your wife, Sir; she's a woman, Sir, and consequently a monster, Sir, a greater monster than a husband, Sir.

SIR JASP. A husband! how, Sir?

HORN.   So, Sir; but I make no more cuckolds, Sir.   [*makes horns*]

SIR JASP.   Ha! ha! ha! Mercury! Mercury!

LADY FID.   Pray, Sir Jasper, let us be gone from this rude fellow.

MRS. DAIN.   Who, by his breeding, would think he had ever been in France?

LADY FID.   Foh! he's but too much a French fellow, such as hate women of quality and virtue for their love to their husbands, Sir Jasper; a woman is hated by 'em as much for loving her husband as for loving their money. But pray, let's be gone.

HORN.   You do well, Madam, for I have nothing that you came for: I have brought over not so much as a bawdy picture, no new postures, nor the second part of the *Escole des Filles;* nor——

QUACK. [*apart to* HORNER]   Hold, for shame, Sir! what d'ye mean? You will ruin yourself for ever with the sex——

SIR JASP.   Ha! ha! ha! he hates women perfectly, I find.

MRS. DAIN.   What pity 'tis he should!

LADY FID.   Ay, he's a base fellow for't. But affectation makes not a woman more odious to them than virtue.

HORN.   Because your virtue is your greatest affectation, Madam.

LADY FID.   How, you saucy fellow! would you wrong my honour?

HORN.   If I could.

LADY FID.   How d'ye mean, Sir?

SIR JASP.   Ha! ha! ha! no, he can't wrong your Ladyship's honour, upon my honour; he, poor man—hark you in your ear—a mere eunuch.

LADY FID.   O filthy French beast! foh! foh! why do we stay? let's be gone: I can't endure the sight of him.

SIR JASP.   Stay but till the chairs come; they'll be here presently.

LADY FID.   No, no.

SIR JASP.   Nor can I stay longer. 'Tis—let me see, a quarter and a half quarter of a minute past eleven. The council will be sat; I must away. Business must be preferred always before love and ceremony with the wise, Mr. Horner.

HORN.   And the impotent, Sir Jasper.

SIR JASP.   Ay, ay, the impotent, Master Horner; ha! ha! ha!

LADY FID.   What, leave us with a filthy man alone in his lodgings?

SIR JASP.   He's an innocent man now, you know. Pray stay, I'll hasten the chairs to you.—— Mr. Horner, your servant; I should be glad to see you at my house. Pray come and dine with me, and play at cards with my wife after dinner; you are fit for women at that game yet, ha! ha!—[*aside*] 'Tis as much a husband's prudence to provide innocent diversion for a wife as to hinder her unlawful pleasures; and he had better employ her than let her employ herself.—— Farewell.

HORN.   Your servant, Sir Jasper.   [*exit* SIR JASPER]

LADY FID.   I will not stay with him, foh!——

HORN.   Nay, Madam, I beseech you stay, if it be but to see I can be as civil to ladies yet as they would desire.

LADY FID.   No, no, foh! you cannot be civil to ladies.

MRS. DAIN.   You as civil as ladies would desire?

LADY FID.   No, no, no, foh! foh! foh!

[*exeunt* LADY FIDGET *and* MRS. DAINTY FIDGET]

QUACK.   Now, I think, I, or you yourself, rather, have done your business with the women.

HORN.   Thou art an ass. Don't you see already, upon the report and my carriage, this grave man of business leaves his wife in my lodgings, invites me to his house and wife, who before would not be acquainted with me out of jealousy?

QUACK.   Nay, by this means you may be the more acquainted with the husbands, but the less with the wives.

HORN.   Let me alone; if I can but abuse the husbands, I'll soon disabuse the wives. Stay—I'll reckon you up the advantages I am like to have by my stratagem. First, I shall be rid of all my old acquaintances, the most insatiable sorts of duns, that invade our lodgings in a morning; and next to the pleasure of making a new mistress is that of being rid of an old one, and of all old debts. Love, when it comes to be so, is paid the most unwillingly.

QUACK.   Well, you may be so rid of your old acquaintances; but how will you get any new ones?

HORN.   Doctor, thou wilt never make a good chemist, thou art so incredulous and impatient. Ask but all the young fellows of the town if they do not lose more time, like huntsmen, in starting the game, than in running it down. One knows not where to find 'em, who will or will not. Women of quality are so civil you can hardly distinguish love from good breeding, and a man is often mistaken: but now I can be sure she that shows an aversion to me loves the sport, as those women that are gone, whom I warrant to be right. And then the next thing is, your women of honour, as you call 'em, are only chary of their reputations, not their persons; and 'tis scandal they would avoid, not men. Now may I have, by the reputation of an eunuch, the privileges of one, and be seen in a lady's chamber in a morning as early as her husband; kiss virgins before their parents or lovers; and maybe, in short, the *passe-partout* of the town. Now, Doctor.

QUACK.   Nay, now you shall be the doctor, and your process is so new that we do not know but it may succeed.

HORN.   Not so new neither; *probatum est*, Doctor.

QUACK.   Well, I wish you luck, and many patients, whilst I go to mine.   [*exit*]

Enter HARCOURT *and* DORILANT *to* HORNER

HAR.   Come, your appearance at the play yesterday has, I hope, hardened you for the future against the women's contempt and the men's raillery; and now you'll abroad as you were wont.

HORN.   Did I not bear it bravely?

DOR.   With a most theatrical impudence, nay, more than the orange-wenches show there, or a drunken vizard-mask, or a great-bellied actress; nay, or the most impudent of creatures, an ill poet; or what is yet more impudent, a second-hand critic.

HORN.   But what say the ladies? have they no pity?

HAR.   What ladies? The vizard-masks, you know, never pity a man when all's gone, though in their service.

DOR.   And for the women in the boxes, you'd never pity them when 'twas in your power.

HAR.   They say 'tis pity but all that deal with common women should be served so.

DOR.   Nay, I dare swear they won't admit you to play at cards with them, go to plays with 'em, or do the little duties which other shadows of men are wont to do for 'em.

HORN.   What do you call shadows of men?

DOR.   Half-men.

HORN.   What, boys?

DOR.   Ay, your old boys, old *beaux garçons*, who, like superannuated stallions, are suffered to run, feed, and whinny with the mares as long as they live, though they can do nothing else.

HORN.   Well, a pox on love and wenching! Women serve but to keep a man from better company. Though I can't enjoy them, I shall you the more. Good fellowship and friendship are lasting, rational, and manly pleasures.

HAR.   For all that, give me some of those pleasures you call effeminate too; they help to relish one another.

HORN.   They disturb one another.

HAR.   No, mistresses are like books. If you pore upon them too much, they doze you, and make you unfit for company; but if used discreetly, you are the fitter for conversation by 'em.

DOR.   A mistress should be like a little country retreat near the town; not to dwell in constantly, but only for a night and away, to taste the town the better when a man returns.

HORN.   I tell you, 'tis as hard to be a good fellow, a good friend, and a lover of women, as 'tis to be a good fellow, a good friend, and a lover of money. You cannot follow both, then choose your side. Wine gives you liberty, loves takes it away.

DOR.   Gad, he's in the right on't.

HORN.   Wine gives you joy; love, grief and tortures, besides the chirurgeon's. Wine makes us witty; love, only sots. Wine makes us sleep; love breaks it.

DOR.   By the world, he has reason, Harcourt.

HORN.   Wine makes——

DOR.   Ay, wine makes us—makes us princes; love makes us beggars, poor rogues, egad—and wine——

HORN.   So, there's one converted.—No, no, love and wine, oil and vinegar.

HAR.   I grant it; love will still be uppermost.

HORN.   Come, for my part, I will have only those glorious manly pleasures of being very drunk and very slovenly.

Enter Boy

BOY.   Mr. Sparkish is below, Sir.   [*exit*]

HAR.   What, my dear friend! a rogue that is fond of me, only I think, for abusing him.

DOR.   No, he can no more think the men laugh at him than that women jilt him, his opinion of himself is so good.

HORN.   Well, there's another pleasure by drinking I thought not of— I shall lose his acquaintance, because he cannot drink: and you know 'tis a very hard thing to be rid of him; for he's one of those nauseous offerers at wit, who, like the worst fiddlers, run themselves into all companies.

HAR.   One that, by being in the company of men of sense, would pass for one.

HORN.   And may so to the short-sighted world, as a false jewel amongst true ones is not discerned at a distance. His company is as troublesome to us as a cuckold's when you have a mind to his wife's.

HAR.   No, the rogue will not let us enjoy one another, but ravishes our conversation, though he signifies no more to't than Sir Martin Marall's gaping, and awkward thrumming upon the lute, does to his man's voice and music.

DOR.   And to pass for a wit in town shows himself a fool every night to us, that are guilty of the plot.

HORN.   Such wits as he are, to a company of reasonable men, like rooks to the gamesters, who only fill a room at the table, but are so far from contributing to the play, that they only serve to spoil the fancy of those that do.

DOR.   Nay, they are used like rooks too, snubbed, checked, and abused; yet the rogues will hang on.

HORN.   A pox on 'em, and all that force nature, and would be still what she forbids 'em! Affectation is her greatest monster.

HAR.   Most men are the contraries to that they would seem. Your bully, you see, is a coward with a long sword; the little humbly fawning physician, with his ebony cane, is he that destroys men.

DOR.'   The usurer, a poor rogue, possessed of mouldy bonds and mortgages; and we they call spendthrifts are only wealthy who lay out his money upon daily new purchases of pleasure.

HORN.   Ay, your arrantest cheat is your trustee or executor, your jealous man, the greatest cuckold, your churchman the greatest atheist, and your noisy pert rogue of a wit, the greatest fop, dullest ass, and worst company, as you shall see; for here he comes.

Enter SPARKISH

SPARK.   How is't, sparks? how is't? Well, faith, Harry, I must rally thee a little, ha! ha! ha! upon the report in town of thee, ha! ha! I can't hold i'faith; shall I speak?

HORN.   Yes; but you'll be so bitter then.

SPARK.   Honest Dick and Frank here shall answer for me, I will not be extreme bitter, by the universe.

HAR.   We will be bound in a ten-thousand-pound bond, he shall not be bitter at all.

DOR.   Nor sharp, nor sweet.

HORN.   What, not downright insipid?

SPARK.   Nay then, since you are so brisk, and provoke me, take what follows. You must know, I was discoursing and rallying with some ladies yesterday, and they happened to talk of the fine new signs in town.

HORN.   Very fine ladies, I believe.

SPARK.   Said I, I know where the best new sign is.—Where? says one of the ladies.—In Covent Garden, I replied.—Said another, In what street?—In Russel Street, answered I.—Lord, says another, I'm sure there was ne'er a fine new sign there yesterday.—Yes, but there was, said I again, and it came out of France, and has been there a fortnight.

DOR.   A pox! I can hear no more, prithee.

HORN.   No, hear him out; let him tune his crowd a while.

HAR.   The worst music, the greatest preparation.

SPARK.   Nay, faith, I'll make you laugh.—It cannot be, says a third lady.—Yes, yes, quoth I again.—Says a fourth lady——

HORN.   Look to't, we'll have no more ladies.

SPARK.   No—then mark, mark, now. Said I to the fourth, Did you never see Mr. Horner? he lodges in Russel Street, and he's a sign of a man, you know, since he came out of France; ha! ha! ha!

HORN.   But the devil take me if thine be the sign of a jest.

SPARK.   With that they all fell a-laughing, till they bepissed themselves. What, but it does not move you, methinks? Well, I see one had as good go to law without a witness, as break a jest without a laugher on one's side.——Come, come, sparks, but where do we dine? I have left at Whitehall an earl to dine with you.

DOR.   Why, I thought thou hadst loved a man with a title better than a suit with a French trimming to't.

HAR.   Go to him again.

SPARK.   No, Sir, a wit to me is the greatest title in the world.

HORN.   But go dine with your earl, Sir; he may be exceptious. We are your friends, and will not take it ill to be left, I do assure you.

HAR.   Nay, faith, he shall go to him.

SPARK.   Nay, pray, gentlemen.

DOR.   We'll thrust you out, if you won't; what, disappoint anybody for us?

SPARK.   Nay, dear gentlemen, hear me.

HORN.   No, no, Sir, by no means; pray go, Sir.

SPARK.   Why, dear rogues——

DOR.   No, no.   [*they all thrust him out of the room*]

ALL.   Ha! ha! ha!

SPARKISH *returns*

SPARK.   But, sparks, pray hear me. What, d'ye think I'll eat then with gay shallow fops and silent coxcombs? I think wit as necessary at dinner as a glass of good wine, and that's the reason I never have any stomach when I eat alone.—Come, but where do we dine?

HORN.   Even where you will.

SPARK.   At Chateline's?

DOR.   Yes, if you will.

SPARK.   Or at the Cock?

DOR.   Yes, if you please.

SPARK.   Or at the Dog and Partridge?

HORN.   Ay, if you have a mind to't; for we shall dine at neither.

SPARK.   Pshaw! with your fooling we shall lose the new play; and I would no more miss seeing a new play the first day, than I would miss sitting in the wits' row. Therefore I'll go fetch my mistress, and away.

[*exit*]

Manent HORNER, HARCOURT, DORILANT: *enter to them* MR. PINCHWIFE

HORN.   Who have we here? Pinchwife?

PINCH.   Gentlemen, your humble servant.

HORN.   Well, Jack, by thy long absence from the town, the grumness of thy countenance, and the slovenliness of thy habit, I should give thee joy, should I not, of marriage?

PINCH. [*aside*]   Death! does he know I'm married too? I thought to

have concealed it from him at least.——My long stay in the country will
excuse my dress; and I have a suit of law that brings me up to town, that
puts me out of humour. Besides, I must give Sparkish to-morrow five
thousand pound to lie with my sister.

HORN.   Nay, you country gentlemen, rather than not purchase, will
buy anything; and he is a cracked title, if we may quibble. Well, but am I
to give thee joy? I heard thou wert married.

PINCH.   What then?

HORN.   Why, the next thing that is to be heard is, thou'rt a cuckold.

PINCH. [*aside*]   Insupportable name!

HORN.   But I did not expect marriage from such a whoremaster as
you, one that knew the town so much, and women so well.

PINCH.   Why, I have married no London wife.

HORN.   Pshaw! that's all one. That grave circumspection in marrying
a country wife, is like refusing a deceitful pampered Smithfield jade, to
go and be cheated by a friend in the country.

PINCH. [*aside*]   A pox on him and his simile!——At least we are a little surer of the breed there, know what her keeping has been, whether
foiled or unsound.

HORN.   Come, come, I have known a clap gotten in Wales; and there
are cuzens, justices' clerks, and chaplains in the country, I won't say
coachmen. But she's handsome and young?

PINCH. [*aside*]   I'll answer as I should do.——No, no; she has no
beauty but her youth, no attraction but her modesty: wholesome,
homely, and huswifely; that's all.

DOR.   He talks as like a grazier as he looks.

PINCH.   She's too awkward, ill-favoured, and silly to bring to town.

HAR.   Then methinks you should bring her to be taught breeding.

PINCH.   To be taught! no, Sir, I thank you. Good wives and private
soldiers should be ignorant—I'll keep her from your instructions, I warrant you.

HAR. [*aside*]   The rogue is as jealous as if his wife were not ignorant.

HORN.   Why, if she be ill-favoured, there will be less danger here for
you than by leaving her in the country. We have such variety of dainties
that we are seldom hungry.

DOR.   But they have always coarse, constant, swingeing stomachs in
the country.

HAR.   Foul feeders indeed!

DOR.   And your hospitality is great there.

HAR.   Open house; every man's welcome.

PINCH.   So, so, gentlemen.

HORN.   But prithee, why wouldst thou marry her? If she be ugly, ill-
bred, and silly, she must be rich then.

PINCH.   As rich as if she brought me twenty thousand pound out of this town; for she'll be as sure not to spend her moderate portion as a London baggage would be to spend hers, let it be what it would: so 'tis all one. Then, because she's ugly, she's the likelier to be my own; and being ill-bred, she'll hate conversation; and since silly and innocent, will not know the difference betwixt a man of one-and-twenty and one of forty.

HORN.   Nine—to my knowledge. But if she be silly, she'll expect as much from a man of forty-nine, as from him of one-and-twenty. But me-thinks wit is more necessary than beauty; and I think no young woman ugly that has it, and no handsome woman agreeable without it.

PINCH.   'Tis my maxim, he's a fool that marries; but he's a greater that does not marry a fool. What is wit in a wife good for, but to make a man a cuckold?

HORN.   Yes, to keep it from his knowledge.

PINCH.   A fool cannot contrive to make her husband a cuckold.

HORN.   No; but she'll club with a man that can: and what is worse, if she cannot make her husband a cuckold, she'll make him jealous, and pass for one: and then 'tis all one.

PINCH.   Well, well, I'll take care for one. My wife shall make me no cuckold, though she had your help, Mr. Horner. I understand the town, Sir.

DOR. [aside]   His help!

HAR. [aside]   He's come newly to town, it seems, and has not heard how things are with him.

HORN.   But tell me, has marriage cured thee of whoring, which it seldom does?

HAR.   'Tis more than age can do.

HORN.   No, the word is, I'll marry and live honest: but a marriage vow is like a penitent gamester's oath, and entering into bonds and penal-ties to stint himself to such a particular small sum at play for the future, which makes him but the more eager; and not being able to hold out, loses his money again, and his forfeit to boot.

DOR.   Ay, ay, a gamester will be a gamester whilst his money lasts, and a whoremaster whilst his vigour.

HAR.   Nay, I have known 'em, when they are broke, and can lose no more, keep a-fumbling with the box in their hands to fool with only, and hinder other gamesters.

DOR.   That had wherewithal to make lusty stakes.

PINCH.   Well, gentlemen, you may laugh at me; but you shall never lie with my wife: I know the town.

HORN.   But prithee, was not the way you were in better? is not keeping better than marriage?

PINCH. A pox on't! the jades would jilt me, I could never keep a whore to myself.

HORN. So, then you only married to keep a whore to yourself. Well, but let me tell you, women, as you say, are like soldiers, made constant and loyal by good pay, rather than by oaths and covenants. Therefore I'd advise my friends to keep rather than marry, since too I find, by your example, it does not serve one's turn; for I saw you yesterday in the eighteen-penny place with a pretty country wench.

PINCH. [*aside*] How the devil! did he see my wife then? I sat there that she might not be seen. But she shall never go to a play again.

HORN. What! dost thou blush at nine-and-forty for having been seen with a wench?

DOR. No, faith, I warrant 'twas his wife, which he seated there out of sight; for he's a cunning rogue, and understands the town.

HAR. He blushes. Then 'twas his wife; for men are now more ashamed to be seen with them in public than with a wench.

PINCH. [*aside*] Hell and damnation! I'm undone, since Horner has seen her, and they know 'twas she.

HORN. But prithee, was it thy wife? She was exceedingly pretty: I was in love with her at that distance.

PINCH. You are like never to be nearer to her. Your servant, gentle-men. [*offers to go*]

HORN. Nay, prithee stay.

PINCH. I cannot; I will not.

HORN. Come, you shall dine with us.

PINCH. I have dined already.

HORN. Come, I know thou hast not: I'll treat thee, dear rogue; thou shalt spend none of thy Hampshire money to-day.

PINCH. [*aside*] Treat me! So, he uses me already like his cuckold.

HORN. Nay, you shall not go.

PINCH. I must; I have business at home. [*exit*]

HAR. To beat his wife. He's as jealous of her as a Cheapside husband of a Covent Garden wife.

HORN. Why, 'tis as hard to find an old whoremaster without jeal-ousy and the gout, as a young one without fear or the pox.

As gout in age from pox in youth proceeds,
So wenching past, then jealousy succeeds;
The worst disease that love and wenching breeds.

[*exeunt*]

ACT II

MRS. MARGERY PINCHWIFE *and* ALITHEA.
PINCHWIFE *peeping behind at the door*

MRS. PINCH.   Pray, Sister, where are the best fields and woods to walk in, in London?

ALITH.   A pretty question!—Why, Sister, Mulberry Garden and St. James's Park; and, for close walks, the New Exchange.

MRS. PINCH.   Pray, Sister, tell me why my husband looks so grum here in town, and keeps me up so close, and will not let me go a-walking, nor let me wear my best gown yesterday.

ALITH.   Oh, he's jealous, Sister.

MRS. PINCH.   Jealous! what's that?

ALITH.   He's afraid you should love another man.

MRS. PINCH.   How should he be afraid of my loving another man, when he will not let me see any but himself?

ALITH.   Did he not carry you yesterday to a play?

MRS. PINCH.   Ay; but we sat amongst ugly people. He would not let me come near the gentry, who sat under us, so that I could not see 'em. He told me none but naughty women sat there, whom they toused and moused. But I would have ventured, for all that.

ALITH.   But how did you like the play?

MRS. PINCH.   Indeed I was weary of the play, but I liked hugeously the actors. They are the goodliest, properest men, Sister!

ALITH.   Oh, but you must not like the actors, Sister.

MRS. PINCH.   Ay, how should I help it, Sister? Pray, Sister, when my husband comes in, will you ask leave for me to go a-walking?

ALITH. [*aside*]   A-walking! ha! ha! Lord, a country-gentlewoman's leisure is the drudgery of a footpost; and she requires as much airing as her husband's horses.——But here comes your husband: I'll ask, though I'm sure he'll not grant it.

MRS. PINCH.   He says he won't let me go abroad for fear of catching the pox.

ALITH.   Fy! the small-pox you should say.

15

Enter PINCHWIFE *to them*

MRS. PINCH.   O my dear, dear bud, welcome home! Why dost thou look so fropish? who has nangered thee?

PINCH.   You're a fool.   [MRS. PINCHWIFE *goes aside, and cries*]

ALITH.   Faith, so she is, for crying for no fault, poor tender creature!

PINCH.   What, you would have her as impudent as yourself, as arrant a jillflirt, a gadder, a magpie; and to say all, a mere notorious town-woman?

ALITH.   Brother, you are my only censurer; and the honour of your family will sooner suffer in your wife there than in me, though I take the innocent liberty of the town.

PINCH.   Hark you, mistress, do not talk so before my wife.—The innocent liberty of the town!

ALITH.   Why, pray, who boasts of any intrigue with me? what lampoon has made my name notorious? what ill women frequent my lodgings? I keep no company with any women of scandalous reputations.

PINCH.   No, you keep the men of scandalous reputations company.

ALITH.   Where? would you not have me civil? answer 'em in a box at the plays, in the drawing-room at Whitehall, in St. James's Park, Mulberry Garden, or——

PINCH.   Hold, hold! Do not teach my wife where the men are to be found: I believe she's the worse for your town-documents already. I bid you keep her in ignorance, as I do.

MRS. PINCH.   Indeed, be not angry with her, bud, she will tell me nothing of the town, though I ask her a thousand times a day.

PINCH.   Then you are very inquisitive to know, I find?

MRS. PINCH.   Not I indeed, dear; I hate London. Our place-house in the country is worth a thousand of 't: would I were there again!

PINCH.   So you shall, I warrant. But were you not talking of plays and players when I came in?——You are her encourager in such discourses.

MRS. PINCH.   No, indeed, dear; she chid me just now for liking the playermen.

PINCH. [*aside*]   Nay, if she be so innocent as to own to me her liking them, there is no hurt in't.——Come, my poor rogue, but thou lik'st none better than me?

MRS. PINCH.   Yes, indeed, but I do. The playermen are finer folks.

PINCH.   But you love none better than me?

MRS. PINCH.   You are my own dear bud, and I know you. I hate a stranger.

PINCH.   Ay, my dear, you must love me only, and not be like the naughty town-women, who only hate their husbands, and love every man else; love plays, visits, fine coaches, fine clothes, fiddles, balls, treats, and so lead a wicked town-life.

MRS. PINCH.   Nay, if to enjoy all these things be a town-life, London is not so bad a place, dear.

PINCH.   How! if you love me, you must hate London.

ALITH. [aside]   The fool has forbid me discovering to her the pleasures of the town, and he is now setting her agog upon them himself.

MRS. PINCH.   But, husband, do the town-women love the playermen too?

PINCH.   Yes, I warrant you.

MRS. PINCH.   Ay, I warrant you.

PINCH.   Why, you do not, I hope?

MRS. PINCH.   No, no, bud. But why have we no playermen in the country?

PINCH.   Ha!—Mrs. Minx, ask me no more to go to a play.

MRS. PINCH.   Nay, why love? I did not care for going: but when you forbid me, you make me, as 'twere, desire it.

ALITH. [aside]   So 'twill be in other things, I warrant.

MRS. PINCH.   Pray let me go to a play, dear.

PINCH.   Hold your peace, I wo' not.

MRS. PINCH.   Why, love?

PINCH.   Why, I'll tell you.

ALITH. [aside]   Nay, if he tell her, she'll give him more cause to forbid her that place.

MRS. PINCH.   Pray why, dear?

PINCH.   First, you like the actors; and the gallants may like you.

MRS. PINCH.   What, a homely country girl! No, bud, nobody will like me.

PINCH.   I tell you yes, they may.

MRS. PINCH.   No, no, you jest—I won't believe you: I will go.

PINCH.   I tell you then, that one of the lewdest fellows in town, who saw you there, told me he was in love with you.

MRS. PINCH.   Indeed! who, who, pray who was't?

PINCH. [aside]   I've gone too far, and slipped before I was aware; how overjoyed she is!

MRS. PINCH.   Was it any Hampshire gallant, any of our neighbours? I promise you, I am beholden to him.

PINCH.   I promise you, you lie; for he would but ruin you, as he has done hundreds. He has no other love for women but that; such as he look upon women, like basilisks, but to destroy 'em.

MRS. PINCH.   Ay, but if he loves me, why should he ruin me? answer me to that. Methinks he should not, I would do him no harm.

ALITH.   Ha! ha! ha!

PINCH.   'Tis very well; but I'll keep him from doing you any harm, or me either. But here comes company; get you in, get you in.

MRS. PINCH.   But, pray, husband, is he a pretty gentleman that loves me?

PINCH.   In, baggage, in.   [*thrusts her in, shuts the door*]

Enter SPARKISH *and* HARCOURT

What, all the lewd libertines of the town brought to my lodging by this easy coxcomb! 'Sdeath, I'll not suffer it.

SPARK.   Here, Harcourt, do you approve my choice?——Dear little rogue, I told you I'd bring you acquainted with all my friends, the wits and——   [HARCOURT *salutes her.*]

PINCH.   Ay, they shall know her, as well as you yourself will, I warrant you.

SPARK.   This is one of those, my pretty rogue, that are to dance at your wedding to-morrow; and him you must bid welcome ever, to what you and I have.

PINCH. [*aside*]   Monstrous!

SPARK.   Harcourt, how dost thou like her, faith? Nay, dear, do not look down; I should hate to have a wife of mine out of countenance at anything.

PINCH. [*aside*]   Wonderful!

SPARK.   Tell me, I say, Harcourt, how dost thou like her? Thou hast stared upon her enough to resolve me.

HAR.   So infinitely well, that I could wish I had a mistress too, that might differ from her in nothing but her love and engagement to you.

ALITH.   Sir, Master Sparkish has often told me that his acquaintance were all wits and railleurs, and now I find it.

SPARK.   No, by the universe, Madam, he does not rally now; you may believe him. I do assure you, he is the honestest, worthiest, true-hearted gentleman—a man of such perfect honour, he would say nothing to a lady he does not mean.

PINCH. [*aside*]   Praising another man to his mistress!

HAR.   Sir, you are so beyond expectation obliging, that——

SPARK.   Nay, egad, I am sure you do admire her extremely; I see't in your eyes.——He does admire you, Madam.——By the world, don't you?

HAR.   Yes, above the world, or the most glorious part of it, her whole sex: and till now I never thought I should have envied you, or any man about to marry, but you have the best excuse for marriage I ever knew.

ALITH.   Nay, now, Sir, I'm satisfied you are of the society of the wits and railleurs, since you cannot spare your friend, even when he is but too civil to you; but the surest sign is, since you are an enemy to marriage, for that I hear you hate as much as business or bad wine.

HAR.   Truly, Madam, I never was an enemy to marriage till now, because marriage was never an enemy to me before.

ALITH.   But why, Sir, is marriage an enemy to you now? Because it robs you of your friend here? for you look upon a friend married as one gone into a monastery, that is, dead to the world.

HAR.   'Tis indeed, because you marry him; I see, Madam, you can guess my meaning. I do confess heartily and openly I wish it were in my power to break the match; by Heavens I would.

SPARK.   Poor Frank!

ALITH.   Would you be so unkind to me?

HAR.   No, no, 'tis not because I would be unkind to you.

SPARK.   Poor Frank! no gad, 'tis only his kindness to me.

PINCH. [aside]   Great kindness to you indeed! Insensible fop, let a man make love to his wife to his face!

SPARK.   Come, dear Frank, for all my wife there, that shall be, thou shalt enjoy me sometimes, dear rogue. By my honour, we men of wit condole for our deceased brother in marriage, as much as for one dead in earnest: I think that was prettily said of me, ha, Harcourt?——But come, Frank, be not melancholy for me.

HAR.   No, I assure you, I am not melancholy for you.

SPARK.   Prithee, Frank, dost think my wife that shall be there, a fine person?

HAR.   I could gaze upon her till I became as blind as you are.

SPARK.   How as I am? how?

HAR.   Because you are a lover, and true lovers are blind, stock blind.

SPARK.   True, true; but by the world she has wit too, as well as beauty: go, go with her into a corner, and try if she has wit; talk to her anything; she's bashful before me.

HAR.   Indeed if a woman wants wit in a corner, she has it nowhere.

ALITH. [aside to SPARKISH]   Sir, you dispose of me a little before your time——

SPARK.   Nay, nay, Madam, let me have an earnest of your obedience, or—go, go, Madam——   [HARCOURT courts ALITHEA aside]

PINCH.   How, Sir! if you are not concerned for the honour of a wife, I am for that of a sister; he shall not debauch her. Be a pander to your own wife! bring men to her! let 'em make love before your face! thrust 'em into a corner together, then leave 'em in private! is this your town wit and conduct?

SPARK.   Ha! ha! ha! a silly wise rogue would make one laugh more than a stark fool, ha! ha! I shall burst. Nay, you shall not disturb 'em; I'll vex thee, by the world.

[struggles with PINCHWIFE to keep him from HARCOURT and ALITHEA]

ALITH.   The writings are drawn, Sir, settlements made: 'tis too late, Sir, and past all revocation.

HAR.   Then so is my death.

ALITH.   I would not be unjust to him.

HAR.   Then why to me so?

ALITH.   I have no obligation to you.

HAR.   My love.

ALITH.   I had his before.

HAR.   You never had it; he wants, you see, jealousy, the only infallible sign of it.

ALITH.   Love proceeds from esteem; he cannot distrust my virtue: besides, he loves me, or he would not marry me.

HAR.   Marrying you is no more sign of his love than bribing your woman, that he may marry you, is a sign of his generosity. Marriage is rather a sign of interest than love; and he that marries a fortune covets a mistress, not loves her. But if you take marriage for a sign of love, take it from me immediately.

ALITH.   No, now you have put a scruple in my head; but in short, Sir, to end our dispute, I must marry him; my reputation would suffer in the world else.

HAR.   No; if you do marry him, with your pardon, Madam, your reputation suffers in the world, and you would be thought in necessity for a cloak.

ALITH.   Nay, now you are rude, Sir.——Mr. Sparkish, pray come hither, your friend here is very troublesome, and very loving.

HAR. [*aside to* ALITHEA]   Hold! hold!——

PINCH.   D'ye hear that?

SPARK.   Why, d'ye think I'll seem to be jealous, like a country bumpkin?

PINCH.   No, rather be a cuckold, like a credulous cit.

HAR.   Madam, you would not have been so little generous as to have told him.

ALITH.   Yes, since you could be so little generous as to wrong him.

HAR.   Wrong him! no man can do't, he's beneath an injury: a bubble, a coward, a senseless idiot, a wretch so contemptible to all the world but you, that——

ALITH.   Hold, do not rail at him, for since he is like to be my husband, I am resolved to like him: nay, I think I am obliged to tell him you are not his friend.——Master Sparkish, Master Sparkish!

SPARK.   What, what?——Now, dear rogue, has not she wit?

HAR.   Not so much as I thought, and hoped she had. [*speaks surlily*]

ALITH.   Mr. Sparkish, do you bring people to rail at you?

HAR.   Madam——

SPARK.   How! no; but if he does rail at me, 'tis but in jest, I warrant: what we wits do for one another, and never take any notice of it.

ALITH.   He spoke so scurrilously of you, I had no patience to hear him; besides, he has been making love to me.

HAR. [*aside*]   True, damned tell-tale woman!

SPARK.   Pshaw! to show his parts—we wits rail and make love often, but to show our parts: as we have no affections, so we have no malice, we——

ALITH.   He said you were a wretch below an injury——

SPARK.   Pshaw!

HAR. [*aside*]   Damned, senseless, impudent, virtuous jade! Well, since she won't let me have her, she'll do as good, she'll make me hate her.

ALITH.   A common bubble——

SPARK.   Pshaw!

ALITH.   A coward——

SPARK.   Pshaw, pshaw!

ALITH.   A senseless, drivelling idiot——

SPARK.   How! did he disparage my parts? Nay, then, my honour's concerned, I can't put up that, Sir, by the world—brother, help me to kill him.—[*aside*] I may draw now, since we have the odds of him—'tis a good occasion, too, before my mistress——   [*offers to draw*]

ALITH.   Hold, hold!

SPARK.   What, what?

ALITH. [*aside*]   I must not let 'em kill the gentleman neither, for his kindness to me: I am so far from hating him, that I wish my gallant had his person and understanding. Nay, if my honour——

SPARK.   I'll be thy death.

ALITH.   Hold, hold! Indeed, to tell the truth, the gentleman said after all, that what he spoke was but out of friendship to you.

SPARK.   How! say, I am—I am a fool, that is no wit, out of friendship to me?

ALITH.   Yes, to try whether I was concerned enough for you; and made love to me only to be satisfied of my virtue, for your sake.

HAR. [*aside*]   Kind, however.

SPARK.   Nay, if it were so, my dear rogue, I ask thee pardon; but why would not you tell me so, faith?

HAR.   Because I did not think on't, faith.

SPARK.   Come, Horner does not come; Harcourt, let's be gone to the new play.—Come, Madam.

ALITH.   I will not go, if you intend to leave me alone in the box and run into the pit, as you use to do.

SPARK.   Pshaw! I'll leave Harcourt with you in the box to entertain you, and that's as good; if I sat in the box, I should be thought no judge but of trimmings.—Come away, Harcourt, lead her down.

                    [*exeunt* SPARKISH, HARCOURT, *and* ALITHEA]

PINCH.   Well, go thy ways, for the flower of the true town fops, such as spend their estates before they come to 'em, and are cuckolds before they're married. But let me go look to my own freehold.——How!

Enter My LADY FIDGET, MRS. DAINTY FIDGET, *and* MRS. SQUEAMISH

LADY FID.   Your servant, Sir: where is your lady? We are come to wait upon her to the new play.

PINCH.   New play!

LADY FID.   And my husband will wait upon you presently.

PINCH. [*aside*]   Damn your civility.——Madam, by no means; I will not see Sir Jasper here till I have waited upon him at home; nor shall my wife see you till she has waited upon your ladyship at your lodgings.

LADY FID.   Now we are here, Sir?

PINCH.   No, Madam.

MRS. DAIN.   Pray, let us see her.

MRS. SQUEAM.   We will not stir till we see her.

PINCH. [*aside*]   A pox on you all!—[*goes to the door, and returns*] She has locked the door, and is gone abroad.

LADY FID.   No, you have locked the door, and she's within.

MRS. DAIN.   They told us below she was here.

PINCH. [*aside*]   Will nothing do?——Well, it must out then. To tell you the truth, ladies, which I was afraid to let you know before, lest it might endanger your lives, my wife has just now the small-pox come out upon her; do not be frightened, but pray be gone, ladies; you shall not stay here in danger of your lives; pray get you gone, ladies.

LADY FID.   No, no, we have all had 'em.

MRS. SQUEAM.   Alack, alack!

MRS. DAIN.   Come, come, we must see how it goes with her; I understand the disease.

LADY FID.   Come!

PINCH. [*aside*]   Well, there is no being too hard for women at their own weapon, lying, therefore I'll quit the field.   [*exit*]

MRS. SQUEAM.   Here's an example of jealousy!

LADY FID.   Indeed, as the world goes, I wonder there are no more jealous, since wives are so neglected.

MRS. DAIN.   Pshaw! as the world goes, to what end should they be jealous?

LADY FID.   Foh! 'tis a nasty world.

MRS. SQUEAM.   That men of parts, great acquaintance, and quality, should take up with and spend themselves and fortunes in keeping little playhouse creatures, foh!

LADY FID.   Nay, that women of understanding, great acquaintance, and good quality, should fall a-keeping too of little creatures, foh!

MRS. SQUEAM.   Why, 'tis the men of quality's fault; they never visit women of honour and reputation as they used to do; and have not so much as common civility for ladies of our rank, but use us with the same indifferency and ill-breeding as if we were all married to 'em.

LADY FID.   She says true; 'tis an arrant shame women of quality should be so slighted; methinks birth—birth should go for something; I have known men admired, courted, and followed for their titles only.

MRS. SQUEAM.   Ay, one would think men of honour should not love, no more than marry, out of their own rank.

MRS. DAIN.   Fy, fy, upon 'em! they are come to think cross breeding for themselves best, as well as for their dogs and horses.

LADY FID.   They are dogs and horses for't.

MRS. SQUEAM.   One would think, if not for love, for vanity a little.

MRS. DAIN.   Nay, they do satisfy their vanity upon us sometimes; and are kind to us in their report, tell all the world they lie with us.

LADY FID.   Damned rascals, that we should be only wronged by 'em! To report a man has had a person, when he has not had a person, is the greatest wrong in the whole world that can be done to a person.

MRS. SQUEAM.   Well, 'tis an arrant shame noble persons should be so wronged and neglected.

LADY FID.   But still 'tis an arranter shame for a noble person to neglect her own honour, and defame her own noble person with little inconsiderable fellows, foh!

MRS. DAIN.   I suppose the crime against our honour is the same with a man of quality as with another.

LADY FID.   How! no, sure, the man of quality is likest one's husband, and therefore the fault should be the less.

MRS. DAIN.   But then the pleasure should be the less.

LADY FID.   Fy, fy, fy, for shame, Sister! whither shall we ramble? Be continent in your discourse, or I shall hate you.

MRS. DAIN.   Besides, an intrigue is so much the more notorious for the man's quality.

MRS. SQUEAM.   'Tis true, that nobody takes notice of a private man, and therefore with him 'tis more secret; and the crime's the less when 'tis not known.

LADY FID.   You say true; i'faith, I think you are in the right on't: 'tis not an injury to a husband till it be an injury to our honours; so that a woman of honour loses no honour with a private person; and to say truth——

MRS. DAIN. [apart to MRS. SQUEAMISH]   So, the little fellow is grown a private person—with her——

LADY FID.   But still my dear, dear honour——

Enter SIR JASPER, HORNER, *and* DORILANT

SIR JASP. Ay, my dear, dear of honour, thou hast still so much honour in thy mouth——

HORN. [*aside*] That she has none elsewhere.

LADY FID. Oh, what d'ye mean to bring in these upon us?

MRS. DAIN. Foh! these are as bad as wits.

MRS. SQUEAM. Foh!

LADY FID. Let us leave the room.

SIR JASP. Stay, stay; faith, to tell you the naked truth——

LADY FID. Fy, Sir Jasper! do not use that word naked.

SIR JASP. Well, well, in short I have business at Whitehall, and cannot
go to the play with you, therefore would have you go——

LADY FID. With those two to a play?

SIR JASP. No, not with t'other, but with Mr. Horner; there can be no
more scandal to go with him than with Mr. Tattle, or Master Limberham.

LADY FID. With that nasty fellow! no—no.

SIR JASP. Nay, prithee, dear, hear me.   [*whispers to* LADY FIDGET]

HORN. Ladies——

[HORNER, DORILANT *drawing near* MRS. SQUEAMISH
and MRS. DAINTY FIDGET]

MRS. DAIN. Stand off.

MRS. SQUEAM. Do not approach us.

MRS. DAIN. You herd with the wits, you are obscenity all over.

MRS. SQUEAM. And I would as soon look upon a picture of Adam
and Eve without fig-leaves, as any of you, if I could help it; therefore keep
off, and do not make us sick.

DOR. What a devil are these?

HORN. Why, these are pretenders to honour, as critics to wit, only
by censuring others; and as every raw, peevish, out-of-humoured, affected, dull, tea-drinking, arithmetical fop, sets up for a wit by railing at
men of sense, so these for honour, by railing at the court, and ladies of as
great honour as quality.

SIR JASP. Come, Mr. Horner, I must desire you to go with these
ladies to the play, Sir.

HORN. I, Sir?

SIR JASP. Ay, ay, come, Sir.

HORN. I must beg your pardon, Sir, and theirs; I will not be seen in
women's company in public again for the world.

SIR JASP. Ha, ha, strange aversion!

MRS. SQUEAM. No, he's for women's company in private.

SIR JASP. He—poor man—he—ha! ha! ha!

MRS. DAIN. 'Tis a greater shame amongst lewd fellows to be seen in
virtuous women's company, than for the women to be seen with them.

HORN. Indeed, Madam, the time was I only hated virtuous women, but now I hate the other too; I beg your pardon, ladies.

LADY FID.   You are very obliging, Sir, because we would not be troubled with you.

SIR JASP.   In sober sadness, he shall go.

DOR.   Nay, if he wo' not, I am ready to wait upon the ladies, and I
think I am the fitter man.

SIR JASP.   You, Sir! no, I thank you for that. Master Horner is a privileged man amongst the virtuous ladies, 'twill be a great while before you
are so; he! he! he! he's my wife's gallant; he! he! he! No, pray withdraw,
Sir, for as I take it, the virtuous ladies have no business with you.

DOR.   And I am sure he can have none with them. 'Tis strange a man
can't come amongst virtuous women now, but upon the same terms as
men are admitted into the Great Turk's seraglio. But heavens keep me
from being an ombre player with 'em!——But where is Pinchwife?

                                                                    [*exit*]

SIR JASP.   Come, come, man; what, avoid the sweet society of womankind? that sweet, soft, gentle, tame, noble creature, woman, made for
man's companion——

HORN.   So is that soft, gentle, tame, and more noble creature a
spaniel, and has all their tricks; can fawn, lie down, suffer beating, and
fawn the more; barks at your friends when they come to see you, makes
your bed hard, gives you fleas, and the mange sometimes. And all the difference is, the spaniel's the more faithful animal, and fawns but upon one
master.

SIR JASP.   He! he! he!

MRS. SQUEAM.   Oh the rude beast!

MRS. DAIN.   Insolent brute!

LADY FID.   Brute! stinking, mortified, rotten French wether, to
dare——

SIR JASP.   Hold, an't please your ladyship.——For shame, Master
Horner! your mother was a woman—[*aside*] Now shall I never reconcile
'em.——[*aside to* LADY FIDGET] Hark you, Madam, take my advice in
your anger. You know you often want one to make up your drolling pack
of ombre players, and you may cheat him easily; for he's an ill gamester,
and consequently loves play. Besides, you know you have but two old
civil gentlemen (with stinking breaths too) to wait upon you abroad; take
in the third into your service. The others are but crazy; and a lady should
have a supernumerary gentleman-usher as a supernumerary coach-horse,
lest sometimes you should be forced to stay at home.

LADY FID.   But are you sure he loves play, and has money?

SIR JASP.   He loves play as much as you, and has money as much as I.

LADY FID.   Then I am contented to make him pay for his scurrility.
Money makes up in a measure all other wants in men.—Those whom

we cannot make hold for gallants, we make fine.

SIR JASP. [*aside*]   So, so; now to mollify, wheedle him.——[*aside to* HORNER] Master Horner, will you never keep civil company? Methinks 'tis time now, since you are only fit for them. Come, come, man, you must e'en fall to visiting our wives, eating at our tables, drinking tea with our virtuous relations after dinner, dealing cards to 'em, reading plays and gazettes to 'em, picking fleas out of their shocks for 'em, collecting receipts, new songs, women, pages, and footmen for 'em.

HORN.   I hope they'll afford me better employment, Sir.

SIR JASP.   He! he! he! 'tis fit you know your work before you come into your place. And since you are unprovided of a lady to flatter, and a good house to eat at, pray frequent mine, and call my wife mistress, and she shall call you gallant, according to the custom.

HORN.   Who, I?

SIR JASP.   Faith, thou shalt for my sake; come, for my sake only.

HORN.   For your sake——

SIR JASP.   Come, come, here's a gamester for you; let him be a little familiar sometimes; nay, what if a little rude? Gamesters may be rude with ladies, you know.

LADY FID.   Yes; losing gamesters have a privilege with women.

HORN.   I always thought the contrary, that the winning gamester had most privilege with women; for when you have lost your money to a man, you'll lose anything you have, all you have, they say, and he may use you as he pleases.

SIR JASP.   He! he! he! well, win or lose, you shall have your liberty with her.

LADY FID.   As he behaves himself; and for your sake I'll give him admittance and freedom.

HORN.   All sorts of freedom, Madam?

SIR JASP.   Ay, ay, ay, all sorts of freedom thou canst take. And so go to her, begin thy new employment; wheedle her, jest with her, and be better acquainted one with another.

HORN. [*aside*]   I think I know her already; therefore may venture with her my secret for hers.   [HORNER *and* LADY FIDGET *whisper*]

SIR JASP.   Sister, cuz, I have provided an innocent playfellow for you there.

MRS. DAIN.   Who, he?

MRS. SQUEAM.   There's a playfellow, indeed!

SIR JASP.   Yes, sure. What, he is good enough to play at cards, blindman's-buff, or the fool with, sometimes!

MRS. SQUEAM.   Foh! we'll have no such playfellows.

MRS. DAIN.   No, Sir; you shan't choose playfellows for us, we thank you.

SIR JASP.   Nay, pray hear me.   [*whispering to them*]

LADY FID.   But, poor gentleman, could you be so generous, so truly a man of honour, as for the sakes of us women of honour, to cause yourself to be reported no man? No man! and to suffer yourself the greatest shame that could fall upon a man, that none might fall upon us women by your conversation? But, indeed, Sir, as perfectly, perfectly the same man as before your going into France, Sir? as perfectly, perfectly, Sir?

HORN.   As perfectly, perfectly, Madam. Nay, I scorn you should take my word; I desire to be tried only, Madam.

LADY FID.   Well, that's spoken again like a man of honour: all men of honour desire to come to the test. But, indeed, generally you men report such things of yourselves, one does not know how or whom to believe; and it is come to that pass we dare not take your words no more than your tailor's, without some staid servant of yours be bound with you. But I have so strong a faith in your honour, dear, dear, noble Sir, that I'd forfeit mine for yours, at any time, dear Sir.

HORN.   No, Madam, you should not need to forfeit it for me; I have given you security already to save you harmless, my late reputation being so well known in the world, Madam.

LADY FID.   But if upon any future falling-out, or upon a suspicion of my taking the trust out of your hands to employ some other, you yourself should betray your trust, dear Sir? I mean, if you'll give me leave to speak obscenely, you might tell, dear Sir.

HORN.   If I did, nobody would believe me. The reputation of impotency is as hardly recovered again in the world as that of cowardice, dear Madam.

LADY FID.   Nay, then, as one may say, you may do your worst, dear, dear Sir.

SIR JASP.   Come, is your ladyship reconciled to him yet? have you agreed on matters? For I must be gone to Whitehall.

LADY FID.   Why, indeed, Sir Jasper, Master Horner is a thousand, thousand times a better man than I thought him. Cousin Squeamish, sister Dainty, I can name him now. Truly, not long ago, you know, I thought his very name obscenity; and I would as soon have lain with him as have named him.

SIR JASP.   Very likely, poor Madam.

MRS. DAIN.   I believe it.

MRS. SQUEAM.   No doubt on't.

SIR JASP.   Well, well—that your ladyship is as virtuous as any she, I know, and him all the town knows—he! he! he! Therefore now you like him, get you gone to your business together; go, go to your business, I say, pleasure; whilst I go to my pleasure, business.

LADY FID.   Come, then, dear gallant.

HORN.   Come away, my dearest mistress.
SIR JASP.   So, so; why, 'tis as I'd have it.   [*exit*]
HORN.   And as I'd have it.
LADY FID.   Who for his business from his wife will run,
              Takes the best care to have her business done.
                                                    [*exeunt omnes*]

ACT III

SCENE I

ALITHEA *and* MRS. PINCHWIFE

ALITH.   Sister, what ails you? You are grown melancholy.

MRS. PINCH.   Would it not make any one melancholy to see you go every day fluttering about abroad, whilst I must stay at home like a poor lonely sullen bird in a cage?

ALITH.   Ay, Sister, but you came young, and just from the nest to your cage, so that I thought you liked it, and could be as cheerful in't as others that took their flight themselves early, and are hopping abroad in the open air.

MRS. PINCH.   Nay, I confess I was quiet enough till my husband told me what pure lives the London ladies live abroad, with their dancing, meetings, and junketings, and dressed every day in their best gowns; and I warrant you, play at nine-pins every day of the week, so they do.

Enter PINCHWIFE

PINCH.   Come, what's here to do? You are putting the town-pleasures in her head, and setting her a-longing.

ALITH.   Yes, after nine-pins. You suffer none to give her those longings you mean but yourself.

PINCH.   I tell her of the vanities of the town like a confessor.

ALITH.   A confessor! just such a confessor as he that, by forbidding a silly ostler to grease the horse's teeth, taught him to do't.

PINCH.   Come, Mistress Flippant, good precepts are lost when bad examples are still before us: the liberty you take abroad makes her hanker after it, and out of humour at home. Poor wretch! she desired not to come to London; I would bring her.

ALITH.   Very well.

PINCH.   She has been this week in town, and never desired till this afternoon to go abroad.

ALITH.   Was she not at a play yesterday?

PINCH.   Yes, but she ne'er asked me; I was myself the cause of her going.

ALITH.   Then if she ask you again, you are the cause of her asking, and not my example.

PINCH.   Well, to-morrow night I shall be rid of you; and the next day, before 'tis light, she and I'll be rid of the town, and my dreadful apprehensions.——Come, be not melancholy; for thou shalt go into the country after to-morrow, dearest.

ALITH.   Great comfort!

MRS. PINCH.   Pish! what d'ye tell me of the country for?

PINCH.   How's this! what, pish at the country?

MRS. PINCH.   Let me alone; I am not well.

PINCH.   Oh, if that be all—what ails my dearest?

MRS. PINCH.   Truly, I don't know: but I have not been well since you told me there was a gallant at the play in love with me.

PINCH.   Ha!——

ALITH.   That's by my example too!

PINCH.   Nay, if you are not well, but are so concerned because a lewd fellow chanced to lie, and say he liked you, you'll make me sick too.

MRS. PINCH.   Of what sickness?

PINCH.   Oh, of that which is worse than the plague, jealousy.

MRS. PINCH.   Pish, you jeer! I'm sure there's no such disease in our receipt-book at home.

PINCH.   No, thou never met'st with it, poor innocent.—[*aside*] Well, if thou cuckold me, 'twill be my own fault—for cuckolds and bastards are generally makers of their own fortune.

MRS. PINCH.   Well, but pray, bud, let's go to a play to-night.

PINCH.   'Tis just done, she comes from it. But why are you so eager to see a play?

MRS. PINCH.   Faith, dear, not that I care one pin for their talk there; but I like to look upon the playermen, and would see, if I could, the gallant you say loves me: that's all, dear bud.

PINCH.   Is that all, dear bud?

ALITH.   This proceeds from my example!

MRS. PINCH.   But if the play be done, let's go abroad, however, dear bud.

PINCH.   Come, have a little patience and thou shalt go into the country on Friday.

MRS. PINCH.   Therefore I would see first some sights to tell my neighbours of. Nay, I will go abroad, that's once.

ALITH.   I'm the cause of this desire too!

PINCH.   But now I think on't, who, who was the cause of Horner's coming to my lodgings to-day? That was you.

ALITH.   No, you, because you would not let him see your handsome wife out of your lodging.

MRS. PINCH.   Why, O Lord! did the gentleman come hither to see me indeed?

PINCH.   No, no. You are not the cause of that damned question too, Mistress Alithea?—[aside] Well, she's in the right of it. He is in love with my wife—and comes after her—'tis so—but I'll nip his love in the bud, lest he should follow us into the country, and break his chariot-wheel near our house, on purpose for an excuse to come to't. But I think I know the town.

MRS. PINCH.   Come, pray, bud, let's go abroad before 'tis late; for I will go, that's flat and plain.

PINCH. [aside]   So! the obstinacy already of the town-wife; and I must, whilst she's here, humour her like one.——Sister, how shall we do, that she may not be seen or known?

ALITH.   Let her put on her mask.

PINCH.   Pshaw! a mask makes people but the more inquisitive, and is as ridiculous a disguise as a stage-beard: her shape, stature, habit will be known. And if we should meet with Horner, he would be sure to take acquaintance with us, must wish her joy, kiss her, talk to her, leer upon her, and the devil and all. No, I'll not use her to a mask, 'tis dangerous, for masks have made more cuckolds than the best faces that ever were known.

ALITH.   How will you do then?

MRS. PINCH.   Nay, shall we go? The Exchange will be shut, and I have a mind to see that.

PINCH.   So—I have it—I'll dress her up in the suit we are to carry down to her brother, little Sir James; nay, I understand the town-tricks. Come, let's go dress her. A mask! no—a woman masked, like a covered dish, gives a man curiosity and appetite; when, it may be, uncovered, 'twould turn his stomach: no, no.

ALITH.   Indeed your comparison is something a greasy one: but I had a gentle gallant used to say, A beauty masked, like the sun in eclipse, gathers together more gazers than if it shined out.   [exeunt]

SCENE II

The Scene Changes to the New Exchange

Enter HORNER, HARCOURT, *and* DORILANT

DOR.   Engaged to women, and not sup with us!

HORN.   Ay, a pox on 'em all!

HAR.   You were much a more reasonable man in the morning, and had as noble resolutions against 'em as a widower of a week's liberty.

DOR. Did I ever think to see you keep company with women in vain?

HORN. In vain: no—'tis since I can't love 'em, to be revenged on 'em.

HAR. Now your sting is gone, you looked in the box amongst all those women like a drone in the hive, all upon you; shoved and ill-used by 'em all, and thrust from one side to t'other.

DOR. Yet he must be buzzing amongst 'em still, like other beetle-headed liquorish drones. Avoid 'em, and hate 'em, as they hate you.

HORN. Because I do hate 'em, and would hate 'em yet more, I'll frequent 'em. You may see by marriage, nothing makes a man hate a woman more than her constant conversation. In short, I converse with 'em, as you do with rich fools, to laugh at 'em and use 'em ill.

DOR. But I would no more sup with women unless I could lie with 'em than sup with a rich coxcomb unless I could cheat him.

HORN. Yes, I have known thee sup with a fool for his drinking; if he could set out your hand that way only, you were satisfied, and if he were a wine-swallowing mouth, 'twas enough.

HAR. Yes, a man drinks often with a fool, as he tosses with a marker, only to keep his hand in use. But do the ladies drink?

HORN. Yes, Sir; and I shall have the pleasure at least of laying 'em flat with a bottle, and bring as much scandal that way upon 'em as formerly t'other.

HAR. Perhaps you may prove as weak a brother amongst 'em that way as t'other.

DOR. Foh! drinking with women is as unnatural as scolding with 'em. But 'tis a pleasure of decayed fornicators, and the basest way of quenching love.

HAR. Nay, 'tis drowning love, instead of quenching it. But leave us for civil women too!

DOR. Ay, when he can't be the better for 'em. We hardly pardon a man that leaves his friend for a wench, and that's a pretty lawful call.

HORN. Faith, I would not leave you for 'em, if they would not drink.

DOR. Who would disappoint his company at Lewis's for a gossiping?

HAR. Foh! Wine and women, good apart, together as nauseous as sack and sugar. But hark you, Sir, before you go, a little of your advice; an old maimed general, when unfit for action, is fittest for counsel. I have other designs upon women than eating and drinking with them; I am in love with Sparkish's mistress, whom he is to marry to-morrow: now how shall I get her?

Enter SPARKISH, *looking about*

HORN.   Why, here comes one will help you to her.

HAR.   He! he, I tell you, is my rival, and will hinder my love.

HORN.   No; a foolish rival and a jealous husband assist their rival's designs, for they are sure to make their women hate them, which is the first step to their love for another man.

HAR.   But I cannot come near his mistress but in his company.

HORN.   Still the better for you; for fools are most easily cheated when they themselves are accessories, and he is to be bubbled of his mistress as of his money, the common mistress, by keeping him company.

SPARK.   Who is that that is to be bubbled? Faith, let me snack; I han't met with a bubble since Christmas. 'Gad, I think bubbles are like their brother woodcocks, go out with the cold weather.

HAR. [*apart to* HORNER]   A pox! he did not hear all, I hope.

SPARK.   Come, you bubbling rogues you, where do we sup?——Oh, Harcourt, my mistress tells me you have been making fierce love to her all the play long: ha! ha! But I——

HAR.   I make love to her!

SPARK.   Nay, I forgive thee, for I think I know thee, and I know her; but I am sure I know myself.

HAR.   Did she tell you so? I see all women are like these of the Exchange; who, to enhance the prize of their commodities, report to their fond customers offers which were never made 'em.

HORN.   Ay, women are apt to tell before the intrigue, as men after it, and so show themselves the vainer sex. But hast thou a mistress, Sparkish? 'Tis as hard for me to believe it as that thou ever hadst a bubble, as you bragged just now.

SPARK.   Oh, your servant, Sir: are you at your raillery, Sir? But we were some of us beforehand with you to-day at the play. The wits were something bold with you, Sir; did you not hear us laugh?

HORN.   Yes; but I thought you had gone to plays to laugh at the poet's wit, not at your own.

SPARK.   Your servant, Sir: no, I thank you. 'Gad, I go to a play as to a country treat; I carry my own wine to one, and my own wit to t'other, or else I'm sure I should not be merry at either. And the reason why we are so often louder than the players is because we think we speak more wit, and so become the poet's rivals in his audience: for to tell you the truth, we hate the silly rogues, nay, so much, that we find fault even with their bawdy upon the stage, whilst we talk nothing else in the pit as loud.

HORN.   But why shouldst thou hate the silly poets? Thou hast too much wit to be one; and they, like whores, are only hated by each other: and thou dost scorn writing, I'm sure.

SPARK.   Yes; I'd have you to know I scorn writing: but women, women, that make men do all foolish things, make 'em write songs too.

Everybody does it. 'Tis even as common with lovers as playing with fans; and you can no more help rhyming to your Phyllis, than drinking to your Phyllis.

HAR.   Nay, poetry in love is no more to be avoided than jealousy.

DOR.   But the poets damned your songs, did they?

SPARK.   Damn the poets! they turned 'em into burlesque, as they call it. That burlesque is a hocus-pocus trick they have got, which, by the virtue of *Hictius doctius, topsy turvy,* they make a wise and witty man in the world, a fool upon the stage you know not how: and 'tis therefore I hate 'em too, for I know not but it may be my own case; for they'll put a man into a play for looking asquint. Their predecessors were contented to make serving-men only their stage-fools: but these rogues must have gentlemen, with a pox to 'em, nay, knights; and, indeed, you shall hardly see a fool upon the stage but he's a knight. And to tell you the truth, they have kept me these six years from being a knight in earnest, for fear of being knighted in a play, and dubbed a fool.

DOR.   Blame 'em not, they must follow their copy, the age.

HAR.   But why shouldst thou be afraid of being in a play, who expose yourself every day in the playhouses, and at public places?

HORN.   'Tis but being on the stage, instead of standing on a bench in the pit.

DOR.   Don't you give money to painters to draw you like? and are you afraid of your pictures at length in a playhouse, where all your mistresses may see you?

SPARK.   A pox! painters don't draw the small-pox or pimples in one's face. Come, damn all your silly authors whatever, all books and booksellers, by the world, and all readers, courteous or uncourteous!

HAR.   But who comes here, Sparkish?

Enter MR. PINCHWIFE *and his Wife in man's clothes,*
ALITHEA, LUCY *her maid*

SPARK.   Oh, hide me! There's my mistress too.

[SPARKISH *hides himself behind* HARCOURT]

HAR.   She sees you.

SPARK.   But I will not see her. 'Tis time to go to Whitehall, and I must not fail the drawing-room.

HAR.   Pray, first carry me, and reconcile me to her.

SPARK.   Another time. Faith, the king will have supped.

HAR.   Not with the worse stomach for thy absence. Thou art one of those fools that think their attendance at the king's meals as necessary as his physicians' when you are more troublesome to him than his doctors or his dogs.

SPARK.   Pshaw! I know my interest, Sir. Prithee hide me.

HORN.   Your servant, Pinchwife.——What, he knows us not!

PINCH. [*to his wife aside*]   Come along.

MRS. PINCH.   Pray, have you any ballads? give me sixpenny worth.

CLASP.   We have no ballads.

MRS. PINCH.   Then give me "Covent Garden Drollery," and a play or two—— Oh, here's "Tarugo's Wiles," and "The Slighted Maiden"; I'll have them.

PINCH. [*apart to her*]   No; plays are not for your reading. Come along; will you discover yourself?

HORN.   Who is that pretty youth with him, Sparkish?

SPARK.   I believe his wife's brother, because he's something like her: but I never saw her but once.

HORN.   Extremely handsome; I have seen a face like it too. Let us follow 'em.   [*exeunt* PINCHWIFE, MRS. PINCHWIFE, ALITHEA, LUCY; HORNER, DORILANT *following them*]

HAR.   Come, Sparkish, your mistress saw you, and will be angry you go not to her. Besides, I would fain be reconciled to her, which none but you can do, dear friend.

SPARK.   Well, that's a better reason, dear friend. I would not go near her now for hers or my own sake; but I can deny you nothing: for though I have known thee a great while, never go, if I do not love thee as well as a new acquaintance.

HAR.   I am obliged to you indeed, dear friend. I would be well with her, only to be well with thee still; for these ties to wives usually dissolve all ties to friends. I would be contented she should enjoy you a-nights, but I would have you to myself a-days as I have had, dear friend.

SPARK.   And thou shalt enjoy me a-days, dear, dear friend, never stir: and I'll be divorced from her, sooner than from thee. Come along.

HAR. [*aside*]   So, we are hard put to't, when we make our rival our procurer; but neither she nor her brother would let me come near her now. When all's done, a rival is the best cloak to steal to a mistress under, without suspicion; and when we have once got to her as we desire, we throw him off like other cloaks.

[*exit* SPARKISH, *and* HARCOURT *following him*]

Re-enter PINCHWIFE, MRS. PINCHWIFE *in man's clothes*

PINCH. [*to* ALITHEA]   Sister, if you will not go, we must leave you.—[*aside*] The fool her gallant and she will muster up all the young saunterers of this place, and they will leave their dear seamstresses to follow us. What a swarm of cuckolds and cuckold-makers are here!—— Come, let's be gone, Mistress Margery.

MRS. PINCH.   Don't you believe that; I han't half my bellyfull of sights yet.

PINCH.   Then walk this way.

MRS. PINCH.   Lord, what a power of brave signs are here! stay—the Bull's-Head, the Ram's-Head, and the Stag's-Head, dear——

PINCH.   Nay, if every husband's proper sign here were visible, they would be all alike.

MRS. PINCH.   What d'ye mean by that, bud?

PINCH.   'Tis no matter—no matter, bud.

MRS. PINCH.   Pray tell me: nay, I will know.

PINCH.   They would be all Bulls', Stags', and Rams'-heads.

[*exeunt* MR. PINCHWIFE *and* MRS. PINCHWIFE]

Re-enter SPARKISH, HARCOURT, ALITHEA, LUCY, *at t'other door*

SPARK.   Come, dear Madam, for my sake you shall be reconciled to him.

ALITH.   For your sake I hate him.

HAR.   That's something too cruel, Madam, to hate me for his sake.

SPARK.   Ay indeed, Madam, too, too cruel to me, to hate my friend for my sake.

ALITH.   I hate him because he is your enemy; and you ought to hate him too, for making love to me, if you love me.

SPARK.   That's a good one! I hate a man for loving you! If he did love you, 'tis but what he can't help; and 'tis your fault, not his, if he admires you. I hate a man for being of my opinion? I'll n'er do't, by the world!

ALITH.   Is it for your honour, or mine, to suffer a man to make love to me, who am to marry you to-morrow?

SPARK.   Is it for your honour, or mine, to have me jealous? That he makes love to you, is a sign you are handsome; and that I am not jealous, is a sign you are virtuous. That I think is for your honour.

ALITH.   But 'tis your honour too I am concerned for.

HAR.   But why, dearest Madam, will you be more concerned for his honour than he is himself? Let his honour alone, for my sake and his. He! he has no honour——

SPARK.   How's that?

HAR.   But what my dear friend can guard himself.

SPARK.   Oh ho—that's right again.

HAR.   Your care of his honour argues his neglect of it, which is no honour to my dear friend here. Therefore once more, let his honour go which way it will, dear Madam.

SPARK.   Ay, ay; were it for my honour to marry a woman whose virtue I suspected, and could not trust her in a friend's hands?

ALITH.   Are you not afraid to lose me?

HAR.   He afraid to lose you, Madam! No, no—you may see how the most estimable and most glorious creature in the world is valued by him. Will you not see it?

SPARK.   Right, honest Frank, I have that noble value for her that I cannot be jealous of her.

ALITH.   You mistake him. He means, you care not for me, nor who has me.

SPARK.   Lord, Madam, I see you are jealous! Will you wrest a poor man's meaning from his words?

ALITH.   You astonish me, Sir, with your want of jealousy.

SPARK.   And you make me giddy, Madam, with your jealousy and fears, and virtue and honour. 'Gad, I see virtue makes a woman as troublesome as a little reading or learning.

ALITH.   Monstrous!

LUCY. [behind]   Well, to see what easy husbands these women of quality can meet with! a poor chambermaid can never have such ladylike luck. Besides, he's thrown away upon her. She'll make no use of her fortune, her blessing, none to a gentleman, for a pure cuckold, for it requires good breeding to be a cuckold.

ALITH.   I tell you then plainly, he pursues me to marry me.

SPARK.   Pshaw!

HAR.   Come, Madam, you see you strive in vain to make him jealous of me. My dear friend is the kindest creature in the world to me.

SPARK.   Poor fellow!

HAR.   But his kindness only is not enough for me, without your favour, your good opinion, dear Madam: 'tis that must perfect my happiness. Good gentleman, he believes all I say: would you would do so! Jealous of me! I would not wrong him nor you for the world.

SPARK.   Look you there. Hear him, hear him, and do not walk away so.   [ALITHEA *walks carelessly to and fro*]

HAR.   I love you, Madam, so——

SPARK.   How's that? Nay, now you begin to go too far indeed.

HAR.   So much, I confess, I say, I love you, that I would not have you miserable, and cast yourself away upon so unworthy and inconsiderable a thing as what you see here.

                    [*clapping his hand on his breast, points at* SPARKISH]

SPARK.   No, faith, I believe thou wouldst not: now his meaning is plain; but I knew before thou wouldst not wrong me, nor her.

HAR.   No, no, Heavens forbid the glory of her sex should fall so low, as into the embraces of such a contemptible wretch, the last of mankind—my friend here—I injure him!   [*embracing* SPARKISH]

ALITH.   Very well.

SPARK.   No, no, dear friend, I knew it.——Madam, you see he will rather wrong himself than me, in giving himself such names.

ALITH.   Do not you understand him yet?

SPARK.   Yes: how modestly he speaks of himself, poor fellow!

ALITH.   Methinks he speaks impudently of yourself, since—before yourself too; insomuch that I can no longer suffer his scurrilous abusiveness to you, no more than his love to me.   [*offers to go*]

SPARK.   Nay, nay, Madam, pray stay—his love to you! Lord, Madam, has he not spoke yet plain enough?

ALITH.   Yes, indeed, I should think so.

SPARK.   Well then, by the world, a man can't speak civilly to a woman now, but presently she says he makes love to her. Nay, Madam, you shall stay, with your pardon, since you have not yet understood him, till he has made an *éclaircissement* of his love to you, that is, what kind of love it is. Answer to thy catechism, friend; do you love my mistress here?

HAR.   Yes, I wish she would not doubt it.

SPARK.   But how do you love her?

HAR.   With all my soul.

ALITH.   I thank him, methinks he speaks plain enough now.

SPARK. [*to* ALITHEA]   You are out still.——But with what kind of love, Harcourt?

HAR.   With the best and the truest love in the world.

SPARK.   Look you there then, that is with no matrimonial love, I'm sure.

ALITH.   How's that? do you say matrimonial love is not best?

SPARK.   'Gad, I went too far ere I was aware. But speak for thyself, Harcourt, you said you would not wrong me nor her.

HAR.   No, no, Madam, e'en take him for Heaven's sake——

SPARK.   Look you there, Madam.

HAR.   Who should in all justice be yours, he that loves you most.
                    [*claps his hand on his breast*]

ALITH.   Look you there, Mr. Sparkish, who's that?

SPARK.   Who should it be?——Go on, Harcourt.

HAR.   Who loves you more than women, titles, or fortune fools.
                    [*points at* SPARKISH]

SPARK.   Look you there, he means me still, for he points at me.

ALITH.   Ridiculous!

HAR.   Who can only match your faith and constancy in love.

SPARK.   Ay.

HAR.   Who knows, if it be possible, how to value so much beauty and virtue.

SPARK.   Ay.

HAR.   Whose love can no more be equalled in the world, than that heavenly form of yours.

SPARK. No.

HAR. Who could no more suffer a rival than your absence, and yet could no more suspect your virtue than his own constancy in his love to you.

SPARK. No.

HAR. Who, in fine, loves you better than his eyes, that first made him love you.

SPARK. Ay—— Nay, Madam, faith, you shan't go till——

ALITH. Have a care, lest you make me stay too long.

SPARK. But till he has saluted you; that I may be assured you are friends, after his honest advice and declaration. Come, pray, Madam, be friends with him.

Enter MASTER PINCHWIFE, MRS. PINCHWIFE

ALITH. You must pardon me, Sir, that I am not yet so obedient to you.

PINCH. What, invite your wife to kiss men? Monstrous! Are you not ashamed? I will never forgive you.

SPARK. Are you not ashamed that I should have more confidence in the chastity of your family than you have? You must not teach me; I am a man of honour, Sir, though I am frank and free; I am frank, Sir——

PINCH. Very frank, Sir, to share your wife with your friends.

SPARK. He is an humble, menial friend, such as reconciles the differences of the marriage bed; you know man and wife do not always agree; I design him for that use, therefore would have him well with my wife.

PINCH. A menial friend!—you will get a great many menial friends, by showing your wife as you do.

SPARK. What then? It may be I have a pleasure in't, as I have to show fine clothes at a playhouse, the first day, and count money before poor rogues.

PINCH. He that shows his wife or money, will be in danger of having them borrowed sometimes.

SPARK. I love to be envied, and would not marry a wife that I alone could love; loving alone is as dull as eating alone. Is it not a frank age? and I am a frank person; and to tell you the truth, it may be I love to have rivals in a wife; they make her seem to a man still but as a kept mistress; and so good night, for I must to Whitehall.——Madam, I hope you are now reconciled to my friend; and so I wish you a good night, Madam, and sleep if you can: for to-morrow you know I must visit you early with a canonical gentleman. Good night, dear Harcourt.   [*exit* SPARKISH]

HAR. Madam, I hope you will not refuse my visit to-morrow, if it should be earlier with a canonical gentleman than Mr. Sparkish's.

PINCH.   This gentlewoman is yet under my care, therefore you must yet forbear your freedom with her, Sir.

[*coming between* ALITHEA *and* HARCOURT]

HAR.   Must, Sir?

PINCH.   Yes, Sir, she is my sister.

HAR.   'Tis well she is, Sir—for I must be her servant, Sir.——Madam——

PINCH.   Come away, Sister, we had been gone, if it had not been for you, and so avoided these lewd rake-hells, who seem to haunt us.

Enter HORNER, DORILANT *to them*

HORN.   How now, Pinchwife!

PINCH.   Your servant.

HORN.   What! I see a little time in the country makes a man turn wild and unsociable, and only fit to converse with his horses, dogs, and his herds.

PINCH.   I have business, Sir, and must mind it; your business is pleasure; therefore you and I must go different ways.

HORN.   Well, you may go on, but this pretty young gentleman——

[*takes hold of* MRS. PINCHWIFE]

HAR.   The lady——

DOR.   And the maid——

HORN.   Shall stay with us; for I suppose their business is the same with ours, pleasure.

PINCH. [*aside*]   'Sdeath, he knows her, she carries it so sillily! Yet if he does not, I should be more silly to discover it first.

ALITH.   Pray, let us go, Sir.

PINCH.   Come, come——

HORN. [*to* MRS. PINCHWIFE]   Had you not rather stay with us?——Prithee, Pinchwife, who is this pretty young gentleman?

PINCH.   One to whom I'm a guardian.—[*aside*] I wish I could keep her out of your hands.

HORN.   Who is he? I never saw anything so pretty in all my life.

PINCH.   Pshaw! do not look upon him so much, he's a poor bashful youth; you'll put him out of countenance.——Come away, brother.

[*offers to take her away*]

HORN.   Oh, your brother!

PINCH.   Yes, my wife's brother.——Come, come, she'll stay supper for us.

HORN.   I thought so, for he is very like her I saw you at the play with, whom I told you I was in love with.

MRS. PINCH. [*aside*]   O jeminy! is that he that was in love with me? I am glad on't, I vow, for he's a curious fine gentleman, and I love him already, too.—[*to* PINCHWIFE] Is this he, bud?

PINCH. [*to his Wife*]   Come away, come away.

HORN.   Why, what haste are you in? why won't you let me talk with him?

PINCH.   Because you'll debauch him; he's yet young and innocent, and I would not have him debauched for anything in the world.—[*aside*] How she gazes on him! the devil!

HORN.   Harcourt, Dorilant, look you here, this is the likeness of that dowdy he told us of, his wife; did you ever see a lovelier creature? The rogue has reason to be jealous of his wife, since she is like him, for she would make all that see her in love with her.

HAR.   And, as I remember now, she is as like him here as can be.

DOR.   She is indeed very pretty, if she be like him.

HORN.   Very pretty? a very pretty commendation!—she is a glorious creature, beautiful beyond all things I ever beheld.

PINCH.   So, so.

HAR.   More beautiful than a poet's first mistress of imagination.

HORN.   Or another man's last mistress of flesh and blood.

MRS. PINCH.   Nay, now you jeer, Sir; pray don't jeer me.

PINCH.   Come, come.—[*aside*] By Heavens, she'll discover herself!

HORN.   I speak of your sister, Sir.

PINCH.   Ay, but saying she was handsome, if like him, made him blush.—[*aside*] I am upon a rack!

HORN.   Methinks he is so handsome he should not be a man.

PINCH. [*aside*]   Oh, there 'tis out! he has discovered her! I am not able to suffer any longer.—[*to his Wife*] Come, come away, I say.

HORN.   Nay, by your leave, Sir, he shall not go yet.—[*aside to them*] Harcourt, Dorilant, let us torment this jealous rogue a little.

HAR. ⎫
DOR. ⎭ How?

HORN.   I'll show you.

PINCH.   Come, pray let him go, I cannot stay fooling any longer; I tell you his sister stays supper for us.

HORN.   Does she? Come then, we'll all go to sup with he and thee.

PINCH.   No, now I think on't, having stayed so long for us, I warrant she's gone to bed.—[*aside*] I wish she and I were well out of their hands.——Come, I must rise early to-morrow, come.

HORN.   Well then, if she be gone to bed, I wish her and you a good night. But pray, young gentleman, present my humble service to her.

MRS. PINCH.   Thank you heartily, Sir.

PINCH. [*aside*]   'Sdeath, she will discover herself yet in spite of me. ——He is something more civil to you, for your kindness to his sister, than I am, it seems.

HORN.   Tell her, dear sweet little gentleman, for all your brother there, that you have revived the love I had for her at first sight in the playhouse.

MRS. PINCH.   But did you love her indeed, and indeed?

PINCH. [*aside*]   So, so.——Away, I say.

HORN.   Nay, stay.——Yes, indeed, and indeed, pray do you tell her so, and give her this kiss from me.   [*kisses her*]

PINCH. [*aside*]   O Heavens! what do I suffer? Now 'tis too plain he knows her, and yet——

HORN.   And this, and this——   [*kisses her again*]

MRS. PINCH.   What do you kiss me for? I am no woman.

PINCH. [*aside*]   So, there, 'tis out.—Come, I cannot, nor will stay any longer.

HORN.   Nay, they shall send your lady a kiss too. Here, Harcourt, Dorilant, will you not?   [*they kiss her*]

PINCH. [*aside*]   How! do I suffer this? Was I not accusing another just now for this rascally patience, in permitting his wife to be kissed before his face? Ten thousand ulcers gnaw away their lips.——Come, come.

HORN.   Good night, dear little gentleman; Madam, good night; farewell, Pinchwife.—[*apart to* HARCOURT *and* DORILANT] Did not I tell you I would raise his jealous gall?

[*exeunt* HORNER, HARCOURT, *and* DORILANT]

PINCH.   So, they are gone at last; stay, let me see first if the coach be at this door.   [*exit*]

HORNER, HARCOURT, *and* DORILANT *return*

HORN.   What, not gone yet? Will you be sure to do as I desired you, sweet Sir?

MRS. PINCH.   Sweet Sir, but what will you give me then?

HORN.   Anything. Come away into the next walk.

[*exit, hauling away* MRS. PINCHWIFE]

ALITH.   Hold! hold! what d'ye do?

LUCY.   Stay, stay, hold——

HAR.   Hold, Madam, hold, let him present him—he'll come presently; nay, I will never let you go till you answer my question.

[ALITHEA, LUCY, *struggling with* HARCOURT *and* DORILANT]

LUCY.   For God's sake, Sir, I must follow 'em.

DOR.   No, I have something to present you with too, you shan't follow them.

PINCHWIFE *returns*

PINCH.   Where?—how—what's become of?—gone!—whither?

LUCY.   He's only gone with the gentleman, who will give him something, an't please your worship.

PINCH.   Something!—give him something, with a pox!—where are
they?

ALITH.   In the next walk only, Brother.

PINCH.   Only, only! where, where?

[*exit* PINCHWIFE *and returns presently, then goes out again*]

HAR.   What's the matter with him? Why so much concerned? But,
dearest Madam——

ALITH.   Pray let me go, Sir; I have said and suffered enough already.

HAR.   Then you will not look upon, nor pity, my sufferings?

ALITH.   To look upon 'em, when I cannot help 'em, were cruelty, not
pity; therefore, I will never see you more.

HAR.   Let me then, Madam, have my privilege of a banished lover,
complaining or railing, and giving you but a farewell reason why, if you
cannot condescend to marry me, you should not take that wretch, my
rival.

ALITH.   He only, not you, since my honour is engaged so far to him,
can give me a reason why I should not marry him; but if he be true, and
what I think him to me, I must be so to him. Your servant, Sir.

HAR.   Have women only constancy when 'tis a vice, and, like
Fortune, only true to fools?

DOR.   Thou shalt not stir, thou robust creature; you see I can deal
with you, therefore you should stay the rather, and be kind.

[*to* LUCY, *who struggles to get from him*]

Enter PINCHWIFE

PINCH.   Gone, gone, not to be found! quite gone! ten thousand
plagues go with 'em! which way went they?

ALITH.   But into t'other walk, Brother.

LUCY.   Their business will be done presently sure, an't please your
worship; it can't be long in doing, I'm sure on't.

ALITH.   Are they not there?

PINCH.   No, you know where they are, you infamous wretch, eternal
shame of your family, which you do not dishonour enough yourself you
think, but you must help her to do it too, thou legion of bawds!

ALITH.   Good Brother——

PINCH.   Damned, damned Sister!

ALITH.   Look you here, she's coming.

Enter MRS. PINCHWIFE *in man's clothes, running, with her hat under
her arm, full of oranges and dried fruit,* HORNER *following*

MRS. PINCH.   O dear bud, look you here what I have got, see!

PINCH. [*aside, rubbing his forehead*]   And what I have got here too, which you can't see.

MRS. PINCH.   The fine gentleman has given me better things yet.

PINCH.   Has he so?—[*aside*] Out of breath and coloured!—I must hold yet.

HORN.   I have only given your little brother an orange, Sir.

PINCH. [*to* HORNER]   Thank you, Sir.—[*aside*] You have only squeezed my orange, I suppose, and given it me again; yet I must have a city patience.—[*to his Wife*] Come, come away.

MRS. PINCH.   Stay, till I have put up my fine things, bud.

Enter SIR JASPER FIDGET

SIR JASP.   O, Master Horner, come, come, the ladies stay for you; your mistress, my wife, wonders you make not more haste to her.

HORN.   I have stayed this half hour for you here, and 'tis your fault I am not now with your wife.

SIR JASP.   But, pray, don't let her know so much; the truth on't is, I was advancing a certain project to his majesty about—I'll tell you.

HORN.   No, let's go, and hear it at your house. Good night, sweet little gentleman; one kiss more, you'll remember me now, I hope.

[*kisses her*]

DOR.   What, Sir Jasper, will you separate friends? He promised to sup with us, and if you take him to your house, you'll be in danger of our company too.

SIR JASP.   Alas! gentlemen, my house is not fit for you; there are none but civil women there, which are not for your turn. He, you know, can bear with the society of civil women now, ha! ha! ha! besides, he's one of my family—he's—he! he! he!

DOR.   What is he?

SIR JASP.   Faith, my eunuch, since you'll have it; he! he! he!

[*Exeunt* SIR JASPER FIDGET *and* HORNER]

DOR.   I rather wish thou wert his or my cuckold. Harcourt, what a good cuckold is lost there for want of a man to make him one! Thee and I cannot have Horner's privilege, who can make use of it.

HAR.   Ay, to poor Horner 'tis like coming to an estate at threescore, when a man can't be the better for't.

PINCH.   Come.

MRS. PINCH.   Presently, bud.

DOR.   Come, let us go too.—[*to* ALITHEA] Madam, your servant.—[*to* LUCY] Good night, strapper.

HAR.   Madam, though you will not let me have a good day or night, I wish you one; but dare not name the other half of my wish.

ALITH.   Good night, Sir, for ever.

MRS. PINCH.   I don't know where to put this here, dear bud, you shall
eat it; nay, you shall have part of the fine gentleman's good things, or treat,
as you call it, when we come home.

PINCH.   Indeed, I deserve it, since I furnished the best part of it.

                                                [*strikes away the orange*]

The gallant treats presents, and gives the ball;
But 'tis the absent cuckold pays for all.

ACT IV

SCENE I

In PINCHWIFE'S *House in the morning*

LUCY, ALITHEA *dressed in new clothes*

LUCY.   Well, Madam,—now have I dressed you, and set you out with so many ornaments, and spent upon you ounces of essence and pulvillio; and all this for no other purpose but as people adorn and perfume a corpse for a stinking second-hand grave: such, or as bad, I think Master Sparkish's bed.

ALITH.   Hold your peace.

LUCY.   Nay, Madam, I will ask you the reason why you would banish poor Master Harcourt for ever from your sight; how could you be so hard-hearted?

ALITH.   'Twas because I was not hard-hearted.

LUCY.   No, no; 'twas stark love and kindness, I warrant.

ALITH.   It was so; I would see him no more because I love him.

LUCY.   Hey day, a very pretty reason!

ALITH.   You do not understand me.

LUCY.   I wish you may yourself.

ALITH.   I was engaged to marry, you see, another man, whom my justice will not suffer me to deceive or injure.

LUCY.   Can there be a greater cheat or wrong done to a man than to give him your person without your heart? I should make a conscience of it.

ALITH.   I'll retrieve it for him after I am married a while.

LUCY.   The woman that marries to love better, will be as much mistaken as the wencher that marries to live better. No, Madam, marrying to increase love is like gaming to become rich; alas! you only lose what little stock you had before.

ALITH.   I find by your rhetoric you have been bribed to betray me.

LUCY.   Only by his merit, that has bribed your heart, you see, against your word and rigid honour. But what a devil is this honour! 'tis sure a

disease in the head, like the megrim or falling-sickness, that always hur-
ries people away to do themselves mischief. Men lose their lives by it;
women, what's dearer to 'em, their love, the life of life.

ALITH. Come, pray talk you no more of honour, nor Master
Harcourt; I wish the other would come to secure my fidelity to him and
his right in me.

LUCY. You will marry him then?

ALITH. Certainly; I have given him already my word, and will my
hand too, to make it good, when he comes.

LUCY. Well, I wish I may never stick pin more, if he be not an arrant
natural to t'other fine gentleman.

ALITH. I own he wants the wit of Harcourt, which I will dispense
withal for another want he has, which is want of jealousy, which men of
wit seldom want.

LUCY. Lord, Madam, what should you do with a fool to your husband? You intend to be honest, don't you? then that husbandly virtue,
credulity, is thrown away upon you.

ALITH. He only that could suspect my virtue should have cause to
do it; 'tis Sparkish's confidence in my truth that obliges me to be so faithful to him.

LUCY. You are not sure his opinion may last.

ALITH. I am satisfied 'tis impossible for him to be jealous after the
proofs I have had of him. Jealousy in a husband—Heaven defend me
from it! it begets a thousand plagues to a poor woman, the loss of her
honour, her quiet, and her——

LUCY. And her pleasure.

ALITH. What d'ye mean, impertinent?

LUCY. Liberty is a great pleasure, Madam.

ALITH. I say, loss of her honour, her quiet, nay, her life sometimes;
and what's as bad almost, the loss of this town; that is, she is sent into the
country, which is the last ill-usage of a husband to a wife, I think.

LUCY [aside] Oh, does the wind lie there?—— Then of necessity,
Madam, you think a man must carry his wife into the country, if he be
wise. The country is as terrible, I find, to our young English ladies, as a
monastery to those abroad; and, on my virginity, I think they would
rather marry a London jailer than a high sheriff of a county, since neither can stir from his employment. Formerly women of wit married fools
for a great estate, a fine seat, or the like; but now 'tis for a pretty seat only
in Lincoln's Inn Fields, St. James's Fields, or the Pall Mall.

Enter to them SPARKISH, *and* HARCOURT, *dressed like a Parson*

SPARK. Madam, your humble servant, a happy day to you, and to us
all.

HAR.   Amen.

ALITH.   Who have we here?

SPARK.   My chaplain, faith—— O Madam, poor Harcourt remembers his humble service to you; and, in obedience to your last commands, refrains coming into your sight.

ALITH.   Is not that he?

SPARK.   No, fy, no; but to show that he ne'er intended to hinder our match, has sent his brother here to join our hands. When I get me a wife, I must get her a chaplain, according to the custom; that is his brother, and my chaplain.

ALITH.   His brother!

LUCY. [*aside*]   And your chaplain, to preach in your pulpit then——

ALITH.   His brother!

SPARK.   Nay, I knew you would not believe it.—— I told you, Sir, she would take you for your brother Frank.

ALITH.   Believe it!

LUCY. [*aside*]   His brother! ha! ha! he! he has a trick left still, it seems.

SPARK.   Come, my dearest, pray let us go to church before the canonical hour is past.

ALITH.   For shame, you are abused still.

SPARK.   By the world, 'tis strange now you are so incredulous.

ALITH.   'Tis strange you are so credulous.

SPARK.   Dearest of my life, hear me. I tell you this is Ned Harcourt of Cambridge, by the world; you see he has a sneaking college look. 'Tis true he's something like his brother Frank; and they differ from each other no more than in their age, for they were twins.

LUCY.   Ha! ha! he!

ALITH.   Your servant, Sir; I cannot be so deceived, though you are. But come, let's hear, how do you know what you affirm so confidently?

SPARK.   Why, I'll tell you all. Frank Harcourt coming to me this morning to wish me joy, and present his service to you, I asked him if he could help me to a parson. Whereupon he told me he had a brother in town who was in orders; and he went straight away, and sent him, you see there, to me.

ALITH.   Yes, Frank goes and puts on a black coat, then tells you he is Ned; that's all you have for't.

SPARK.   Pshaw! pshaw! I tell you, by the same token, the midwife put her garter about Frank's neck, to know 'em asunder, they were so like.

ALITH.   Frank tells you this too?

SPARK.   Ay, and Ned there too: nay, they are both in a story.

ALITH.   So, so; very foolish.

SPARK.   Lord, if you won't believe one, you had best try him by your chambermaid there; for chambermaids must needs know chaplains from other men, they are so used to 'em.

LUCY.   Let's see: nay, I'll be sworn he has the canonical smirk, and the filthy clammy palm of a chaplain.

ALITH.   Well, most reverend Doctor, pray let us make an end of this fooling.

HAR.   With all my soul, divine heavenly creature, when you please.

ALITH.   He speaks like a chaplain indeed.

SPARK.   Why, was there not soul, divine, heavenly, in what he said?

ALITH.   Once more, most impertinent black coat, cease your persecution, and let us have a conclusion of this ridiculous love.

HAR. [*aside*]   I had forgot; I must suit my style to my coat, or I wear it in vain.

ALITH.   I have no more patience left; let us make once an end of this troublesome love, I say.

HAR.   So be it, seraphic lady, when your honour shall think it meet and convenient so to do.

SPARK.   'Gad, I'm sure none but a chaplain could speak so, I think.

ALITH.   Let me tell you, Sir, this dull trick will not serve your turn; though you delay our marriage, you shall not hinder it.

HAR.   Far be it from me, munificent patroness, to delay your marriage; I desire nothing more than to marry you presently, which I might do, if you yourself would; for my noble, good-natured, and thrice generous patron here would not hinder it.

SPARK.   No, poor man, not I, faith.

HAR.   And now, Madam, let me tell you plainly nobody else shall marry you, by Heavens! I'll die first, for I'm sure I should die after it.

LUCY.   How his love has made him forget his function, as I have seen it in real parsons!

ALITH.   That was spoken like a chaplain too? Now you understand him, I hope.

SPARK.   Poor man, he takes it heinously to be refused; I can't blame him, 'tis putting an indignity upon him, not to be suffered; but you'll pardon me, Madam, it shan't be; he shall marry us; come away, pray, Madam.

LUCY.   Ha! ha! he! more ado! 'tis late.

ALITH.   Invincible stupidity! I tell you, he would marry me as your rival, not as your chaplain.

SPARK.   Come, come, Madam.   [*pulling her away*]

LUCY.   I pray, Madam, do not refuse this reverend divine the honour and satisfaction of marrying you; for I dare say he has set his heart upon't, good Doctor.

ALITH.   What can you hope or design by this?

HAR. [*aside*]   I could answer her, a reprieve for a day only, often revokes a hasty doom. At worst, if she will not take mercy on me, and let me marry her, I have at least the lover's second pleasure, hindering my rival's enjoyment, though but for a time.

SPARK.   Come, Madam, 'tis e'en twelve o'clock, and my mother charged me never to be married out of the canonical hours. Come, come; Lord, here's such a deal of modesty, I warrant, the first day.

LUCY.   Yes, an't please your worship, married women show all their modesty the first day, because married men show all their love the first day.   [*exeunt* SPARKISH, ALITHEA, HARCOURT, *and* LUCY]

SCENE II

The Scene changes to a Bedchamber, where appear PINCHWIFE *and* MRS. PINCHWIFE

PINCH.   Come, tell me, I say.

MRS. PINCH.   Lord! han't I told it a hundred times over?

PINCH. [*aside*]   I would try, if in the repetition of the ungrateful tale, I could find her altering it in the least circumstance; for if her story be false, she is so too.—— Come, how was't, baggage?

MRS. PINCH.   Lord, what pleasure you take to hear it, sure!

PINCH.   No, you take more in telling it I find; but speak, how was't?

MRS. PINCH.   He carried me up into the house next to the Exchange.

PINCH.   So, and you two were only in the room!

MRS. PINCH.   Yes, for he sent away a youth that was there, for some dried fruit, and China oranges.

PINCH.   Did he so? Damn him for it—and for——

MRS. PINCH.   But presently came up the gentlewoman of the house.

PINCH.   Oh, 'twas well she did; but what did he do whilst the fruit came?

MRS. PINCH.   He kissed me an hundred times, and told me he fancied he kissed my fine sister, meaning me, you know, whom he said he loved with all his soul, and bid me be sure to tell her so, and to desire her to be at her window, by eleven of the clock this morning, and he would walk under it at that time.

PINCH. [*aside*]   And he was as good as his word, very punctual; a pox reward him for't.

MRS. PINCH.   Well, and he said if you were not within, he would come up to her, meaning me, you know, bud, still.

PINCH. [*aside*]   So—he knew her certainly; but for this confession, I am obliged to her simplicity.——But what, you stood very still when he kissed you?

MRS. PINCH.   Yes, I warrant you; would you have had me discover myself?

PINCH.   But you told me he did some beastliness to you, as you call it; what was't?

MRS. PINCH.   Why, he put——

PINCH.   What?

MRS. PINCH.   Why, he put the tip of his tongue between my lips, and so moused me—and I said, I'd bite it.

PINCH.   An eternal canker seize it, for a dog!

MRS. PINCH.   Nay, you need not be so angry with him neither, for to say truth, he has the sweetest breath I ever knew.

PINCH.   The devil! you were satisfied with it then, and would do it again?

MRS. PINCH.   Not unless he should force me.

PINCH.   Force you, changeling! I tell you, no woman can be forced.

MRS. PINCH.   Yes, but she may sure, by such a one as he, for he's a proper, goodly, strong man; 'tis hard, let me tell you, to resist him.

PINCH. [aside]   So, 'tis plain she loves him, yet she has not love enough to make her conceal it from me; but the sight of him will increase her aversion for me and love for him; and that love instruct her how to deceive me and satisfy him, all idiot as she is. Love! 'twas he gave women first their craft, their art of deluding. Out of Nature's hands they came plain, open, silly, and fit for slaves, as she and Heaven intended 'em; but damned Love—well—I must strangle that little monster whilst I can deal with him.—— Go fetch pen, ink, and paper out of the next room.

MRS. PINCH.   Yes, bud.   [exit]

PINCH.   Why should women have more invention in love than men? It can only be, because they have more desires, more soliciting passions, more lust, and more of the devil.

MRS. PINCHWIFE returns

Come, minx, sit down and write.

MRS. PINCH.   Ay, dear bud, but I can't do't very well.

PINCH.   I wish you could not at all.

MRS. PINCH.   But what should I write for?

PINCH.   I'll have you write a letter to your lover.

MRS. PINCH.   O Lord, to the fine gentleman a letter!

PINCH.   Yes, to the fine gentleman.

MRS. PINCH.   Lord, you do but jeer: sure you jest.

PINCH.   I am not so merry: come, write as I bid you.

MRS. PINCH.   What, do you think I am a fool?

PINCH. [aside]   She's afraid I would not dictate any love to him, therefore she's unwilling.—But you had best begin.

MRS. PINCH.   Indeed, and indeed, but I won't, so I won't.

PINCH.   Why?

MRS. PINCH.   Because he's in town; you may send for him if you will.

PINCH.   Very well, you would have him brought to you; is it come to this? I say, take the pen and write, or you'll provoke me.

MRS. PINCH.   Lord, what d'ye make a fool of me for? Don't I know that letters are never writ but from the country to London, and from London into the country? Now he's in town, and I am in town too; therefore I can't write to him, you know.

PINCH. [*aside*]   So, I am glad it is no worse; she is innocent enough yet.—— Yes, you may, when your husband bids you, write letters to people that are in town.

MRS. PINCH.   Oh, may I so? then I'm satisfied.

PINCH.   Come, begin [*dictates*]—"Sir"——

MRS. PINCH.   Shan't I say, "Dear Sir?" You know one says always something more than bare "Sir."

PINCH.   Write as I bid you, or I will write whore with this penknife in your face.

MRS. PINCH.   Nay, good bud [*she writes*]—"Sir"——

PINCH.   "Though I suffered last night your nauseous, loathed kisses and embraces"—— Write!

MRS. PINCH.   Nay, why should I say so? You know I told you he had a sweet breath.

PINCH.   Write!

MRS. PINCH.   Let me but put out "loathed."

PINCH.   Write, I say!

MRS. PINCH.   Well then.   [*writes*]

PINCH.   Let's see, what have you writ?—[*takes the paper and reads*] "Though I suffered last night your kisses and embraces"—— Thou impudent creature! where is "nauseous" and "loathed"?

MRS. PINCH.   I can't abide to write such filthy words.

PINCH.   Once more write as I'd have you, and question it not, or I will spoil thy writing with this. I will stab out those eyes that cause my mischief.   [*holds up the penknife*]

MRS. PINCH.   O Lord! I will.

PINCH.   So—so—let's see now.—[*reads*] "Though I suffered last night your nauseous, loathed kisses and embraces"—go on—"yet I would not have you presume that you shall ever repeat them"—so——   [*she writes*]

MRS. PINCH.   I have writ it.

PINCH.   On, then—"I then concealed myself from your knowledge, to avoid your insolencies."——   [*she writes*]

MRS. PINCH.   So——

PINCH.   "The same reason, now I am out of your hands"——

                                                               [*she writes*]

MRS. PINCH.   So——

PINCH.   "Makes me own to you my unfortunate, though innocent frolic, of being in man's clothes"——   [*she writes*]

MRS. PINCH.   So——

PINCH.   "That you may for evermore cease to pursue her, who hates and detests you"——   [*she writes on*]

MRS. PINCH.   So-h——   [*sighs*]

PINCH.   What, do you sigh?—"detests you—as much as she loves her husband and her honour."

MRS. PINCH.   I vow, husband, he'll ne'er believe I should write such a letter.

PINCH.   What, he'd expect a kinder from you? Come, now your name only.

MRS. PINCH.   What, shan't I say "Your most faithful humble servant till death?"

PINCH.   No, tormenting fiend!—[*aside*] Her style, I find, would be very soft.—— Come, wrap it up now, whilst I go fetch wax and a candle; and write on the backside, "For Mr. Horner."   [*exit* PINCHWIFE]

MRS. PINCH.   "For Mr. Horner."—— So, I am glad he has told me his name. Dear Mr. Horner! But why should I send thee such a letter that will vex thee, and make thee angry with me?—— Well, I will not send it.—— Ay, but then my husband will kill me—for I see plainly he won't let me love Mr. Horner—but what care I for my husband? I won't, so I won't, send poor Mr. Horner such a letter—— But then my husband—but oh, what if I writ at bottom my husband made me write it?—— Ay, but then my husband would see't—Can one have no shift? Ah, a London woman would have had a hundred presently. Stay—what if I should write a letter, and wrap it up like this, and write upon't too? Ay, but then my husband would see't—I don't know what to do.—But yet evads I'll try, so I will—for I will not send this letter to poor Mr. Horner, come what will on't.

"Dear, sweet Mr. Horner"—[*she writes and repeats what she hath writ*]—so—"my husband would have me send you a base, rude, unmannerly letter; but I won't"—so—"and would have me forbid you loving me; but I won't"—so—"and would have me say to you, I hate you, poor Mr. Horner; but I won't tell a lie for him"—there—"for I'm sure if you and I were in the country at cards together"—so—"I could not help treading on your toe under the table"—so—"or rubbing knees with you, and staring in your face, till you saw me"—very well—"and then looking down, and blushing for an hour together"—so— "but I must make haste before my husband come: and now he has taught me to write letters, you shall have longer ones from me, who am, dear, dear, poor, dear Mr. Horner, your most humble friend, and servant to command till death,— Margery Pinchwife."

Stay, I must give him a hint at bottom—so—now wrap it up just like t'other—so—now write "For Mr. Horner"—But oh now, what shall I do with it? for here comes my husband.

Enter PINCHWIFE

PINCH. [*aside*]   I have been detained by a sparkish coxcomb, who pretended a visit to me; but I fear 'twas to my wife——— What, have you done?

MRS. PINCH.   Ay, ay, bud, just now.

PINCH.   Let's see't: what d'ye tremble for? what, you would not have it go?

MRS. PINCH.   Here—[*aside*] No, I must not give him that: so I had been served if I had given him this.   [*he opens and reads the first letter*]

PINCH.   Come, where's the wax and seal?

MRS. PINCH. [*aside*]   Lord, what shall I do now? Nay, then I have it——— Pray let me see't. Lord, you think me so arrant a fool I cannot seal a letter; I will do't, so I will.   [*snatches the letter from him, changes it for the other, seals it, and delivers it to him*]

PINCH.   Nay, I believe you will learn that, and other things too, which I would not have you.

MRS. PINCH.   So, han't I done it curiously?—[*aside*] I think I have; there's my letter going to Mr. Horner, since he'll needs have me send letters to folks.

PINCH.   'Tis very well; but I warrant, you would not have it go now?

MRS. PINCH.   Yes, indeed, but I would, bud, now.

PINCH.   Well, you are a good girl then. Come, let me lock you up in your chamber till I come back; and be sure you come not within three strides of the window when I am gone, for I have a spy in the street.— [*exit* MRS. PINCHWIFE, PINCHWIFE *locks the door*] At least, 'tis fit she think so. If we do not cheat women, they'll cheat us, and fraud may be justly used with secret enemies, of which a wife is the most dangerous; and he that has a handsome one to keep, and a frontier town, must provide against treachery, rather than open force. Now I have secured all within, I'll deal with the foe without, with false intelligence.

[*holds up the letter; exit* PINCHWIFE]

SCENE III

The Scene changes to HORNER'S *Lodging*

QUACK *and* HORNER

QUACK.   Well, Sir, how fadges the new design? Have you not the luck of all your brother projectors, to deceive only yourself at last?

HORN.   No, good domine Doctor, I deceive you, it seems, and others too; for the grave matrons, and old, rigid husbands think me as unfit for love as they are; but their wives, sisters, and daughters know, some of 'em, better things already.

QUACK.   Already!

HORN.   Already, I say. Last night I was drunk with half-a-dozen of your civil persons, as you call 'em, and people of honour, and so was made free of their society and dressing-rooms for ever hereafter; and am already come to the privileges of sleeping upon their pallets, warming smocks, tying shoes and garters, and the like, Doctor, already, already, Doctor.

QUACK.   You have made good use of your time, Sir.

HORN.   I tell thee, I am now no more interruption to 'em when they sing, or talk, bawdy, than a little squab French page who speaks no English.

QUACK.   But do civil persons and women of honour drink, and sing bawdy songs?

HORN.   Oh, amongst friends, amongst friends. For your bigots in honour are just like those in religion; they fear the eye of the world more than the eye of Heaven, and think there is no virtue but railing at vice, and no sin but giving scandal. They rail at a poor little kept player, and keep themselves some young modest pulpit comedian to be privy to their sins in their closets, not to tell 'em of them in their chapels.

QUACK.   Nay, the truth on't is priests, amongst the women now, have quite got the better of us lay-confessors, physicians.

HORN.   And they are rather their patients; but——

Enter MY LADY FIDGET, *looking about her*

Now we talk of women of honour, here comes one. Step behind the screen there, and but observe if I have not particular privileges with the women of reputation already, Doctor, already.   [QUACK *retires*]

LADY FID.   Well, Horner, am not I a woman of honour? You see, I'm as good as my word.

HORN.   And you shall see, Madam, I'll not behindhand with you in honour; and I'll be as good as my word too, if you please but to withdraw into the next room.

LADY FID.   But first, my dear Sir, you must promise to have a care of my dear honour.

HORN.   If you talk a word more of your honour, you'll make me incapable to wrong it. To talk of honour in the mysteries of love, is like talking of Heaven or the Deity in an operation of witchcraft just when you are employing the devil: it makes the charm impotent.

LADY FID.   Nay, fy! let us not be smutty. But you talk of mysteries and bewitching to me; I don't understand you.

HORN.   I tell you, Madam, the word money in a mistress's mouth, at such a nick of time, is not a more disheartening sound to a younger brother, than that of honour to an eager lover like myself.

LADY FID.   But you can't blame a lady of my reputation to be chary.

HORN.   Chary! I have been chary of it already, by the report I have caused of myself.

LADY FID.   Ay, but if you should ever let other women know that dear secret, it would come out. Nay, you must have a great care of your conduct; for my acquaintance are so censorious (oh, 'tis a wicked, censorious world, Mr. Horner!), I say, are so censorious and detracting that perhaps they'll talk to the prejudice of my honour, though you should not let them know the dear secret.

HORN.   Nay, Madam, rather than they shall prejudice your honour, I'll prejudice theirs; and, to serve you, I'll lie with 'em all, make the secret their own, and then they'll keep it. I am a Machiavel in love, Madam.

LADY FID.   Oh, no, Sir, not that way.

HORN.   Nay, the devil take me, if censorious women are to be silenced any other way.

LADY FID.   A secret is better kept, I hope, by a single person than a multitude; therefore pray do not trust anybody else with it, dear, dear Mr. Horner.   [*embracing him*]

Enter SIR JASPER FIDGET

SIR JASP.   How now!

LADY FID. [*aside*]   Oh my husband!—prevented—and what's almost as bad, found with my arms about another man—that will appear too much—what shall I say?—— Sir Jasper, come hither: I am trying if Mr. Horner were ticklish, and he's as ticklish as can be. I love to torment the confounded toad; let you and I tickle him.

SIR JASP.   No, your ladyship will tickle him better without me, I suppose. But is this your buying china? I thought you had been at the china-house.

HORN. [*aside*]   China-house! that's my cue, I must take it.—— A pox! can't you keep your impertinent wives at home? Some men are troubled with the husbands, but I with the wives; but I'd have you to know, since I cannot be your journeyman by night, I will not be your drudge by day, to squire your wife about, and be your man of straw or scarecrow only to pies and jays, that would be nibbling at your forbidden fruit; I shall be shortly the hackney gentleman-usher of the town.

SIR JASP. [*aside*]   He! he! he! poor fellow, he's in the right on't, faith. To squire women about for other folks is as ungrateful an employment, as to tell money for other folks.—— He! he! he! be'n't angry, Horner.

LADY FID.   No, 'tis I have more reason to be angry, who am left by you to go abroad indecently alone; or, what is more indecent, to pin myself upon such ill-bred people of your acquaintance as this is.

SIR JASP.   Nay, prithee, what has he done?

LADY FID.   Nay, he has done nothing.

SIR JASP.   But what d'ye take ill, if he has done nothing?

LADY FID.   Ha! ha! ha! faith, I can't but laugh, however; why, d'ye think the unmannerly toad would come down to me to the coach? I was fain to come up to fetch him, or go without him, which I was resolved not to do; for he knows china very well, and has himself very good, and will not let me see it lest I should beg some; but I will find it out, and have what I came for yet.

HORN. [*apart to* LADY FIDGET]   Lock the door, Madam.—[*exit* LADY FIDGET, *and* locks the door followed by HORNER to the door]—— So, she has got into my chamber and locked me out. Oh the impertinency of womankind! Well, Sir Jasper, plain-dealing is a jewel; if ever you suffer your wife to trouble me again here she shall carry you home a pair of horns; by my lord mayor she shall; though I cannot furnish you myself, you are sure, yet I'll find a way.

SIR JASP.   Ha! ha! he!—[*aside*] At my first coming in, and finding her arms about him, tickling him it seems, I was half jealous, but now I see my folly.—— He! he! he! poor Horner.

HORN.   Nay, though you laugh now, 'twill be my turn ere long. Oh, women, more impertinent, more cunning, and more mischievous than their monkeys, and to me almost as ugly!—Now is she throwing my things about and rifling all I have; but I'll get in to her the back way, and so rifle her for it.

SIR JASP.   Ha! ha! ha! poor angry Horner.

HORN.   Stay here a little, I'll ferret her out to you presently, I warrant.   [*exit at t'other door*]

[SIR JASPER *calls through the door to his Wife; she answers from within*]

SIR JASP.   Wife! my Lady Fidget! wife! he is coming in to you the back way.

LADY FID.   Let him come, and welcome, which way he will.

SIR JASP.   He'll catch you, and use you roughly, and be too strong for you.

LADY FID.   Don't you trouble yourself, let him if he can.

QUACK. [*behind*]   This indeed I could not have believed from him, nor any but my own eyes.

Enter MRS. SQUEAMISH

MRS. SQUEAM.   Where's this woman-hater, this toad, this ugly, greasy, dirty sloven?

SIR JASP. [*aside*]   So, the women all will have him ugly: methinks he is a comely person, but his wants make his form contemptible to 'em; and 'tis e'en as my wife said yesterday, talking of him, that a proper handsome eunuch was as ridiculous a thing as a gigantic coward.

MRS. SQUEAM.   Sir Jasper, your servant: where is the odious beast?

SIR JASP.   He's within in his chamber, with my wife; she's playing the wag with him.

MRS. SQUEAM.   Is she so? and he's a clownish beast, he'll give her no quarter, he'll play the wag with her again, let me tell you: come, let's go help her.—What, the door's locked?

SIR JASP.   Ay, my wife locked it.

MRS. SQUEAM.   Did she so? Let's break it open then.

SIR JASP.   No, no; he'll do her no hurt.

MRS. SQUEAM.   No.—[*aside*] But is there no other way to get in to 'em? Whither goes this? I will disturb 'em.

[*exit* MRS. SQUEAMISH *at another door*]

Enter OLD LADY SQUEAMISH

LADY SQUEAM.   Where is this harlotry, this impudent baggage, this ràmbling tomrigg? O Sir Jasper, I'm glad to see you here; did you not see my vile grandchild come in hither just now?

SIR JASP.   Yes.

LADY SQUEAM.   Ay, but where is she then? where is she? Lord, Sir Jasper, I have e'en rattled myself to pieces in pursuit of her: but can you tell what she makes here? They say below, no woman lodges here.

SIR JASP.   No.

LADY SQUEAM.   No! what does she here then? Say, if it be not a woman's lodging, what makes she here? But are you sure no woman lodges here?

SIR JASP.   No, nor no man neither; this is Mr. Horner's lodging.

LADY SQUEAM.   Is it so, are you sure?

SIR JASP.   Yes, yes.

LADY SQUEAM.   So; then there's no hurt in't, I hope. But where is he?

SIR JASP.   He's in the next room with my wife.

LADY SQUEAM.   Nay, if you trust him with your wife, I may with my Biddy. They say, he's a merry harmless man now, e'en as harmless a man as ever came out of Italy with a good voice, and as pretty, harmless company for a lady as a snake without his teeth.

SIR JASP.   Ay, ay, poor man.

Enter MRS. SQUEAMISH

MRS. SQUEAM.   I can't find 'em.—— Oh, are you here, Grandmother? I followed, you must know, my Lady Fidget hither; 'tis the prettiest lodging, and I have been staring on the prettiest pictures——

Enter LADY FIDGET *with a piece of china in her hand, and* HORNER *following*

LADY FID.   And I have been toiling and moiling for the prettiest piece of china, my dear. .

HORN.   Nay, she has been too hard for me, do what I could.

MRS. SQUEAM.   O Lord, I'll have some china too. Good Mr. Horner, don't think to give other people china, and me none; come in with me too.

HORN.   Upon my honour, I have none left now.

MRS. SQUEAM.   Nay, nay, I have known you deny your china before now, but you shan't put me off so. Come.

HORN.   This lady had the last there.

LADY FID.   Yes, indeed, Madam, to my certain knowledge, he has no more left.

MRS. SQUEAM.   Oh, but it may be he may have some you could not find.

LADY FID.   What, d'ye think if he had had any left, I would not have had it too? for we women of quality never think we have china enough.

HORN.   Do not take it ill, I cannot make china for you all, but I will have a roll-waggon for you too, another time.

MRS. SQUEAM.   Thank you, dear toad.

LADY FID. [*aside to* HORNER]   What do you mean by that promise?

HORN. [*aside to* LADY FIDGET]   Alas, she has an innocent, literal understanding.

LADY SQUEAM.   Poor Mr. Horner! he has enough to do to please you all, I see.

HORN.   Ay, Madam, you see how they use me.

LADY SQUEAM.   Poor gentleman, I pity you.

HORN.   I thank you, Madam: I could never find pity but from such reverend ladies as you are; the young ones will never spare a man.

MRS. SQUEAM.   Come, come, beast, and go dine with us; for we shall want a man at ombre after dinner.

HORN.   That's all their use of me, Madam, you see.

MRS. SQUEAM.   Come, sloven, I'll lead you, to be sure of you.

[*pulls him by the cravat*]

LADY SQUEAM.   Alas, poor man, how she tugs him! Kiss, kiss her; that's the way to make such nice women quiet.

HORN.   No, Madam, that remedy is worse than the torment; they know I dare suffer anything rather than do it.

LADY SQUEAM.   Prithee kiss her, and I'll give you her picture in little, that you admired so last night; prithee do.

HORN.   Well, nothing but that could bribe me: I love a woman only in effigy and good painting, as much as I hate them. I'll do't, for I could adore the devil well painted.   [*kisses* MRS. SQUEAMISH]

MRS. SQUEAM.   Foh, you filthy toad! nay, now I've done jesting.

LADY SQUEAM.   Ha! ha! ha! I told you so.

MRS. SQUEAM.   Foh! a kiss of his——

SIR JASP.   Has no more hurt in't than one of my spaniel's.

MRS. SQUEAM.   Nor no more good neither.

QUACK. [*behind*]   I will now believe anything he tells me.

Enter PINCHWIFE

LADY FID.   O Lord, here's a man! Sir Jasper, my mask, my mask! I would not be seen here for the world.

SIR JASP.   What, not when I am with you?

LADY FID.   No, no, my honour—let's be gone.

MRS. SQUEAM.   O Grandmother, let us be gone; make haste, make haste, I know not how he may censure us.

LADY FID.   Be found in the lodging of anything like a man!—Away.

[*exeunt* SIR JASPER FIDGET, LADY FIDGET,
OLD LADY SQUEAMISH, MRS. SQUEAMISH]

QUACK. [*behind*]   What's here? another cuckold? he looks like one, and none else sure have any business with him.

HORN.   Well, what brings my dear friend hither?

PINCH.   Your impertinency.

HORN.   My impertinency!—why, you gentlemen that have got handsome wives think you have a privilege of saying anything to your friends, and are as brutish as if you were our creditors.

PINCH.   No, Sir, I'll ne'er trust you any way.

HORN.   But why not, dear Jack? Why diffide in me thou know'st so well?

PINCH.   Because I do know you so well.

HORN.   Han't I been always thy friend, honest Jack, always ready to serve thee, in love or battle, before thou wert married, and am so still?

PINCH.   I believe so; you would be my second now, indeed.

HORN.   Well then, dear Jack, why so unkind, so grum, so strange to me? Come, prithee kiss me, dear rogue: gad, I was always, I say, and am still as much thy servant as——

PINCH.   As I am yours, Sir. What, you would send a kiss to my wife, is that it?

HORN.   So, there 'tis—a man can't show his friendship to a married man, but presently he talks of his wife to you. Prithee, let thy wife alone, and let thee and I be all one, as we were wont. What, thou art as shy of my kindness as a Lombard Street alderman of a courtier's civility at Locket's!

PINCH.   But you are overkind to me, as kind as if I were your cuckold already; yet I must confess you ought to be kind and civil to me, since I am so kind, so civil to you, as to bring you this: look you there, Sir.

                                    [*delivers him a letter*]

HORN.   What is't?

PINCH.   Only a love letter, Sir.

HORN.   From whom?—how! this is from your wife—hum—and hum——   [*reads*]

PINCH.   Even from my wife, Sir: am I not wondrous kind and civil to you now too?—[*aside*] But you'll not think her so.

HORN. [*aside*]   Ha! is this a trick of his or hers?

PINCH.   The gentleman's surprised I find.—What, you expected a kinder letter?

HORN.   No faith, not I, how could I?

PINCH.   Yes, yes, I'm sure you did. A man so well made as you are must needs be disappointed, if the women declare not their passion at first sight or opportunity.

HORN. [*aside*]   But what should this mean? Stay, the postscript.— [*reads aside*] "Be sure you love me, whatsoever my husband says to the contrary, and let him not see this, lest he should come home and pinch me, or kill my squirrel."—It seems he knows not what the letter contains.

PINCH.   Come, ne'er wonder at it so much.

HORN.   Faith, I can't help it.

PINCH.   Now, I think I have deserved your infinite friendship and kindness, and have showed myself sufficiently an obliging kind friend and husband; am I not so, to bring a letter from my wife to her gallant?

HORN.   Ay, the devil take me, art thou, the most obliging, kind friend and husband in the world, ha! ha!

PINCH.   Well, you may be merry, Sir; but in short I must tell you, Sir, my honour will suffer no jesting.

HORN.   What dost thou mean?

PINCH.   Does the letter want a comment? Then, know, Sir, though I have been so civil a husband as to bring you a letter from my wife, to let you kiss and court her to my face, I will not be a cuckold, Sir, I will not.

HORN.   Thou art mad with jealousy. I never saw thy wife in my life but at the play yesterday, and I know not if it were she or no. I court her, kiss her!

PINCH.   I will not be a cuckold, I say; there will be danger in making me a cuckold.

HORN.   Why, wert thou not well cured of thy last clap?

PINCH.   I wear a sword.

HORN.   It should be taken from thee, lest thou shouldst do thyself a mischief with it; thou art mad, man.

PINCH.   As mad as I am, and as merry as you are, I must have more reason from you ere we part. I say again, though you kissed and courted last night my wife in man's clothes, as she confesses in her letter——

HORN. [*aside*]   Ha!

PINCH.   Both she and I say you must not design it again, for you have mistaken your woman, as you have done your man.

HORN. [*aside*]   Oh—I understand something now—— Was that thy wife! Why wouldst thou not tell me 'twas she? Faith, my freedom with her was your fault, not mine.

PINCH. [*aside*]   Faith, so 'twas.

HORN.   Fy! I'd never do't to a woman before her husband's face, sure.

PINCH.   But I had rather you should do't to my wife before my face, than behind my back; and that you shall never do.

HORN.   No—you will hinder me.

PINCH.   If I would not hinder you, you see by her letter she would.

HORN.   Well, I must e'en acquiesce then, and be contented with what she writes.

PINCH.   I'll assure you 'twas voluntarily writ; I had no hand in't, you may believe me.

HORN.   I do believe thee, faith.

PINCH.   And believe her too, for she's an innocent creature, has no dissembling in her: and so fare you well, Sir.

HORN.   Pray, however, present my humble service to her, and tell her I will obey her letter to a tittle, and fulfil her desires, be what they will, or with what difficulty soever I do't; and you shall be no more jealous of me, I warrant her, and you.

PINCH.   Well then, fare you well; and play with any man's honour but mine, kiss any man's wife but mine, and welcome.

[*exit* MR. PINCHWIFE]

HORN.   Ha! ha! ha! Doctor.

QUACK.   It seems he has not heard the report of you, or does not believe it.

HORN.   Ha! ha!—now, Doctor, what think you?

QUACK.   Pray let's see the letter—hum—[*reads the letter*]—"for—dear—love you——"

HORN.   I wonder how she could contrive it! What say'st thou to't? 'Tis an original.

QUACK.   So are your cuckolds, too, originals: for they are like no other common cuckolds, and I will henceforth believe it not impossible for you to cuckold the Grand Signior amidst his guards of eunuchs, that I say.

HORN.   And I say for the letter, 'tis the first love-letter that ever was without flames, darts, fates, destinies, lying and dissembling in't.

Enter SPARKISH *pulling in* MR. PINCHWIFE

SPARK.   Come back, you are a pretty brother-in-law, neither go to church nor to dinner with your sister bride!

PINCH.   My sister denies her marriage, and you see is gone away from you dissatisfied.

SPARK.   Pshaw! upon a foolish scruple, that our parson was not in lawful orders, and did not say all the common prayer; but 'tis her modesty only I believe. But let women be never so modest the first day, they'll be sure to come to themselves by night, and I shall have enough of her then. In the meantime, Harry Horner, you must dine with me: I keep my wedding at my aunt's in the Piazza.

HORN.   Thy wedding! what stale maid has lived to despair of a husband, or what young one of a gallant?

SPARK.   Oh, your servant, Sir—this gentleman's sister then,—no stale maid.

HORN.   I'm sorry for't.

PINCH. [*aside*]   How comes he so concerned for her?

SPARK.   You sorry for't? Why, do you know any ill by her?

HORN.   No, I know none but by thee; 'tis for her sake, not yours, and another man's sake that might have hoped, I thought.

SPARK.   Another man! another man! What is his name?

HORN.   Nay, since 'tis past, he shall be nameless.—[*aside*] Poor Harcourt! I am sorry thou hast missed her.

PINCH. [*aside*]   He seems to be much troubled at the match.

SPARK.   Prithee, tell me—— Nay, you shan't go, Brother.

PINCH.   I must of necessity, but I'll come to you to dinner.

[*exit* PINCHWIFE]

SPARK.   But, Harry, what, have I a rival in my wife already? But with all my heart, for he may be of use to me hereafter; for though my hunger is now my sauce, and I can fall on heartily without, the time will come when a rival will be as good sauce for a married man to a wife, as an orange to veal.

HORN.   O thou damned rogue! thou hast set my teeth on edge with thy orange.

SPARK.   Then let's to dinner—there I was with you again. Come.

HORN.   But who dines with thee?

SPARK.   My friends and relations, my brother Pinchwife, you see, of your acquaintance.

HORN.   And his wife?

SPARK.   No, 'gad, he'll ne'er let her come amongst us good fellows; your stingy country coxcomb keeps his wife from his friends, as he does his little firkin of ale for his own drinking, and a gentleman can't get a smack on't; but his servants, when his back is turned, broach it at their pleasures, and dust it away, ha! ha! ha!—'Gad, I am witty, I think, considering I was married to-day, by the world; but come——

HORN.   No, I will not dine with you, unless you can fetch her too.

SPARK.   Pshaw! what pleasure canst thou have with women now, Harry?

HORN.   My eyes are not gone; I love a good prospect yet, and will not dine with you unless she does too; go fetch her, therefore, but do not tell her husband 'tis for my sake.

SPARK.   Well, I'll go try what I can do; in the meantime, come away to my aunt's lodging, 'tis in the way to Pinchwife's.

HORN.   The poor woman has called for aid, and stretched forth her hand, Doctor; I cannot but help her over the pale out of the briars.

[*exeunt* SPARKISH, HORNER, QUACK]

SCENE IV

The Scene changes to PINCHWIFE'S *House*

MRS. PINCHWIFE *alone, leaning on her elbow. A table, pen, ink, and paper*

MRS. PINCH.   Well, 'tis e'en so, I have got the London disease they call love; I am sick of my husband, and for my gallant. I have heard this distemper called a fever, but methinks 'tis like an ague; for when I think of my husband, I tremble, and am in a cold sweat, and have inclinations to vomit; but when I think of my gallant, dear Mr. Horner, my hot fit comes, and I am all in a fever indeed; and, as in other fevers, my own chamber is tedious to me, and I would fain be removed to his, and then methinks I should be well. Ah, poor Mr. Horner! Well, I cannot, will not stay here; therefore I'll make an end of my letter to him, which shall be a finer letter than my last, because I have studied it like anything. Oh sick, sick! [*takes the pen and writes*]

Enter PINCHWIFE, *who, seeing her writing, steals softly behind her, and, looking over her shoulder, snatches the paper from her*

PINCH.   What, writing more letters?

MRS. PINCH.   O Lord, bud, why d'ye fright me so?

[*she offers to run out; he stops her, and reads*]

PINCH.   How's this? nay, you shall not stir, Madam:—"Dear, dear, dear Mr. Horner"—very well—I have taught you to write letters to good purpose—but let's see't. "First, I am to beg your pardon for my boldness in writing to you, which I'd have you to know I would not have done, had not you said first you loved me so extremely, which if you do, you will never suffer me to lie in the arms of another man whom I loathe, nauseate, and detest."—Now you can write these filthy words. But what follows?—"Therefore, I hope you will speedily find some way to free me from this unfortunate match, which was never, I assure you, of my choice, but I'm afraid 'tis already too far gone; however, if you love me, as I do you, you will try what you can do; but you must help me away before to-morrow, or else, alas! I shall be for ever out of your reach, for I can defer no longer our—our——" [*the letter concludes*] what is to follow "our"?—speak, what?—Our journey into the country I suppose—Oh woman, damned woman! and Love, damned Love, their old tempter! for this is one of his miracles; in a moment he can make those blind that could see, and those see that were blind, those dumb that could speak, and those prattle who were dumb before; nay, what is more than all, make these dough-baked, senseless, indocile animals, women, too hard for us, their politic lords and rulers, in a moment. But make an end of your letter, and then I'll make an end of you thus, and all my plagues together.   [*draws his sword*]

MRS. PINCH.   O Lord, O Lord, you are such a passionate man, bud!

Enter SPARKISH

SPARK.   How now, what's here to do?

PINCH.   This fool here now!

SPARK.   What! drawn upon your wife? You should never do that, but at night in the dark, when you can't hurt her. This is my sister-in-law, is it not? ay, faith, e'en our country Margery [*pulls aside her handkerchief*]; one may know her. Come, she and you must go dine with me; dinner's ready, come. But where's my wife? Is she not come home yet? Where is she?

PINCH.   Making you a cuckold; 'tis that they all do, as soon as they can.

SPARK.   What, the wedding-day? No, a wife that designs to make a cully of her husband will be sure to let him win the first stake of love, by the world. But come, they stay dinner for us: come, I'll lead down our Margery.

MRS. PINCH.   No—Sir, go, we'll follow you.

SPARK.   I will not wag without you.

PINCH. [*aside*]   This coxcomb is a sensible torment to me amidst the greatest in the world.

SPARK.   Come, come, Madam Margery.

PINCH.   No; I'll lead her my way: what, would you treat your friends with mine, for want of your own wife?—[*leads her to t'other door, and locks her in and returns*] I am contented my rage should take breath——

SPARK. [*aside*]   I told Horner this.

PINCH.   Come now.

SPARK. Lord, how shy you are of your wife! But let me tell you, Brother, we men of wit have amongst us a saying that cuckolding, like the small-pox, comes with a fear; and you may keep your wife as much as you will out of danger of infection, but if her constitution incline her to't, she'll have it sooner or later, by the world, say they.

PINCH. [*aside*] What a thing is a cuckold, that every fool can make him ridiculous!—— Well, Sir—but let me advise you, now you are come to be concerned, because you suspect the danger, not to neglect the means to prevent it, especially when the greatest share of the malady will light upon your own head, for

> Hows'e'er the kind wife's belly comes to swell,
> The husband breeds for her, and first is ill.

ACT V

SCENE I

MR. PINCHWIFE'S *House*

Enter MR. PINCHWIFE *and* MRS. PINCHWIFE. *A table and candle*

PINCH.   Come, take the pen and make an end of the letter, just as you intended; if you are false in a tittle, I shall soon perceive it, and punish you with this as you deserve.—[*lays his hand on his sword*] Write what was to follow—let's see—"You must make haste, and help me away before to-morrow, or else I shall be for ever out of your reach, for I can defer no longer our"—What follows "our"?

MRS. PINCH.   Must all out, then, bud?—Look you there, then.

[MRS. PINCHWIFE *takes the pen and writes*]

PINCH.   Let's see—"For I can defer no longer our—wedding—Your slighted Alithea."—What's the meaning of this? my sister's name to't? Speak, unriddle.

MRS. PINCH.   Yes, indeed, bud.

PINCH.   But why her name to't? Speak—speak, I say.

MRS. PINCH.   Ay, but you'll tell her then again. If you would not tell her again——

PINCH.   I will not:—I am stunned, my head turns round.—Speak.

MRS. PINCH.   Won't you tell her, indeed, and indeed?

PINCH.   No; speak, I say.

MRS. PINCH.   She'll be angry with me; but I had rather she should be angry with me than you, bud; and, to tell you the truth, 'twas she made me write the letter, and taught me what I should write.

PINCH. [*aside*]   Ha! I thought the style was somewhat better than her own.—— But how could she come to you to teach you, since I had locked you up alone?

MRS. PINCH.   Oh, through the keyhole, bud.

PINCH.   But why should she make you write a letter for her to him, since she can write herself?

MRS. PINCH.   Why, she said because—for I was unwilling to do it——

67

PINCH. Because what—because?

MRS. PINCH. Because, lest Mr. Horner should be cruel, and refuse her; or be vain afterwards, and show the letter, she might disown it, the hand not being hers.

PINCH. [*aside*] How's this? Ha!—then I think I shall come to myself again. This changeling could not invent this lie: but if she could, why should she? she might think I should soon discover it.—Stay—now I think on't too, Horner said he was sorry she had married Sparkish; and her disowning her marriage to me makes me think she has evaded it for Horner's sake: yet why should she take this course? But men in love are fools; women may well be so—— But hark you, Madam, your sister went out in the morning, and I have not seen her within since.

MRS. PINCH. Alack-a-day, she has been crying all day above, it seems, in a corner.

PINCH. Where is she? Let me speak with her.

MRS. PINCH. [*aside*] O Lord, then she'll discover all!—— Pray hold, bud; what, d'ye mean to discover me? she'll know I have told you then. Pray, bud, let me talk with her first.

PINCH. I must speak with her, to know whether Horner ever made her any promise, and whether she be married to Sparkish or no.

MRS. PINCH. Pray, dear bud, don't, till I have spoken with her, and told her that I have told you all; for she'll kill me else.

PINCH. Go then, and bid her come out to me.

MRS. PINCH. Yes, yes, bud.

PINCH. Let me see——

MRS. PINCH. [*aside*] I'll go, but she is not within to come to him: I have just got time to know of Lucy her maid, who first set me on work, what lie I shall tell next; for I am e'en at my wit's end.

[*exit* MRS. PINCHWIFE]

PINCH. Well, I resolve it, Horner shall have her: I'd rather give him my sister than lend him my wife; and such an alliance will prevent his pretensions to my wife, sure. I'll make him of kin to her, and then he won't care for her.

MRS. PINCHWIFE *returns*

MRS. PINCH. O Lord, bud! I told you what anger you would make me with my sister.

PINCH. Won't she come hither?

MRS. PINCH. No, no. Alack-a-day, she's ashamed to look you in the face: and she says, if you go in to her, she'll run away downstairs, and shamefully go herself to Mr. Horner, who has promised her marriage, she says; and she will have no other, so she won't.

PINCH. Did he so?—promise her marriage!—then she shall have no other. Go tell her so; and if she will come and discourse with me a little concerning the means, I will about it immediately. Go.——[*exit* MRS. PINCHWIFE] His estate is equal to Sparkish's, and his extraction as much better than his as his parts are; but my chief reason is I'd rather be akin to him by the name of brother-in-law than that of cuckold.

Enter MRS. PINCHWIFE

Well, what says she now?

MRS. PINCH.   Why, she says, she would only have you lead her to Horner's lodging; with whom she first will discourse the matter before she talks with you, which yet she cannot do; for alack, poor creature, she says she can't so much as look you in the face, therefore she'll come to you in a mask. And you must excuse her if she make you no answer to any question of yours, till you have brought her to Mr. Horner; and if you will not chide her, nor question her, she'll come out to you immediately.

PINCH.   Let her come: I will not speak a word to her, nor require a word from her.

MRS. PINCH.   Oh, I forgot: besides, she says she cannot look you in the face, though through a mask; therefore would desire you to put out the candle.

PINCH.   I agree to all. Let her make haste.——There, 'tis out.——[*puts out the candle; exit* MRS. PINCHWIFE] My case is something better: I'd rather fight with Horner for not lying with my sister, than for lying with my wife; and of the two, I had rather find my sister too forward than my wife. I expected no other from her free education, as she calls it, and her passion for the town. Well, wife and sister are names which make us expect love and duty, pleasure and comfort; but we find 'em plagues and torments, and are equally, though differently, troublesome to their keeper; for we have as much ado to get people to lie with our sisters as to keep 'em from lying with our wives.

Enter MRS. PINCHWIFE *masked, and in hoods and scarfs, and a night-gown and petticoat of* ALITHEA'S, *in the dark*

What, are you come, Sister? let us go then.——But first, let me lock up my wife. Mrs. Margery, where are you?

MRS. PINCH.   Here, bud.

PINCH.   Come hither, that I may lock you up: get you in.——[*locks the door*] Come, Sister, where are you now?

[MRS. PINCHWIFE *gives him her hand; but when he lets her go,
she steals softly on to t'other side of him,
and is led away by him for his sister,* ALITHEA]

SCENE II

The Scene changes to HORNER'S *Lodging*

QUACK, HORNER

QUACK.   What, all alone? not so much as one of your cuckolds here, nor one of their wives! They use to take their turns with you, as if they were to watch you.

HORN.   Yes, it often happens that a cuckold is but his wife's spy, and is more upon family duty when he is with her gallant abroad, hindering his pleasure, than when he is at home with her playing the gallant. But the hardest duty a married woman imposes upon a lover is keeping her husband company always.

QUACK.   And his fondness wearies you almost as soon as hers.

HORN.   A pox! keeping a cuckold company, after you have had his wife, is as tiresome as the company of a country squire to a witty fellow of the town, when he has got all his money.

QUACK.   And as at first a man makes a friend of the husband to get the wife, so at last you are fain to fall out with the wife to be rid of the husband.

HORN.   Ay, most cuckold-makers are true courtiers; when once a poor man has cracked his credit for 'em, they can't abide to come near him.

QUACK.   But at first, to draw him in, are so sweet, so kind, so dear! just as you are to Pinchwife. But what becomes of that intrigue with his wife?

HORN.   A pox! he's as surly as an alderman that has been bit; and since he's so coy, his wife's kindness is in vain, for she's a silly innocent.

QUACK.   Did she not send you a letter by him?

HORN.   Yes; but that's a riddle I have not yet solved. Allow the poor creature to be willing, she is silly too, and he keeps her up so close——

QUACK.   Yes, so close, that he makes her but the more willing, and adds but revenge to her love; which two, when met, seldom fail of satisfying each other one way or other.

HORN.   What! here's the man we are talking of, I think.

Enter MR. PINCHWIFE, *leading in his Wife masked, muffled, and in her Sister's gown*

Pshaw!

QUACK.   Bringing his wife to you is the next thing to bringing a love letter from her.

HORN.   What means this?

PINCH.   The last time, you know, Sir, I brought you a love letter; now, you see, a mistress; I think you'll say I am a civil man to you.

HORN.   Ay, the devil take me, will I say thou art the civilest man I ever met with; and I have known some. I fancy I understand thee now better than I did the letter. But, hark thee, in thy ear——

PINCH.   What?

HORN.   Nothing but the usual question, man: is she sound, on thy word?

PINCH.   What, you take her for a wench, and me for a pimp?

HORN.   Pshaw! wench and pimp, paw words; I know thou art an honest fellow, and hast a great acquaintance among the ladies, and per-haps hast made love for me, rather than let me make love to thy wife.

PINCH.   Come, Sir, in short, I am for no fooling.

HORN.   Nor I neither: therefore prithee, let's see her face presently. Make her show, man: art thou sure I don't know her?

PINCH.   I am sure you do know her.

HORN.   A pox! why dost thou bring her to me then?

PINCH.   Because she's a relation of mine——

HORN.   Is she, faith, man? then thou art still more civil and obliging, dear rogue.

PINCH.   Who desired me to bring her to you.

HORN.   Then she is obliging, dear rogue.

PINCH.   You'll make her welcome for my sake, I hope.

HORN.   I hope she is handsome enough to make herself welcome. Prithee let her unmask.

PINCH.   Do you speak to her; she would never be ruled by me.

HORN.   Madam—— [MRS. PINCHWIFE *whispers to* HORNER] She says she must speak with me in private. Withdraw, prithee.

PINCH. [*aside*]   She's unwilling, it seems, I should know all her unde-cent conduct in this business.—— Well then, I'll leave you together, and hope when I am gone, you'll agree; if not, you and I shan't agree, Sir.

HORN.   What means the fool? if she and I agree 'tis no matter what you and I do.   [*whispers to* MRS. PINCHWIFE,
                                        who makes signs with her hand for him to be gone]

PINCH.   In the meantime I'll fetch a parson, and find out Sparkish, and disabuse him. You would have me fetch a parson, would you not? Well then—now I think I am rid of her, and shall have no more trouble with her—our sisters and daughters, like usurers' money, are safest when put out; but our wives, like their writings, never safe but in our closets under lock and key.   [*exit* MR. PINCHWIFE]

Enter Boy

BOY.   Sir Jasper Fidget, Sir, is coming up.   [*exit*]

HORN.   Here's the trouble of a cuckold now we are talking of. A pox on him! has he not enough to do to hinder his wife's sport, but he must other women's too?—Step in here, Madam.   [*exit* MRS. PINCHWIFE]

Enter SIR JASPER

SIR JASP.   My best and dearest friend.

HORN. [*aside to* QUACK]   The old style, Doctor.—— Well, be short, for I am busy. What would your impertinent wife have now?

SIR JASP.   Well guessed, i'faith; for I do come from her.

HORN.   To invite me to supper! Tell her, I can't come: go.

SIR JASP.   Nay, now you are out, faith; for my lady, and the whole knot of the virtuous gang, as they call themselves, are resolved upon a frolic of coming to you to-night in masquerade, and are all dressed already.

HORN.   I shan't be at home.

SIR JASP. [*aside*]   Lord, how churlish he is to women!—— Nay, prithee don't disappoint 'em; they'll think 'tis my fault: prithee don't. I'll send in the banquet and the fiddles. But make no noise on't; for the poor virtuous rogues would not have it known, for the world, that they go a-masquerading; and they would come to no man's ball but yours.

HORN.   Well, well—get you gone; and tell 'em, if they come, 'twill be at the peril of their honour and yours.

SIR JASP.   He! he! he!—we'll trust you for that: farewell.

[*exit* SIR JASPER]

HORN.   Doctor, anon you too shall be my guest,
         But now I'm going to a private feast.   [*exeunt*]

SCENE III

The Scene changes to the Piazza of Covent Garden

SPARKISH, PINCHWIFE

SPARK. [*with the letter in his hand*]   But who would have thought a woman could have been false to me? By the world, I could not have thought it.

PINCH.   You were for giving and taking liberty: she has taken it only, Sir, now you find in that letter. You are a frank person, and so is she, you see there.

SPARK.   Nay, if this be her hand—for I never saw it.

PINCH.   'Tis no matter whether that be her hand or no; I am sure this hand, at her desire, led her to Mr. Horner, with whom I left her just now, to go fetch a parson to 'em at their desire too, to deprive you of her for ever; for it seems yours was but a mock marriage.

SPARK.   Indeed, she would needs have it that 'twas Harcourt himself, in a parson's habit, that married us; but I'm sure he told me 'twas his brother Ned.

PINCH.   Oh, there 'tis out; and you were deceived, not she: for you are such a frank person. But I must be gone.—You'll find her at Mr. Horner's. Go, and believe your eyes.   [*exit* MR. PINCHWIFE]

SPARK.   Nay, I'll to her, and call her as many crocodiles, sirens, harpies, and other heathenish names, as a poet would do a mistress who had refused to hear his suit, nay more, his verses on her.—But stay, is not that she following a torch at t'other end of the Piazza? and from Horner's certainly—'tis so.

Enter ALITHEA *following a torch, and* LUCY *behind*

You are well met, Madam, though you don't think so. What, you have made a short visit to Mr. Horner? But I suppose you'll return to him presently; by that time the parson can be with him.

ALITH.   Mr. Horner and the parson, Sir!

SPARK.   Come, Madam, no more dissembling, no more jilting; for I am no more a frank person.

ALITH.   How's this?

LUCY. [*aside*]   So, 'twill work, I see.

SPARK.   Could you find out no easy country fool to abuse? none but me, a gentleman of wit and pleasure about the town? But it was your pride to be too hard for a man of parts, unworthy false woman! false as a friend that lends a man money to lose; false as dice, who undo those that trust all they have to 'em.

LUCY [*aside*]   He has been a great bubble, by his similes, as they say.

ALITH.   You have been too merry, Sir, at your wedding-dinner, sure.

SPARK.   What, d'ye mock me too?

ALITH.   Or you have been deluded.

SPARK.   By you.

ALITH.   Let me understand you.

SPARK.   Have you the confidence—I should call it something else, since you know your guilt—to stand my just reproaches? You did not write an impudent letter to Mr. Horner? who I find now has clubbed with you in deluding me with his aversion for women, that I might not, forsooth, suspect him for my rival.

LUCY. [*aside*]   D'ye think the gentleman can be jealous now, Madam?

ALITH.   I write a letter to Mr. Horner!

SPARK.   Nay, Madam, do not deny it. Your brother showed it me just now; and told me likewise, he left you at Horner's lodging to fetch a parson to marry you to him: and I wish you joy, Madam, joy, joy; and to him too, much joy; and to myself more joy, for not marrying you.

ALITH. [*aside*]   So, I find my brother would break off the match; and I can consent to't, since I see this gentleman can be made jealous.—— O Lucy, by his rude usage and jealousy, he makes me almost afraid I am married to him. Art thou sure 'twas Harcourt himself, and no parson, that married us?

SPARK.   No, Madam, I thank you. I suppose, that was a contrivance too of Mr. Horner's and yours, to make Harcourt play the parson; but I would as little as you have him one now, no, not for the world. For shall I tell you another truth? I never had any passion for you till now, for now I hate you. 'Tis true, I might have married your portion, as other men of parts of the town do sometimes: and so, your servant. And to show my unconcernedness, I'll come to your wedding, and resign you with as much joy as I would a stale wench to a new cully; nay, with as much joy as I would after the first night, if I had been married to you. There's for you; and so your servant, servant.   [*exit* SPARKISH]

ALITH.   How was I deceived in a man!

LUCY.   You'll believe then a fool may be made jealous now? for that easiness in him that suffers him to be led by a wife, will likewise permit him to be persuaded against her by others.

ALITH.   But marry Mr. Horner! my brother does not intend it, sure: if I thought he did, I would take thy advice, and Mr. Harcourt for my husband. And now I wish that if there be any over-wise woman of the town, who, like me, would marry a fool for fortune, liberty, or title, first, that her husband may love play, and be a cully to all the town but her, and suffer none but Fortune to be mistress of his purse; then, if for liberty, that he may send her into the country, under the conduct of some huswifely mother-in-law; and if for title, may the world give 'em none but that of cuckold.

LUCY.   And for her greater curse, Madam, may he not deserve it.

ALITH.   Away, impertinent! Is not this my old Lady Lanterlu's?

LUCY.   Yes, Madam.—[*aside*] And here I hope we shall find Mr. Harcourt.   [*exeunt*]

SCENE IV

The Scene changes again to HORNER'S *Lodging*

HORNER, LADY FIDGET, MRS. DAINTY FIDGET, MRS. SQUEAMISH

A table, banquet, and bottles

HORN. [*aside*]   A pox! they are come too soon—before I have sent back my new mistress. All I have now to do is to lock her in, that they may not see her.

LADY FID.   That we may be sure of our welcome, we have brought our entertainment with us, and are resolved to treat thee, dear toad.

MRS. DAIN.   And that we may be merry to purpose, have left Sir Jasper and my old Lady Squeamish quarrelling at home at backgammon.

MRS. SQUEAM.   Therefore let us make use of our time, lest they should chance to interrupt us.

LADY FID.   Let us sit then.

HORN.   First, that you may be private, let me lock this door and that, and I'll wait upon you presently.

LADY FID.   No, Sir, shut 'em only, and your lips for ever; for we must trust you as much as our women.

HORN.   You know all vanity's killed in me; I have no occasion for talking.

LADY FID.   Now, ladies, supposing we had drank each of us two bottles, let us speak the truth of our hearts.

MRS. DAIN. and MRS. SQUEAM.   Agreed.

LADY FID.   By this brimmer, for truth is nowhere else to be found— [*aside to* HORNER] not in thy heart, false man!

HORN. [*aside to* Lady Fidget]   You have found me a true man, I'm sure.

LADY FID. [*aside to* HORNER]   Not every way.—— But let us sit and be merry.   [LADY FIDGET *sings*]

1

    Why should our damn'd tyrants oblige us to live
    On the pittance of pleasure which they only give?
        We must not rejoice
        With wine and with noise:
    In vain we must wake in a dull bed alone,
    Whilst to our warm rival the bottle, they're gone.
        Then lay aside charms,
        And take up these arms.⋆

2

    'Tis wine only gives 'em their courage and wit;
    Because we live sober, to men we submit.
        If for beauties you'd pass,
        Take a lick of the glass,
    'Twill mend your complexions, and when they are gone,
     The best red we have is the red of the grape:
    Then, sisters, lay't on,
        And damn a good shape.

⋆The glasses.

MRS. DAIN.   Dear brimmer! Well, in token of our openness and plain-dealing, let us throw our masks over our heads.

HORN.   So, 'twill come to the glasses anon.

MRS. SQUEAM.   Lovely brimmer! let me enjoy him first.

LADY FID.   No, I never part with a gallant till I've tried him. Dear brimmer! that makest our husbands short-sighted.

MRS. DAIN.   And our bashful gallants bold.

MRS. SQUEAM.   And, for want of a gallant, the butler lovely in our eyes.—— Drink, eunuch.

LADY FID.   Drink, thou representative of a husband.—Damn a husband!

MRS. DAIN.   And, as it were a husband, an old keeper.

MRS. SQUEAM.   And an old grandmother.

HORN.   And an English bawd, and a French chirurgeon.

LADY FID.   Ay, we have all reason to curse 'em.

HORN.   For my sake, ladies?

LADY FID.   No, for our own; for the first spoils all young gallants' industry.

MRS. DAIN.   And the other's art makes 'em bold only with common women.

MRS. SQUEAM.   And rather run the hazard of the vile distemper amongst them, than of a denial amongst us.

MRS. DAIN.   The filthy toads choose mistresses now as they do stuffs, for having been fancied and worn by others.

MRS. SQUEAM.   For being common and cheap.

LADY FID.   Whilst women of quality, like the richest stuffs, lie untumbled, and unasked for.

HORN.   Ay, neat, and cheap, and new, often they think best.

MRS. DAIN.   No, Sir, the beasts will be known by a mistress longer than by a suit.

MRS. SQUEAM.   And 'tis not for cheapness neither.

LADY FID.   No; for the vain fops will take up druggets and embroider 'em. But I wonder at the depraved appetites of witty men; they use to be out of the common road, and hate imitation. Pray tell me, beast, when you were a man, why you rather chose to club with a multitude in a common house for an entertainment than to be the only guest at a good table.

HORN.   Why, faith, ceremony and expectation are unsufferable to those that are sharp bent. People always eat with the best stomach at an ordinary, where every man is snatching for the best bit.

LADY FID.   Though he get a cut over the fingers.—But I have heard people eat most heartily of another man's meat, that is, what they do not pay for.

HORN.   When they are sure of their welcome and freedom; for ceremony in love and eating is as ridiculous as in fighting: falling on briskly is all should be done on those occasions.

LADY FID.   Well then, let me tell you, Sir, there is nowhere more freedom than in our houses; and we take freedom from a young person as a sign of good breeding; and a person may be as free as he pleases with us, as frolic, as gamesome, as wild as he will.

HORN.   Han't I heard you all declaim against wild men?

LADY FID.   Yes; but for all that, we think wildness in a man as desirable a quality as in a duck or rabbit: a tame man! foh!

HORN.   I know not, but your reputations frightened me as much as your faces invited me.

LADY FID.   Our reputation! Lord, why should you not think that we women make use of our reputation, as you men of yours, only to deceive the world with less suspicion? Our virtue is like the statesman's religion, the Quaker's word, the gamester's oath, and the great man's honour—but to cheat those that trust us.

MRS. SQUEAM.   And that demureness, coyness, and modesty that you see in our faces in the boxes at plays, is as much a sign of a kind woman, as a vizard-mask in the pit.

MRS. DAIN.   For, I assure you, women are least masked when they have the velvet vizard on.

LADY FID.   You would have found us modest women in our denials only.

MRS. SQUEAM.   Our bashfulness is only the reflection of the men's.

MRS. DAIN.   We blush when they are shamefaced.

HORN.   I beg your pardon, ladies, I was deceived in you devilishly. But why that mighty pretence to honour?

LADY FID.   We have told you; but sometimes 'twas for the same reason you men pretend business often, to avoid ill company, to enjoy the better and more privately those you love.

HORN.   But why would you ne'er give a friend a wink then?

LADY FID.   Faith, your reputation frightened us as much as ours did you, you were so notoriously lewd.

HORN.   And you so seemingly honest.

LADY FID.   Was that all that deterred you?

HORN.   And so expensive—you allow freedom, you say——

LADY FID.   Ay, ay.

HORN.   That I was afraid of losing my little money, as well as my little time, both which my other pleasures required.

LADY FID.   Money! foh! you talk like a little fellow now: do such as we expect money?

HORN.   I beg your pardon, Madam, I must confess, I have heard that great ladies, like great merchants, set but the higher prices upon what they have, because they are not in necessity of taking the first offer.

MRS. DAIN.   Such as we make sale of our hearts?

MRS. SQUEAM.   We bribed for our love? foh!

HORN.   With your pardon, ladies, I know, like great men in offices, you seem to exact flattery and attendance only from your followers; but you have receivers about you, and such fees to pay, a man is afraid to pass your grants. Besides, we must let you win at cards, or we lose your hearts; and if you make an assignation, 'tis at a goldsmith's, jeweller's, or china-house; where for your honour you deposit to him, he must pawn his to the punctual cit, and so paying for what you take up, pays for what he takes up.

MRS. DAIN.   Would you not have us assured of our gallants' love?

MRS. SQUEAM.   For love is better known by liberality than by jealousy.

LADY FID.   For one may be dissembled, the other not.—[*aside*] But my jealousy can be no longer dissembled, and they are telling ripe.—— Come, here's to our gallants in waiting, whom we must name, and I'll begin. This is my false rogue.   [*claps him on the back*]

MRS. SQUEAM.   How!

HORN.   So, all will out now.

MRS. SQUEAM. [*aside to* HORNER]   Did you not tell me 'twas for my sake only you reported yourself no man?

MRS. DAIN. [*aside to* HORNER]   Oh, wretch! did you not swear to me, 'twas for my love and honour you passed for that thing you do?

HORN.   So, so.

LADY FID.   Come, speak, ladies: this is my false villain.

MRS. SQUEAM.   And mine too.

MRS. DAIN.   And mine.

HORN.   Well then, you are all three my false rogues too, and there's an end on't.

LADY FID.   Well then, there's no remedy; sister sharers, let us not fall out, but have a care of our honour. Though we get no presents, no jewels of him, we are savers of our honour, the jewel of most value and use, which shines yet to the world unsuspected, though it be counterfeit.

HORN.   Nay, and is e'en as good as if it were true, provided the world think so; for honour, like beauty now, only depends on the opinion of others.

LADY FID.   Well, Harry Common, I hope you can be true to three. Swear; but 'tis to no purpose to require your oath, for you are as often forsworn as you swear to new women.

HORN.   Come, faith, Madam, let us e'en pardon one another; for all the difference I find betwixt we men and you women, we forswear ourselves at the beginning of an amour, you as long as it lasts.

Enter SIR JASPER FIDGET, *and* OLD LADY SQUEAMISH

SIR JASP.   Oh, my Lady Fidget, was this your cunning, to come to Mr. Horner without me? But you have been nowhere else, I hope.

LADY FID.   No, Sir Jasper.

LADY SQUEAM.   And you came straight hither, Biddy?

MRS. SQUEAM.   Yes, indeed, lady Grandmother.

SIR JASP.   'Tis well, 'tis well; I knew when once they were thoroughly acquainted with poor Horner, they'd ne'er be from him: you may let her masquerade it with my wife and Horner, and I warrant her reputation safe.

Enter Boy

BOY.   O Sir, here's the gentleman come, whom you bid me not suffer to come up without giving you notice, with a lady too, and other gentlemen.

HORN.   Do you all go in there, whilst I send 'em away; and, boy, do you desire 'em to stay below till I come, which shall be immediately.

[*exeunt* SIR JASPER, LADY SQUEAMISH, LADY FIDGET, MRS. DAINTY, MRS. SQUEAMISH]

BOY.   Yes, sir.   [*exit*]

[*exit* HORNER *at t'other door, and returns with* MRS. PINCHWIFE]

HORN.   You would not take my advice, to be gone home before your husband came back; he'll now discover all. Yet pray, my dearest, be persuaded to go home, and leave the rest to my management; I'll let you down the back way.

MRS. PINCH.   I don't know the way home, so I don't.

HORN.   My man shall wait upon you.

MRS. PINCH.   No, don't you believe that I'll go at all; what, are you weary of me already?

HORN.   No, my life, 'tis that I may love you long, 'tis to secure my love, and your reputation with your husband; he'll never receive you again else.

MRS. PINCH.   What care I? d'ye think to frighten me with that? I don't intend to go to him again; you shall be my husband now.

HORN.   I cannot be your husband, dearest, since you are married to him.

MRS. PINCH.   Oh, would you make me believe that? Don't I see every day at London here, women leave their first husbands, and go and live with other men as their wives? Pish, pshaw! you'd make me angry, but that I love you so mainly.

HORN.   So, they are coming up—In again, in, I hear 'em.—[*exit*

MRS. PINCHWIFE] Well, a silly mistress is like a weak place, soon got, soon lost, a man has scarce time for plunder; she betrays her husband first to her gallant, and then her gallant to her husband.

Enter PINCHWIFE, ALITHEA, HARCOURT, SPARKISH, LUCY, *and a* PARSON

PINCH.   Come, Madam, 'tis not the sudden change of your dress, the confidence of your asseverations, and your false witness there, shall persuade me I did not bring you hither just now; here's my witness, who cannot deny it, since you must be confronted.—— Mr. Horner, did not I bring this lady to you just now?

HORN. [*aside*]   Now must I wrong one woman for another's sake— but that's no new thing with me, for in these cases I am still on the criminal's side against the innocent.

ALITH.   Pray speak, Sir.

HORN. [*aside*]   It must be so. I must be impudent, and try my luck; impudence uses to be too hard for truth.

PINCH.   What, you are studying an evasion or excuse for her! Speak, Sir.

HORN.   No, faith, I am something backward only to speak in women's affairs or disputes.

PINCH.   She bids you speak.

ALITH.   Ah, pray, Sir, do, pray satisfy him.

HORN.   Then truly, you did bring that lady to me just now.

PINCH.   Oh ho!

ALITH.   How, Sir?

HAR.   How, Horner?

ALITH.   What mean you, Sir? I always took you for a man of honour.

HORN. [*aside*]   Ay, so much a man of honour, that I must save my mistress, I thank you, come what will on't.

SPARK.   So, if I had had her, she'd have made me believe the moon had been made of a Christmas pie.

LUCY. [*aside*]   Now could I speak, if I durst, and solve the riddle, who am the author of it.

ALITH.   Oh unfortunate woman! A combination against my honour! which most concerns me now, because you share in my disgrace, Sir, and it is your censure, which I must now suffer, that troubles me, not theirs.

HAR.   Madam, then have no trouble, you shall now see 'tis possible for me to love too, without being jealous; I will not only believe your innocence myself, but make all the world believe it.—[*apart to* HORNER] Horner, I must now be concerned for this lady's honour.

HORN.   And I must be concerned for a lady's honour too.

HAR.   This lady has her honour, and I will protect it.

HORN.   My lady has not her honour, but has given it me to keep, and I will preserve it.

HAR.   I understand you not.

HORN.   I would not have you.

MRS. PINCH. [*peeping in behind*]   What's the matter with 'em all?

PINCH.   Come, come, Mr. Horner, no more disputing; here's the parson, I brought him not in vain.

HAR.   No, Sir, I'll employ him, if this lady please.

PINCH.   How! what d'ye mean?

SPARK.   Ay, what does he mean?

HORN.   Why, I have resigned your sister to him; he has my consent.

PINCH.   But he has not mine, Sir; a woman's injured honour, no more than a man's, can be repaired or satisfied by any but him that first wronged it; and you shall marry her presently, or——

[*lays his hand on his sword*]

Enter to them MRS. PINCHWIFE

MRS. PINCH. [*aside*]   O Lord, they'll kill poor Mr. Horner! besides, he shan't marry her whilst I stand by, and look on; I'll not lose my second husband so.

PINCH.   What do I see?

ALITH.   My sister in my clothes!

SPARK.   Ha!

MRS. PINCH. [*to* MR. PINCHWIFE]   Nay, pray now don't quarrel about finding work for the parson: he shall marry me to Mr. Horner; for now, I believe, you have enough of me.

HORN. [*aside*]   Damned, damned loving changeling!

MRS. PINCH.   Pray, Sister, pardon me for telling so many lies of you.

HORN.   I suppose the riddle is plain now.

LUCY.   No, that must be my work.—— Good Sir, hear me.

[*kneels to* MR. PINCHWIFE, *who stands doggedly with his hat over his eyes*]

PINCH.   I will never hear woman again, but make 'em all silent thus——   [*offers to draw upon his Wife*]

HORN.   No, that must not be.

PINCH.   You then shall go first, 'tis all one to me.

[*offers to draw on* HORNER, *stopped by* HARCOURT]

HAR.   Hold!

Enter SIR JASPER FIDGET, LADY FIDGET, LADY SQUEAMISH,
MRS. DAINTY FIDGET, MRS. SQUEAMISH

SIR JASP.   What's the matter? what's the matter? pray, what's the matter, Sir? I beseech you communicate, Sir.

PINCH.   Why, my wife has communicated, Sir, as your wife may have done too, Sir, if she knows him, Sir.

SIR JASP.   Pshaw, with him! ha! ha! he!

PINCH.   D'ye mock me, Sir? A cuckold is a kind of a wild beast; have a care, Sir.

SIR JASP.   No, sure, you mock me, Sir. He cuckold you! it can't be, ha! ha! he! why, I'll tell you, Sir——   [*offers to whisper*]

PINCH.   I tell you again, he has whored my wife, and yours too, if he knows her, and all the women he comes near; 'tis not his dissembling, his hypocrisy, can wheedle me.

SIR JASP.   How! does he dissemble? is he a hypocrite? Nay, then— how—wife—sister, is he a hypocrite?

LADY SQUEAM.   An hypocrite! a dissembler! Speak, young harlotry, speak, how?

SIR JASP.   Nay, then—Oh my head too!—Oh thou libidinous lady!

LADY SQUEAM.   Oh thou harloting harlotry! hast thou done't then?

SIR JASP.   Speak, good Horner, art thou a dissembler, a rogue? hast thou——

HORN.   Soh!

LUCY. [*apart to* HORNER]   I'll fetch you off, and her too, if she will but hold her tongue.

HORN. [*apart to* LUCY]   Can'st thou? I'll give thee——

LUCY [*to Mr.* PINCHWIFE]   Pray have but patience to hear me, Sir, who am the unfortunate cause of all this confusion. Your wife is innocent, I only culpable; for I put her upon telling you all these lies concerning my mistress, in order to the breaking off the match between Mr. Sparkish and her, to make way for Mr. Harcourt.

SPARK.   Did you so, eternal rotten tooth? Then, it seems, my mistress was not false to me, I was only deceived by you. Brother, that should have been, now man of conduct, who is a frank person now, to bring your wife to her lover, ha?

LUCY.   I assure you, Sir, she came not to Mr. Horner out of love, for she loves him no more——

MRS. PINCH.   Hold, I told lies for you, but you shall tell none for me, for I do love Mr. Horner with all my soul, and nobody shall say me nay; pray, don't you go to make poor Mr. Horner believe to the contrary; 'tis spitefully done of you, I'm sure.

HORN. [*aside to* MRS. PINCHWIFE]   Peace, dear idiot.

MRS. PINCH.   Nay, I will not peace.

PINCH.   Not till I make you.

Enter DORILANT, QUACK

DOR.   Horner, your servant; I am the doctor's guest, he must excuse our intrusion.

QUACK.   But what's the matter, gentlemen? for Heaven's sake, what's the matter?

HORN.   Oh, 'tis well you are come. 'Tis a censorious world we live in; you may have brought me a reprieve, or else I had died for a crime I never committed, and these innocent ladies had suffered with me; therefore, pray satisfy these worthy, honourable, jealous gentlemen—that——
                                                                            [*whispers*]

QUACK.   Oh, I understand you, is that all?—— Sir Jasper, by Heavens, and upon the word of a physician, Sir——   [*whispers to* SIR JASPER]

SIR JASP.   Nay, I do believe you truly.—— Pardon me, my virtuous lady, and dear of honour.

LADY SQUEAM.   What, then all's right again?

SIR JASP.   Ay, ay, and now let us satisfy him too.
                                                [*they whisper with* MR. PINCHWIFE]

PINCH.   An eunuch! Pray, no fooling with me.

QUACK.   I'll bring half the chirurgeons in town to swear it.

PINCH.   They!—they'll swear a man that bled to death through his wounds died of an apoplexy.

QUACK.   Pray, hear me, Sir—why, all the town has heard the report of him.

PINCH.   But does all the town believe it?

QUACK.   Pray, inquire a little, and first of all these.

PINCH.   I'm sure when I left the town, he was the lewdest fellow in't.

QUACK.   I tell you, Sir, he has been in France since; pray, ask but these ladies and gentlemen, your friend Mr. Dorilant. Gentlemen and ladies, han't you all heard the late sad report of poor Mr. Horner?

ALL THE LADIES.   Ay, ay, ay.

DOR.   Why, thou jealous fool, dost thou doubt it? he's an arrant French capon.

MRS. PINCH.   'Tis false, Sir, you shall not disparage poor Mr. Horner, for to my certain knowledge——

LUCY.   Oh, hold!

MRS. SQUEAM. [*aside to* LUCY]   Stop her mouth!

LADY FID. [*to* PINCHWIFE]   Upon my honour, Sir, 'tis as true——

MRS. DAIN.   D'ye think we would have been seen in his company?

MRS. SQUEAM.   Trust our unspotted reputations with him?

LADY FID. [*aside to* HORNER]   This you get, and we too, by trusting your secret to a fool.

HORN.   Peace, Madam.—[*aside to* QUACK] Well, Doctor, is not this a good design, that carries man on unsuspected, and brings him off safe?

PINCH. [*aside*]   Well, if this were true—but my wife——
                                        [DORILANT *whispers with* MRS. PINCHWIFE]

ALITH.   Come, Brother, your wife is yet innocent, you see; but have a care of too strong an imagination, lest, like an over-concerned timorous gamester, by fancying an unlucky cast, it should come. Women and fortune are truest still to those that trust 'em.

LUCY.   And any wild thing grows but the more fierce and hungry for being kept up, and more dangerous to the keeper.

ALITH.   There's doctrine for all husbands, Mr. Harcourt.

HAR.   I edify, Madam, so much, that I am impatient till I am one.

DOR.   And I edify so much by example, I will never be one.

SPARK.   And because I will not disparage my parts, I'll ne'er be one.

HORN.   And I, alas! can't be one.

PINCH.   But I must be one—against my will to a country wife, with a country murrain to me!

MRS. PINCH. [*aside*]   And I must be a country wife still too, I find; for I can't, like a city one, be rid of my musty husband, and do what I list.

HORN.   Now, Sir, I must pronounce your wife innocent, though I blush whilst I do it; and I am the only man by her now exposed to shame, which I will straight drown in wine, as you shall your suspicion; and the ladies' troubles we'll divert with a ballad.—— Doctor, where are your maskers?

LUCY.   Indeed, she's innocent, Sir, I am her witness; and her end of coming out was but to see her sister's wedding; and what she has said to your face of her love to Mr. Horner was but the usual innocent revenge on a husband's jealousy—was it not, Madam, speak?

MRS. PINCH. [*aside to* LUCY *and* HORNER]   Since you'll have me tell more lies—— Yes, indeed, bud.

PINCH.

> For my own sake fain I would all believe;
> Cuckolds, like lovers, should themselves deceive.
> But—— [*sighs*] his honour is least safe (too late I find)
> Who trusts it with a foolish wife or friend.

A Dance of Cuckolds

HORN.

> Vain fops but court and dress, and keep a pother,
> To pass for women's men with one another;
> But he who aims by women to be priz'd,
> First by the men, you see, must be despis'd.

EPILOGUE

Spoken by MY LADY FIDGET

Now you the vigorous, who daily here
O'er vizard-mask in public domineer,
And what you'd do to her, if in place where;
Nay, have the confidence to cry, "Come out!"
Yet when she says, "Lead on!" you are not stout;
But to your well-dress'd brother straight turn round,
And cry, "Pox on her, Ned, she can't be sound!"
Then slink away, a fresh one to engage,
With so much seeming heat and loving rage,
You'd frighten listening actress on the stage;
Till she at last has seen you huffing come,
And talk of keeping in the tiring-room,
Yet cannot be provok'd to lead her home.
Next, you Falstaffs of fifty, who beset
Your buckram maidenheads, which your friends get;
And whilst to them you of achievements boast,
They share the booty, and laugh at your cost.
In fine, you essenc'd boys, both old and young,
Who would be thought so eager, brisk, and strong,
Yet do the ladies, not their husbands wrong;
Whose purses for your manhood make excuse,
And keep your Flanders mares for show not use;
Encourag'd by our woman's man to-day,
A Horner's part may vainly think to play;
And may intrigues so bashfully disown,
That they may doubted be by few or none;
May kiss the cards at picquet, ombre, loo,
And so be taught to kiss the lady too;
But, gallants, have a care, faith, what you do.
The world, which to no man his due will give,
You by experience know you can deceive,
And men may still believe you vigorous,
But then we women—there's no cozening us.

The Man of Mode;
or, Sir Fopling Flutter
Sir George Etherege

Dramatis Personae

GENTLEMEN:
   MR. DORIMANT
   MR. MEDLEY
   OLD HARRY BELLAIR
   YOUNG HARRY BELLAIR
   SIR FOPLING FLUTTER
GENTLEWOMEN:
   LADY TOWNLEY
   EMILIA
   MRS. LOVEIT
   BELLINDA
   LADY WOODVILL, *and*
   HARRIET, *her daughter*
WAITING WOMEN:
   PERT *and* BUSY
TOM, *a Shoemaker*
NAN, *an Orange-Woman*
Three Slovenly Bullies
Two Chairmen
MR. SMIRK, *a Parson*
HANDY, *a* Valet-de-chambre
Pages, Footmen, &c.

PROLOGUE

By SIR CAR SCROOPE, BARONET

Like dancers on the ropes poor poets fare,
Most perish young, the rest in danger are;
This (one would think) should make our authors wary,
But, gamester-like, the giddy fools miscarry.
A lucky hand or two so tempts 'em on,
They cannot leave off play till they're undone.
With modest fears a Muse does first begin,
Like a young wench newly entic'd to sin;
But tickl'd once with praise, by her good will,
The wanton fool would never more lie still.
'Tis an old mistress you'll meet here to-night,
Whose charms you once have look'd on with delight.
But now of late such dirty drabs have known ye,
A Muse o'th' better sort's ashamed to own ye.
Nature well drawn, and wit, must now give place
To gaudy nonsense and to dull grimace;
Nor is it strange that you should like so much
That kind of wit, for most of yours is such.
But I'm afraid that while to France we go,
To bring you home fine dresses, dance, and show,
The stage, like you, will but more foppish grow.
Of foreign wares, why should we fetch the scum,
When we can be so richly serv'd at home?
For heav'n be thank'd, 'tis not so wise an age
But your own follies may supply the stage.
Tho' often plough'd, there's no great fear the soil
Should barren grow by the too frequent toil;
While at your doors are to be daily found
Such loads of dunghill to manure the ground.
'Tis by your follies that we players thrive,
As the physicians by diseases live;

89

And as each year some new distemper reigns,
Whose friendly poison helps to increase their gains,
So, among you, there starts up every day
Some new, unheard-of fool for us to play.
Then, for your own sakes be not too severe,
Nor what you all admire at home, damn here;
Since each is fond of his own ugly face,
Why should you, when we hold it, break the glass?

ACT I

SCENE: *A dressing-room; a table covered with a toilet, clothes laid ready*

Enter DORIMANT *in his gown and slippers, with a note in his hand,
made up, repeating verses*

DOR.

Now for some ages had the pride of Spain
Made the sun shine on half the world in vain.

[*then looking on the note*]
"For Mrs. Loveit." What a dull, insipid thing is a billet-doux written in cold blood, after the heat of the business is over! It is a tax upon good nature which I have here been labouring to pay, and have done it, but with as much regret as ever fanatic paid the Royal Aid or church duties. 'Twill have the same fate, I know, that all my notes to her have had of late: 'twill not be thought kind enough. 'Faith, women are i'the right when they jealously examine our letters, for in them we always first discover our decay of passion.—Hey! Who waits?

Enter HANDY

HAND.   Sir——
DOR.   Call a footman.
HAND.   None of 'em are come yet.
DOR.   Dogs! Will they ever lie snoring abed till noon?
HAND.   'Tis all one, Sir; if they're up, you indulge 'em so they're ever poaching after whores all the morning.
DOR.   Take notice henceforward who's wanting in his duty; the next clap he gets, he shall rot for an example. What vermin are those chattering without?
HAND.   Foggy Nan, the orange-woman, and Swearing Tom, the shoemaker.
DOR.   Go, call in that overgrown jade with the flasket of guts before her; fruit is refreshing in a morning.   [*exit* HANDY]

It is not that I love you less
Than when before your feet I lay——

Enter Orange-Woman and HANDY

——How now, double tripe, what news do you bring?

OR. WOM.   News! Here's the best fruit has come to town t'year; gad, I was up before four o'clock this morning and bought all the choice i'the market.

DOR.   The nasty refuse of your shop.

OR. WOM.   You need not make mouths at it; I assure you, 'tis all culled ware.

DOR.   The citizens buy better on a holiday in their walk to Tottenham.

OR. WOM.   Good or bad, 'tis all one; I never knew you commend anything. Lord! would the ladies had heard you talk of 'em as I have done! [*sets down the fruit*] Here, bid your man give me an angel.

DOR.   Give the bawd her fruit again.

OR. WOM.   Well, on my conscience, there never was the like of you! God's my life, I had almost forgot to tell you there is a young gentlewoman lately come to town with her mother, that is so taken with you.

DOR.   Is she handsome?

OR. WOM.   Nay, gad, there are few finer women, I tell you but so, and a hugeous fortune, they say. Here, eat this peach. It comes from the stone; 'tis better than any Newington y'have tasted.

DOR. [*taking the peach*]   This fine woman, I'll lay my life, is some awkward, ill-fashioned country toad who, not having above four dozen of black hairs on her head, has adorned her baldness with a large, white fruz, that she may look sparkishly in the forefront of the King's box at an old play.

OR. WOM.   Gad, you'd change your note quickly if you did but see her.

DOR.   How came she to know me?

OR. WOM.   She saw you yesterday at the Change; she told me you came and fooled with the woman at the next shop.

DOR.   I remember there was a mask observed me, indeed. Fooled, did she say?

OR. WOM.   Ay; I vow she told me twenty things you said, too, and acted with head and with her body so like you——

Enter MEDLEY

MED.   Dorimant, my life, my joy, my darling sin! how dost thou?

OR. WOM.   Lord, what a filthy trick these men have got of kissing one another!   [*she spits*]

MED. Why do you suffer this cartload of scandal to come near you and make your neighbors think you so improvident to need a bawd?

OR. WOM. Good, now! we shall have it you did but want him to help you! Come, pay me for my fruit.

MED. Make us thankful for it, huswife, bawds are as much out of fashion as gentlemen-ushers; none but old formal ladies use the one, and none but foppish old stagers employ the other. Go! You are an insignificant brandy bottle.

DOR. Nay, there you wrong her; three quarts of Canary is her business.

OR. WOM. What you please, gentlemen.

DOR. To him! give him as good as he brings.

OR. WOM. Hang him, there is not such another heathen in the town again, except it be the shoemaker without.

MED. I shall see you hold up your hand at the bar next sessions for murder, huswife; that shoemaker can take his oath you are in fee with the doctors to sell green fruit to the gentry that the crudities may breed diseases.

OR. WOM. Pray, give me my money.

DOR. Not a penny! When you bring the gentlewoman hither you spoke of, you shall be paid.

OR. WOM. The gentlewoman! the gentlewoman may be as honest as your sisters for aught as I know. Pray, pay me, Mr. Dorimant, and do not abuse me so; I have an honester way of living—you know it.

MED. Was there ever such a resty bawd?

DOR. Some jade's tricks she has, but she makes amends when she's in good humour.—— Come, tell me the lady's name and Handy shall pay you.

OR. WOM. I must not; she forbid me.

DOR. That's a sure sign she would have you.

MED. Where does she live?

OR. WOM. They lodge at my house.

MED. Nay, then she's in a hopeful way.

OR. WOM. Good Mr. Medley, say your pleasure of me, but take heed how you affront my house! God's my life!—"in a hopeful way"!

DOR. Prithee, peace! What kind of woman's the mother?

OR. WOM. A goodly grave gentlewoman. Lord, how she talks against the wild young men o' the town! As for your part, she thinks you an arrant devil; should she see you, on my conscience she would look if you had not a cloven foot.

DOR. Does she know me?

OR. WOM. Only by hearsay; a thousand horrid stories have been told her of you, and she believes 'em all.

MED.   By the character this should be the famous Lady Woodvill and her daughter Harriet.

OR. WOM.   The devil's in him for guessing, I think.

DOR.   Do you know 'em?

MED.   Both very well; the mother's a great admirer of the forms and civility of the last age.

DOR.   An antiquated beauty may be allowed to be out of humour at the freedoms of the present. This is a good account of the mother; pray, what is the daughter?

MED.   Why, first, she's an heiress—vastly rich.

DOR.   And handsome?

MED.   What alteration a twelvemonth may have bred in her I know not, but a year ago she was the beautifullest creature I ever saw: a fine, easy, clean shape; light brown hair in abundance; her features regular; her complexion clear and lively; large, wanton eyes; but above all, a mouth that has made me kiss it a thousand times in imagination; teeth white and even, and pretty, pouting lips, with a little moisture ever hanging on them, that look like the Provins rose fresh on the bush, ere the morning sun has quite drawn up the dew.

DOR.   Rapture! mere rapture!

OR. WOM.   Nay, gad, he tells you true; she's a delicate creature.

DOR.   Has she wit?

MED.   More than is usual in her sex, and as much malice. Then, she's as wild as you would wish her, and has a demureness in her looks that makes it so surprising.

DOR.   Flesh and blood cannot hear this and not long to know her.

MED.   I wonder what makes her mother bring her up to town; an old doting keeper cannot be more jealous of his mistress.

OR. WOM.   She made me laugh yesterday; there was a judge came to visit 'em, and the old man, she told me, did so stare upon her, and when he saluted her smacked so heartily. Who would think it of 'em?

MED.   God-a-mercy, judge!

DOR.   Do 'em right; the gentlemen of the long robe have not been wanting by their good examples to countenance the crying sin o' the nation.

MED.   Come, on with your trappings; 'tis later than you imagine.

DOR.   Call in the shoemaker, Handy.

OR. WOM.   Good Mr. Dorimant, pay me. Gad, I had rather give you my fruit than stay to be abused by that foul-mouthed rogue; what you gentlemen say, it matters not much, but such a dirty fellow does one more disgrace.

DOR.   Give her ten shillings, and be sure you tell the young gentle-woman I must be acquainted with her.

Or. Wom.   Now do you long to be tempting this pretty creature. Well, heavens mend you!

Med.   Farewell, bog!   [*exit Orange-Woman and* Handy]
Dorimant, when did you see your *pisaller,* as you call her, Mrs. Loveit?

Dor.   Not these two days.

Med.   And how stand affairs between you?

Dor.   There has been great patching of late, much ado; we make a shift to hang together.

Med.   I wonder how her mighty spirit bears it.

Dor.   Ill enough, on all conscience; I never knew so violent a creature.

Med.   She's the most passionate in her love and the most extravagant in her jealousy of any woman I ever heard of. What note is that?

Dor.   An excuse I am going to send her for the neglect I am guilty of.

Med.   Prithee, read it.

Dor.   No; but if you will take the pains, you may.

Med. [*reads*]   I never was a lover of business, but now I have a just reason to hate it, since it has kept me these two days from seeing you. I intend to wait upon you in the afternoon, and in the pleasure of your conversation forget all I have suffered during this tedious absence.

This business of yours, Dorimant, has been with a vizard at the playhouse; I have had an eye on you. If some malicious body should betray you, this kind note would hardly make your peace with her.

Dor.   I desire no better.

Med.   Why, would her knowledge of it oblige you?

Dor.   Most infinitely; next to the coming to a good understanding with a new mistress, I love a quarrel with an old one. But the devil's in't, there has been such a calm in my affairs of late, I have not had the pleasure of making a woman so much as break her fan, to be sullen, or forswear herself, these three days.

Med.   A very great misfortune. Let me see; I love mischief well enough to forward this business myself. I'll about it presently, and though I know the truth of what y'ave done will set her a-raving, I'll heighten it a little with invention, leave her in a fit o' the mother, and be here again before y'are ready.

Dor.   Pray, stay; you may spare yourself the labour. The business is undertaken already by one who will manage it with as much address, and I think with a little more malice, than you can.

Med.   Who i'the devil's name can this be!

Dor.   Why, the vizard—that very vizard you saw me with.

Med.   Does she love mischief so well as to betray herself to spite another?

DOR.   Not so neither, Medley. I will make you comprehend the mystery: this mask, for a farther confirmation of what I have been these two days swearing to her, made me yesterday at the playhouse make her a promise before her face utterly to break off with Loveit, and, because she tenders my reputation and would not have me do a barbarous thing, has contrived a way to give me a handsome occasion.

MED.   Very good.

DOR.   She intends about an hour before me, this afternoon, to make Loveit a visit, and, having the privilege, by reason of a professed friend-ship between 'em, to talk of her concerns——

MED.   Is she a friend?

DOR.   Oh, an intimate friend!

MED.   Better and better; pray, proceed.

DOR.   She means insensibly to insinuate a discourse of me and arti-ficially raise her jealousy to such a height that, transported with the first motions of her passion, she shall fly upon me with all the fury imagin-able as soon as ever I enter; the quarrel being thus happily begun, I am to play my part, confess and justify all my roguery, swear her imperti-nence and ill-humour makes her intolerable, tax her with the next fop that comes into my head, and in a huff march away, slight her, and leave her to be taken by whosoever thinks it worth his time to lie down be-fore her.

MED.   This vizard is a spark and has a genius that makes her worthy of yourself, Dorimant.

Enter HANDY, *Shoemaker, and Footman*

DOR.   You rogue there who sneak like a dog that has flung down a dish, if you do not mend your waiting, I'll uncase you and turn you loose to the wheel of fortune. Handy, seal this and let him run with it presently.

[*exit Footman*]

MED.   Since y'are resolved on a quarrel, why do you send her this kind note?

DOR.   To keep her at home in order to the business.—[*to the Shoe-maker*] How now, you drunken sot?

SHOEM.   'Zbud, you have no reason to talk; I have not had a bottle of sack of yours in my belly this fortnight.

MED.   The orange-woman says your neighbours take notice what a heathen you are, and design to inform the bishop and have you burned for an atheist.

SHOEM.   Damn her, dunghill, if her husband does not remove her, she stinks so, the parish intend to indict him for a nuisance.

MED.   I advise you like a friend; reform your life. You have brought the envy of the world upon you by living above yourself. Whoring and swearing are vices too genteel for a shoemaker.

SHOEM.   'Zbud, I think you men of quality will grow as unreasonable as the women. You would ingross the sins of the nation; poor folks can no sooner be wicked but th'are railed at by their betters.

DOR.   Sirrah, I'll have you stand i'the pillory for this libel!

SHOEM.   Some of you deserve it, I'm sure; there are so many of 'em, that our journeymen nowadays, instead of harmless ballads, sing nothing but your damned lampoons.

DOR.   Our lampoons, you rogue!

SHOEM.   Nay, good Master, why should not you write your own commentaries as well as Cæsar?

MED.   The rascal's read, I perceive.

SHOEM.   You know the old proverb—ale and history.

DOR.   Draw on my shoes, Sirrah.

SHOEM.   Here's a shoe——!

DOR.   Sits with more wrinkles than there are in an angry bully's forehead!

SHOEM.   'Zbud, as smooth as your mistress's skin does upon her! So; strike your foot in home. 'Zbud, if e'er a monsieur of 'em all make more fashionable ware, I'll be content to have my ears whipped off with my own paring knife.

MED.   And served up in a ragout instead of coxcombs to a company of French shoemakers for a collation.

SHOEM.   Hold, hold! Damn 'em, caterpillars! let 'em feed upon cabbage. Come Master, your health this morning next my heart now!

DOR.   Go, get you home and govern your family better! Do not let your wife follow you to the ale-house, beat your whore, and lead you home in triumph.

SHOEM.   'Zbud, there's never a man i'the town lives more like a gentleman with his wife than I do. I never mind her motions, she never inquires into mine; we speak to one another civilly, hate one another heartily, and because 'tis vulgar to lie and soak together, we have each of us our several settle-bed.

DOR.   Give him half a crown.

MED.   Not without he will promise to be bloody drunk.

SHOEM.   "Tope"'s the word i'the eye of the world, for my master's honor, Robin!

DOR.   Do not debauch my servants, Sirrah.

SHOEM.   I only tip him the wink; he knows an ale-house from a hovel.   [*exit Shoemaker*]

DOR.   My clothes, quickly.

MED.   Where shall we dine today?

Enter YOUNG BELLAIR

DOR.   Where you will; here comes a good third man.

Y. BELL.   Your servant, gentlemen.

MED.   Gentle Sir, how will you answer this visit to your honourable mistress? 'Tis not her interest you should keep company with men of sense who will be talking reason.

Y. BELL.   I do not fear her pardon; do you but grant me yours for my neglect of late.

MED.   Though y'ave made us miserable by the want of your good company, to show you I am free from all resentment, may the beautiful cause of our misfortune give you all the joys happy lovers have shared ever since the world began.

Y. BELL.   You wish me in heaven, but you believe me on my journey to hell.

MED.   You have a good strong faith, and that may contribute much towards your salvation. I confess I am but of an untoward constitution, apt to have doubts and scruples, and in love they are no less distracting than in religion. Were I so near marriage, I should cry out by fits as I ride in my coach, "Cuckold, cuckold!" with no less fury than the mad fanatic does "glory!" in Bethlem.

Y. BELL.   Because religion makes some run mad must I live an atheist?

MED.   Is it not great indiscretion for a man of credit, who may have money enough on his word, to go and deal with Jews, who for little sums make men enter into bonds and give judgments?

Y. BELL.   Preach no more on this text. I am determined, and there is no hope of my conversion.

DOR. [*to* HANDY, *who is fiddling about him*]   Leave your unnecessary fiddling; a wasp that's buzzing about a man's nose at dinner is not more troublesome than thou art.

HAND.   You love to have your clothes hang just, Sir.

DOR.   I love to be well dressed, Sir, and think it no scandal to my understanding.

HAND.   Will you use the essence or orange flower water?

DOR.   I will smell as I do to-day, no offence to the ladies' noses.

HAND.   Your pleasure, Sir.   [*exit* HANDY]

DOR.   That a man's excellency should lie in neatly tying of a ribband or a cravat! How careful's nature in furnishing the world with necessary coxcombs!

Y. BELL.   That's a mighty pretty suit of yours, Dorimant.

DOR.   I am glad't has your approbation.

Y. Bell.   No man in town has a better fancy in his clothes than you have.

Dor.   You will make me have an opinion of my genius.

Med.   There is a great critic, I hear, in these matters, lately arrived piping hot from Paris.

Y. Bell.   Sir Fopling Flutter, you mean.

Med.   The same.

Y. Bell.   He thinks himself the pattern of modern gallantry.

Dor.   He is indeed the pattern of modern foppery.

Med.   He was yesterday at the play, with a pair of gloves up to his elbows, and a periwig more exactly curled than a lady's head newly dressed for a ball.

Y. Bell.   What a pretty lisp he has!

Dor.   Ho! that he affects in imitation of the people of quality of France.

Med.   His head stands, for the most part, on one side, and his looks are more languishing than a lady's when she lolls at stretch in her coach or leans her head carelessly against the side of a box i'the playhouse.

Dor.   He is a person indeed of great acquired follies.

Med.   He is like many others, beholding to his education for making him so eminent a coxcomb; many a fool had been lost to the world had their indulgent parents wisely bestowed neither learning nor good breeding on 'em.

Y. Bell.   He has been, as the sparkish word is, "brisk upon the ladies" already. He was yesterday at my Aunt Townley's and gave Mrs. Loveit a catalogue of his good qualities under the character of a complete gentleman, who, according to Sir Fopling, ought to dress well, dance well, fence well, have a genius for love letters, an agreeable voice for a chamber, be very amorous, something discreet, but not overconstant.

Med.   Pretty ingredients to make an accomplished person!

Dor.   I am glad he pitched upon Loveit.

Y. Bell.   How so?

Dor.   I wanted a fop to lay to her charge, and this is as pat as may be.

Y. Bell.   I am confident she loves no man but you.

Dor.   The good fortune were enough to make me vain, but that I am in my nature modest.

Y. Bell.   Hark you, Dorimant.—— With your leave, Mr. Medley; 'tis only a secret concerning a fair lady.

Med.   Your good breeding, Sir, gives you too much trouble; you might have whispered without all this ceremony.

Y. Bell. [*to* Dorimant]   How stand your affairs with Bellinda of late?

Dor.   She's a little jilting baggage.

Y. Bell.   Nay, I believe her false enough, but she's ne'er the worse for your purpose; she was with you yesterday in a disguise at the play.

Dor.   There we fell out and resolved never to speak to one another more.

Y. Bell.   The occasion?

Dor.   Want of courage to meet me at the place appointed. These young women apprehend loving as much as the young men do fighting, at first; but, once entered, like them too, they all turn bullies straight.

Enter HANDY

Hand. [*to* Young Bellair]   Sir, your man without desires to speak with you.

Y. Bell.   Gentlemen, I'll return immediately. [*exit* Young Bellair]

Med.   A very pretty fellow this.

Dor.   He's handsome, well-bred, and by much the most tolerable of all the young men that do not abound in wit.

Med.   Ever well dressed, always complaisant, and seldom impertinent. You and he are grown very intimate, I see.

Dor.   It is our mutual interest to be so: it makes the women think the better of his understanding, and judge more favourably of my reputation; it makes him pass upon some for a man of very good sense, and I upon others for a very civil person.

Med.   What was that whisper?

Dor.   A thing which he would fain have known, but I did not think it fit to tell him; it might have frighted him from his honourable intentions of marrying.

Med.   Emilia, give her her due, has the best reputation of any young woman about the town who has beauty enough to provoke detraction; her carriage is unaffected, her discourse modest, not at all censorious nor pretending, like the counterfeits of the age.

Dor.   She's a discreet maid, and I believe nothing can corrupt her but a husband.

Med.   A husband?

Dor.   Yes, a husband: I have known many women make a difficulty of losing a maidenhead, who have afterwards made none of making a cuckold.

Med.   This prudent consideration, I am apt to think, has made you confirm poor Bellair in the desperate resolution he has taken.

Dor.   Indeed, the little hope I found there was of her, in the state she was in, has made me by my advice contribute something towards the changing of her condition.

Enter YOUNG BELLAIR

Dear Bellair, by heavens, I thought we had lost thee; men in love are never to be reckoned on when we would form a company.

Y. BELL.   Dorimant, I am undone. My man has brought the most surprising news i'the world.

DOR.   Some strange misfortune is befallen your love.

Y. BELL.   My father came to town last night and lodges i'the very house where Emilia lies.

MED.   Does he know it is with her you are in love?

Y. BELL.   He knows I love, but knows not whom, without some officious sot has betrayed me.

DOR.   Your Aunt Townley is your confidante and favours the business.

Y. BELL.   I do not apprehend any ill office from her. I have received a letter in which I am commanded by my father to meet him at my aunt's this afternoon. He tells me farther he has made a match for me and bids me resolve to be obedient to his will or expect to be disinherited.

MED.   Now's your time, Bellair; never had lover such an opportunity of giving a generous proof of his passion.

Y. BELL.   As how, I pray?

MED.   Why, hang an estate, marry Emilia out of hand, and provoke your father to do what he threatens; 'tis but despising a coach, humbling yourself to a pair of goloshes, being out of countenance when you meet your friends, pointed at and pitied wherever you go by all the amorous fops that know you, and your fame will be immortal.

Y. BELL.   I could find in my heart to resolve not to marry at all.

DOR.   Fie, fie! That would spoil a good jest and disappoint the well-natured town of an occasion of laughing at you.

Y. BELL.   The storm I have so long expected hangs o'er my head and begins to pour down upon me; I am on the rack and can have no rest till I'm satisfied in what I fear. Where do you dine?

DOR.   At Long's or Locket's.

MED.   At Long's let it be.

Y. BELL.   I'll run and see Emilia and inform myself how matters stand. If my misfortunes are not so great as to make me unfit for company, I'll be with you.   [*exit* YOUNG BELLAIR]

Enter a Footman with a letter

FOOT. [*to* DORIMANT]   Here's a letter, Sir.

DOR.   The superscription's right: "For Mr. Dorimant."

MED.   Let's see; the very scrawl and spelling of a true-bred whore.

DOR.   I know the hand; the style is admirable, I assure you.

MED.   Prithee, read it.

DOR. [*reads*]   I told a you you dud not love me, if you dud, you would have seen me again ere now. I have no money and am very mallicolly; pray send me a guynie to see the operies.

Your servant to command,

Molly.

MED.   Pray, let the whore have a favourable answer, that she may spark it in a box and do honour to her profession.

DOR.   She shall, and perk up i'the face of quality. Is the coach at door?

HAND.   You did not bid me send for it.

DOR.   Eternal blockhead! [HANDY *offers to go out*] Hey, sot——

HAND.   Did you call me, Sir?

DOR.   I hope you have no just exception to the name, Sir?

HAND.   I have sense, Sir.

DOR.   Not so much as a fly in winter.—— How did you come, Medley?

MED.   In a chair.

FOOT.   You may have a hackney coach if you please, Sir.

DOR.   I may ride the elephant if I please, Sir. Call another chair and let my coach follow to Long's.

Be calm, ye great parents, etc.   [*exeunt, singing*]

ACT II

SCENE I

Enter MY LADY TOWNLEY *and* EMILIA

L. TOWN.   I was afraid, Emilia, all had been discovered.

EMIL.   I tremble with the apprehension still.

L. TOWN.   That my brother should take lodgings i'the very house where you lie!

EMIL.   'Twas lucky we had timely notice to warn the people to be secret. He seems to be a mighty good-humoured old man.

L. TOWN.   He ever had a notable smirking way with him.

EMIL.   He calls me rogue, tells me he can't abide me, and does so bepat me.

L. TOWN.   On my word, you are much in his favour then.

EMIL.   He has been very inquisitive, I am told, about my family, my reputation, and my fortune.

L. TOWN.   I am confident he does not i'the least suspect you are the woman his son's in love with.

EMIL.   What should make him, then, inform himself so particularly of me?

L. TOWN.   He was always of a very loving temper himself; it may be he has a doting fit upon him—who knows?

EMIL.   It cannot be.

Enter YOUNG BELLAIR

L. TOWN.   Here comes my nephew.—— Where did you leave your father?

Y. BELL.   Writing a note within. Emilia, this early visit looks as if some kind jealousy would not let you rest at home.

EMIL.   The knowledge I have of my rival gives me a little cause to fear your constancy.

Y. BELL.   My constancy! I vow——

102

EMIL.   Do not vow. Our love is frail as is our life and full as little in our power; and are you sure you shall outlive this day?

Y. BELL.   I am not; but when we are in perfect health, 'twere an idle thing to fright ourselves with the thoughts of sudden death.

L. TOWN.   Pray, what has passed between you and your father i'the garden?

Y. BELL.   He's firm in his resolution, tells me I must marry Mrs. Harriet, or swears he'll marry himself and disinherit me. When I saw I could not prevail with him to be more indulgent, I dissembled an obedience to his will, which has composed his passion and will give us time, and, I hope, opportunity, to deceive him.

Enter OLD BELLAIR *with a note in his hand*

L. TOWN.   Peace, here he comes!

O. BELL.   Harry, take this and let your man carry it for me to Mr. Fourbe's chamber, my lawyer i'the Temple.   [*exit* YOUNG BELLAIR] [*to* EMILIA] Neighbour, a dod! I am glad to see thee here. Make much of her, Sister; she's one of the best of your acquaintance. I like her countenance and her behaviour well; she has a modesty that is not common i'this age, a dod, she has!

L. TOWN.   I know her value, Brother, and esteem her accordingly.

O. BELL.   Advise her to wear a little more mirth in her face; a dod, she's too serious.

L. TOWN.   The fault is very excusable in a young woman.

O. BELL.   Nay, a dod, I like her ne'er the worse. A melancholy beauty has her charms. I love a pretty sadness in a face, which varies now and then, like changeable colours, into a smile.

L. TOWN.   Methinks you speak very feelingly, Brother.

O. BELL.   I am but five and fifty, Sister, you know, an age not altogether unsensible.—[*to* EMILIA] Cheer up, sweetheart! I have a secret to tell thee may chance to make thee merry. We three will make collation together anon; i'the meantime, mum, I can't abide you! go, I can't abide you!

Enter YOUNG BELLAIR

Harry, come! you must along with me to my Lady Woodvill's. I am going to slip the boy at a mistress.

Y. BELL.   At a wife, Sir, you would say.

O. BELL.   You need not look so glum, Sir; a wife is no curse when she brings the blessing of a good estate with her; but an idle town flirt, with a painted face, a rotten reputation, and a crazy fortune, a dod! is the devil and all, and such a one I hear you are in league with.

Y. BELL.   I cannot help detraction, Sir.

O. BELL. Out! A pise o' their breeches, there are keeping fools enough for such flaunting baggages, and they are e'en too good for 'em.—[*to* EMILIA] Remember 'night. Go, y'are a rogue, y'are a rogue! Fare you well, fare you well!—— Come, come, come along, Sir!

[*exeunt* OLD *and* YOUNG BELLAIR]

L. TOWN. On my word, the old man comes on apace; I'll lay my life he's smitten.

EMIL. This is nothing but the pleasantness of his humour.

L. TOWN. I know him better than you. Let it work; it may prove lucky.

Enter a Page

PAGE. Madam, Mr. Medley has sent to know whether a visit will not be troublesome this afternoon.

L. TOWN. Send him word his visits never are so.   [*exit Page*]

EMIL. He's a very pleasant man.

L. TOWN. He's a very necessary man among us women; he's not scandalous i'the least, perpetually contriving to bring good company together, and always ready to stop up a gap at ombre; then, he knows all the little news o'the town.

EMIL. I love to hear him talk o'the intrigues; let 'em be never so dull in themselves, he'll make 'em pleasant i'the relation.

L. TOWN. But he improves things so much one can take no measure of the truth from him. Mr. Dorimant swears a flea or a maggot is not made more monstrous by a magnifying glass than a story is by his telling it.

Enter MEDLEY

EMIL. Hold, here he comes.

L. TOWN. Mr. Medley.

MED. Your servant, Madam.

L. TOWN. You have made yourself a stranger of late.

EMIL. I believe you took a surfeit of ombre last time you were here.

MED. Indeed, I had my bellyful of that termagant, Lady Dealer. There never was so unsatiable a carder; an old gleeker never loved to sit to't like her. I have played with her now at least a dozen times till she's worn out all her fine complexion and her tour would keep in curl no longer.

L. TOWN. Blame her not, poor woman; she loves nothing so well as a black ace.

MED. The pleasure I have seen her in when she has had hope in drawing for a matadore!

EMIL. 'Tis as pretty sport to her as persuading masks off is to you, to make discoveries.

L. TOWN.   Pray, where's your friend Mr. Dorimant?

MED.   Soliciting his affairs; he's a man of great employment, has more mistresses now depending than the most eminent lawyer in England has causes.

EMIL.   Here has been Mrs. Loveit so uneasy and out of humour these two days.

L. TOWN.   How strangely love and jealousy rage in that poor woman!

MED.   She could not have picked out a devil upon earth so proper to torment her; he's made her break a dozen or two of fans already, tear half a score points in pieces, and destroy hoods and knots without number.

L. TOWN.   We heard of a pleasant serenade he gave her t'other night.

MED.   A Danish serenade with kettle-drums and trumpets.

EMIL.   Oh, barbarous!

MED.   What! You are of the number of the ladies whose ears are grown so delicate since our operas you can be charmed with nothing but *flûtes douces* and French hautboys?

EMIL.   Leave your raillery, and tell us, is there any new wit come forth, songs or novels?

MED.   A very pretty piece of gallantry, by an eminent author, called *The Diversions of Bruxelles,* very necessary to be read by all old ladies who are desirous to improve themselves at questions and commands, blind-man's buff, and the like fashionable recreations.

EMIL.   Oh, ridiculous!

MED.   Then there is *The Art of Affectation,* written by a late beauty of quality, teaching you how to draw up your breasts, stretch up your neck, to thrust out your breech, to play with your head, to toss up your nose, to bite your lips, to turn up your eyes, to speak in a silly, soft tone of a voice, and use all the foolish French words that will infallibly make your person and conversation charming; with a short apology at the latter end in the behalf of young ladies who notoriously wash and paint though they have naturally good complexions.

EMIL.   What a deal of stuff you tell us!

MED.   Such as the town affords, Madam. The Russians, hearing the great respect we have for foreign dancing, have lately sent over some of their best balladines, who are now practising a famous ballet which will be suddenly danced at the Bear Garden.

L. TOWN.   Pray, forbear your idle stories, and give us an account of the state of love as it now stands.

MED.   Truly, there has been some revolutions in those affairs, great chopping and changing among the old, and some new lovers whom malice, indiscretion, and misfortune have luckily brought into play.

L. TOWN.   What think you of walking into the next room and sitting down before you engage in this business?

MED.   I wait upon you, and I hope (though women are commonly unreasonable) by the plenty of scandal I shall discover, to give you very good content, ladies.   [*exeunt*]

SCENE II

Enter MRS. LOVEIT *and* PERT. MRS. LOVEIT *putting up a letter, then pulling out her pocket-glass and looking in it*

LOV.   Pert.

PERT.   Madam?

LOV.   I hate myself, I look so ill today.

PERT.   Hate the wicked cause on't, that base man Mr. Dorimant, who makes you torment and vex yourself continually.

LOV.   He is to blame, indeed.

PERT.   To blame to be two days without sending, writing, or coming near you, contrary to his oath and covenant! 'Twas to much purpose to make him swear! I'll lay my life there's not an article but he has broken— talked to the vizards i'the pit, waited upon the ladies from the boxes to their coaches, gone behind the scenes, and fawned upon those little insignificant creatures, the players. 'Tis impossible for a man of his inconstant temper to forbear, I'm sure.

LOV.   I know he is a devil, but he has something of the angel yet undefaced in him, which makes him so charming and agreeable that I must love him, be he never so wicked.

PERT.   I little thought, Madam, to see your spirit tamed to this degree, who banished poor Mr. Lackwit but for taking up another lady's fan in your presence.

LOV.   My knowing of such odious fools contributes to the making of me love Dorimant the better.

PERT.   Your knowing of Mr. Dorimant, in my mind, should rather make you hate all mankind.

LOV.   So it does, besides himself.

PERT.   Pray, what excuse does he make in his letter?

LOV.   He has had business.

PERT.   Business in general terms would not have been a current excuse for another. A modish man is always very busy when he is in pursuit of a new mistress.

LOV.   Some fop has bribed you to rail at him. He had business; I will believe it, and will forgive him.

PERT.   You may forgive him anything, but I shall never forgive him his turning me into ridicule, as I hear he does.

LOV.   I perceive you are of the number of those fools his wit has made his enemies.

PERT.   I am of the number of those he's pleased to rally, Madam, and if we may believe Mr. Wagfan and Mr. Caperwell, he sometimes makes merry with yourself too, among his laughing companions.

LOV.   Blockheads are as malicious to witty men as ugly women are to the handsome; 'tis their interest, and they make it their business to defame 'em.

PERT.   I wish Mr. Dorimant would not make it his business to defame you.

LOV.   Should he, I had rather be made infamous by him than owe my reputation to the dull discretion of those fops you talk of.

Enter BELLINDA

Bellinda!   [*running to her*]

BELL.   My dear!

LOV.   You have been unkind of late.

BELL.   Do not say unkind—say unhappy.

LOV.   I could chide you. Where have you been these two days?

BELL.   Pity me rather, my dear, where I have been—so tired with two or three country gentlewomen, whose conversation has been more unsufferable than a country fiddle.

LOV.   Are they relations?

BELL.   No, Welsh acquaintance I made when I was last year at St. Winifred's. They have asked me a thousand questions of the modes and intrigues of the town, and I have told 'em almost as many things for news that hardly were so when their gowns were in fashion.

LOV.   Provoking creatures! How could you endure 'em?

BELL. [*aside*]   Now to carry on my plot. Nothing but love could make me capable of so much falsehood. 'Tis time to begin, lest Dorimant should come before her jealousy has stung her.—[*laughs, and then speaks on*] I was yesterday at a play with 'em, where I was fain to show 'em the living as the man at Westminster does the dead: "That is Mrs. Such-a-one, admired for her beauty; that is Mr. Such-a-one, cried up for a wit; that is sparkish Mr. Such-a-one, who keeps reverend Mrs. Such-a-one; and there sits fine Mrs. Such-a-one who was lately cast off by my Lord Such-a-one."

LOV.   Did you see Dorimant there?

BELL.   I did, and imagine you were there with him and have no mind to own it.

LOV.   What should make you think so?

BELL.   A lady masked in a pretty *déshabillé,* whom Dorimant entertained with more respect than the gallants do a common vizard.

LOV. [*aside*]   Dorimant at the play entertaining a mask! Oh, heavens!

BELL. [*aside*]   Good!

Lov.   Did he stay all the while?

Bell.   Till the play was done, and then led her out, which confirms me it was you.

Lov.   Traitor!

Pert.   Now you may believe he had business, and you may forgive him too.

Lov.   Ingrateful, perjured man!

Bell.   You seem so much concerned, my dear, I fear I have told you unawares what I had better have concealed for your quiet.

Lov.   What manner of shape had she?

Bell.   Tall and slender. Her motions were very genteel; certainly she must be some person of condition.

Lov.   Shame and confusion be ever in her face when she shows it!

Bell.   I should blame your discretion for loving that wild man, my dear, but they say he has a way so bewitching that few can defend their hearts who know him.

Lov.   I will tear him from mine or die i'the attempt.

Bell.   Be more moderate.

Lov.   Would I had daggers, darts, or poisoned arrows in my breast, so I could but remove the thoughts of him from thence!

Bell.   Fie, fie! your transports are too violent, my dear; this may be but an accidental gallantry, and 'tis likely ended at her coach.

Pert.   Should it proceed farther, let your comfort be, the conduct Mr. Dorimant affects will quickly make you know your rival, ten to one let you see her ruined, her reputation exposed to the town—a happiness none will envy her but yourself, Madam.

Lov.   Whoe'er she be, all the harm I wish her is, may she love him as well as I do and may he give her as much cause to hate him.

Pert.   Never doubt the latter end of your curse, Madam.

Lov.   May all the passions that are raised by neglected love—jealousy, indignation, spite, and thirst of revenge—eternally rage in her soul, as they do now in mine.   [*walks up and down with a distracted air*]

Enter a Page

Page.   Madam, Mr. Dorimant——

Lov.   I will not see him.

Page.   I told him you were within, Madam.

Lov.   Say you lied—say I'm busy—shut the door—say anything!

Page.   He's here, Madam.

Enter Dorimant

Dor.   They taste of death who do at heaven arrive;
But we this paradise approach alive.

[*to* MISTRESS LOVEIT] What, dancing *The Galloping Nag* without a fiddle? [*offers to catch her by the hand; she flings away and walks on, he pursuing her*] I fear this restlessness of the body, Madam, proceeds from an unquietness of the mind. What unlucky accident puts you out of humour? A point ill washed, knots spoiled i'the making up, hair shaded awry, or some other little mistake in setting you in order?

PERT.   A trifle, in my opinion, Sir, more inconsiderable than any you mention.

DOR.   O Mrs. Pert! I never knew you sullen enough to be silent; come, let me know the business.

PERT.   The business, Sir, is the business that has taken you up these two days. How have I seen you laugh at men of business, and now to become a man of business yourself!

DOR.   We are not masters of our own affections; our inclinations daily alter: now we love pleasure, and anon we shall dote on business. Human frailty will have it so, and who can help it?

LOV.   Faithless, inhuman, barbarous man——

DOR. [*aside*]   Good! Now the alarm strikes.

LOV.   Without sense of love, of honour, or of gratitude, tell me, for I will know, what devil masked she was you were with at the play yesterday?

DOR.   Faith, I resolved as much as you, but the devil was obstinate and would not tell me.

LOV.   False in this as in your vows to me!—you do know.

DOR.   The truth is, I did all I could to know.

LOV.   And dare you own it to my face? Hell and furies!

[*tears her fan in pieces*]

DOR.   Spare your fan, Madam; you are growing hot and will want it to cool you.

LOV.   Horror and distraction seize you! Sorrow and remorse gnaw your soul, and punish all your perjuries to me!   [*weeps*]

DOR. [*turning to* BELLINDA]

So thunder breaks the cloud in twain
And makes a passage for the rain.

[*to* BELLINDA] Bellinda, you are the devil that have raised this storm; you were at the play yesterday and have been making discoveries to your dear.

BELL.   Y'are the most mistaken man i'the world.

DOR.   It must be so, and here I vow revenge—resolve to pursue and persecute you more impertinently than ever any loving fop did his mistress, hunt you i'the Park, trace you i'the Mail, dog you in every visit you make, haunt you at the plays and i'the drawing-room, hang my nose in your neck and talk to you whether you will or no, and ever look upon you with such dying eyes till your friends grow jealous of me, send you

out of town, and the world suspect your reputation.—[*in a lower voice*] At
my Lady Townley's when we go from hence.

[*he looks kindly on* BELLINDA]

BELL.   I'll meet you there.

DOR.   Enough.

LOV. [*pushing* DORIMANT *away*]   Stand off! You sha' not stare upon her
so.

DOR.   Good; there's one made jealous already.

LOV.   Is this the constancy you vowed?

DOR.   Constancy at my years! 'Tis not a virtue in season; you might
as well expect the fruit the autumn ripens i'the spring.

LOV.   Monstrous principle!

DOR.   Youth has a long journey to go, Madam; should I have set up
my rest at the first inn I lodged at, I should never have arrived at the happiness I now enjoy.

LOV.   Dissembler, damned dissembler!

DOR.   I am so, I confess: good nature and good manners corrupt me.
I am honest in my inclinations, and would not, wer't not to avoid offence,
make a lady a little in years believe I think her young, willfully mistake
art for nature, and seem as fond of a thing I am weary of as when I doted
on't in earnest.

LOV.   False man!

DOR.   True woman!

LOV.   Now you begin to show yourself.

DOR.   Love gilds us over and makes us show fine things to one another for a time, but soon the gold wears off and then again the native
brass appears.

LOV.   Think on your oaths, your vows and protestations, perjured man!

DOR.   I made 'em when I was in love.

LOV.   And therefore ought they not to bind? Oh, impious!

DOR.   What we swear at such a time may be a certain proof of a present passion, but, to say truth, in love there is no security to be given for
the future.

LOV.   Horrid and ingrateful, begone, and never see me more!

DOR.   I am not one of those troublesome coxcombs who, because
they were once well received, take the privilege to plague a woman with
their love ever after. I shall obey you, Madam, though I do myself some
violence.   [*he offers to go and* MRS. LOVEIT *pulls him back*]

LOV.   Come back! You sha' not go! Could you have the ill-nature to
offer it?

DOR.   When love grows diseased, the best thing we can do is to put
it to a violent death. I cannot endure the torture of a lingering and con-
sumptive passion.

Lov.   Can you think mine sickly?

Dor.   Oh, 'tis desperately ill. What worse symptoms are there than your being always uneasy when I visit you, your picking quarrels with me on slight occasions, and in my absence kindly listening to the impertinences of every fashionable fool that talks to you?

Lov.   What fashionable fool can you lay to my charge?

Dor.   Why, the very cock-fool of all those fools—Sir Fopling Flutter.

Lov.   I never saw him in my life but once.

Dor.   The worse woman you, at first sight to put on all your charms, to entertain him with that softness in your voice, and all that wanton kindness in your eyes you so notoriously affect when you design a conquest.

Lov.   So damned a lie did never malice yet invent. Who told you this?

Dor.   No matter. That ever I should love a woman that can dote on a senseless caper, a tawdry French ribband, and a formal cravat!

Lov.   You make me mad.

Dor.   A guilty conscience may do much. Go on, be the game-mistress o' the town, and enter all our young fops as fast as they come from travel.

Lov.   Base and scurrilous!

Dor.   A fine mortifying reputation 'twill be for a woman of your pride, wit, and quality!

Lov.   This jealousy's a mere pretence, a cursed trick of your own devising. I know you.

Dor.   Believe it and all the ill of me you can: I would not have a woman have the least good thought of me that can think well of Fopling. Farewell! Fall to, and much good may do you with your coxcomb.

Lov.   Stay, oh stay! and I will tell you all.

Dor.   I have been told too much already.   [*exit* DORIMANT]

Lov.   Call him again!

Pert.   E'en let him go—a fair riddance.

Lov.   Run, I say! call him again! I will have him called!

Pert.   The devil should carry him away first were it my concern.

[*exit* PERT]

Bell.   He's frighted me from the very thoughts of loving men. For heaven's sake, my dear, do not discover what I told you! I dread his tongue as much as you ought to have done his friendship.

Enter PERT

Pert.   He's gone, Madam.

Lov.   Lightning blast him!

Pert.   When I told him you desired him to come back, he smiled, made a mouth at me, flung into his coach, and said——

LOV.   What did he say?

PERT.   "Drive away!" and then repeated verses.

LOV.   Would I had made a contract to be a witch when first I entertained this greater devil, monster, barbarian! I could tear myself in pieces. Revenge—nothing but revenge can ease me. Plague, war, famine, fire— all that can bring universal ruin and misery on mankind—with joy I'd perish to have you in my power but this moment.   [*exit* MRS. LOVEIT]

PERT.   Follow, Madam; leave her not in this outrageous passion!

[PERT *gathers up the things*]

BELL. [*aside*]   He's given me the proof which I desired of his love,
But 'tis a proof of his ill-nature too.
I wish I had not seen him use her so.
I sigh to think that Dorimant may be
One day as faithless and unkind to me.

[*exeunt*]

ACT III

SCENE I

Enter Harriet *and* Busy, *her woman*

Busy. Dear Madam, let me set that curl in order.

Har. Let me alone; I will shake 'em all out of order.

Busy. Will you never leave this wildness?

Har. Torment me not.

Busy. Look! There's a knot falling off.

Har. Let it drop.

Busy. But one pin, dear Madam.

Har. How do I daily suffer under thy officious fingers!

Busy. Ah, the difference that is between you and my Lady Dapper! how uneasy she is if the least thing be amiss about her!

Har. She is indeed most exact; nothing is ever wanting to make her ugliness remarkable.

Busy. Jeering people say so.

Har. Her powdering, painting, and her patching never fail in public to draw the tongues and eyes of all the men upon her.

Busy. She is, indeed, a little too pretending.

Har. That women should set up for beauty as much in spite of nature as some men have done for wit!

Busy. I hope without offence one may endeavour to make one's self agreeable.

Har. Not when 'tis impossible. Women then ought to be no more fond of dressing than fools should be of talking; hoods and modesty, masks and silence, things that shadow and conceal—they should think of nothing else.

Busy. Jesu! Madam, what will your mother think is become of you? For heaven's sake go in again!

Har. I won't.

BUSY.   This is the extravagantest thing that ever you did in your life, to leave her and a gentleman who is to be your husband.

HAR.   My husband! Hast thou so little wit to think I spoke what I meant when I overjoyed her in the country with a low curtsey and "What you please, Madam; I shall ever be obedient"?

BUSY.   Nay, I know not, you have so many fetches.

HAR.   And this was one, to get her up to London! Nothing else, I assure thee.

BUSY.   Well, the man, in my mind, is a fine man.

HAR.   The man indeed wears his clothes fashionably and has a pretty, negligent way with him, very courtly and much affected; he bows, and talks, and smiles so agreeably, as he thinks.

BUSY.   I never saw anything so genteel.

HAR.   Varnished over with good breeding, many a blockhead makes a tolerable show.

BUSY.   I wonder you do not like him.

HAR.   I think I might be brought to endure him, and that is all a reasonable woman should expect in a husband; but there is duty i'the case, and like the haughty Merab, I

> Find much aversion in my stubborn mind,

Which

> Is bred by being promis'd and design'd.

BUSY.   I wish you do not design your own ruin. I partly guess your inclinations, Madam—that Mr. Dorimant——

HAR.   Leave your prating and sing some foolish song or other.

BUSY.   I will—the song you love so well ever since you saw Mr. Dorimant.

SONG

> When first Amintas charm'd my heart,
> My heedless sheep began to stray;
> The wolves soon stole the greatest part,
> And all will now be made a prey.
> Ah, let not love your thoughts possess,
> 'Tis fatal to a shepherdess;
> The dang'rous passion you must shun,
> Or else like me be quite undone.

HAR.   Shall I be paid down by a covetous parent for a purchase? I need no land; no, I'll lay myself out all in love. It is decreed—

Enter YOUNG BELLAIR

Y. BELL.   What generous resolution are you making, Madam?

HAR.   Only to be disobedient, Sir.

Y. BELL.   Let me join hands with you in that.

HAR.   With all my heart; I never thought I should have given you mine so willingly. Here I, Harriet——

Y. BELL.   And I, Harry——

HAR.   Do solemnly protest——

Y. BELL.   And vow——

HAR.   That I with you——

Y. BELL.   And I with you——

BOTH.   Will never marry.

HAR.   A match!

Y. BELL.   And no match! How do you like this indifference now?

HAR.   You expect I should take it ill, I see.

Y. BELL.   'Tis not unnatural for you women to be a little angry: you miss a conquest, though you would slight the poor man were he in your power.

HAR.   There are some, it may be, have an eye like Bart'lomew—big enough for the whole fair; but I am not of the number, and you may keep your gingerbread. 'Twill be more acceptable to the lady whose dear image it wears, Sir.

Y. BELL.   I must confess, Madam, you came a day after the fair.

HAR.   You own then you are in love?

Y. BELL.   I do.

HAR.   The confidence is generous, and in return I could almost find in my heart to let you know my inclinations.

Y. BELL.   Are you in love?

HAR.   Yes, with this dear town, to that degree I can scarce endure the country in landscapes and in hangings.

Y. BELL.   What a dreadful thing 'twould be to be hurried back to Hampshire!

HAR.   Ah, name it not!

Y. BELL.   As for us, I find we shall agree well enough. Would we could do something to deceive the grave people!

HAR.   Could we delay their quick proceeding, 'twere well. A reprieve is a good step towards the getting of a pardon.

Y. BELL.   If we give over the game, we are undone. What think you of playing it on booty?

HAR.   What do you mean?

Y. BELL.   Pretend to be in love with one another; 'twill make some dilatory excuses we may feign pass the better.

HAR.   Let us do't, if it be but for the dear pleasure of dissembling.

Y. BELL.   Can you play your part?

HAR.   I know not what it is to love, but I have made pretty remarks by being now and then where lovers meet. Where did you leave their gravities?

Y. BELL.   I'th' next room. Your mother was censuring our modern gallant.

Enter OLD BELLAIR *and* LADY WOODVILL

HAR.   Peace! here they come. I will lean against this wall and look bashfully down upon my fan, while you, like an amorous spark, modishly entertain me.

L. WOOD.   Never go about to excuse 'em; come, come, it was not so when I was a young woman.

O. BELL.   A dod, they're something disrespectful——

L. WOOD.   Quality was then considered, and not rallied by every fleering fellow.

O. BELL.   Youth will have its jest, a dod, it will.

L. WOOD.   'Tis good breeding now to be civil to none but players and Exchange women; they are treated by 'em as much above their condition as others are below theirs.

O. BELL.   Out! a pise on 'em! talk no more. The rogues ha' got an ill habit of preferring beauty no matter where they find it.

L. WOOD.   See your son and my daughter; they have improved their acquaintance since they were within.

O. BELL.   A dod, methinks they have! Let's keep back and observe.

Y. BELL.   Now for a look and gestures that may persuade 'em I am saying all the passionate things imaginable.

HAR.   Your head a little more on one side. Ease yourself on your left leg and play with your right hand.

Y. BELL.   Thus, is it not?

HAR.   Now set your right leg firm on the ground, adjust your belt, then look about you.

Y. BELL.   A little exercising will make me perfect.

HAR.   Smile, and turn to me again very sparkish.

Y. BELL.   Will you take your turn and be instructed?

HAR.   With all my heart!

Y. BELL.   At one motion play your fan, roll your eyes, and then settle a kind look upon me.

HAR.   So!

Y. BELL.   Now spread your fan, look down upon it, and tell the sticks with a finger.

HAR.   Very modish!

Y. BELL.   Clap your hand up to your bosom, hold down your gown. Shrug a little, draw up your breasts, and let 'em fall again gently, with a sigh or two, etc.

HAR.   By the good instructions you give, I suspect you for one of those malicious observers who watch people's eyes, and from innocent looks make scandalous conclusions.

Y. BELL.   I know some, indeed, who out of mere love to mischief are as vigilant as jealousy itself, and will give you an account of every glance that passes at a play and i'th' Circle.

HAR.   'Twill not be amiss now to seem a little pleasant.

Y. BELL.   Clap your fan, then, in both your hands, snatch it to your mouth, smile, and with a lively motion fling your body a little forwards. So! Now spread it, fall back on the sudden, cover your face with it and break out into a loud laughter—take up, look grave, and fall a-fanning of yourself.—Admirably well acted!

HAR.   I think I am pretty apt at these matters.

O. BELL.   A dod, I like this well!

L. WOOD.   This promises something.

O. BELL.   Come! there is love i'th' case, a dod there is, or will be. What say you, young lady?

HAR.   All in good time, Sir; you expect we should fall to and love as game-cocks fight, as soon as we are set together. A dod, y'are unreasonable!

O. BELL.   A dod, Sirrah, I like thy wit well.

Enter a Servant

SERV.   The coach is at the door, Madam.

O. BELL.   Go, get you and take the air together.

L. WOOD.   Will not you go with us?

O. BELL.   Out! a pise! A dod, I ha' business and cannot. We shall meet at night at my sister Townley's.

Y. BELL. [*aside*]   He's going to Emilia. I overheard him talk of a collation.   [*exeunt*]

SCENE II

Enter LADY TOWNLEY, EMILIA, *and* MR. MEDLEY

L. TOWN.   I pity the young lovers we last talked of, though to say truth their conduct has been so indiscreet they deserve to be unfortunate.

MED.   Y'have had an exact account, from the great lady i'th' box down to the little orange wench.

EMIL.   Y'are a living libel, a breathing lampoon. I wonder you are not torn in pieces.

MED.   What think you of setting up an office of intelligence for these matters? The project may get money.

L. TOWN.   You would have great dealings with country ladies.

MED.   More than Muddiman has with their husbands.

Enter BELLINDA

L. TOWN.   Bellinda, what has become of you? We have not seen you here of late with your friend Mrs. Loveit.

BELL.   Dear creature, I left her but now so sadly afflicted!

L. TOWN.   With her old distemper, jealousy!

MED.   Dorimant has played her some new prank.

BELL.   Well, that Dorimant is certainly the worst man breathing.

EMIL.   I once thought so.

BELL.   And you do not think so still?

EMIL.   No, indeed!

BELL.   Oh, Jesu!

EMIL.   The town does him a great deal of injury, and I will never believe what it says of a man I do not know, again, for his sake.

BELL.   You make me wonder.

L. TOWN.   He's a very well-bred man.

BELL.   But strangely ill-natured.

EMIL.   Then he's a very witty man.

BELL.   But a man of no principles.

MED.   Your man of principles is a very fine thing, indeed.

BELL.   To be preferred to men of parts by women who have regard to their reputation and quiet. Well, were I minded to play the fool, he should be the last man I'd think of.

MED.   He has been the first in many ladies' favours, though you are so severe, Madam.

L. TOWN.   What he may be for a lover, I know not; but he's a very pleasant acquaintance, I am sure.

BELL.   Had you seen him use Mrs. Loveit as I have done, you would never endure him more.

EMIL.   What, he has quarreled with her again!

BELL.   Upon the slightest occasion; he's jealous of Sir Fopling.

L. TOWN.   She never saw him in her life but yesterday, and that was here.

EMIL.   On my conscience, he's the only man in town that's her aversion! How horribly out of humour she was all the while he talked to her!

BELL.   And somebody has wickedly told him——

EMIL.   Here he comes.

Enter DORIMANT

MED.   Dorimant! you are luckily come to justify yourself: here's a lady——

BELL.   Has a word or two to say to you from a disconsolate person.

DOR.   You tender your reputation too much, I know, Madam, to whisper with me before this good company.

BELL.   To serve Mrs. Loveit I'll make a bold venture.

DOR.   Here's Medley, the very spirit of scandal.

BELL.   No matter!

EMIL.   'Tis something you are unwilling to hear, Mr. Dorimant.

L. TOWN.   Tell him, Bellinda, whether he will or no.

BELL. [aloud]   Mrs. Loveit——

DOR.   Softly! these are laughers; you do not know 'em.

BELL. [to DORIMANT apart]   In a word, y'ave made me hate you, which I thought you never could have done.

DOR.   In obeying your commands.

BELL.   'Twas a cruel part you played. How could you act it?

DOR.   Nothing is cruel to a man who could kill himself to please you. Remember five o'clock to-morrow morning!

BELL.   I tremble when you name it.

DOR.   Be sure you come!

BELL.   I sha' not.

DOR.   Swear you will!

BELL.   I dare not.

DOR.   Swear, I say!

BELL.   By my life——by all the happiness I hope for——

DOR.   You will.

BELL.   I will!

DOR.   Kind!

BELL.   I am glad I've sworn. I vow I think I should ha' failed you else!

DOR.   Surprisingly kind! In what temper did you leave Loveit?

BELL.   Her raving was prettily over, and she began to be in a brave way of defying you and all your works. Where have you been since you went from thence?

DOR.   I looked in at the play.

BELL.   I have promised, and must return to her again.

DOR.   Persuade her to walk in the Mail this evening.

BELL.   She hates the place and will not come.

DOR.   Do all you can to prevail with her.

BELL.   For what purpose?

DOR.   Sir Fopling will be here anon; I'll prepare him to set upon her there before me.

BELL.   You persecute her too much, but I'll do all you'll ha' me.

DOR. [aloud]   Tell her plainly 'tis grown so dull a business I can drudge on no longer.

EMIL.   There are afflictions in love, Mr. Dorimant.

DOR.   You women make 'em, who are commonly as unreasonable in that as you are at play—without the advantage be on your side, a man can never quietly give over when he's weary.

MED.   If you would play without being obliged to complaisance, Dorimant, you should play in public places.

DOR.   Ordinaries were a very good thing for that, but gentlemen do not of late frequent 'em. The deep play is now in private houses.

[BELLINDA *offering to steal away*]

L. TOWN.   Bellinda, are you leaving us so soon?

BELL.   I am to go to the Park with Mrs. Loveit, Madam.

[*exit* BELLINDA]

L. TOWN.   This confidence will go nigh to spoil this young creature.

MED.   'Twill do her good, Madam. Young men who are brought up under practising lawyers prove the abler counsel when they come to be called to the bar themselves.

DOR.   The town has been very favourable to you this afternoon, my Lady Townley; you use to have an *embarras* of chairs and coaches at your door, an uproar of footmen in your hall, and a noise of fools above here.

L. TOWN.   Indeed, my house is the general rendezvous, and next to the playhouse is the common refuge of all the young idle people.

EMIL.   Company is a very good thing, Madam, but I wonder you do not love it a little more chosen.

L. TOWN.   'Tis good to have an universal taste; we should love wit, but for variety be able to divert ourselves with the extravagancies of those who want it.

MED.   Fools will make you laugh.

EMIL.   For once or twice, but the repetition of their folly after a visit or two grows tedious and unsufferable.

L. TOWN.   You are a little too delicate, Emilia.

Enter a Page

PAGE.   Sir Fopling Flutter, Madam, desires to know if you are to be seen.

L. TOWN.   Here's the freshest fool in town, and one who has not cloyed you yet.—— Page!

PAGE.   Madam!

L. TOWN.   Desire him to walk up.   [*exit Page*]

DOR.   Do not you fall on him, Medley, and snub him. Soothe him up in his extravagance; he will show the better.

MED.   You know I have a natural indulgence for fools and need not this caution, Sir.

Enter SIR FOPLING FLUTTER *with his Page after him*

SIR FOP.   Page, wait without. [*exit Page*] [*to* LADY TOWNLEY] Madam, I kiss your hands. I see yesterday was nothing of chance; the *belles assem-*

blées form themselves here every day. [*to* EMILIA] Lady, your servant.——
Dorimant, let me embrace thee! Without lying, I have not met with any
of my acquaintance who retain so much of Paris as thou dost—the very
air thou hadst when the marquise mistook thee i'th' Tuileries and cried,
"Hey, Chevalier!" and then begged thy pardon.

DOR.   I would fain wear in fashion as long as I can, Sir; 'tis a thing to
be valued in men as well as baubles.

SIR FOP.   Thou art a man of wit and understands the town. Prithee,
let thee and I be intimate; there is no living without making some good
man the confidant of our pleasures.

DOR.   'Tis true! but there is no man so improper for such a business
as I am.

SIR FOP.   Prithee, why hast thou so modest an opinion of thyself?

DOR.   Why, first, I could never keep a secret in my life; and then,
there is no charm so infallibly makes me fall in love with a woman as my
knowing a friend loves her. I deal honestly with you.

SIR FOP.   Thy humour's very gallant, or let me perish! I knew a
French count so like thee!

L. TOWN.   Wit, I perceive, has more power over you than beauty, Sir
Fopling, else you would not have let this lady stand so long neglected.

SIR FOP. [*to* EMILIA]   A thousand pardons, Madam; some civility's due
of course upon the meeting a long absent friend. The *éclat* of so much
beauty, I confess, ought to have charmed me sooner.

EMIL.   The *brillant* of so much good language, Sir, has much more
power than the little beauty I can boast.

SIR FOP.   I never saw anything prettier than this high work on your
point d'Espagne.

EMIL.   'Tis not so rich as *point de Venise*.

SIR FOP.   Not altogether, but looks cooler and is more proper for the
season.—— Dorimant, is not that Medley?

DOR.   The same, Sir.

SIR FOP.   Forgive me, Sir; in this *embarras* of civilities I could not
come to have you in my arms sooner. You understand an equipage the
best of any man in town, I hear.

MED.   By my own you would not guess it.

SIR FOP.   There are critics who do not write, Sir.

MED.   Our peevish poets will scarce allow it.

SIR FOP.   Damn 'em, they'll allow no man wit who does not play the
fool like themselves and show it! Have you taken notice of the gallesh I
brought over?

MED.   Oh, yes! 't has quite another air than th' English makes.

SIR FOP.   'Tis as easily known from an English tumbril as an Inns of
Court man is from one of us.

DOR.   Truly; there is a *bel air* in galleshes as well as men.

MED.   But there are few so delicate to observe it.

SIR FOP.   The world is generally very *grossier* here, indeed.

L. TOWN.   He's very fine.

EMIL.   Extreme proper.

SIR FOP.   A slight suit I made to appear in at my first arrival—not worthy your consideration, ladies.

DOR.   The pantaloon is very well mounted.

SIR FOP.   The tassels are new and pretty.

MED.   I never saw a coat better cut.

SIR FOP.   It makes me show long-waisted, and, I think, slender.

DOR.   That's the shape our ladies dote on.

MED.   Your breech, though, is a handful too high, in my eye, Sir Fopling.

SIR FOP.   Peace, Medley! I have wished it lower a thousand times, but a pox on't! 'twill not be.

L. TOWN.   His gloves are well fringed, large and graceful.

SIR FOP.   I was always eminent for being *bien ganté*.

EMIL.   He wears nothing but what are originals of the most famous hands in Paris.

SIR FOP.   You are in the right, Madam.

L. TOWN.   The suit!

SIR FOP.   Barroy.

EMIL.   The garniture!

SIR FOP.   Le Gras.

MED.   The shoes!

SIR FOP.   Piccar.

DOR.   The periwig!

SIR FOP.   Chedreux.

L. TOWN. ⎱ The gloves!
EMIL.   ⎰

SIR FOP.   Orangerie—you know the smell, ladies.—— Dorimant, I could find in my heart for an amusement to have a gallantry with some of our English ladies.

DOR.   'Tis a thing no less necessary to confirm the reputation of your wit than a duel will be to satisfy the town of your courage.

SIR FOP.   Here was a woman yesterday——

DOR.   Mistress Loveit.

SIR FOP.   You have named her.

DOR.   You cannot pitch on a better for your purpose.

SIR FOP.   Prithee, what is she?

DOR.   A person of quality, and one who has a rest of reputation enough to make the conquest considerable; besides, I hear she likes you too.

Sir Fop.   Methoughts she seemed, though, very reserved and uneasy all the time I entertained her.

Dor.   Grimace and affectation! You will see her i'th' Mail to-night.

Sir Fop.   Prithee, let thee and I take the air together.

Dor.   I am engaged to Medley, but I'll meet you at St. James's and give you some information upon the which you may regulate your proceedings.

Sir Fop.   All the world will be in the Park to-night. Ladies, 'twere pity to keep so much beauty longer within doors and rob the Ring of all those charms that should adorn it.—— Hey, Page!

Enter Page

See that all my people be ready.   [*Page goes out again*]
—Dorimant, *au revoir.*   [*exit*]

Med.   A fine mettled coxcomb.

Dor.   Brisk and insipid.

Med.   Pert and dull.

Emil.   However you despise him, gentlemen, I'll lay my life he passes for a wit with many.

Dor.   That may very well be; Nature has her cheats, stums a brain, and puts sophisticate dulness often on the tasteless multitude for true wit and good humour. Medley, come!

Med.   I must go a little way; I will meet you i'the Mail.

Dor.   I'll walk through the garden thither.—[*to the women*] We shall meet anon and bow.

L. Town.   Not to-night. We are engaged about a business the knowledge of which may make you laugh hereafter.

Med.   Your servant, ladies.

Dor.   *Au revoir,* as Sir Fopling says.

[*exeunt* Medley *and* Dorimant]

L. Town.   The old man will be here immediately.

Emil.   Let's expect him i'th' garden.

L. Town.   Go! you are a rogue.

Emil.   I can't abide you.   [*exeunt*]

SCENE III

Scene: *The Mail*

Enter Harriet *and* Young Bellair, *she pulling him*

Har.   Come along.

Y. Bell.   And leave your mother!

HAR.   Busy will be sent with a hue and cry after us, but that's no matter.

Y. BELL.   'Twill look strangely in me.

HAR.   She'll believe it a freak of mine and never blame your manners.

Y. BELL.   What reverend acquaintance is that she has met?

HAR.   A fellow-beauty of the last king's time, though by the ruins you would hardly guess it.   [*exeunt*]

Enter DORIMANT *and crosses the stage*
Enter YOUNG BELLAIR *and* HARRIET

Y. BELL.   By this time your mother is in a fine taking.

HAR.   If your friend Mr. Dorimant were but here now, that she might find me talking with him!

Y. BELL.   She does not know him, but dreads him, I hear, of all mankind.

HAR.   She concludes if he does but speak to a woman, she's undone—is on her knees every day to pray heaven defend me from him.

Y. BELL.   You do not apprehend him so much as she does?

HAR.   I never saw anything in him that was frightful.

Y. BELL.   On the contrary, have you not observed something extreme delightful in his wit and person?

HAR.   He's agreeable and pleasant, I must own, but he does so much affect being so, he displeases me.

Y. BELL.   Lord, Madam! all he does and says is so easy and so natural.

HAR.   Some men's verses seem so to the unskillful, but labour i'the one and affectation in the other to the judicious plainly appear.

Y. BELL.   I never heard him accused of affectation before.

Enter DORIMANT *and stares upon her*

HAR.   It passes on the easy town, who are favourably pleased in him to call it humour.   [*exeunt* YOUNG BELLAIR *and* HARRIET]

DOR.   'Tis she! it must be she—that lovely hair, that easy shape, those wanton eyes, and all those melting charms about her mouth which Medley spoke of! I'll follow the lottery and put in for a prize with my friend Bellair.   [*exeunt* DORIMANT *repeating:*
            In love the victors from the vanquish'd fly;
            They fly that wound, and they pursue that die.]

Enter YOUNG BELLAIR *and* HARRIET
and after them DORIMANT *standing at a distance*

Y. BELL.   Most people prefer High Park to this place.

HAR.   It has the better reputation, I confess; but I abominate the dull diversions there—the formal bows, the affected smiles, the silly by-words and amorous tweers in passing. Here one meets with a little conversation now and then.

Y. BELL.   These conversations have been fatal to some of your sex, Madam.

HAR.   It may be so; because some who want temper have been undone by gaming, must others who have it wholly deny themselves the pleasure of play?

DOR. [*coming up gently and bowing to her*]   Trust me, it were unreasonable, Madam.

HAR. [*she starts and looks grave*]   Lord, who's this?

Y. BELL.   Dorimant!

DOR.   Is this the woman your father would have you marry?

Y. BELL.   It is.

DOR.   Her name?

Y. BELL.   Harriet.

DOR.   I am not mistaken; she's handsome.

Y. BELL.   Talk to her; her wit is better than her face. We were wishing for you but now.

DOR. [*to* HARRIET]   Overcast with seriousness o'the sudden! A thousand smiles were shining in that face but now; I never saw so quick a change of weather.

HAR. [*aside*]   I feel as great a change within, but he shall never know it.

DOR.   You were talking of play, Madam. Pray, what may be your stint?

HAR.   A little harmless discourse in public walks, or at most an appointment in a box, barefaced, at the playhouse: you are for masks and private meetings, where women engage for all they are worth, I hear.

DOR.   I have been used to deep play, but I can make one at small game when I like my gamester well.

HAR.   And be so unconcerned you'll ha' no pleasure in't.

DOR.   Where there is a considerable sum to be won, the hope of drawing people in makes every trifle considerable.

HAR.   The sordidness of men's natures, I know, makes 'em willing to flatter and comply with the rich, though they are sure never to be the better for 'em.

DOR.   'Tis in their power to do us good, and we despair not but at some time or other they may be willing.

HAR.   To men who have fared in this town like you, 'twould be a great mortification to live on hope. Could you keep a Lent for a mistress?

Dor.   In expectation of a happy Easter and, though time be very precious, think forty days well lost to gain your favour.

Har.   Mr. Bellair, let us walk; 'tis time to leave him. Men grow dull when they begin to be particular.

Dor.   Y'are mistaken; flattery will not ensue, though I know y'are greedy of the praises of the whole Mail.

Har.   You do me wrong.

Dor.   I do not. As I followed you, I observed how you were pleased when the fops cried, "She's handsome, very handsome! by God she is!" and whispered aloud your name; the thousand several forms you put your face into; then, to make yourself more agreeable, how wantonly you played with your head, flung back your locks, and looked smilingly over your shoulder at 'em!

Har.   I do not go begging the men's, as you do the ladies', good liking, with a sly softness in your looks and a gentle slowness in your bows as you pass by 'em—as thus, Sir. [*acts him*] Is not this like you?

Enter Lady Woodvill *and* Busy

Y. Bell.   Your mother, Madam.

[*pulls* Harriet; *she composes herself*]

L. Wood.   Ah, my dear child Harriet!

Busy.   Now is she so pleased with finding her again she cannot chide her.

L. Wood.   Come away!

Dor.   'Tis now but high Mail, Madam, the most entertaining time of all the evening.

Har.   I would fain see that Dorimant, Mother, you so cry out of for a monster; he's in the Mail, I hear.

L. Wood.   Come away then! The plague is here and you should dread the infection.

Y. Bell.   You may be misinformed of the gentleman.

L. Wood.   Oh, no! I hope you do not know him. He is the prince of all the devils in the town—delights in nothing but in rapes and riots!

Dor.   If you did but hear him speak, Madam!

L. Wood.   Oh, he has a tongue, they say, would tempt the angels to a second fall.

Enter Sir Fopling *with his equipage, six Footmen and a Page*

Sir Fop.   Hey! Champagne, Norman, La Rose, La Fleur, La Tour, La Verdure!—— Dorimant——

L. Wood.   Here, here he is among this rout! He names him! Come away, Harriet; come away!

[*exeunt* Lady Woodvill, Harriet, Busy, *and* Young Bellair]

DOR.   This fool's coming has spoiled all. She's gone, but she has left a pleasing image of herself behind that wanders in my soul—it must not settle there.

SIR FOP.   What reverie is this? Speak, man!

DOR.   Snatcht from myself, how far behind
        Already I behold the shore!

Enter MEDLEY

MED.   Dorimant, a discovery! I met with Bellair.

DOR.   You can tell me no news, Sir; I know all.

MED.   How do you like the daughter?

DOR.   You never came so near truth in your life as you did in her description.

MED.   What think you of the mother?

DOR.   Whatever I think of her, she thinks very well of me, I find.

MED.   Did she know you?

DOR.   She did not; whether she does now or no, I know not. Here was a pleasant scene towards, when in came Sir Fopling, mustering up his equipage, and at the latter end named me and frighted her away.

MED.   Loveit and Bellinda are not far off; I saw 'em alight at St. James's.

DOR.   Sir Fopling! Hark you, a word or two. [*whispers*] Look you do not want assurance.

SIR FOP.   I never do on these occasions.

DOR.   Walk on; we must not be seen together. Make your advantage of what I have told you. The next turn you will meet the lady.

SIR FOP.   Hey! Follow me all! [*exeunt* SIR FOPLING *and his equipage*]

DOR.   Medley, you shall see good sport anon between Loveit and this Fopling.

MED.   I thought there was something toward, by that whisper.

DOR.   You know a worthy principle of hers?

MED.   Not to be so much as civil to a man who speaks to her in the presence of him she professes to love.

DOR.   I have encouraged Fopling to talk to her to-night.

MED.   Now you are here, she will go nigh to beat him.

DOR.   In the humour she's in, her love will make her do some very extravagant thing doubtless.

MED.   What was Bellinda's business with you at my Lady Townley's?

DOR.   To get me to meet Loveit here in order to an *éclaircissement*. I made some difficulty of it and have prepared this rencounter to make good my jealousy.

MED.   Here they come.

Enter MRS. LOVEIT, BELLINDA, *and* PERT

DOR.   I'll meet her and provoke her with a deal of dumb civility in passing by, then turn short and be behind her when Sir Fopling sets upon her——

> See how unregarded now
> That piece of beauty passes.

[exeunt DORIMANT *and* MEDLEY]

BELL.   How wonderful respectfully he bowed!

PERT.   He's always over-mannerly when he has done a mischief.

BELL.   Methoughts, indeed, at the same time he had a strange, despising countenance.

PERT.   The unlucky look he thinks becomes him.

BELL.   I was afraid you would have spoke to him, my dear.

LOV.   I would have died first; he shall no more find me the loving fool he has done.

BELL.   You love him still?

LOV.   No!

PERT.   I wish you did not.

LOV.   I do not, and I will have you think so.—What made you hale me to this odious place, Bellinda?

BELL.   I hate to be hulched up in a coach; walking is much better.

LOV.   Would we could meet Sir Fopling now!

BELL.   Lord, would you not avoid him?

LOV.   I would make him all the advances that may be.

BELL.   That would confirm Dorimant's suspicion, my dear.

LOV.   He is not jealous; but I will make him so, and be revenged a way he little thinks on.

BELL. [*aside*]   If she should make him jealous, that may make him fond of her again. I must dissuade her from it.—— Lord, my dear, this will certainly make him hate you.

LOV.   'Twill make him uneasy, though he does not care for me. I know the effects of jealousy on men of his proud temper.

BELL.   'Tis a fantastic remedy; its operations are dangerous and uncertain.

LOV.   'Tis the strongest cordial we can give to dying love: it often brings it back when there's no sign of life remaining. But I design not so much the reviving of his, as my revenge.

Enter SIR FOPLING *and his equipage*

SIR FOP.   Hey! Bid the coachman send home four of his horses and bring the coach to Whitehall; I'll walk over the Park.—— Madam, the honour of kissing your fair hands is a happiness I missed this afternoon at my Lady Townley's.

Lov.   You were very obliging, Sir Fopling, the last time I saw you there.

Sir Fop.   The preference was due to your wit and beauty.—— Madam, your servant; there never was so sweet an evening.

Bell.   'T has drawn all the rabble of the town hither.

Sir Fop.   'Tis pity there's not an order made that none but the *beau monde* should walk here.

Lov.   'Twould add much to the beauty of the place. See what a sort of nasty fellows are coming!

Enter four ill-fashioned fellows, singing:
               'Tis not for kisses alone, etc.

Lov.   Fo! Their periwigs are scented with tobacco so strong——

Sir Fop.   It overcomes our pulvillio. Methinks I smell the coffee-house they come from.

1 Man.   Dorimant's convenient, Madam Loveit.

2 Man.   I like the oily buttock with her.

3 Man.   What spruce prig is that?

1 Man.   A caravan lately come from Paris.

2 Man.   Peace! they smoke.   [*all of them coughing; exeunt singing:*
               There's something else to be done, etc.*]

Enter Dorimant *and* Medley

Dor.   They're engaged.

Med.   She entertains him as if she liked him!

Dor.   Let us go forward—seem earnest in discourse and show ourselves; then you shall see how she'll use him.

Bell.   Yonder's Dorimant, my dear.

Lov. [*aside*]   I see him. He comes insulting, but I will disappoint him in his expectation. [*to* Sir Fopling] I like this pretty, nice humour of yours, Sir Fopling.—— With what a loathing eye he looked upon those fellows!

Sir Fop.   I sat near one of 'em at a play to-day and was almost poisoned with a pair of cordovan gloves he wears.

Lov.   Oh, filthy cordovan! How I hate the smell!
                              [*laughs in a loud, affected way*]

Sir Fop.   Did you observe, Madam, how their cravats hung loose an inch from their neck and what a frightful air it gave 'em?

Lov.   Oh, I took particular notice of one that is always spruced up with a deal of dirty sky-coloured ribband.

Bell.   That's one of the walking flageolets who haunt the Mail o'nights.

Lov.   Oh, I remember him; h'has a hollow tooth enough to spoil the sweetness of an evening.

Sir Fop.   I have seen the tallest walk the streets with a dainty pair of boxes neatly buckled on.

Lov.   And a little foot-boy at his heels, pocket-high, with a flat cap, a dirty face——

Sir Fop.   And a snotty nose.

Lov.   Oh, odious!—There's many of my own sex with that Holborn equipage trig to Gray's Inn Walks and now and then travel hither on a Sunday.

Med.   She takes no notice of you.

Dor.   Damn her! I am jealous of a counterplot.

Lov.   Your liveries are the finest, Sir Fopling—oh, that page! that page is the prettily'st dressed—they are all Frenchmen.

Sir Fop.   There's one damned English blockhead among 'em; you may know him by his mien.

Lov.   Oh, that's he—that's he! What do you call him?

Sir Fop.   Hey—I know not what to call him——

Lov.   What's your name?

Footm.   John Trott, Madam.

Sir Fop.   Oh, unsufferable! Trott, Trott, Trott! There's nothing so barbarous as the names of our English servants.—— What countryman are you, Sirrah?

Footm.   Hampshire, Sir.

Sir Fop.   Then Hampshire be your name. Hey, Hampshire!

Lov.   Oh, that sound—that sound becomes the mouth of a man of quality!

Med.   Dorimant, you look a little bashful on the matter.

Dor.   She dissembles better than I thought she could have done.

Med.   You have tempted her with too luscious a bait. She bites at the coxcomb.

Dor.   She cannot fall from loving me to that.

Med.   You begin to be jealous in earnest.

Dor.   Of one I do not love——

Med.   You did love her.

Dor.   The fit has long been over.

Med.   But I have known men fall into dangerous relapses when they have found a woman inclining to another.

Dor. [*to himself*]   He guesses the secret of my heart. I am concerned, but dare not show it, lest Bellinda should mistrust all I have done to gain her.

Bell. [*aside*]   I have watched his look and find no alteration there. Did he love her, some signs of jealousy would have appeared.

DOR.   I hope this happy evening, Madam, has reconciled you to the scandalous Mail. We shall have you now hankering here again——

LOV.   Sir Fopling, will you walk?

SIR FOP.   I am all obedience, Madam.

LOV.   Come along then, and let's agree to be malicious on all the ill-fashioned things we meet.

SIR FOP.   We'll make a critique on the whole Mail, Madam.

LOV.   Bellinda, you shall engage——

BELL.   To the reserve of our friends, my dear.

LOV.   No! no exceptions!

SIR FOP.   We'll sacrifice all to our diversion.

LOV.   All—all.

SIR FOP.   All.

BELL.   All? Then let it be.

[*exeunt* SIR FOPLING, MRS. LOVEIT, BELLINDA, *and* PERT, *laughing*]

MED.   Would you had brought some more of your friends, Dorimant, to have been witnesses of Sir Fopling's disgrace and your triumph.

DOR.   'Twere unreasonable to desire you not to laugh at me; but pray do not expose me to the town this day or two.

MED.   By that time you hope to have regained your credit.

DOR.   I know she hates Fopling and only makes use of him in hope to work me on again; had it not been for some powerful considerations which will be removed to-morrow morning, I had made her pluck off this mask and show the passion that lies panting under.

Enter a Footman

MED.   Here comes a man from Bellair with news of your last adventure.

DOR.   I am glad he sent him; I long to know the consequence of our parting.

FOOTM.   Sir, my master desires you to come to my Lady Townley's presently and bring Mr. Medley with you. My Lady Woodvill and her daughter are there.

MED.   Then all's well, Dorimant.

FOOTM.   They have sent for the fiddles and mean to dance. He bid me tell you, Sir, the old lady does not know you, and would have you own yourself to be Mr. Courtage. They are all prepared to receive you by that name.

DOR.   That foppish admirer of quality, who flatters the very meat at honourable tables and never offers love to a woman below a lady-grandmother.

MED.   You know the character you are to act, I see.

DOR.   This is Harriet's contrivance—wild, witty, lovesome, beautiful, and young!—Come along, Medley.

MED.   This new woman would well supply the loss of Loveit.

DOR.   That business must not end so; before to-morrow sun is set I will revenge and clear it.

And you and Loveit, to her cost, shall find,
I fathom all the depths of womankind.

[*exeunt*]

ACT IV

SCENE I

The Scene opens with the Fiddles playing a Country Dance.

Enter DORIMANT *and* LADY WOODVILL, YOUNG BELLAIR
and MRS. HARRIET, OLD BELLAIR *and* EMILIA, MR. MEDLEY
and LADY TOWNLEY, *as having just ended the Dance*

O. BELL.   So, so, so!—a smart bout, a very smart bout, a dod!

L. TOWN.   How do you like Emilia's dancing, Brother?

O. BELL.   Not at all—not at all!

L. TOWN.   You speak not what you think, I am sure.

O. BELL.   No matter for that; go, bid her dance no more. It don't become her—it don't become her. Tell her I say so. [*aside*] A dod, I love her!

DOR.   [*to* LADY WOODVILL]   All people mingle nowadays, Madam. And in public places women of quality have the least respect showed 'em.

L. WOOD.   I protest you say the truth, Mr. Courtage.

DOR.   Forms and ceremonies, the only things that uphold quality and greatness, are now shamefully laid aside and neglected.

L. WOOD.   Well, this is not the women's age, let 'em think what they will. Lewdness is the business now; love was the business in my time.

DOR.   The women, indeed, are little beholding to the young men of this age; they're generally only dull admirers of themselves, and make their court to nothing but their periwigs and their cravats, and would be more concerned for the disordering of 'em, though on a good occasion, than a young maid would be for the tumbling of her head or handkercher.

L. WOOD.   I protest you hit 'em.

DOR.   They are very assiduous to show themselves at court, well dressed, to the women of quality, but their business is with the stale mistresses of the town, who are prepared to receive their lazy addresses by industrious old lovers who have cast 'em off and made 'em easy.

HAR.   He fits my mother's humour so well, a little more and she'll dance a kissing dance with him anon.

MED.   Dutifully observed, Madam.

DOR.   They pretend to be great critics in beauty. By their talk you would think they liked no face, and yet can dote on an ill one if it belong to a laundress or a tailor's daughter. They cry, "A woman's past her prime at twenty, decayed at four-and-twenty, old and unsufferable at thirty."

L. WOOD.   Unsufferable at thirty! That they are in the wrong, Mr. Courtage, at five-and-thirty, there are living proofs enough to convince 'em.

DOR.   Ay, Madam. There's Mrs. Setlooks, Mrs. Droplip, and my Lady Lowd; show me among all our opening buds a face that promises so much beauty as the remains of theirs.

L. WOOD.   The depraved appetite of this vicious age tastes nothing but green fruit, and loathes it when 'tis kindly ripened.

DOR.   Else so many deserving women, Madam, would not be so untimely neglected.

L. WOOD.   I protest, Mr. Courtage, a dozen such good men as you would be enough to atone for that wicked Dorimant and all the under debauchees of the town. [HARRIET, EMILIA, YOUNG BELLAIR, MEDLEY, LADY TOWNLEY *break out into a laughter*]—— What's the matter there?

MED.   A pleasant mistake, Madam, that a lady has made, occasions a little laughter.

O. BELL.   Come, come, you keep 'em idle! They are impatient till the fiddles play again.

DOR.   You are not weary, Madam?

L. WOOD.   One dance more; I cannot refuse you, Mr. Courtage.

> [*they dance; after the dance,* OLD BELLAIR,
> *singing and dancing up to* EMILIA]

EMILIA.   You are very active, Sir.

O. BELL.   A dod, Sirrah! when I was a young fellow I could ha' capered up to my woman's gorget.

DOR.   You are willing to rest yourself, Madam——

L. TOWN.   We'll walk into my chamber and sit down.

MED.   Leave us Mr. Courtage; he's a dancer, and the young ladies are not weary yet.

L. WOOD.   We'll send him out again.

HAR.   If you do not quickly, I know where to send for Mr. Dorimant.

L. WOOD.   This girl's head, Mr. Courtage, is ever running on that wild fellow.

DOR.   'Tis well you have got her a good husband, Madam; that will settle it.

> [*exeunt* LADY TOWNLEY, LADY WOODVILL, *and* DORIMANT]

O. BELL. [*to* EMILIA]   A dod, sweetheart, be advised and do not throw thyself away on a young, idle fellow.

EMIL.   I have no such intention, Sir.

O. BELL.   Have a little patience! Thou shalt have the man I spake of. A dod, he loves thee and will make a good husband—but no words!

EMIL.   But, Sir——

O. BELL.   No answer—out a pise! peace! and think on't.

Enter DORIMANT

DOR.   Your company is desired within, Sir.

O. BELL.   I go, I go! Good Mr. Courtage, fare you well!—[*to* EMILIA] Go, I'll see you no more!

EMIL.   What have I done, Sir?

O. BELL.   You are ugly, you are ugly!—Is she not, Mr. Courtage?

EMIL.   Better words or I shan't abide you.

O. BELL.   Out a pise; a dod, what does she say? Hit her a pat for me there.   [*exit* OLD BELLAIR]

MED.   You have charms for the whole family.

DOR.   You'll spoil all with some unseasonable jest, Medley.

MED.   You see I confine my tongue and am content to be a bare spectator, much contrary to my nature.

EMIL.   Methinks, Mr. Dorimant, my Lady Woodvill is a little fond of you.

DOR.   Would her daughter were!

MED.   It may be you may find her so. Try her—you have an opportunity.

DOR.   And I will not lose it.—— Bellair, here's a lady has something to say to you.

Y. BELL.   I wait upon her.—— Mr. Medley, we have both business with you.

DOR.   Get you all together then. [*to* HARRIET] That demure curtsey is not amiss in jest, but do not think in earnest it becomes you.

HAR.   Affectation is catching, I find; from your grave bow I got it.

DOR.   Where had you all that scorn and coldness in your look?

HAR.   From nature, Sir; pardon my want of art. I have not learnt those softnesses and languishings which now in faces are so much in fashion.

DOR.   You need 'em not; you have a sweetness of your own, if you would but calm your frowns and let it settle.

HAR.   My eyes are wild and wandering like my passions, and cannot yet be tied to rules of charming.

DOR.   Women, indeed, have commonly a method of managing those messengers of love. Now they will look as if they would kill, and anon they will look as if they were dying. They point and rebate their glances, the better to invite us.

HAR.   I like this variety well enough, but hate the set face that always looks as it would say, "Come love me!"—a woman who at plays makes the *doux yeux* to a whole audience and at home cannot forbear 'em to her monkey.

DOR.   Put on a gentle smile and let me see how well it will become you.

HAR.   I am sorry my face does not please you as it is, but I shall not be complaisant and change it.

DOR.   Though you are obstinate, I know 'tis capable of improvement, and shall do you justice, Madam, if I chance to be at Court when the critics of the Circle pass their judgment; for thither you must come.

HAR.   And expect to be taken in pieces, have all my features examined, every motion censured, and on the whole be condemned to be but pretty, or a beauty of the lowest rate. What think you?

DOR.   The women—nay, the very lovers who belong to the drawing-room—will maliciously allow you more than that: they always grant what is apparent, that they may the better be believed when they name concealed faults they cannot easily be disproved in.

HAR.   Beauty runs as great a risk exposed at Court as wit does on the stage, where the ugly and the foolish all are free to censure.

DOR. [*aside*]   I love her and dare not let her know it; I fear sh'as an ascendant o'er me and may revenge the wrongs I have done her sex. [*to her*] Think of making a party, Madam; love will engage.

HAR.   You make me start! I did not think to have heard of love from you.

DOR.   I never knew what 'twas to have a settled ague yet, but now and then have had irregular fits.

HAR.   Take heed! sickness after long health is commonly more violent and dangerous.

DOR. [*aside*]   I have took the infection from her, and feel the disease now spreading in me. [*to her*] Is the name of love so frightful that you dare not stand it?

HAR.   'Twill do little execution out of your mouth on me, I am sure.

DOR.   It has been fatal——

HAR.   To some easy women, but we are not all born to one destiny. I was informed you use to laugh at love and not make it.

DOR.   The time has been, but now I must speak——

HAR.   If it be on that idle subject, I will put on my serious look, turn my head carelessly from you, drop my lip, let my eyelids fall and hang half o'er my eyes—thus—while you buzz a speech of an hour long in my ear, and I answer never a word. Why do you not begin?

DOR.   That the company may take notice how passionately I make advances of love, and how disdainfully you receive 'em!

HAR.   When your love's grown strong enough to make you bear being laughed at, I'll give you leave to trouble me with it. Till then pray forbear, Sir.

Enter SIR FOPLING *and others in masks*

DOR.   What's here—masquerades?

HAR.   I thought that foppery had been left off, and people might have been in private with a fiddle.

DOR.   'Tis endeavoured to be kept on foot still by some who find themselves the more acceptable the less they are known.

Y. BELL.   This must be Sir Fopling.

MED.   That extraordinary habit shows it.

Y. BELL.   What are the rest?

MED.   A company of French rascals whom he picked up in Paris and has brought over to be his dancing equipage on these occasions. Make him own himself; a fool is very troublesome when he presumes he is incognito.

SIR FOP. [*to* HARRIET]   Do you know me?

HAR.   Ten to one but I guess at you?

SIR FOP.   Are you women as fond of a vizard as we men are?

HAR.   I am very fond of a vizard that covers a face I do not like, Sir.

Y. BELL.   Here are no masks, you see, Sir, but those which came with you. This was intended a private meeting; but because you look like a gentleman, if you will discover yourself and we know you to be such, you shall be welcome.

SIR FOP. [*pulling off his mask*]   Dear Bellair!

MED.   Sir Fopling! How came you hither?

SIR FOP.   Faith, as I was coming late from Whitehall, after the King's *couchée,* one of my people told me he had heard fiddles at my Lady Townley's, and——

DOR.   You need not say any more, Sir.

SIR FOP.   Dorimant, let me kiss thee.

DOR.   Hark you, Sir Fopling——   [*whispers*]

SIR FOP.   Enough, enough, Courtage.—— A pretty kind of young woman that, Medley. I observed her in the Mail—more *éveillée* than our English women commonly are. Prithee, what is she?

MED.   The most noted coquette in town. Beware of her.

SIR FOP.   Let her be what she will, I know how to take my measures. In Paris the mode is to flatter the *prude,* laugh at the *faux-prude,* make serious love to the *demi-prude,* and only rally with the *coquette.* Medley, what think you?

MED.   That for all this smattering of the mathematics, you may be out in your judgment at tennis.

SIR FOP.   What a *coq-à-l'âne* is this? I talk of women and thou answer'st tennis.

MED.   Mistakes will be for want of apprehension.

SIR FOP.   I am very glad of the acquaintance I have with this family.

MED.   My lady truly is a good woman.

SIR FOP.   Ah, Dorimant—Courtage, I would say—would thou hadst spent the last winter in Paris with me! When thou wert there, La Corneus and Sallyes were the only habitudes we had: a comedian would have been a *bonne fortune*. No stranger ever passed his time so well as I did some months before I came over. I was well received in a dozen families where all the women of quality used to visit; I have intrigues to tell thee more pleasant than ever thou read'st in a novel.

HAR.   Write 'em Sir, and oblige us women. Our language wants such little stories.

SIR FOP.   Writing, Madam, 's a mechanic part of wit. A gentleman should never go beyond a song or a *billet*.

HAR.   Bussy was a gentleman.

SIR FOP.   Who, d'Ambois?

MED.   Was there ever such a brisk blockhead?

HAR.   Not d'Ambois, Sir, but Rabutin—he who writ the loves of France.

SIR FOP.   That may be, Madam; many gentlemen do things that are below 'em. Damn your authors, Courtage; women are the prettiest things we can fool away our time with.

HAR.   I hope ye have wearied yourself to-night at Court, Sir, and will not think of fooling with anybody here.

SIR FOP.   I cannot complain of my fortune there, Madam.—— Dorimant——

DOR.   Again!

SIR FOP.   Courtage—a pox on't!—I have something to tell thee. When I had made my court within, I came out and flung myself upon the mat under the state i'th' outward room, i'th' midst of half a dozen beauties who were withdrawn to jeer among themselves, as they called it.

DOR.   Did you know 'em?

SIR FOP.   Not one of 'em, by heavens!—not I. But they were all your friends.

DOR.   How are you sure of that?

SIR FOP.   Why, we laughed at all the town—spared nobody but yourself. They found me a man for their purpose.

DOR.   I know you are malicious, to your power.

SIR FOP.   And faith, I had occasion to show it, for I never saw more gaping fools at a ball or on a birthday.

DOR.   You learned who the women were?

SIR FOP.   No matter; they frequent the drawing-room.

DOR.   And entertain themselves pleasantly at the expense of all the fops who come there.

SIR FOP.   That's their business. Faith, I sifted 'em, and find they have a sort of wit among them.—— Ah, filthy!   [*pinches a tallow candle*]

DOR.   Look, he has been pinching the tallow candle.

SIR FOP.   How can you breathe in a room where there's grease frying?—— Dorimant, thou art intimate with my lady; advise her, for her own sake and the good company that comes hither, to burn wax lights.

HAR.   What are these masquerades who stand so obsequiously at a distance?

SIR FOP.   A set of balladines whom I picked out of the best in France and brought over with a *flûte-douce* or two—my servants. They shall entertain you.

HAR.   I had rather see you dance yourself, Sir Fopling.

SIR FOP.   And I had rather do it—all the company knows it—but, Madam——

MED.   Come, come, no excuses, Sir Fopling!

SIR FOP.   By heavens, Medley——

MED.   Like a woman I find you must be struggled with before one brings you to what you desire.

HAR. [*aside*]   Can he dance?

EMIL.   And fence and sing too, if you'll believe him.

DOR.   He has no more excellence in his heels than in his head. He went to Paris a plain, bashful English blockhead, and is returned a fine undertaking French fop.

MED.   I cannot prevail.

SIR FOP.   Do not think it want of complaisance, Madam.

HAR.   You are too well bred to want that, Sir Fopling. I believe it want of power.

SIR FOP.   By heavens, and so it is! I have sat up so damned late and drunk so cursed hard since I came to this lewd town, that I am fit for nothing but low dancing now—a *courante,* a *bourrée,* or a *menuet.* But St. André tells me, if I will but be regular, in one month I shall rise again. Pox on this debauchery!   [*endeavours at a caper*]

EMIL.   I have heard your dancing much commended.

SIR FOP.   It had the good fortune to please in Paris. I was judged to rise within an inch as high as the Basque in an entry I danced there.

HAR.   I am mightily taken with this fool; let us sit.—— Here's a seat, Sir Fopling.

SIR FOP. At your feet, Madam; I can be nowhere so much at ease.—— By your leave, gown.

HAR. ⎫
EMIL. ⎭ Ah, you'll spoil it!

SIR FOP. No matter; my clothes are my creatures. I make 'em to make my court to you ladies.—— Hey! *Qu'on commence!* [*dance*]—— To an English dancer, English motions. I was forced to entertain this fellow, one of my set miscarrying.—— Oh, horrid! Leave your damned manner of dancing and put on the French air: have you not a pattern before you?—— Pretty well! imitation in time may bring him to something.

After the dance, enter OLD BELLAIR, LADY WOODVILL, *and* LADY TOWNLEY

O. BELL. Hey, a dod, what have we here—a mumming?

L. WOOD. Where's my daughter? Harriet!

DOR. Here, here, Madam! I know not but under these disguises there may be dangerous sparks; I gave the young lady warning.

L. WOOD. Lord! I am so obliged to you, Mr. Courtage.

HAR. Lord, how you admire this man!

L. WOOD. What have you to except against him?

HAR. He's a fop.

L. WOOD. He's not a Dorimant, a wild extravagant fellow of the times.

HAR. He's a man made up of forms and commonplaces sucked out of the remaining lees of the last age.

L. WOOD. He's so good a man that, were you not engaged——

L. TOWN. You'll have but little night to sleep in.

L. WOOD. Lord, 'tis perfect day.

DOR. [*aside*] The hour is almost come I appointed Bellinda, and I am not so foppishly in love here to forget. I am flesh and blood yet.

L. TOWN. I am very sensible, Madam.

L. WOOD. Lord, Madam!

HAR. Look! in what a struggle is my poor mother yonder!

Y. BELL. She has much ado to bring out the compliment.

DOR. She strains hard for it.

HAR. See, see! her head tottering, her eyes staring, and her under lip trembling——

DOR. Now—now she's in the very convulsion of her civility. [*aside*] 'Sdeath, I shall lose Bellinda! I must fright her hence; she'll be an hour in this fit of good manners else. [*to* LADY WOODVILL] Do you not know Sir Fopling, Madam?

L. WOOD. I have seen that face—oh, heaven! 'tis the same we met in the Mail. How came he here?

DOR. A fiddle, in this town, is a kind of fop-call; no sooner it strikes up but the house is besieged with an army of masquerades straight.

L. WOOD.   Lord! I tremble, Mr. Courtage. For certain, Dorimant is in the company.

DOR.   I cannot confidently say he is not. You had best be gone. I will wait upon you; your daughter is in the hands of Mr. Bellair.

L. WOOD.   I'll see her before me.—— Harriet, come away.

Y. BELL.   Lights! lights!

L. TOWN.   Light, down there!

O. BELL.   A dod, it needs not——

DOR.   Call my Lady Woodvill's coach to the door quickly.

[*exeunt* YOUNG BELLAIR, HARRIET, LADY TOWNLEY,
DORIMANT, *and* LADY WOODVILL]

O. BELL.   Stay, Mr. Medley: let the young fellows do that duty; we will drink a glass of wine together. 'Tis good after dancing. What mumming spark is that?

MED.   He is not to be comprehended in few words.

SIR FOP.   Hey, La Tour!

MED.   Whither away, Sir Fopling?

SIR FOP.   I have business with Courtage.

MED.   He'll but put the ladies into their coach and come up again.

O. BELL.   In the meantime I'll call for a bottle.   [*exit* OLD BELLAIR]

Enter YOUNG BELLAIR

MED.   Where's Dorimant?

Y. BELL.   Stolen home. He has had business waiting for him there all this night, I believe, by an impatience I observed in him.

MED.   Very likely; 'tis but dissembling drunkenness, railing at his friends, and the kind soul will embrace the blessing and forget the tedious expectation.

SIR FOP.   I must speak with him before I sleep.

Y. BELL.   Emilia and I are resolved on that business.

MED.   Peace! here's your father.

Enter OLD BELLAIR *and Butler with a bottle of wine*

O. BELL.   The women are all gone to bed.—— Fill, boy!—— Mr. Medley, begin a health.

MED. [*whispers*]   To Emilia!

O. BELL.   Out a pise! she's a rogue, and I'll not pledge you.

MED.   I know you will.

O. BELL.   A dod, drink it, then!

SIR FOP.   Let us have the new bacchic.

O. BELL.   A dod, that is a hard word. What does it mean, Sir?

MED.   A catch or drinking-song.

O. BELL. Let us have it then.

SIR FOP. Fill the glasses round and draw up in a body.—— Hey, music!   [*they sing*]

> The pleasures of love and the joys of good wine
> To perfect our happiness wisely we join.
> We to beauty all day
> Give the sovereign sway
> And her favourite nymphs devoutly obey.
> At the plays we are constantly making our court,
> And when they are ended we follow the sport
> To the Mall and the Park,
> Where we love till 'tis dark;
> Then sparkling champagne
> Puts an end to their reign;
> It quickly recovers
> Poor languishing lovers;
> Makes us frolic and gay, and drowns all our sorrow.
> But alas! we relapse again on the morrow.
> Let every man stand
> With his glass in his hand,
> And briskly discharge at the word of command:
> Here's a health to all those
> Whom to-night we depose!
> Wine and beauty by turns great souls should inspire;
> Present all together! and now, boys, give fire!

O. BELL. A dod, a pretty business and very merry!

SIR FOP. Hark you, Medley, let you and I take the fiddles and go waken Dorimant.

MED. We shall do him a courtesy, if it be as I guess. For after the fatigue of this night he'll quickly have his belly full and be glad of an occasion to cry, "Take away, Handy!"

Y. BELL. I'll go with you, and there we'll consult about affairs, Medley.

O. BELL. [*looks on his watch*] A dod, 'tis six o'clock!

SIR FOP. Let's away, then.

O. BELL. Mr. Medley, my sister tells me you are an honest man—and a dod, I love you. Few words and hearty—that's the way with old Harry, old Harry.

SIR FOP. Light your flambeaux. Hey!

O. BELL. What does the man mean?

MED. 'Tis day, Sir Fopling.

SIR FOP. No matter; our serenade will look the greater.

[*exeunt omnes*]

SCENE II

SCENE: DORIMANT'S *lodging;*
a table, a candle, a toilet, etc. HANDY, *tying up linen*

Enter DORIMANT *in his gown, and* BELLINDA

DOR.   Why will you be gone so soon?

BELL.   Why did you stay out so late?

DOR.   Call a chair, Handy.——What makes you tremble so?

BELL.   I have a thousand fears about me. Have I not been seen, think you?

DOR.   By nobody but myself and trusty Handy.

BELL.   Where are all your people?

DOR.   I have dispersed 'em on sleeveless errands. What does that sigh mean?

BELL.   Can you be so unkind to ask me? Well—[*sighs*]—were it to do again——

DOR.   We should do it, should we not?

BELL.   I think we should—the wickeder man you to make me love so well. Will you be discreet now?

DOR.   I will.

BELL.   You cannot.

DOR.   Never doubt it.

BELL.   I will not expect it.

DOR.   You do me wrong.

BELL.   You have no more power to keep the secret than I had not to trust you with it.

DOR.   By all the joys I have had and those you keep in store——

BELL.   You'll do for my sake what you never did before.

DOR.   By that truth thou hast spoken, a wife shall sooner betray herself to her husband.

BELL.   Yet I had rather you should be false in this than in another thing you promised me.

DOR.   What's that?

BELL.   That you would never see Loveit more but in public places—in the Park, at Court and plays.

DOR.   'Tis not likely a man should be fond of seeing a damned old play when there is a new one acted.

BELL.   I dare not trust your promise.

DOR.   You may——

BELL.   This does not satisfy me. You shall swear you never will see her more.

DOR.   I will, a thousand oaths. By all——

BELL.   Hold! You shall not, now I think on't better.

DOR.   I will swear!

BELL.   I shall grow jealous of the oath and think I owe your truth to that, not to your love.

DOR.   Then, by my love; no other oath I'll swear.

Enter HANDY

HAND.   Here's a chair.

BELL.   Let me go.

DOR.   I cannot.

BELL.   Too willingly, I fear.

DOR.   Too unkindly feared. When will you promise me again?

BELL.   Not this fortnight.

DOR.   You will be better than your word.

BELL.   I think I shall. Will it not make you love me less? [*starting*] Hark! what fiddles are these?   [*fiddles without*]

DOR.   Look out, Handy.   [*exit* HANDY *and returns*]

HAND.   Mr. Medley, Mr. Bellair, and Sir Fopling; they are coming up.

DOR.   How got they in?

HAND.   The door was open for the chair.

BELL.   Lord, let me fly!

DOR.   Here, here, down the back stairs! I'll see you into your chair.

BELL.   No, no! Stay and receive 'em. And be sure you keep your word and never see Loveit more. Let it be a proof of your kindness.

DOR.   It shall.—— Handy, direct her. [*kissing her hand*] Everlasting love go along with thee.   [*exeunt* BELLINDA *and* HANDY]

Enter YOUNG BELLAIR, MEDLEY, *and* SIR FOPLING

Y. BELL.   Not abed yet?

MED.   You have had an irregular fit, Dorimant.

DOR.   I have.

Y. BELL.   And is it off already?

DOR.   Nature has done her part, gentlemen; when she falls kindly to work, great cures are effected in little time, you know.

SIR FOP.   We thought there was a wench in the case, by the chair that waited. Prithee, make us a *confidence*.

DOR.   Excuse me.

SIR FOP.   *Le sage* Dorimant! Was she pretty?

DOR.   So pretty she may come to keep her coach and pay parish duties if the good humour of the age continue.

MED.   And be of the number of the ladies kept by public-spirited men for the good of the whole town.

SIR FOP. [*dancing by himself*]   Well said, Medley.

Y. BELL.   See Sir Fopling dancing!

DOR.   You are practising and have a mind to recover, I see.

SIR FOP.   Prithee, Dorimant, why hast not thou a glass hung up here? A room is the dullest thing without one.

Y. BELL.   Here is company to entertain you.

SIR FOP.   But I mean in case of being alone. In a glass a man may entertain himself——

DOR.   The shadow of himself, indeed.

SIR FOP.   Correct the errors of his motions and his dress.

MED.   I find, Sir Fopling, in your solitude you remember the saying of the wise man, and study yourself.

SIR FOP.   'Tis the best diversion in our retirements. Dorimant, thou art a pretty fellow and wear'st thy clothes well, but I never saw thee have a handsome cravat. Were they made up like mine, they'd give another air to thy face. Prithee, let me send my man to dress thee but one day; by heavens, an Englishman cannot tie a ribbon.

DOR.   They are something clumsy fisted——

SIR FOP.   I have brought over the prettiest fellow that ever spread a toilet. He served some time under Merille, the greatest *genie* in the world for a *valet-de-chambre*.

DOR.   What! he who formerly belonged to the Duke of Candale?

SIR FOP.   The same, and got him his immortal reputation.

DOR.   Y'have a very fine brandenburgh on, Sir Fopling.

SIR FOP.   It serves to wrap me up after the fatigue of a ball.

MED.   I see you often in it, with your periwig tied up.

SIR FOP.   We should not always be in a set dress; 'tis more *en cavalier* to appear now and then in a *deshabillé*.

MED.   Pray, how goes your business with Loveit?

SIR FOP.   You might have answered yourself in the Mail last night. Dorimant, did you not see the advances she made me? I have been endeavouring at a song.

DOR.   Already!

SIR FOP.   'Tis my *coup d'essai* in English: I would fain have thy opinion of it.

DOR.   Let's see it.

SIR FOP.   Hey, page, give me my song.—— Bellair, here; thou hast a pretty voice—sing it.

Y. BELL.   Sing it yourself, Sir Fopling.

SIR FOP.   Excuse me.

Y. BELL.   You learnt to sing in Paris.

SIR FOP.   I did—of Lambert, the greatest master in the world. But I have his own fault, a weak voice, and care not to sing out of a *ruelle*.

DOR. [*aside*]   A *ruelle* is a pretty cage for a singing fop, indeed.

Y. BELL. [*reads the song*]

    How charming Phillis is, how fair!
     Ah, that she were as willing
    To ease my wounded heart of care,
     And make her eyes less killing.
    I sigh, I sigh, I languish now,
     And love will not let me rest;
    I drive about the Park and bow,
     Still as I meet my dearest.

SIR FOP. Sing it! sing it, man; it goes to a pretty new tune which I am confident was made by Baptiste.

MED. Sing it yourself, Sir Fopling; he does not know the tune.

SIR FOP. I'll venture.   [SIR FOPLING *sings*]

DOR. Ay, marry! now 'tis something. I shall not flatter you, Sir Fopling; there is not much thought in't, but 'tis passionate and well turned.

MED. After the French way.

SIR FOP. That I aimed at. Does it not give you a lively image of the thing? Slap! down goes the glass, and thus we are at it.

DOR. It does, indeed, I perceive, Sir Fopling. You'll be the very head of the sparks who are lucky in compositions of this nature.

Enter SIR FOPLING'S *Footman*

SIR FOP. La Tour, is the bath ready?

FOOTM. Yes, Sir.

SIR FOP. *Adieu donc, mes chers.*   [*exit* SIR FOPLING]

MED. When have you your revenge on Loveit, Dorimant?

DOR. I will but change my linen and about it.

MED. The powerful considerations which hindered have been removed then?

DOR. Most luckily this morning. You must along with me; my reputation lies at stake there.

MED. I am engaged to Bellair.

DOR. What's your business?

MED. Ma-tri-mony, an't like you.

DOR. It does not, Sir.

Y. BELL. It may in time, Dorimant: what think you of Mrs. Harriet?

DOR. What does she think of me?

Y. BELL. I am confident she loves you.

DOR. How does it appear?

Y. BELL. Why, she's never well but when she's talking of you—but then, she finds all the faults in you she can. She laughs at all who commend you—but then, she speaks ill of all who do not.

Dor. Women of her temper betray themselves by their overcunning. I had once a growing love with a lady who would always quarrel with me when I came to see her, and yet was never quiet if I stayed a day from her.

Y. Bell. My father is in love with Emilia.

Dor. That is a good warrant for your proceedings. Go on and prosper; I must to Loveit. Medley, I am sorry you cannot be a witness.

Med. Make her meet Sir Fopling again in the same place and use him ill before me.

Dor. That may be brought about, I think. I'll be at your aunt's anon and give you joy, Mr. Bellair.

Y. Bell. You had not best think of Mrs. Harriet too much; without church security there's no taking up there.

Dor. I may fall into the snare too. But——
    The wise will find a difference in our fate;
    You wed a woman, I a good estate.   [exeunt]

SCENE III

Enter the chair with Bellinda;
the men set it down and open it. Bellinda *starting*

Bell. [*surprised*] Lord, where am I?—in the Mail! Whither have you brought me?

I Chairm. You gave us no directions, Madam.

Bell. [*aside*] The fright I was in made me forget it.

I Chairm. We use to carry a lady from the Squire's hither.

Bell. [*aside*] This is Loveit: I am undone if she sees me.—Quickly, carry me away!

I Chairm. Whither, an't like your honour?

Bell. Ask no questions——

Enter Mrs. Loveit's *Footman*

Footm. Have you seen my Lady, Madam?

Bell. I am just come to wait upon her.

Footm. She will be glad to see you, Madam. She sent me to you this morning to desire your company, and I was told you went out by five o'clock.

Bell. [*aside*] More and more unlucky!

Footm. Will you walk in, Madam?

Bell. I'll discharge my chair and follow. Tell your mistress I am here. [*exit Footman*] [*gives the Chairmen money*] Take this, and if ever you should be examined, be sure you say you took me up in the Strand over against the Exchange, as you will answer it to Mr. Dorimant.

CHAIRM.   We will, an't like your honour.   [*exeunt Chairmen*]
BELL.   Now to come off, I must on——
          In confidence and lies some hope is left;
          'Twere hard to be found out in the first theft.   [*exit*]

ACT V

SCENE I

Enter Mrs. Loveit *and* Pert, *her woman*

Pert.   Well! in my eyes Sir Fopling is no such despicable person.

Lov.   You are an excellent judge!

Pert.   He's as handsome as man as Mr. Dorimant, and as great a gallant.

Lov.   Intolerable! Is't not enough I submit to his impertinences, but must I be plagued with yours too?

Pert.   Indeed, Madam——

Lov.   'Tis false, mercenary malice——

Enter her Footman

Footm.   Mrs. Bellinda, Madam.

Lov.   What of her?

Footm.   She's below.

Lov.   How came she?

Footm.   In a chair; Ambling Harry brought her.

Lov.   He bring her! His chair stands near Dorimant's door and always brings me from thence.—— Run and ask him where he took her up. [*exit Footman*] Go! there is no truth in friendship neither. Women, as well as men, all are false—or all are so to me, at least.

Per.   You are jealous of her too?

Lov.   You had best tell her I am. 'Twill become the liberty you take of late. This fellow's bringing of her, her going out by five o'clock—I know not what to think.

Enter Bellinda

Bellinda, you are grown an early riser, I hear.

Bell.   Do you not wonder, my dear, what made me abroad so soon?

Lov.   You do not use to be so.

Bell.   The country gentlewomen I told you of (Lord, they have the

149

oddest diversions!) would never let me rest till I promised to go with them to the markets this morning to eat fruit and buy nosegays.

LOV.   Are they so fond of a filthy nosegay?

BELL.   They complain of the stinks of the town, and are never well but when they have their noses in one.

LOV.   There are essences and sweet waters.

BELL.   Oh, they cry out upon perfumes, they are unwholesome; one of 'em was falling into a fit with the smell of these *nerolii*.

LOV.   Methinks in complaisance you should have had a nosegay too.

BELL.   Do you think, my dear, I could be so loathsome to trick my-self up with carnations and stock-gillyflowers? I begged their pardon and told them I never wore anything but orange flowers and tuberose. That which made me willing to go was a strange desire I had to eat some fresh nectarines.

LOV.   And had you any?

BELL.   The best I ever tasted.

LOV.   Whence came you now?

BELL.   From their lodgings, where I crowded out of a coach and took a chair to come and see you, my dear.

LOV.   Whither did you send for that chair?

BELL.   'Twas going by empty.

LOV.   Where do these country gentlewomen lodge, I pray?

BELL.   In the Strand over against the Exchange.

PERT.   That place is never without a nest of 'em. They are always, as one goes by, fleering in balconies or staring out of windows.

Enter Footman

LOV. [*to the Footman*]   Come hither!   [*whispers*]

BELL. [*aside*]   This fellow by her order has been questioning the chair-men. I threatened 'em with the name of Dorimant; if they should have told truth, I am lost forever.

LOV.   In the Strand, said you?

FOOTM.   Yes, Madam; over against the Exchange.   [*exit Footman*]

LOV. [*aside*]   She's innocent, and I am much to blame.

BELL. [*aside*]   I am so frighted, my countenance will betray me.

LOV.   Bellinda, what makes you look so pale?

BELL.   Want of my usual rest and jolting up and down so long in an odious hackney.

Footman returns

FOOTM.   Madam, Mr. Dorimant.

LOV.   What makes him here?

BELL. [aside]   Then I am betrayed, indeed. He's broke his word, and I love a man that does not care for me!

LOV.   Lord, you faint, Bellinda!

BELL.   I think I shall—such an oppression here on the sudden.

PERT.   She has eaten too much fruit, I warrant you.

LOV.   Not unlikely.

PERT.   'Tis that lies heavy on her stomach.

LOV.   Have her into my chamber, give her some surfeit water, and let her lie down a little.

PERT.   Come, Madam! I was a strange devourer of fruit when I was young—so ravenous——   [exeunt BELLINDA, and PERT, leading her off]

LOV.   Oh, that my love would be but calm awhile, that I might receive this man with all the scorn and indignation he deserves!

Enter DORIMANT

DOR.   Now for a touch of Sir Fopling to begin with. Hey, page, give positive order that none of my people stir. Let the *canaille* wait as they should do. Since noise and nonsense have such powerful charms,

> I, that I may successful prove,
> Transform myself to what you love.

LOV.   If that would do, you need not change from what you are: you can be vain and loud enough.

DOR.   But not with so good a grace as Sir Fopling. Hey, Hampshire! Oh, that sound, that sound becomes the mouth of a man of quality!

LOV.   Is there a thing so hateful as a senseless mimic?

DOR.   He's a great grievance indeed to all who, like yourself, Madam, love to play the fool in quiet.

LOV.   A ridiculous animal, who has more of the ape than the ape has of the man in him!

DOR.   I have as mean an opinion of a sheer mimic as yourself; yet were he all ape, I should prefer him to the gay, the giddy, brisk, insipid noisy fool you dote on.

LOV.   Those noisy fools, however you despise 'em, have good qualities which weigh more (or ought at least) with us women than all the pernicious wit you have to boast of.

DOR.   That I may hereafter have a just value for their merit, pray do me the favour to name 'em.

LOV.   You'll despise 'em as the dull effects of ignorance and vanity; yet I care not if I mention some. First, they really admire us, while you at best but flatter us well.

DOR.   Take heed! Fools can dissemble too.

LOV.   They may, but not so artificially as you. There is no fear they should deceive us. Then, they are assiduous, Sir; they are ever offering us their service, and always waiting on our will.

DOR.   You owe that to their excessive idleness. They know not how to entertain themselves at home, and find so little welcome abroad they are fain to fly to you who countenance 'em, as a refuge against the solitude they would be otherwise condemned to.

LOV.   Their conversation, too, diverts us better.

DOR.   Playing with your fan, smelling to your gloves, commending your hair, and taking notice how 'tis cut and shaded after the new way——

LOV.   Were it sillier than you can make it, you must allow 'tis pleasanter to laugh at others than to be laughed at ourselves, though never so wittily. Then, though they want skill to flatter us, they flatter themselves so well they save us the labour. We need not take that care and pains to satisfy 'em of our love, which we so often lose on you.

DOR.   They commonly, indeed, believe too well of themselves, and always better of you than you deserve.

LOV.   You are in the right. They have an implicit faith in us which keeps 'em from prying narrowly into our secrets and saves us the vexatious trouble of clearing doubts which your subtle and causeless jealousies every moment raise.

DOR.   There is an inbred falsehood in women which inclines 'em still to them whom they may most easily deceive.

LOV.   The man who loves above his quality does not suffer more from the insolent impertinence of his mistress than the woman who loves above her understanding does from the arrogant presumptions of her friend.

DOR.   You mistake the use of fools; they are designed for properties, and not for friends. You have an indifferent stock of reputation left yet. Lose it all like a frank gamester on the square; 'twill then be time enough to turn rook and cheat it up again on a good, substantial bubble.

LOV.   The old and the ill-favoured are only fit for properties, indeed, but young and handsome fools have met with kinder fortunes.

DOR.   They have, to the shame of your sex be it spoken! 'Twas this, the thought of this, made me by a timely jealousy endeavour to prevent the good fortune you are providing for Sir Fopling. But against a woman's frailty all our care is vain.

LOV.   Had I not with a dear experience bought the knowledge of your falsehood, you might have fooled me yet. This is not the first jealousy you have feigned, to make a quarrel with me and get a week to throw away on some such unknown, inconsiderable slut as you have been lately lurking with at plays.

DOR.   Women, when they would break off with a man, never want th' address to turn the fault on him.

LOV.   You take a pride of late in using of me ill, that the town may know the power you have over me, which now (as unreasonably as yourself) expects that I (do me all the injuries you can) must love you still.

DOR.   I am so far from expecting that you should, I begin to think you never did love me.

LOV.   Would the memory of it were so wholly worn out in me, that I did doubt it too! What made you come to disturb my growing quiet?

DOR.   To give you joy of your growing infamy.

LOV.   Insupportable! Insulting devil!—this from you, the only author of my shame! This from another had been but justice, but from you 'tis a hellish and inhumane outrage. What have I done?

DOR.   A thing that puts you below my scorn, and makes my anger as ridiculous as you have made my love.

LOV.   I walked last night with Sir Fopling.

DOR.   You did, Madam, and you talked and laughed aloud, "Ha, ha, ha!"—Oh, that laugh! that laugh becomes the confidence of a woman of quality.

LOV.   You who have more pleasure in the ruin of a woman's reputation than in the endearments of her love, reproach me not with yourself—and I defy you to name the man can lay a blemish on my fame.

DOR.   To be seen publicly so transported with the vain follies of that notorious fop, to me is an infamy below the sin of prostitution with another man.

LOV.   Rail on! I am satisfied in the justice of what I did; you had provoked me to't.

DOR.   What I did was the effect of a passion whose extravagancies you have been willing to forgive.

LOV.   And what I did was the effect of a passion you may forgive if you think fit.

DOR.   Are you so indifferent grown?

LOV.   I am.

DOR.   Nay, then 'tis time to part. I'll send you back your letters you have so often asked for. I have two or three of 'em about me.

LOV.   Give 'em me.

DOR.   You snatch as if you thought I would not. There! and may the perjuries in 'em be mine if e'er I see you more!

                                        [*offers to go; she catches him*]

LOV.   Stay!

DOR.   I will not.

LOV.   You shall.

DOR.   What have you to say?

LOV.   I cannot speak it yet.

DOR.   Something more in commendation of the fool.——Death, I want patience; let me go!

LOV.   I cannot. [*aside*] I can sooner part with the limbs that hold him.—— I hate that nauseous fool; you know I do.

DOR.   Was it the scandal you were fond of then?

LOV.   Y'had raised my anger equal to my love—a thing you ne'er could do before, and in revenge I did—I know not what I did. Would you would not think on't any more!

DOR.   Should I be willing to forget it, I shall be daily minded of it; 'twill be a commonplace for all the town to laugh at me, and Medley, when he is rhetorically drunk, will ever be declaiming on it in my ears.

LOV.   'Twill be believed a jealous spite. Come, forget it.

DOR.   Let me consult my reputation; you are too careless of it. [*pauses*] You shall meet Sir Fopling in the Mail again to-night.

LOV.   What mean you?

DOR.   I have thought on it, and you must. 'Tis necessary to justify my love to the world. You can handle a coxcomb as he deserves when you are not out of humour, Madam.

LOV.   Public satisfaction for the wrong I have done you! This is some new device to make me more ridiculous.

DOR.   Hear me!

LOV.   I will not.

DOR.   You will be persuaded.

LOV.   Never!

DOR.   Are you so obstinate?

LOV.   Are you so base?

DOR.   You will not satisfy my love?

LOV.   I would die to satisfy that; but I will not, to save you from a thousand racks, do a shameless thing to please your vanity.

DOR.   Farewell, false woman!

LOV.   Do! go!

DOR.   You will call me back again.

LOV.   Exquisite fiend, I knew you came but to torment me!

Enter BELLINDA *and* PERT

DOR. [*surprised*]   Bellinda here!

BELL. [*aside*]   He starts and looks pale! The sight of me has touched his guilty soul.

PERT.   'Twas but a qualm, as I said—a little indigestion; the surfeit water did it, Madam, mixed with a little mirabilis.

DOR. [*aside*]   I am confounded, and cannot guess how she came hither!

LOV.   'Tis your fortune, Bellinda, ever to be here when I am abused by this prodigy of ill-nature.

BELL.   I am amazed to find him here. How has he the face to come near you?

DOR. [*aside*]   Here is fine work towards! I never was at such a loss before.

BELL.   One who makes a public profession of breach of faith and ingratitude—I loathe the sight of him.

DOR. [*aside*]   There is no remedy; I must submit to their tongues now, and some other time bring myself off as well as I can.

BELL.   Other men are wicked, but then, they have some sense of shame. He is never well but when he triumphs—nay, glories to a woman's face in his villainies.

LOV.   You are in the right, Bellinda, but methinks your kindness for me makes you concern yourself too much with him.

BELL.   It does indeed, my dear. His barbarous carriage to you yesterday made me hope you ne'er would see him more, and the very next day to find him here again, provokes me strangely. But because I know you love him, I have done.

DOR.   You have reproached me handsomely, and I deserve it for coming hither; but——

PERT.   You must expect it, Sir. All women will hate you for my lady's sake.

DOR. [*aside to* BELLINDA]   Nay, if she begins too, 'tis time to fly; I shall be scolded to death else.—— I am to blame in some circumstances, I confess; but as to the main, I am not so guilty as you imagine. I shall seek a more convenient time to clear myself.

LOV.   Do it now. What impediments are here?

DOR.   I want time, and you want temper.

LOV.   These are weak pretences.

DOR.   You were never more mistaken in your life; and so farewell.

[DORIMANT *flings off*]

LOV.   Call a footman, Pert, quickly; I will have him dogged.

PERT.   I wish you would not, for my quiet and your own.

LOV.   I'll find out the infamous cause of all our quarrels, pluck her mask off, and expose her barefaced to the world!   [*exit* PERT]

BELL. [*aside*]   Let me but escape this time, I'll never venture more.

LOV.   Bellinda, you shall go with me.

BELL.   I have such a heaviness hangs on me with what I did this morning, I would fain go home and sleep, my dear.

LOV.   Death and eternal darkness! I shall never sleep again. Raging fevers seize the world and make mankind as restless all as I am!

[*exit* MRS. LOVEIT]

BELL.   I knew him false and helped to make him so. Was not her ruin enough to fright me from the danger? It should have been, but love can take no warning. [*exit* BELLINDA]

SCENE II

SCENE: LADY TOWNLEY'S *house*

Enter MEDLEY, YOUNG BELLAIR, LADY TOWNLEY, EMILIA, *and* SMIRK

MED.   Bear up, Bellair, and do not let us see that repentance in thine we daily do in married faces.

L. TOWN.   This wedding will strangely surprise my brother when he knows it.

MED.   Your nephew ought to conceal it for a time, Madam; since marriage has lost its good name, prudent men seldom expose their own reputations till 'tis convenient to justify their wives.

O. BELL. [*without*]   Where are you all there? Out, a dod! will nobody hear?

L. TOWN.   My brother! Quickly, Mr. Smirk, into this closet! you must not be seen yet. [SMIRK *goes into the closet*]

Enter OLD BELLAIR *and* LADY TOWNLEY'S *Page*

O. BELL.   Desire Mr. Fourbe to walk into the lower parlour; I will be with him presently. [*to* YOUNG BELLAIR] Where have you been, Sir, you could not wait on me to-day?

Y. BELL.   About a business.

O. BELL.   Are you so good at business? A dod, I have a business, too, you shall dispatch out of hand, Sir.—— Send for a parson, Sister; my Lady Woodvill and her daughter are coming.

L. TOWN.   What need you huddle up things thus?

O. BELL.   Out a pise! youth is apt to play the fool, and 'tis not good it should be in their power.

L. TOWN.   You need not fear your son.

O. BELL.   He's been idling this morning, and a dod, I do not like him. [*to* EMILIA] How dost thou do, sweetheart?

EMIL.   You are very severe, Sir—married in such haste.

O. BELL.   Go to, thou'rt a rogue, and I will talk with thee anon. Here's my Lady Woodvill come.

Enter LADY WOODVILL, HARRIET, *and* BUSY

Welcome, Madam; Mr. Fourbe's below with the writings.

L. WOOD.   Let us down and make an end then.

O. BELL.   Sister, show the way. [*to* YOUNG BELLAIR, *who is talking to*

HARRIET] Harry, your business lies not there yet.—— Excuse him till we
have done, lady, and then, a dod, he shall be for thee. Mr. Medley, we must
trouble you to be a witness.

MED.   I luckily came for that purpose, Sir.

> [*exeunt* OLD BELLAIR, MEDLEY, YOUNG BELLAIR,
> LADY TOWNLEY, *and* LADY WOODVILL]

BUSY.   What will you do, Madam?

HAR.   Be carried back and mewed up in the country again—run
away here—anything rather than be married to a man I do not care for!
Dear Emilia, do thou advise me.

EMIL.   Mr. Bellair is engaged, you know.

HAR.   I do, but know not what the fear of losing an estate may fright
him to.

EMIL.   In the desperate condition you are in, you should consult with
some judicious man. What think you of Mr. Dorimant?

HAR.   I do not think of him at all.

BUSY. [*aside*]   She thinks of nothing else, I am sure.

EMIL.   How fond your mother was of Mr. Courtage!

HAR.   Because I contrived the mistake to make a little mirth, you believe I like the man.

EMIL.   Mr. Bellair believes you love him.

HAR.   Men are seldom in the right when they guess at a woman's
mind. Would she whom he loves loved him no better!

BUSY. [*aside*]   That's e'en well enough, on all conscience.

EMIL.   Mr. Dorimant has a great deal of wit.

HAR.   And takes a great deal of pains to show it.

EMIL.   He's extremely well fashioned.

HAR.   Affectedly grave, or ridiculously wild and apish.

BUSY.   You defend him still against your mother!

HAR.   I would not were he justly rallied, but I cannot hear anyone
undeservedly railed at.

EMIL.   Has your woman learnt the song you were so taken with?

HAR.   I was fond of a new thing; 'tis dull at second hearing.

EMIL.   Mr. Dorimant made it.

BUSY.   She knows it, Madam, and has made me sing it at least a dozen
times this morning.

HAR.   Thy tongue is as impertinent as thy fingers.

EMIL.   You have provoked her.

BUSY.   'Tis but singing the song and I shall appease her.

EMIL.   Prithee, do.

HAR.   She has a voice will grate your ears worse than a cat-call, and
dresses so ill she's scarce fit to trick up a yeoman's daughter on a holiday.

> [BUSY *sings*]

SONG

BY SIR C. S.

As Amoret with Phillis sat,
    One evening on the plain,
And saw the charming Strephon wait
    To tell the nymph his pain;

The threat'ning danger to remove,
    She whisper'd in her ear,
"Ah, Phillis, if you would not love,
    This shepherd do not hear!

"None ever had so strange an art,
    His passion to convey
Into a list'ning virgin's heart,
    And steal her soul away.

"Fly, fly betimes, for fear you give
    Occasion for your fate."
"In vain," said she; "in vain I strive!
    Alas, 'tis now too late."

Enter DORIMANT

DOR.   Music so softens and disarms the mind——

HAR.   That not one arrow does resistance find.

DOR.   Let us make use of the lucky minute, then.

HAR. [*aside, turning from* DORIMANT]   My love springs with my blood into my face; I dare not look upon him yet.

DOR.   What have we here? the picture of celebrated beauty giving audience in public to a declared lover?

HAR.   Play the dying fop and make the piece complete, Sir.

DOR.   What think you if the hint were well improved—the whole mystery of making love pleasantly designed and wrought in a suit of hangings?

HAR.   'Twere needless to execute fools in effigy who suffer daily in their own persons.

DOR. [*to* EMILIA, *aside*]   Mrs. Bride, for such I know this happy day has made you——

EMIL. [*aside*]   Defer the formal joy you are to give me, and mind your business with her. [*aloud*] Here are dreadful preparations, Mr. Dorimant—writings, sealing, and a parson sent for.

DOR.   To marry this lady——

BUSY.   Condemned she is, and what will become of her I know not, without you generously engage in a rescue.

DOR.   In this sad condition, Madam, I can do no less than offer you my service.

HAR.   The obligation is not great; you are the common sanctuary for all young women who run from their relations.

DOR.   I have always my arms open to receive the distressed. But I will open my heart and receive you, where none yet did ever enter. You have filled it with a secret, might I but let you know it——

HAR.   Do not speak it if you would have me believe it; your tongue is so famed for falsehood, 'twill do the truth an injury.

[turns away her head]

DOR.   Turn not away, then, but look on me and guess it.

HAR.   Did you not tell me there was no credit to be given to faces? that women nowadays have their passions as much at will as they have their complexions, and put on joy and sadness, scorn and kindness, with the same ease they do their paint and patches? Are they the only counterfeits?

DOR.   You wrong your own while you suspect my eyes. By all the hope I have in you, the inimitable colour in your cheeks is not more free from art than are the sighs I offer.

HAR.   In men who have been long hardened in sin we have reason to mistrust the first signs of repentance.

DOR.   The prospect of such a heaven will make me persevere and give you marks that are infallible.

HAR.   What are those?

DOR.   I will renounce all the joys I have in friendship and in wine, sacrifice to you all the interest I have in other women——

HAR.   Hold! Though I wish you devout, I would not have you turn fanatic. Could you neglect these a while and make a journey into the country?

DOR.   To be with you, I could live there and never send one thought to London.

HAR.   Whate'er you say, I know all beyond High Park's a desert to you, and that no gallantry can draw you farther.

DOR.   That has been the utmost limit of my love; but now my passion knows no bounds, and there's no measure to be taken of what I'll do for you from anything I ever did before.

HAR.   When I hear you talk thus in Hampshire I shall begin to think there may be some truth enlarged upon.

DOR.   Is this all? Will you not promise me——

HAR.   I hate to promise; what we do then is expected from us and wants much of the welcome it finds when it surprises.

DOR.   May I not hope?

HAR.   That depends on you and not on me, and 'tis to no purpose to forbid it.   [*turns to* BUSY]

BUSY.   Faith, Madam, now I perceive the gentleman loves you too, e'en let him know your mind, and torment yourselves no longer.

HAR.   Dost think I have no sense of modesty?

BUSY.   Think, if you lose this you may never have another opportunity.

HAR.   May he hate me (a curse that frights me when I speak it), if ever I do a thing against the rules of decency and honour.

DOR. [*to* EMILIA]   I am beholding to you for your good intentions, Madam.

EMIL.   I thought the concealing of our marriage from her might have done you better service.

DOR.   Try her again.

EMIL.   What have you resolved, Madam? The time draws near.

HAR.   To be obstinate and protest against this marriage.

Enter LADY TOWNLEY *in haste*

L. TOWN. [*to* EMILIA]   Quickly, quickly! let Mr. Smirk out of the closet.   [SMIRK *comes out of the closet*]

HAR.   A parson! Had you laid him in here?

DOR.   I knew nothing of him.

HAR.   Should it appear you did, your opinion of my easiness may cost you dear.

Enter OLD BELLAIR, YOUNG BELLAIR, MEDLEY, *and* LADY WOODVILL

O. BELL.   Out a pise! the canonical hour is almost past. Sister, is the man of God come?

L. TOWN.   He waits your leisure.

O. BELL.   By your favour, Sir.—— A dod, a pretty spruce fellow. What may we call him?

L. TOWN.   Mr. Smirk—my Lady Biggot's chaplain.

O. BELL.   A wise woman! a dod, she is. The man will serve for the flesh as well as the spirit. Please you, Sir, to commission a young couple to go to bed together a God's name?—— Harry!

Y. BELL.   Here, Sir.

O. BELL.   Out a pise! Without your mistress in your hand!

SMIRK.   Is this the gentleman?

O. BELL.   Yes, Sir.

SMIRK.   Are you not mistaken, Sir?

O. BELL.   A dod, I think not, Sir.

SMIRK.   Sure, you are, Sir!

O. BELL.   You look as if you would forbid the banns, Mr. Smirk. I hope you have no pretension to the lady.

SMIRK.   Wish him joy, Sir; I have done him the good office to-day already.

O. BELL.   Out a pise! What do I hear?

L. TOWN.   Never storm, Brother; the truth is out.

O. BELL.   How say you, Sir? Is this your wedding day?

Y. BELL.   It is, Sir.

O. BELL.   And a dod, it shall be mine too. [to EMILIA] Give me thy hand, sweetheart. What dost thou mean? Give me thy hand, I say.

[EMILIA *kneels and* YOUNG BELLAIR]

L. TOWN.   Come, come! give her your blessing; this is the woman your son loved and is married to.

O. BELL.   Ha! cheated! cozened! and by your contrivance, Sister!

L. TOWN.   What would you do with her? She's a rogue and you can't abide her.

MED.   Shall I hit her a pat for you, Sir?

O. BELL.   A dod, you are all rogues, and I never will forgive you.

L. TOWN.   Whither? Whither away?

MED.   Let him go and cool awhile.

L. WOOD. [*to* DORIMANT]   Here's a business broke out now, Mr. Courtage; I am made a fine fool of.

DOR.   You see the old gentleman knew nothing of it.

L. WOOD.   I find he did not. I shall have some trick put upon me if I stay in this wicked town any longer.—— Harriet, dear child, where art thou? I'll into the country straight.

O. BELL.   A dod, Madam, you shall hear me first.

Enter MRS. LOVEIT *and* BELLINDA

LOV.   Hither my man dogged him.

BELL.   Yonder he stands, my dear.

LOV.   I see him [*aside*] and with him the face that has undone me. Oh, that I were but where I might throw out the anguish of my heart! Here it must rage within and break it.

L. TOWN.   Mrs. Loveit! Are you afraid to come forward?

LOV.   I was amazed to see so much company here in a morning. The occasion sure is extraordinary.

DOR. [*aside*]   Loveit and Bellinda! The devil owes me a shame to-day and I think never will have done paying it.

LOV.   Married! dear Emilia! How am I transported with the news!

HAR. [*to* DORIMANT]   I little thought Emilia was the woman Mr. Bellair was in love with. I'll chide her for not trusting me with the secret.

DOR.   How do you like Mrs. Loveit?

HAR.   She's a famed mistress of yours, I hear.

DOR.   She has been, on occasion.

O. BELL. [*to* LADY WOODVILL]   A dod, Madam, I cannot help it.

L. WOOD.   You need make no more apologies, Sir.

EMIL. [*to* MRS. LOVEIT]   The old gentleman's excusing himself to my Lady Woodvill.

LOV.   Ha, ha, ha! I never heard of anything so pleasant!

HAR. [*to* DORIMANT]   She's extremely overjoyed at something.

DOR.   At nothing. She is one of those hoyting ladies who gaily fling themselves about and force a laugh when their aching hearts are full of discontent and malice.

LOV.   O heaven! I was never so near killing myself with laughing.—— Mr. Dorimant, are you a brideman?

L. WOOD.   Mr. Dorimant!—Is this Mr. Dorimant, Madam?

LOV.   If you doubt it, your daughter can resolve you, I suppose.

L. WOOD.   I am cheated too—basely cheated!

O. BELL.   Out a pise! what's here? More knavery yet?

L. WOOD.   Harriet, on my blessing come away, I charge you!

HAR.   Dear Mother, do but stay and hear me.

L. WOOD.   I am betrayed and thou art undone, I fear.

HAR.   Do not fear it; I have not, nor never will, do anything against my duty—believe me, dear Mother, do!

DOR. [*to* MRS. LOVEIT]   I had trusted you with this secret but that I knew the violence of your nature would ruin my fortune, as now unluckily it has. I thank you, Madam.

LOV.   She's an heiress, I know, and very rich.

DOR.   To satisfy you, I must give up my interest wholly to my love. Had you been a reasonable woman, I might have secured 'em both and been happy.

LOV.   You might have trusted me with anything of this kind—you know you might. Why did you go under a wrong name?

DOR.   The story is too long to tell you now. Be satisfied, this is the business; this is the mask has kept me from you.

BELL. [*aside*]   He's tender of my honour though he's cruel to my love.

LOV.   Was it no idle mistress, then?

DOR.   Believe me, a wife to repair the ruins of my estate, that needs it.

LOV.   The knowledge of this makes my grief hang lighter on my soul, but I shall never more be happy.

DOR.   Bellinda!

BELL.   Do not think of clearing yourself with me; it is impossible. Do all men break their words thus?

DOR.   Th'extravagant words they speak in love. 'Tis as unreasonable to expect we should perform all we promise then, as do all we threaten when we are angry. When I see you next——

BELL.   Take no notice of me, and I shall not hate you.

DOR.   How came you to Mrs. Loveit?

BELL.   By a mistake the chairmen made for want of my giving them directions.

DOR.   'Twas a pleasant one. We must meet again.

BELL.   Never.

DOR.   Never!

BELL.   When we do, may I be as infamous as you are false.

L. TOWN.   Men of Mr. Dorimant's character always suffer in the general opinion of the world.

MED.   You can make no judgment of a witty man from common fame, considering the prevailing faction, Madam.

O. BELL.   A dod, he's in the right.

MED.   Besides, 'tis a common error among women to believe too well of them they know, and too ill of them they don't.

O. BELL.   A dod, he observes well.

L. TOWN.   Believe me, Madam, you will find Mr. Dorimant as civil a gentleman as you thought Mr. Courtage.

HAR.   If you would but know him better——

L. WOOD.   You have a mind to know him better! Come away! You shall never see him more.

HAR.   Dear Mother, stay!

L. WOOD.   I wo'not be consenting to your ruin.

HAR.   Were my fortune in your power——

L. WOOD.   Your person is.

HAR.   Could I be disobedient, I might take it out of yours and put it into his.

L. WOOD.   'Tis that you would be at; you would marry this Dorimant.

HAR.   I cannot deny it; I would, and never will marry any other man.

L. WOOD.   Is this the duty that you promised?

HAR.   But I will never marry him against your will.

L. WOOD. [aside]   She knows the way to melt my heart.—[to HARRIET] Upon yourself light your undoing!

MED. [to OLD BELLAIR]   Come, Sir, you have not the heart any longer to refuse your blessing.

O. BELL.   A dod, I ha' not.—— Rise, and God bless you both! Make much of her, Harry; she deserves thy kindness. [to EMILIA] A dod, Sirrah, I did not think it had been in thee.

Enter SIR FOPLING *and Page*

SIR FOP.   'Tis a damned windy day.—— Hey, page, is my periwig right?

PAGE.   A little out of order, Sir.

SIR FOP.   Pox o' this apartment! It wants an antechamber to adjust oneself in. [*to* MRS. LOVEIT] Madam, I came from your house, and your servants directed me hither.

LOV.   I will give order hereafter they shall direct you better.

SIR FOP.   The great satisfaction I had in the Mail last night has given me much disquiet since.

LOV.   'Tis likely to give me more than I desire.

SIR FOP. [*aside*]   What the devil makes her so reserved?—— Am I guilty of an indiscretion, Madam?

LOV.   You will be of a great one if you continue your mistake, Sir.

SIR FOP.   Something puts you out of humour.

LOV.   The most foolish, inconsiderable thing that ever did.

SIR FOP.   Is it in my power?

LOV.   To hang or drown it. Do one of 'em and trouble me no more.

SIR FOP.   So *fière? Serviteur,* Madam!—— Medley, where's Dorimant?

MED.   Methinks the lady has not made you those advances to-day she did last night, Sir Fopling.

SIR FOP.   Prithee, do not talk of her!

MED.   She would be a *bonne fortune.*

SIR FOP.   Not to me at present.

MED.   How so?

SIR FOP.   An intrigue now would be but a temptation to me to throw away that vigour on one which I mean shall shortly make my court to the whole sex in a ballet.

MED.   Wisely considered, Sir Fopling.

SIR FOP.   No one woman is worth the loss of a cut in a caper.

MED.   Not when 'tis so universally designed.

L. WOOD.   Mr. Dorimant, everyone has spoke so much in your behalf that I can no longer doubt but I was in the wrong.

LOV.   There's nothing but falsehood and impertinence in this world; all men are villains or fools. Take example from my misfortunes. Bellinda, if thou wouldst be happy, give thyself wholly up to goodness.

HAR. [*to* MRS. LOVEIT]   Mr. Dorimant has been your God Almighty long enough; 'tis time to think of another.

LOV.   Jeered by her! I will lock myself up in my house and never see the world again.

HAR.   A nunnery is the more fashionable place for such a retreat, and has been the fatal consequence of many a *belle passion.*

LOV. [*aside*]   Hold, heart, till I get home! Should I answer, 'twould make her triumph greater.   [*is going out*]

DOR.   Your hand, Sir Fopling——

SIR FOP.   Shall I wait upon you, Madam?

LOV.   Legion of fools, as many devils take thee!   [*exit* MRS. LOVEIT]

MED.   Dorimant, I pronounce thy reputation clear; and hencefor-ward when I would know anything of woman, I will consult no other oracle.

SIR FOP.   Stark mad, by all that's handsome!—— Dorimant, thou hast engaged me in a pretty business.

DOR.   I have not leisure now to talk about it.

O. BELL.   Out a pise! what does this man of mode do here again?

L. TOWN.   He'll be an excellent entertainment within, Brother, and is luckily come to raise the mirth of the company.

L. WOOD.   Madam, I take my leave of you.

L. TOWN.   What do you mean, Madam?

L. WOOD.   To go this afternoon part of my way to Hartly.

O. BELL.   A dod, you shall stay and dine first! Come, we will all be good friends, and you shall give Mr. Dorimant leave to wait upon you and your daughter in the country.

L. WOOD.   If his occasions bring him that way, I have now so good an opinion of him, he shall be welcome.

HAR.   To a great rambling, lone house that looks as it were not in-habited, the family's so small. There you'll find my mother, an old lame aunt, and myself, Sir, perched up on chairs at a distance in a large parlour, sitting moping like three or four melancholy birds in a spacious volary. Does not this stagger your resolution?

DOR.   Not at all, Madam. The first time I saw you you left me with the pangs of love upon me, and this day my soul has quite given up her liberty.

HAR.   This is more dismal than the country! Emilia, pity me, who am going to that sad place. Methinks I hear the hateful noise of rooks al-ready—kaw, kaw, kaw! There's music in the worst cry in London—My dill and cowcumbers to pickle!

O. BELL.   Sister, knowing of this matter, I hope you have provided us some good cheer.

L. TOWN.   I have, Brother, and the fiddles too.

O. BELL.   Let 'em strike up, then; the young lady shall have a dance before she departs.   [*dance*]

[*after the dance*]—— So! now we'll in and make this an arrant wedding-day.   [*to the pit*]

> And if these honest gentlemen rejoice,
> A dod, the boy has made a happy choice.

[*exeunt omnes*]

EPILOGUE

By Mr. Dryden

Most modern wits such monstrous fools have shown,
They seem'd not of heav'n's making, but their own.
Those nauseous harlequins in farce may pass,
But there goes more to a substantial ass.
Something of man must be expos'd to view
That, gallants, they may more resemble you.
Sir Fopling is a fool so nicely writ,
The ladies would mistake him for a wit;
And when he sings, talks loud, and cocks, would cry,
"I vow, methinks he's pretty company!
So brisk, so gay, so travell'd, so refin'd,
As he took pains to graff upon his kind."
True fops help nature's work and go to school,
To file and finish God A'mighty's fool.
Yet none Sir Fopling him, or him, can call;
He's knight o'th' shire, and represents ye all.
From each he meets, he culls whate'er he can;
Legion's his name, a people in a man.
His bulky folly gathers as it goes
And, rolling o'er you, like a snowball grows.
His various modes from various fathers follow;
One taught the toss, and one the new French wallow.
His sword-knot, this; his cravat, this design'd;
And this, the yard-long snake he twirls behind.
From one the sacred periwig he gain'd,
Which wind ne'er blew, nor touch of hat profan'd.
Another's diving bow he did adore,
Which with a shog casts all the hair before
Till he with full decorum brings it back,
And rises with a water spaniel shake.
As for his songs (the ladies' dear delight),
Those sure he took from most of you who write.
Yet every man is safe from what he feared,
For no one fool is hunted from the herd.

The Rover
or
The Banished Cavaliers
Aphra Behn

Dramatis Personae

DON ANTONIO, *the viceroy's son*
DON PEDRO, *a noble Spaniard, his friend*
BELVILE, *an English colonel in love with* FLORINDA
WILLMORE, *the Rover*
FREDERICK, *an English gentleman, and friend to* BELVILE *and* BLUNT
BLUNT, *an English country gentleman*
STEPHANO, *servant to* DON PEDRO
PHILIPPO, LUCETTA'S *gallant*
SANCHO, *pimp to* LUCETTA
BISKEY, ⎫
          ⎬ *two bravoes to* ANGELLICA
SEBASTIAN, ⎭
Officers and Soldiers
DIEGO, *page to* DON ANTONIO

FLORINDA, *sister to* DON PEDRO
HELLENA, *a gay young woman designed for a nun, and sister to* FLORINDA
VALERIA, *a kinswoman to* FLORINDA
ANGELLICA BIANCA, *a famous courtesan*
MORETTA, *her woman*
CALLIS, *governess to* FLORINDA *and* HELLENA
LUCETTA, *a jilting wench*

Servants, Other Masqueraders (men and women)

SCENE—*Naples, in carnival time*

PROLOGUE

Wits, like physicians, never can agree,
When of a different society.
And Rabel's drops were never more cried down
By all the learned doctors of the town,
Than a new play whose author is unknown.
Nor can those doctors with more malice sue
(And powerful purses) the dissenting few,
Than those with an insulting pride do rail
At all who are not of their own cabal.
    If a young poet hit your humour right,
You judge him then out of revenge and spite.
So amongst men there are ridiculous elves,
Who monkeys hate for being too like themselves.
So that the reason of the grand debate,
Why wit so oft is damned when good plays take,
Is that you censure as you love, or hate.
    Thus like a learned conclave poets sit,
Catholic judges both of sense and wit,
And damn or save as they themselves think fit.
Yet those who to others' faults are so severe,
Are not so perfect but themselves may err.
Some write correct indeed, but then the whole
(Bating their own dull stuff i'th' play) is stole.
As bees do suck from flowers their honeydew,
So they rob others, striving to please you.
    Some write their characters genteel and fine,
But then they do so toil for every line,
That what to you does easy seem and plain,
Is the hard issue of their labouring brain.
And some th'effects of all their pains we see,
Is but to mimic good extempore.

Others by long converse about the town,
Have wit enough to write a lewd lampoon,
But their chief skill lies in a bawdy song.
In short, the only wit that's now in fashion,
Is but the gleanings of good conversation.
As for the author of this coming play,
I asked him what he thought fit I should say,
In thanks for your good company today:
He called me fool, and said it was well known,
You came not here for our sakes, but your own.
New plays are stuffed with wits, and with debauches,
That crowd and sweat like cits in May–Day coaches.

Written by a person of quality.

ACT I

SCENE I—*A chamber*

Enter FLORINDA *and* HELLENA

FLORINDA   What an impertinent thing is a young girl bred in a nunnery! How full of questions! Prithee no more, Hellena, I have told thee more than thou understand'st already.

HELLENA   The more's my grief. I would fain know as much as you, which makes me so inquisitive; nor is't enough I know you're a lover, unless you tell me too, who 'tis you sigh for.

FLORINDA   When you're a lover, I'll think you fit for a secret of that nature.

HELLENA   'Tis true, I was never a lover yet—but I begin to have a shrewd guess what 'tis to be so, and fancy it very pretty to sigh and sing, and blush and wish, and dream and wish, and long and wish to see the man; and when I do, look pale and tremble; just as you did when my brother brought home the fine English colonel to see you—what do you call him, Don Belvile?

FLORINDA   Fie, Hellena.

HELLENA   That blush betrays you—I am sure 'tis so—or is it Don Antonio, the viceroy's son? Or perhaps the rich Old Don Vincentio, whom my father designs you for a husband? Why do you blush again?

FLORINDA   With indignation, and how near soever my father thinks I am to marrying that hated object, I shall let him see I understand better what's due to my beauty, birth and fortune, and more to my soul, than to obey those unjust commands.

HELLENA   Now hang me, if I don't love thee for that dear disobedience. I love mischief strangely, as most of our sex do who are come to love nothing else—but tell me, dear Florinda, don't you love that fine *Anglese?*—For I vow, next to loving him myself, 'twill please me most that you do so, for he is so gay and so handsome.

FLORINDA   Hellena, a maid designed for a nun ought not to be so curious in a discourse of love.

HELLENA   And dost thou think that ever I'll be a nun? Or at least till I'm so old, I'm fit for nothing else—faith no, sister; and that which makes me long to know whether you love Belvile, is because I hope he has some mad companion or other that will spoil my devotion. Nay, I'm resolved to provide myself this carnival, if there be e'er a handsome proper fellow of my humour above ground, though I ask first.

FLORINDA   Prithee be not so wild.

HELLENA   Now you have provided yourself with a man you take no care for poor me—prithee tell me, what dost thou see about me that is unfit for love? Have I not a world of youth? A humour gay? A beauty passable? A vigour desirable? Well-shaped? Clean-limbed? Sweet-breathed? And sense enough to know how all these ought to be employed to the best advantage? Yes, I do, and will. Therefore lay aside your hopes of my fortune by my being a devote, and tell me how you came acquainted with this Belvile—for I perceive you knew him before he came to Naples.

FLORINDA   Yes, I knew him at the siege of Pamplona. He was then a colonel of French horse, who, when the town was ransacked, nobly treated my brother and myself, preserving us from all insolences; and I must own (besides great obligations) I have I know not what that pleads kindly for him about my heart, and will suffer no other to enter.—But see, my brother.

Enter DON PEDRO, STEPHANO *with a masquing habit, and* CALLIS

PEDRO   Good morrow, sister—pray, when saw you your lover Don Vincentio?

FLORINDA   I know not, sir—Callis, when was he here? For I consider it so little, I know not when it was.

PEDRO   I have a command from my father here to tell you you ought not to despise him, a man of so vast a fortune, and such a passion for you—Stephano, my things.   [*puts on his masquing habit*]

FLORINDA   A passion for me? 'Tis more than e'er I saw, or he had a desire should be shown. I hate Vincentio, sir, and I would not have a man so dear to me as my brother follow the ill custom of our country, and make a slave of his sister—and, sir, my father's will I'm sure you may divert.

PEDRO I know not how dear I am to you, but I wish only to be ranked in your esteem equal with the English colonel Belvile—why do you frown and blush? Is there any guilt belongs to the name of that cavalier?

FLORINDA I'll not deny I value Belvile. When I was exposed to such dangers as the licensed lust of common soldiers threatened, when rage and conquest flew through the city; then Belvile, this criminal for my sake, threw himself into all dangers to save my honour, and will not you allow him my esteem?

PEDRO Yes, pay him what you will in honour—but you must consider Don Vincentio's fortune, and the jointure he'll make you.

FLORINDA Let him consider my youth, beauty and fortune, which ought not to be thrown away on his age and jointure.

PEDRO 'Tis true he's not so young and fine a gentleman as that Belvile—but what jewels will that cavalier present you with? Those of his eyes and heart?

HELLENA And are not those better than any Don Vincentio has brought from the Indies?

PEDRO Why, how now! Has your nunnery breeding taught you to understand the value of hearts and eyes?

HELLENA Better than to believe Vincentio's deserve value from any woman—he may perhaps increase her bags but not her family.

PEDRO This is fine! Go—up to your devotion. You are not designed for the conversation of lovers.

HELLENA [aside] Nor saints yet awhile, I hope.—Is't not enough you make a nun of me, but you must cast my sister away too, exposing her to a worse confinement than a religious life?

PEDRO The girl's mad! It is a confinement to be carried into the country, to an ancient villa belonging to the family of the Vincentios these five hundred years, and have no other prospect than that pleasing one of seeing all her own that meets her eyes—a fine air, large fields, and gardens, where she may walk and gather flowers!

HELLENA When, by moonlight? For I am sure she dares not encounter with the heat of the sun. That were a task only for Don Vincentio and his Indian breeding, who loves it in the dog days. And if these be her daily divertisements, what are those of the night? To lie in a wide moth-eaten bedchamber, with furniture in the fashion in the reign of King Sancho the First;—the bed, that which his forefathers lived and died in.

PEDRO Very well.

HELLENA This apartment (new furbished and fitted out for the young wife), he (out of freedom) makes his dressing-room, and being a frugal and a jealous coxcomb, instead of a valet to uncase his feeble carcase, he desires you to do that office—signs of favour I'll assure you, and such as you must not hope for unless your woman be out of the way.

PEDRO   Have you done yet?

HELLENA   That honour being past, the giant stretches itself, yawns and sighs a belch or two loud as a musket, throws himself into bed, and expects you in his foul sheets, and ere you can get yourself undressed, calls you with a snore or two—and are not these fine blessings to a young lady?

PEDRO   Have you done yet?

HELLENA   And this man you must kiss, nay you must kiss none but him, too—and nuzzle through his beard to find his lips. And this you must submit to for threescore years, and all for a jointure.

PEDRO   For all your character of Don Vincentio, she is as like to marry him as she was before.

HELLENA   Marry Don Vincentio! Hang me! Such a wedlock would be worse than adultery with another man. I had rather see her in the Hôtel de Dieu, to waste her youth there in vows, and be a handmaid to lazars and cripples, than to lose it in such a marriage.

PEDRO   You have considered, sister, that Belvile has no fortune to bring you to, banished his country, despised at home, and pitied abroad.

HELLENA   What then? The viceroy's son is better than that old Sir Fifty. Don Vincentio! Don Indian! He thinks he's trading to Gambo still, and would barter himself (that bell and bauble) for your youth and fortune.

PEDRO   Callis, take her hence, and lock her up all this carnival, and at Lent she shall begin her everlasting penance in a monastery.

HELLENA   I care not, I had rather be a nun than be obliged to marry as you would have me, if I were designed for't.

PEDRO   Do not fear the blessing of that choice—you shall be a nun.

HELLENA   Shall I so? You may chance to be mistaken in my way of devotion—a nun! Yes, I am like to make a fine nun! I have an excellent humour for a grate. [aside] No, I'll have a saint of my own to pray to shortly, if I like any that dares venture on me.

PEDRO   Callis, make it your business to watch this wild cat. As for you, Florinda, I've only tried you all this while and urged my father's will; but mine is that you would love Antonio. He is brave and young, and all that can complete the happiness of a gallant maid. This absence of my father will give us opportunity to free you from Vincentio by marrying here, which you must do tomorrow.

FLORINDA   Tomorrow!

PEDRO   Tomorrow, or 'twill be too late. 'Tis not my friendship to Antonio which makes me urge this, but love to thee, and hatred to Vincentio—therefore resolve upon tomorrow.

FLORINDA   Sir, I shall strive to do as shall become your sister.

PEDRO   I'll both believe and trust you. Adieu.

[exeunt PEDRO and STEPHANO]

HELLENA   As becomes his sister! That is to be as resolved your way, as he is his.   [HELLENA *goes to* CALLIS]

FLORINDA   I ne'er till now perceived my ruin near:
            I've no defence against Antonio's love,
            For he has all the advantages of nature,
            The moving arguments of youth and fortune.

HELLENA   But hark you, Callis, you will not be so cruel to lock me up indeed, will you?

CALLIS   I must obey the commands I hate—besides, do you consider what a life you are going to lead?

HELLENA   Yes, Callis, that of a nun: and till then I'll be indebted a world of prayers to you if you let me now see, what I never did, the divertisements of a carnival.

CALLIS   What, go in masquerade? 'Twill be a fine farewell to the world I take it—pray what would you do there?

HELLENA   That which all the world does, as I am told—be as mad as the rest, and take all innocent freedoms. Sister, you'll go too, will you not? Come, prithee be not sad. We'll outwit twenty brothers, if you'll be ruled by me. Come, put off this dull humour with your clothes, and assume one as gay, and as fantastic as the dress my cousin Valeria and I have provided, and let's ramble.

FLORINDA   Callis, will you give us leave to go?

CALLIS [*aside*]   I have a youthful itch of going myself.—Madam, if I thought your brother might not know it, and I might wait on you, for by my troth I'll not trust young girls alone.

FLORINDA   Thou see'st my brother's gone already, and thou shalt attend and watch us.

Enter STEPHANO

STEPHANO   Madam, the habits are come, and your cousin Valeria is dressed and stays for you.

FLORINDA   'Tis well. I'll write a note, and if I chance to see Belvile and want an opportunity to speak to him, that shall let him know what I've resolved in favour of him.

HELLENA   Come, let's in and dress us.   [*exeunt*]

SCENE II

A long street

Enter BELVILE, *melancholy;* BLUNT *and* FREDERICK

FREDERICK   Why what the devil ails the colonel? In a time when all the world is gay, to look like mere Lent thus? Hadst thou been long enough in Naples to have been in love, I should have sworn some such judgement had befallen thee.

BELVILE   No, I have made no new amours since I came to Naples.

FREDERICK   You have left none behind you in Paris?

BELVILE   Neither.

FREDERICK   I cannot divine the cause then, unless the old cause, the want of money.

BLUNT   And another old cause, the want of a wench—would not that revive you?

BELVILE   You are mistaken, Ned.

BLUNT   Nay, 'sheartlikins, then thou'rt past cure.

FREDERICK   I have found it out: thou hast renewed thy acquaintance with the lady that cost thee so many sighs at the siege of Pamplona—pox on't, what d'ye call her—her brother's a noble Spaniard—nephew to the dead general—Florinda—aye, Florinda—and will nothing serve thy turn but that damned virtuous woman? Whom on my conscience thou lovest in spite too, because thou seest little or no possibility of gaining her?

BELVILE   Thou art mistaken. I have interest enough in that lovely virgin's heart to make me proud and vain, were it not abated by the severity of a brother, who, perceiving my happiness—

FREDERICK   Has civilly forbid thee the house?

BELVILE   'Tis so, to make way for a powerful rival, the viceroy's son, who has the advantage of me in being a man of fortune, a Spaniard, and her brother's friend; which gives him liberty to make his court, while I have recourse only to letters, and distant looks from her window, which are as soft and kind as those which heaven sends down on penitents.

BLUNT   Heyday! 'Sheartlikins, simile! By this light, the man is quite spoiled. Fred, what the devil are we made of, that we cannot be thus concerned for a wench? 'Sheartlikins, our cupids are like the cooks of the camp, they can roast or boil a woman, but they have none of the fine tricks to set 'em off, no hogoes to make the sauce pleasant and the stomach sharp.

FREDERICK   I dare swear I have had a hundred as young, kind and handsome as this Florinda; and dogs eat me, if they were not as troublesome to me i' the morning, as they were welcome o'er night.

BLUNT   And yet I warrant he would not touch another woman if he might have her for nothing.

BELVILE   That's thy joy, a cheap whore.

BLUNT   Why, 'sheartlikins, I love a frank soul—when did you ever hear of an honest woman that took a man's money? I warrant 'em good ones—but gentlemen, you may be free, you have been kept so poor with parliaments and protectors that the little stock you have is not worth preserving—but I thank my stars, I had more grace than to forfeit my estate by cavaliering.

BELVILE   Methinks only following the court should be sufficient to entitle 'em to that.

BLUNT   'Sheartlikins, they know I follow it to do it no good, unless they pick a hole in my coat for lending you money now and then, which is a greater crime to my conscience, gentlemen, than to the Commonwealth.

Enter WILLMORE

WILLMORE   Ha! Dear Belvile! Noble colonel!

BELVILE   Willmore! Welcome ashore, my dear rover! What happy wind blew us this good fortune?

WILLMORE   Let me salute my dear Fred, and then command me. How is't, honest lad?

FREDERICK   Faith, sir, the old complement, infinitely the better to see my dear mad Willmore again. Prithee, why cam'st thou ashore? And where's the prince?

WILLMORE   He's well, and reigns still lord of the watery element. I must aboard again within a day or two, and my business ashore was only to enjoy myself a little this carnival.

BELVILE   Pray know our new friend, sir; he's but bashful, a raw traveller, but honest, stout, and one of us.   [*embraces* BLUNT]

WILLMORE   That you esteem him gives him an interest here.

BLUNT   Your servant, sir.

WILLMORE   But well—faith, I'm glad to meet you again in a warm climate, where the kind sun has its god-like power still over the wine and women. Love and mirth are my business in Naples, and if I mistake not the place, here's an excellent market for chapmen of my humour.

BELVILE   See, here be those kind merchants of love you look for.

Enter several men in masquing habits, some playing on music, others dancing after; women dressed like courtesans, with papers pinned on their breasts, and baskets of flowers in their hands

BLUNT   'Sheartlikins, what have we here?

FREDERICK   Now the game begins.

WILLMORE   Fine pretty creatures! May a stranger have leave to look and love? What's here—[*reads the papers*] "Roses for every month"?

BLUNT   "Roses for every month"? What means that?

BELVILE   They are, or would have you think they're courtesans, who here in Naples are to be hired by the month.

WILLMORE   Kind and obliging to inform us—pray, where do these roses grow? I would fain plant some of 'em in a bed of mine.

WOMAN Beware such roses, sir.

WILLMORE A pox of fear! I'll be baked with thee between a pair of sheets, and that's thy proper still; so I might but strew such roses over me and under me. Fair one, would you give me leave to gather at your bush this idle month, I would go near to make somebody smell of it all the year after.

BELVILE And thou hast need of such a remedy, for thou stink'st of tar and ropes' ends like a dock or pest-house.

[*the woman puts herself into the hands of a man and exeunt*]

WILLMORE Nay, nay, you shall not leave me so.

BELVILE By all means use no violence here.

WILLMORE Death! Just as I was going to be damnably in love, to have her led off! I could pluck that rose out of his hand, and even kiss the bed the bush grew in.

FREDERICK No friend to love like a long voyage at sea.

BLUNT Except a nunnery, Fred.

WILLMORE Death! But will they not be kind? Quickly be kind? Thou know'st I'm no tame fighter, but a rampant lion of the forest.

Advances from the farther end of the scenes two men dressed all over with horns of several sorts, making grimaces at one another, with papers pinned on their backs

BELVILE Oh the satirical rogues, how they're dressed! 'Tis a satire against the whole sex.

WILLMORE Is this a fruit that grows in the warm country?

BELVILE Yes, 'tis pretty to see these Italians start, swell and stab at the word cuckold, and yet stumble at horns on every threshold.

WILLMORE See what's on their back—[*reads*] "Flowers of every night." Ah, rogue! And more sweet than roses of every month! This is a gardener of Adam's own breeding.   [*they dance*]

BELVILE What think you of those grave people? Is a wake in Essex half so mad or extravagant?

WILLMORE I like their sober, grave way; 'tis a kind of legal authorised fornication, where the men are not chid for't, nor the women despised, as amongst our dull English; even the monsieurs want that part of good manners.

BELVILE But here in Italy, a monsieur is the humblest, best-bred gentleman. Duels are so baffled by bravoes that an age shows not one but between a Frenchman and a hangman, who is as much too hard for him on the piazza as they are for a Dutchman on the New Bridge—but see, another crew.

Enter FLORINDA, HELLENA *and* VALERIA, *dressed like gypsies;* CALLIS *and* STEPHANO, LUCETTA, PHILIPPO *and* SANCHO *in masquerade*

HELLENA   Sister, there's your Englishman, and with him a handsome proper fellow—I'll to him, and instead of telling him his fortune, try my own.

WILLMORE   Gypsies, on my life. Sure these will prattle if a man cross their hands. [*goes to* HELLENA] Dear, pretty (and I hope) young devil, will you tell an amorous stranger what luck he's like to have?

HELLENA·   Have a care how you venture with me, sir, lest I pick your pocket, which will more vex your English humour than an Italian fortune will please you.

WILLMORE   How the devil cam'st thou to know my country and humour?

HELLENA   The first I guess by a certain forward impudence, which does not displease me at this time; and the loss of your money will vex you, because I hope you have but very little to lose.

WILLMORE   Egad, child, thou'rt i'th'right; it is so little I dare not offer it thee for a kindness—but cannot you divine what other things of more value I have about me, that I would more willingly part with?

HELLENA   Indeed, no, that's the business of a witch, and I am but a gypsy yet. Yet without looking in your hand, I have a parlous guess, 'tis some foolish heart you mean, an inconstant English heart, as little worth stealing as your purse.

WILLMORE   Nay, then thou dost deal with the devil, that's certain—thou hast guessed as right as if thou hadst been one of that number it has languished for. I find you'll be better acquainted with it, nor can you take it in a better time; for I am come from sea, child, and Venus not being propitious to me in her own element, I have a world of love in store—would you would be good-natured, and take some on't off my hands.

HELLENA   Why—I could be inclined that way—but for a foolish vow I am going to make—to die a maid.

WILLMORE   Then thou art damned without redemption, and as I am a good Christian, I ought in charity to divert so wicked a design—therefore prithee, dear creature, let me know quickly when and where I shall begin to set a helping hand to so good a work.

HELLENA   If you should prevail with my tender heart (as I begin to fear you will, for you have horrible loving eyes), there will be difficulty in't that you'll hardly undergo for my sake.

WILLMORE   Faith, child, I have been bred in dangers, and wear a sword that has been employed in a worse cause than for a handsome kind woman. Name the danger—let it be anything but a long siege—and I'll undertake it.

HELLENA   Can you storm?

WILLMORE   Oh, most furiously.

HELLENA   What think you of a nunnery wall? For he that wins me must gain that first.

WILLMORE   A nun! Oh, how I love thee for't! There's no sinner like a young saint—nay, now there's no denying me, the old law had no curse (to a woman) like dying a maid; witness Jephthah's daughter.

HELLENA   A very good text this, if well handled, and I perceive, Father Captain, you would impose no severe penance on her who were inclined to console herself before she took orders.

WILLMORE   If she be young and handsome.

HELLENA   Ay, there's it—but if she be not—

WILLMORE   By this hand, child, I have an implicit faith, and dare venture on thee with all faults—besides, 'tis more meritorious to leave the world when thou hast tasted and proved the pleasure on't. Then 'twill be a virtue in thee, which now will be pure ignorance.

HELLENA   I perceive, good Father Captain, you design only to make me fit for heaven—but if, on the contrary, you should quite divert me from it and bring me back to the world again, I should have a new man to seek I find. And what a grief that will be—for when I begin, I fancy I shall love like anything; I never tried yet.

WILLMORE   Egad, and that's kind. Prithee, dear creature, give me credit for a heart, for faith I'm a very honest fellow. Oh, I long to come first to the banquet of love! And such a swingeing appetite I bring—oh, I'm impatient. Thy lodging, sweetheart, thy lodging, or I'm a dead man!

HELLENA   Why must we be either guilty of fornication or murder if we converse with you men—and is there no difference between leave to love me, and leave to lie with me?

WILLMORE   Faith, child, they were made to go together.

LUCETTA   Are you sure this is the man?   [*pointing to* BLUNT]

SANCHO   When did I mistake your game?

LUCETTA   This is a stranger, I know by his gazing; if he be brisk he'll venture to follow me, and then, if I understand my trade, he's mine. He's English too, and they say that's a sort of good-natured, loving people, and have generally so kind an opinion of themselves, that a woman with any wit may flatter 'em into any sort of fool she pleases.

> [*she often passes by* BLUNT, *and gazes on him;*
> *he struts and cocks, and walks and gazes on her*]

BLUNT   'Tis so—she is taken—I have beauties which my false glass at home did not discover.

FLORINDA   This woman watches me so, I shall get no opportunity to discover myself to him, and so miss the intent of my coming—but as I was saying, sir—[*looking in his hand*] by this line you should be a lover.

BELVILE   I thought how right you guessed, all men are in love, or pretend to be so—come, let me go, I'm weary of this fooling.   [*walks away*]

FLORINDA   I will not, till you have confessed whether the passion that you have vowed for Florinda be true or false.

[*she holds him, he strives to get from her; turns quick towards her*]

BELVILE   Florinda!

FLORINDA   Softly.

BELVILE   Thou hast named one will fix me here for ever.

FLORINDA   She'll be disappointed then, who expects you this night at the garden gate, and if you fail not as—let me see the other hand—you will go near to do—she vows to die or make you happy.

[*looks on* CALLIS *who observes 'em*]

BELVILE   What canst thou mean?

FLORINDA   That which I say. Farewell.   [*offers to go*]

BELVILE   Oh, charming sybil, stay, complete that joy which as it is will turn into distraction! Where must I be? At the garden gate? I know it— at night you say? I'll sooner forfeit heaven than disobey.

Enter DON PEDRO *and other masquers, and pass over the stage*

CALLIS   Madam, your brother's here.

FLORINDA   Take this to instruct you farther.

[*gives him a letter, and goes off*]

FREDERICK   Have a care, sir, what you promise. This may be a trap laid by her brother to ruin you.

BELVILE   Do not disturb my happiness with doubts.   [*opens the letter*]

WILLMORE   My dear pretty creature, a thousand blessings on thee! Still in this habit you say? And after dinner at this place?

HELLENA   Yes, if you will swear to keep your heart and not bestow it between this and that.

WILLMORE   By all the little gods of love, I swear I'll leave it with you, and if you run away with it, those deities of justice will revenge me.

[*exeunt all the women except* LUCETTA]

FREDERICK   Do you know the hand?

BELVILE   'Tis Florinda's.

All blessings fall upon the virtuous maid.

FREDERICK   Nay, no idolatry; a sober sacrifice I'll allow you.

BELVILE   Oh friends, the welcom'st news! The softest letter! Nay, you shall all see it! And could you now be serious, I might be made the happiest man the sun shines on!

WILLMORE   The reason of this mighty joy?

BELVILE   See how kindly she invites me to deliver her from the threatened violence of her brother—will you not assist me?

WILLMORE   I know not what thou mean'st, but I'll make one at any mischief where a woman's concerned—but she'll be grateful to us for the favour, will she not?

BELVILE   How mean you?

WILLMORE   How should I mean? Thou know'st there's but one way for a woman to oblige me.

BELVILE   Do not profane—the maid is nicely virtuous.

WILLMORE   Who, pox, then she's fit for nothing but a husband. Let her e'en go, colonel.

FREDERICK   Peace, she's the colonel's mistress, sir.

WILLMORE   Let her be the devil; if she be thy mistress, I'll serve her—name the way.

BELVILE   Read here this postscript.   [*gives him a letter*]

WILLMORE [*reads*]   "At ten at night—at the garden gate—of which, if I cannot get the key, I will contrive a way over the wall—come attended with a friend or two." Kind heart, if we three cannot weave a string to let her down a garden wall, 'twere pity but the hangman wove one for us all.

FREDERICK   Let her alone for that; your woman's wit, your fair kind woman will out-trick a broker or a Jew, and contrive like a Jesuit in chains! But see, Ned, Blunt is stolen out after the lure of a damsel.

[*exeunt* BLUNT *and* LUCETTA]

BELVILE   So, he'll scarce find his way home again unless we get him cried by the bellman in the market-place, and 'twould sound prettily—a lost English boy of thirty.

FREDERICK   I hope 'tis some common crafty sinner, one that will fit him. It may be she'll sell him for Peru: the rogue's sturdy and would work well in a mine. At least I hope she'll dress him for our mirth, cheat him of all, then have him well-favouredly banged, and turned out naked at midnight.

WILLMORE   Prithee, what humour is he of, that you wish him so well?

BELVILE   Why, of an English elder brother's humour: educated in a nursery, with a maid to tend him till fifteen, and lies with his grandmother till he's of age. One that knows no pleasure beyond riding to the next fair, or going up to London with his right worshipful father in parliament-time; wearing gay clothes, or making honourable love to his lady mother's laundry maid; gets drunk at a hunting match, and ten to one then gives some proof of his prowess. A pox upon him, he's our banker, and has all our cash about him, and if he fail, we are all broke.

FREDERICK   Oh, let him alone for that matter, he's of a damned stingy quality that will secure our stock. I know not in what danger it were indeed if the jilt should pretend she's in love with him, for 'tis a kind believing coxcomb. Otherwise, if he part with more than a piece of eight—geld him—for which offer he may chance to be beaten if she be a whore of the first rank.

BELVILE   Nay, the rogue will not be easily beaten, he's stout enough. Perhaps if they talk beyond his capacity, he may chance to exercise his courage upon some of them, else I'm sure they'll find it as difficult to beat as to please him.

WILLMORE   'Tis a lucky devil to light upon so kind a wench!

FREDERICK   Thou hadst a great deal of talk with thy little gypsy, coudst thou do no good upon her? For mine was hard-hearted.

WILLMORE   Hang her, she was some damned honest person of quality I'm sure, she was so very free and witty. If her face be but answerable to her wit and humour, I would be bound to constancy this month to gain her—in the meantime, have you made no kind acquaintance since you came to town? You do not use to be honest so long, gentlemen.

FREDERICK   Faith, love has kept us honest: we have been all fired with a beauty newly come to town, the famous Paduana Angellica Bianca.

WILLMORE   What, the mistress of the dead Spanish general?

BELVILE   Yes, she's now the only adored beauty of all the youth in Naples, who put on all their charms to appear lovely in her sight, their coaches, liveries, and themselves, all gay as on a monarch's birthday, to attract the eyes of this fair charmer, while she has the pleasure to behold all languish for her that see her.

FREDERICK   'Tis pretty to see with how much love the men regard her, and how much envy the women.

WILLMORE   What gallant has she?

BELVILE   None, she's exposed to sale, and four days in the week she's yours—for so much a month.

WILLMORE   The very thought of it quenches all manner of fire in me—yet prithee, let's see her.

BELVILE   Let's first to dinner, and after that we'll pass the day as you please—but at night ye must all be at my devotion.

WILLMORE   I will not fail you.   [*exeunt*]

ACT II

SCENE I

The long street

Enter BELVILE *and* FREDERICK *in masquing habits,*
and WILLMORE *in his own clothes, with a vizard in his hand*

WILLMORE   But why thus disguised and muzzled?

BELVILE   Because whatever extravagances we commit in these faces,
our own may not be obliged to answer 'em.

WILLMORE   I should have changed my eternal buff too; but no matter, my little gypsy would not have found me out then, unless I should
hear her prattle. A pox on't, I cannot get her out of my head: pray heaven,
if I ever do see her again, she prove damnable ugly, that I may fortify myself against her tongue.

BELVILE   Have a care of love, for o' my conscience she was not of a
quality to give thee any hopes.

WILLMORE   Pox on 'em, why do they draw a man in then? She has
played with my heart so, that 'twill never lie still till I have met with some
kind wench that will play the game out with me. Oh, for my arms full
of soft, white, kind—woman! Such as I fancy Angellica.

BELVILE   This is her house, if you were but in stock to get admittance.
They have not yet dined yet; I perceive the picture is not out.

Enter BLUNT

WILLMORE   I long to see the shadow of the fair substance; a man may
gaze on that for nothing.

BLUNT   Colonel, thy hand—and thine, Fred. I have been an ass, a deluded fool, a very coxcomb from my birth till this hour, and heartily repent my little faith.

BELVILE   What the devil's the matter with thee, Ned?

BLUNT   Oh, such a mistress, Fred, such a girl!

WILLMORE   Ha! Where?

FREDERICK   Aye, where?

BLUNT   So fond, so amorous, so toying and so fine! And all for sheer love, ye rogue! Oh, how she looked and kissed! And soothed my heart from my bosom—I cannot think I was awake, and yet methinks I see and feel her charms still—Fred, try if she have not left the taste of her balmy breath upon my lips.   [*kisses him*]

BELVILE   Ha, ha, ha!

WILLMORE   Death, man, where is she?

BLUNT   What a dog was I to stay in dull England so long. How have I laughed at the colonel when he sighed for love! But now the little archer has revenged him! And by this one dart I can guess at all his joys, which then I took for fancies, mere dreams and fables. Well, I'm resolved to sell all in Essex, and plant here forever.

BELVILE   What a blessing 'tis thou hast a mistress thou dar'st boast of, for I know thy humour is rather to have a proclaimed clap than a secret amour.

WILLMORE   Dost know her name?

BLUNT   Her name? No, 'sheartlikins, what care I for names? She's fair, young, brisk and kind—even to ravishment! And what a pox care I for knowing her by any other title?

WILLMORE   Didst give her anything?

BLUNT   Give her! Ha, ha, ha! Why, she's a person of quality—that's a good one, give her! 'Sheartlikins, dost think such creatures are to be bought? Or are we provided for such a purchase? Give her, quoth ye? Why, she presented me with this bracelet for the toy of a diamond I used to wear. No, gentlemen, Ned Blunt is not everybody—she expects me again tonight.

WILLMORE   Egad, that's well; we'll all go.

BLUNT   Not a soul. No, gentlemen, you are wits; I am a dull country rogue, I.

FREDERICK   Well, sir, for all your person of quality, I shall be very glad to understand your purse be secure; 'tis our whole estate at present, which we are loath to hazard in one bottom. Come, sir, unlade.

BLUNT   Take the necessary trifle useless now to me, that am beloved by such a gentlewoman—'sheartlikins, money! Here, take mine, too.

FREDERICK   No, keep that to be cozened, that we may laugh.

WILLMORE   Cozened—death! would I could meet with one that would cozen me of all the love I could spare tonight.

FREDERICK   Pox, 'tis some common whore, upon my life.

BLUNT   A whore? Yes, with such clothes, such jewels, such a house, such furniture, and so attended! A whore!

BELVILE   Why yes, sir, they are whores, though they'll neither entertain you with drinking, swearing, or bawdry; are whores in all those gay clothes and right jewels; are whores with those great houses richly furnished with velvet beds, store of plate, handsome attendance and fine coaches; are whores, and arrant ones.

WILLMORE   Pox on't, where do these fine whores live?

BELVILE   Where no rogue in office ycleped constables dare give 'em laws, nor the wine-inspired bullies of the town break their windows; yet they are whores, though this Essex calf believe 'em persons of quality.

BLUNT   'Sheartlikins, y'are all fools. There are things about this Essex calf that shall take with the ladies, beyond all your wit and parts—this shape and size, gentlemen, are not to be despised—my waste too, tolerably long, with other inviting signs that shall be nameless.

WILLMORE   Egad, I believe he may have met with some person of quality that may be kind to him.

BELVILE   Dost thou perceive any such tempting things about him that should make a fine woman, and of quality, pick him out from all mankind to throw away her youth and beauty upon, nay, and her dear heart too? No, no, Angellica has raised the price too high.

WILLMORE   May she languish for mankind till she die, and be damned for that one sin alone.

Enter two BRAVOES *and hang up a great picture of* ANGELLICA'S
against the balcony; and two little ones at each side of the door

BELVILE   See there, the fair sign to the inn where a man may lodge that's fool enough to give her price.   [WILLMORE *gazes on the picture*]

BLUNT   'Sheartlikins, gentlemen, what's this?

BELVILE   A famous courtesan, that's to be sold.

BLUNT   How? To be sold? Nay then, I have nothing to say to her—sold! What impudence is practised in this country! With what order and decency whoring's established here by virtue of the Inquisition. Come, let's be gone, I'm sure we're no chapmen for this commodity.

FREDERICK   Thou art none, I'm sure, unless thou couldst have her in thy bed at the price of a coach in the street.

WILLMORE   How wondrous fair she is—"a thousand crowns a month"—by heaven, as many kingdoms were too little. A plague of this poverty—of which I ne'er complain but when it hinders my approach to beauty, which virtue ne'er could purchase.   [*turns away from the picture*]

BLUNT   What's this? [*reads*] "A thousand crowns a month"! 'Sheartlikins, here's a sum! Sure 'tis a mistake.—Hark you friend, does she take or give so much by the month?

FREDERICK   A thousand crowns! Why, 'tis a portion for the Infanta.

BLUNT   Hark ye friends, won't she trust?

BRAVO   This is a trade, sir, that cannot live by credit.

Enter DON PEDRO *in masquerade, followed by* STEPHANO

BELVILE   See, here's more company, let's walk off a while.

[*exeunt the* ENGLISH; PEDRO *reads*]

Enter ANGELLICA *and* MORETTA *in the balcony, and draw a silk curtain*

PEDRO   Fetch me a thousand crowns, I never wished to buy this beauty at an easier rate.   [*passes off the stage*]

ANGELLICA   Prithee, what said those fellows to thee?

BRAVO   Madam, the first were admirers of your beauty only, but no purchasers: they were merry with your price and picture, laughed at the sum, and so passed off.

ANGELLICA   No matter, I'm not displeased with their rallying; their wonder feeds my vanity, and he that wishes but to buy gives me more pride than he that gives my price can make me pleasure.

BRAVO   Madam, the last I knew through all his disguises to be Don Pedro, nephew to the general, and who was with him in Pamplona.

ANGELLICA   Don Pedro! My old gallant's nephew. When his uncle died he left him a vast sum of money; it is he who was so in love with me at Padua, and who used to make the general so jealous.

MORETTA   Is this he that used to prance before our window, and took such care to show himself an amorous ass? If I am not mistaken, he is the likeliest man to give your price.

ANGELLICA   The man is brave and generous, but of an humour so uneasy and inconstant that the victory over his heart is as soon lost as won, a slave that can add little to the triumph of the conqueror. But inconstancy's the sin of all mankind, therefore I'm resolved that nothing but gold shall charm my heart.

MORETTA   I'm glad on't; 'tis only interest that women of our profession ought to consider, though I wonder what has kept you from that general disease of our sex so long—I mean that of being in love.

ANGELLICA   A kind but sullen star, under which I had the happiness to be born. Yet I have had no time for love; the bravest and noblest of mankind have purchased my favours at so dear a rate, as if no coin but gold were current with our trade—but here's Don Pedro again, fetch me my lute—for 'tis for him or Don Antonio, the viceroy's son, that I have spread my nets.

Enter at one door DON PEDRO, STEPHANO, DON ANTONIO *and* DIEGO *at the other door, with people following him in masquerade, anticly attired, some with music; they both go up to the picture*

ANTONIO   A thousand crowns! Had not the painter flattered her, I should not think it dear.

PEDRO   Flattered her! By heaven, he cannot; I have seen the original,

nor is there one charm here more than adorns her face and eyes; all this
soft and sweet, with a certain languishing air that no artist can represent.

ANTONIO   What I heard of her beauty before had fired my soul, but
this confirmation of it has blown it to a flame.

PEDRO   Ha!

DIEGO   Sir, I have known you throw away a thousand crowns on a
worse face, and though y'are near your marriage, you may venture a little love here, Florinda will not miss it.

PEDRO [aside]   Ha! Florinda! Sure 'tis Antonio.

ANTONIO   Florinda! Name not those distant joys, there's not one
thought of her will check my passion here.

PEDRO   Florinda scorned! And all my hopes defeated of the possession of Angellica! Her injuries, by heaven, he shall not boast of!

[a noise of a lute above; ANTONIO gazes up; song to a lute above]

SONG

When Damon first began to love
He languished in a soft desire,
And knew not how the gods to move,
To lessen or increase his fire.
For Celia in her charming eyes
Wore all love's sweets, and all his cruelties.

2

But as beneath a shade he lay,
Weaving of flowers for Celia's hair,
She chanced to lead her flock that way,
And saw the am'rous shepherd there.
She gazed around upon the place,
And saw the grove (resembling night)
To all the joys of love invite,
Whilst guilty smiles and blushes dressed her face.
At last the bashful youth all transport grew,
And with kind force he taught the virgin how
To yield what all his sighs could never do.

[ANGELLICA throws open the curtains and bows to ANTONIO, who pulls off
his vizard and bows and blows up kisses; PEDRO unseen looks in his face]

ANTONIO   By heaven, she's charming fair!

PEDRO   'Tis he, the false Antonio!

ANTONIO [to the BRAVO]   Friend, where must I pay my offering of
love? My thousand crowns, I mean.

PEDRO   That offering I have designed to make.
             And yours will come too late.
ANTONIO   Prithee begone, I shall grow angry else.
             And then thou art not safe.
PEDRO   My anger may be fatal, sir, as yours;
             And he that enters here may prove this truth.
ANTONIO   I know not who thou art, but I am sure thou'rt worth my
killing for aiming at Angellica.   [*they draw and fight*]

                    Enter WILLMORE *and* BLUNT

BLUNT   'Sheartlikins, here's fine doings.
WILLMORE   Tilting for the wench I'm sure—nay, gad, if that would
win her, I have as good a sword as the best of ye.
             [WILLMORE *and* BLUNT *draw and part* PEDRO *and* ANTONIO]
Put up, put up, and take another time and place, for this is designed for
lovers only.   [*they all put up*]
PEDRO   We are prevented; dare you meet me tomorrow on the
             Molo?
             For I've a title to a better quarrel,
             That of Florinda, in whose credulous heart
             Thou'st made an interest and destroyed my hopes.
ANTONIO   Dare!
             I'll meet thee there as early as the day.
PEDRO   We will come thus disguised, that whosoever chance to get
the better, he may escape unknown.
ANTONIO   It shall be so.   [*exeunt* PEDRO *and* STEPHANO]
             Who should this rival be, unless the English colonel, of
             whom I've often heard Don Pedro speak?
             It must be he, and time he were removed,
             Who lays a claim to all my happiness.
                    [WILLMORE, *having gazed all this while on the picture,
                                pulls down a little one*]
WILLMORE   This posture's loose and negligent,
             The sight on't would beget a warm desire
             In souls whom impotence and age had chilled.
             This must along with me.
BRAVO   What means this rudeness, sir? Restore the picture.
ANTONIO   Ha! Rudeness committed to the fair Angellica!
             Restore the picture, sir—
WILLMORE   Indeed I will not, sir.
ANTONIO   By heaven, but you shall.
WILLMORE   Nay, do not show your sword; if you do, by this dear
beauty—I will show mine too.

ANTONIO   What right can you pretend to't?

WILLMORE   That of possession which I will maintain—you perhaps have a thousand crowns to give for the original.

ANTONIO   No matter, sir, you shall restore the picture.

[ANGELLICA *and* MORETTA *above*]

ANGELLICA   Oh, Moretta! What's the matter?

WILLMORE   Death! You lie—I will do neither.

[*they fight; the* SPANIARDS *join with* ANTONIO;
BLUNT *laying on like mad*]

ANGELLICA   Hold, I command you, if for me you fight.

[*they leave off and bow*]

WILLMORE   How heavenly fair she is! Ah, plague of her price.

ANGELLICA   You sir, in buff, you that appear a soldier, that first began this insolence—

WILLMORE   'Tis true, I did so, if you call it insolence for a man to preserve himself. I saw your charming picture and was wounded: quite through my soul each pointed beauty ran, and wanting a thousand crowns to procure my remedy, I laid this little picture to my bosom— which if you cannot allow me, I'll resign.

ANGELLICA   No, you may keep the trifle.

ANTONIO   You shall first ask my leave, and this. [*fight again as before*]

Enter BELVILE *and* FREDERICK *who join with the* ENGLISH

ANGELLICA   Hold! Will you ruin me? Biskey—Sebastian—part 'em.

[*the* SPANIARDS *are beaten off; exeunt all the* MEN]

MORETTA   Oh madam, we're undone. A pox upon that rude fellow, he's set on to ruin us; we shall never see good days till all these fighting poor rogues are sent to the galleys.

Enter BELVILE, BLUNT, FREDERICK *and* WILLMORE *with his shirt bloody*

BLUNT   'Sheartlikins, beat me at this sport and I'll ne'er wear sword more.

BELVILE [*to* WILLMORE]   The devil's in thee for a mad fellow, thou art always one at an unlucky adventure—come, let's be gone whilst we're safe, and remember these are Spaniards, a sort of people that know how to revenge an affront.

FREDERICK   You bleed! I hope you are not wounded.

WILLMORE   Not much—a plague on your dons, if they fight no better they'll ne'er recover Flanders. What the devil was't to them that I took down the picture?

BLUNT   Took it! 'Sheartlikins, we'll have the great one too; 'tis ours by conquest. Prithee help me up, and I'll pull it down—

ANGELLICA   Stay, sir, and ere you affront me farther, let me know how

you durst commit this outrage—to you I speak, sir, for you appear a gentleman.

WILLMORE   To me, madam?—Gentlemen, your servant.

[BELVILE *stays him*]

BELVILE   Is the devil in thee? Dost know the danger of entering the
house of an incensed courtesan?

WILLMORE   I thank you for your care—but there are other matters
in hand, there are, though we have no great temptation. Death! Let me
go!

FREDERICK   Yes, to your lodging if you will, but not in here. Damn
these gay harlots—by this hand, I'll have as sound and handsome a whore
for a patacoon. Death, man, she'll murder thee.

WILLMORE   Oh, fear me not. Shall I not venture where a beauty
calls? A lovely charming beauty! For fear of danger! When, by heaven,
there's none so great as to long for her whilst I want money to purchase
her.

FREDERICK   Therefore 'tis loss of time unless you had the thousand
crowns to pay.

WILLMORE   It may be she may give a favour; at least I shall have the
pleasure of saluting her when I enter, and when I depart.

BELVILE   Pox, she'll as soon lie with thee as kiss thee, and sooner stab
than do either—you shall not go.

ANGELLICA   Fear not, sir, all I have to wound with is my eyes.

BLUNT   Let him go, 'sheartlikins, I believe the gentlewoman means
well.

BELVILE   Well, take thy fortune, we'll expect you in the next street.
Farewell, fool—farewell.

WILLMORE   'Bye, colonel—   [*goes in*]

FREDERICK   The rogue's stark mad for a wench.   [*exeunt*]

SCENE II

A fine chamber

Enter WILLMORE, ANGELLICA *and* MORETTA

ANGELLICA   Insolent sir, how durst you pull down my picture?

WILLMORE   Rather, how durst you set it up, to tempt poor amorous
mortals with so much excellence? Which I find you have but too well
consulted by the unmerciful price you set upon't. Is all this heaven of
beauty shown to move despair in those that cannot buy? And can you
think th'effects of that despair should be less extravagant than I have
shown?

ANGELLICA   I sent for you to ask my pardon, sir, not to aggravate your crime—I thought I should have seen you at my feet imploring it.

WILLMORE   You are deceived; I came to rail at you, and rail such truths too, as shall let you see the vanity of that pride which taught you how to set such a price on sin.

For such it is, whilst that which is love's due
Is meanly bartered for.

ANGELLICA   Ha! Ha! Ha! Alas, good captain, what pity 'tis your edifying doctrine will do no good upon me—Moretta! Fetch the gentleman a glass and let him survey himself to see what charms he has—[*aside in a soft tone*] and guess my business.

MORETTA   He knows himself of old; I believe those breeches and he have been acquainted ever since he was beaten at Worcester.

ANGELLICA   Nay, do not abuse the poor creature—

MORETTA   Good weather-beaten corporal, will you march off? We have no need of your doctrine, though you have of our charity, but at present we have no scraps, we can afford no kindness for God's sake. In fine, sirrah, the price is too high i'th'mouth for you, therefore troop, I say.

WILLMORE   Here, good forewoman of the shop, serve me, and I'll be gone.

MORETTA   Keep it to pay your laundress, your linen stinks of the gunroom; for here's no selling by retail.

WILLMORE   Thou hast sold plenty of thy stale ware at a cheap rate.

MORETTA   Aye, the more silly kind heart I, but this is an age wherein beauty is at higher rates. In fine, you know the price of this.

WILLMORE   I grant you 'tis here set down a thousand crowns a month—pray how much may come to my share for a pistole? Bawd, take your black lead and sum it up, that I may have a pistole's worth of this vain gay thing, and I'll trouble you no more.

MORETTA   Pox on him, he'll fret me to death.—Abominable fellow, I tell thee, we only sell by the whole piece.

WILLMORE   'Tis very hard, the whole cargo or nothing. Faith, madam, my stock will not reach it; I cannot be your chapman. Yet I have countrymen in town, merchants of love like me: I'll see if they'll put in for a share. We cannot lose much by it, and what we have no use for we'll sell upon the Friday's mart at "Who gives more?" I am studying, madam, how to purchase you, though at present I am unprovided of money.

ANGELLICA [*aside*]   Sure, this from any other man would anger me— nor shall he know the conquest he has made.—Poor angry man, how I despise this railing.

WILLMORE   Yes, I am poor—but I'm a gentleman,
And one that scorns this baseness which you practise;

Poor as I am, I would not sell myself,
No, not to gain your charming high-prized person.
Though I admire you strangely for your beauty,
Yet I contemn your mind.
—And yet I would at any rate enjoy you,
At your own rate—but cannot—see here
The only sum I can command on earth;
I know not where to eat when this is gone.
Yet such a slave I am to love and beauty
This last reserve I'll sacrifice to enjoy you.
—Nay, do not frown, I know you're to be bought,
And would be bought by me, by me,
For a mean trifling sum if I could pay it down;
Which happy knowledge I will still repeat,
And lay it to my heart, it has a virtue in't,
And soon will cure those wounds your eyes have made.
—And yet—there's something so divinely powerful there—
Nay, I will gaze—to let you see my strength.
                    [*holds her, looks on her, and pauses and sighs*]
By heaven, bright creature, I would not for the world
Thy fame were half so fair as is thy face.
                              [*turns her away from him*]

ANGELLICA [*aside*]   His words go through me to the very soul.
        —If you have nothing else to say to me—
WILLMORE   Yes, you shall hear how infamous you are—
        For which I do not hate thee—
        But that secures my heart, and all the flames it feels
        Are but so many lusts—
        I know it by their sudden bold intrusion.
        The fire's impatient and betrays, 'tis false—
        For had it been the purer flame of love,
        I should have pined and languished at your feet,
        Ere found the impudence to have discovered it.
        I now dare stand your scorn and your denial.

MORETTA   Sure, she's bewitched that she can stand thus tamely and
hear his saucy railing.—Sirrah, will you be gone?

ANGELLICA [*to* MORETTA]   How dare you take this liberty! Withdraw.—Pray tell me, sir, are not you guilty of the same mercenary crime?
When a lady is proposed to you for a wife, you never ask how fair, discreet, or virtuous she is; but what's her fortune—which if but small, you
cry "She will not do my business," and basely leave her, though she languish for you. Say, is not this as poor?

WILLMORE   It is a barbarous custom, which I will scorn to defend in
our sex, and do despise in yours.

ANGELLICA   Thou'rt a brave fellow! Put up thy gold, and know,
        That were thy fortune large as is thy soul,
        Thou shouldst not buy my love,
        Couldst thou forget those mean effects of vanity
        Which set me out to sale,
        And, as a lover, prize my yielding joys?
        Canst thou believe they'll be entirely thine,
        Without considering they were mercenary?

WILLMORE   I cannot tell, I must bethink me first. [*aside*]—Ha, death,
I'm going to believe her.

ANGELLICA   Prithee confirm that faith—or if thou canst not—Flatter
me a little, 'twill please me from thy mouth.

WILLMORE [*aside*]   Curse on thy charming tongue! Dost thou return
        My feigned contempt with so much subtlety?
        Thou'st found the easiest way into my heart,
        Though I yet know that all thou say'st is false.
                                        [*turning from her in rage*]

ANGELLICA   By all that's good 'tis real;
        I never loved before, though oft a mistress.
        Shall my first vows be slighted?

WILLMORE [*aside*]   What can she mean?

ANGELLICA [*in an angry tone*]   I find you cannot credit me.

WILLMORE   I know you take me for an arrant ass,
        An ass that may be soothed into belief,
        And then be used at pleasure.
        —But, madam, I have been so often cheated
        By perjured, soft, deluding hypocrites,
        That I've no faith left for the cozening sex;
        Especially for women of your trade.

ANGELLICA   The low esteem you have of me, perhaps
        May bring my heart again:
        For I have pride, that yet surmounts my love.
                                        [*she turns with pride; he holds her*]

WILLMORE   Throw off this pride, this enemy to bliss,
        And show the power of love: 'tis with those arms
        I can be only vanquished, made a slave.

ANGELLICA   Is all my mighty expectation vanished?
        No, I will not hear thee talk—thou hast a charm
        In every word that draws my heart away.
        And all the thousand trophies I designed

Thou hast undone—why art thou soft?
Thy looks are bravely rough, and meant for war.
Couldst thou not storm on still?
I then perhaps had been as free as thou.

WILLMORE [*aside*]   Death, how she throws her fire about my soul!
—Take heed, fair creature, how you raise my hopes,
Which once assumed pretend to all dominion.
There's not a joy thou hast in store,
I shall not then command.
For which I'll pay thee back my soul, my life!
Come, let's begin th'account this happy minute!

ANGELLICA   And will you pay me then the price I ask?

WILLMORE   Oh, why dost thou draw me from an awful worship
By showing thou art no divinity?
Conceal the fiend, and show me all the angel!
Keep me but ignorant, and I'll be devout
And pay my vows for ever at this shrine.

[*kneels and kisses her hand*]

ANGELLICA   The pay I mean is but thy love for mine. Can you give that?

WILLMORE   Entirely—come, let's withdraw! Where I'll renew my vows, and breathe 'em with such ardour thou shalt not doubt my zeal.

ANGELLICA   Thou hast a power too strong to be resisted.

[*exeunt* WILLMORE *and* ANGELLICA]

MORETTA   Now, my curse go with you—is all our project fallen to this? To love the only enemy to our trade? Nay, to love such a shameroon, a very beggar, nay a pirate beggar, whose business is to rifle and be gone; a no-purchase, no-pay tatterdemalion, and English picaroon. A rogue that fights for daily drink, and takes a pride in being loyally lousy! Oh, I could curse now, if I durst. This is the fate of most whores.

Trophies, which from believing fops we win,
Are spoils to those who cozen us again.

ACT III

SCENE I

A street

Enter FLORINDA, VALERIA, HELLENA, *in antic different dresses from what they were in before;* CALLIS *attending*

FLORINDA   I wonder what should make my brother in so ill a humour? I hope he has not found out our ramble this morning.

HELLENA   No, if he had, we should have heard on't at both ears, and have been mewed up this afternoon; which I would not for the world should have happened—hey ho, I'm as sad as a lover's lute.

VALERIA   Well, methinks we have learnt this trade of gypsies as readily as if we had been bred upon the road to Loretto; and yet I did so fumble when I told the stranger his fortune that I was afraid I should have told my own and yours by mistake—but, methinks Hellena has been very serious ever since.

FLORINDA   I would give my garters she were in love, to be revenged upon her for abusing me—how is't, Hellena?

HELLENA   Ah—would I had never seen my mad monsieur—and yet for all your laughing, I am not in love—and yet this small acquaintance, o' my conscience, will never out of my head.

VALERIA   Ha, ha, ha,—I laugh to think how thou art fitted with a lover, a fellow that I warrant loves every new face he sees.

HELLENA   Hum—he has not kept his word with me here—and may be taken up—that thought is not very pleasant to me—what the deuce should this be now, that I feel?

VALERIA   What is't like?

HELLENA   Nay, the Lord knows—but if I should be hanged I cannot choose but be angry and afraid, when I think that mad fellow should be in love with anybody but me. What to think of myself, I know not—would I could meet with some true damned gypsy, that I might know my fortune.

VALERIA   Know it! Why there's nothing so easy; thou wilt love this wandering inconstant till thou find thyself hanged about his neck, and then be as mad to get free again.

FLORINDA   Yes, Valeria, we shall see her astride his baggage horse, and follow him to the campaign.

HELLENA   So, so, now you are provided for, there's no care taken of poor me. But since you have set my heart a-wishing, I am resolved to know for what; I will not die of the pip, so I will not.

FLORINDA   Art thou mad to talk so? Who will like thee well enough to have thee, that hears what a mad wench thou art?

HELLENA   Like me! I don't intend every he that likes me shall have me, but he that I like. I should have stayed in the nunnery still, if I had liked my Lady Abbess as well as she liked me—no, I came thence not (as my wise brother imagines) to take an eternal farewell of the world, but to love and to be beloved, and I will be beloved, or I'll get one of your men, so I will.

VALERIA   Am I put into the number of lovers?

HELLENA   You? Why, coz, I know thou'rt too good-natured to leave us in any design: thou wouldst venture a cast though thou comest off a loser, especially with such a gamester. I observe your man, and your willing ear incline that way; and if you are not a lover, 'tis an art soon learnt— that I find. [*sighs*]

FLORINDA   I wonder you learnt to love so easily, I had a thousand charms to meet my eyes and ears e'er I could yield, and 'twas the knowledge of Belvile's merit, not the surprising person, took my soul. Thou art too rash, to give a heart at first sight.

HELLENA   Hang your considering lover! I never thought beyond the fancy that 'twas a very pretty, idle, silly kind of pleasure to pass one's time with, to write little soft nonsensical billets, and with great difficulty and danger receive answers in which I shall have my beauty praised, my wit admired (though little or none), and have the vanity and power to know I am desirable; then I have the more inclination that way because I am to be a nun, and so shall not be suspected to have any such earthly thoughts about me—but when I walk thus—and sigh thus—they'll think my mind's upon my monastery, and cry "How happy 'tis she's so resolved."—But not a word of man.

FLORINDA   What mad creature's this?

HELLENA   I'll warrant if my brother hears either of you sigh, he cries (gravely)—"I fear you have the indiscretion to be in love, but take heed of the honour of our house, and your own unspotted fame," and so he conjures on till he has laid the soft-winged god in your hearts, or broke the bird's nest—but see, here comes your lover, but where's my inconstant? Let's step aside, and we may learn something.   [*go aside*]

Enter BELVILE, FREDERICK *and* BLUNT

BELVILE   What means this? The picture's taken in.

BLUNT   It may be the wench is good-natured, and will be kind gratis. Your friend's a proper, handsome fellow.

BELVILE   I rather think she has cut his throat and is fled: I am mad he should throw himself into dangers—pox on't, I shall want him, too, at night—let's knock and ask for him.

HELLENA   My heart goes a-pit-a-pat, for fear 'tis my man they talk of.

[*knock,* MORETTA *above*]

MORETTA   What would you have?

BELVILE   Tell the stranger that entered here about two hours ago, that his friends stay here for him.

MORETTA   A curse upon him for Moretta, would he were at the devil—but he's coming to you.

Enter WILLMORE

HELLENA   Aye, aye, 'tis he! Oh, how this vexes me.

BELVILE   And how and how, dear lad, has fortune smiled? Are we to break her windows? Or raise up altars to her, hah?

WILLMORE   Does not my fortune sit triumphant on my brow? Dost not see the little wanton god there all gay and smiling? Have I not an air about my face and eyes that distinguish me from the crowd of common lovers? By heaven, Cupid's quiver has not half so many darts as her eyes! Oh, such a *bona roba!* To sleep in her arms is lying in *fresco,* all perfumed air about me.

HELLENA [*aside*]   Here's fine encouragement for me to fool on.

WILLMORE   Harkee, where didst thou purchase that rich Canary we drank today? Tell me, that I may adore the spigot and sacrifice to the butt! The juice was divine, into which I must dip my rosary, and then bless all things that I would have bold or fortunate.

BELVILE   Well, sir, let's go take a bottle, and hear the story of your success.

FREDERICK   Would not French wine do better?

WILLMORE   Damn the hungry balderdash; cheerful sack has a generous virtue in't, inspiring a successful confidence, gives eloquence to the tongue, and vigour to the soul! And has in a few hours completed all my hopes and wishes! There's nothing left to raise a new desire in me—come, let's be gay and wanton—and, gentlemen, study, study what you want, for here are friends, that will supply gentlemen. [*jingles gold*] Hark what a charming sound they make! 'Tis he and she gold whilst here, and shall beget new pleasures every moment.

BLUNT   But harkee, sir, you are not married are you?

WILLMORE   All the honey of matrimony, but none of the sting, friend!

BLUNT   'Sheartlikins, thou'rt a fortunate rogue!

WILLMORE   I am so, sir, let these—inform you!—Ha, how sweetly they chime!—Pox of poverty, it makes a man a slave, makes wit and honour sneak. My soul grew lean and rusty for want of credit.

BLUNT   'Sheartlikins, this I like well; it looks like my lucky bargain! Oh how I long for the approach of my squire, that is to conduct me to her house again. Why, here's two provided for!

FREDERICK   By this light y'are happy men.

BLUNT   Fortune is pleased to smile on us, gentlemen—to smile on us.

Enter SANCHO *and pulls down* BLUNT *by the sleeve*

SANCHO   Sir, my lady expects you—[*they go aside*]—She has removed all that might oppose your will and pleasure, and is impatient till you come.

BLUNT   Sir, I'll attend you—oh, the happiest rogue! I'll take no leave, lest they either dog me, or stay me.   [*exit with* SANCHO]

BELVILE   But then the little gypsy is forgot?

WILLMORE   A mischief on thee for putting her into my thoughts! I had quite forgot her else, and this night's debauch had drunk her quite down.

HELLENA   Had it so, good captain? [*claps him on the back*]

WILLMORE [*aside*]   Hah! I hope she did not hear me.

HELLENA   What, afraid of such a champion?

WILLMORE   Oh! You're a fine lady of your word, are you not? To make a man languish a whole day—

HELLENA   In tedious search of me.

WILLMORE   Egad, child, thou'rt in the right. Hadst thou seen what a melancholy dog I have been ever since I was a lover, how I have walked the streets like a Capuchin with my hands in my sleeves—faith, sweetheart, thou wouldst pity me.

HELLENA [*aside*]   Now, if I should be hanged, I can't be angry with him, he dissembles so heartily.—Alas, good captain, what pains you have taken—now were I ungrateful not to reward so true a servant.

WILLMORE   Poor soul! That's kindly said, I see thou bearest a conscience. Come then, for a beginning show me thy dear face.

HELLENA   I'm afraid, my small acquaintance, you have been staying that swingeing stomach you boasted of this morning; I then remember my little collation would have gone down with you without the sauce of a handsome face—is your stomach so queasy now?

WILLMORE   Faith, long fasting, child, spoils a man's appetite—yet if you durst treat, I could so lay about me still—

HELLENA   And would you fall to, before a priest says grace?

WILLMORE   Oh fie, fie! What an old, out-of-fashioned thing hast thou named! Thou couldst not dash me more out of countenance shouldst thou show me an ugly face.

Whilst he is seemingly courting HELLENA, *enter* ANGELLICA,
MORETTA, BISKEY *and* SEBASTIAN *all in masquerade;*
ANGELLICA *sees* WILLMORE *and stares*

ANGELLICA   Heavens, 'tis he! And passionately fond to see another woman.

MORETTA   What could you less expect from such a swaggerer?

ANGELLICA   Expect? As much as I paid him, a heart entire,
        Which I had pride enough to think whene'er I gave,
        It would have raised the man above the vulgar,
        Made him all soul, and that all soft and constant.

HELLENA   You see, captain, how willing I am to be friends with you till time and ill luck make us lovers, and ask you the question first, rather than put your modesty to the blush by asking me. For (alas!) I know you captains are such strict men, and such severe observers of your vows to chastity, that 'twill be hard to prevail with your tender conscience to marry a young willing maid.

WILLMORE   Do not abuse me, for fear I should take thee at thy word and marry thee indeed, which I'm sure will be revenge sufficient.

HELLENA   O' my conscience, that will be our destiny, because we are both of one humour. I am as inconstant as you, for I have considered, captain, that a handsome woman has a great deal to do whilst her face is good, for then is our harvest-time to gather friends; and should I in these days of my youth, catch a fit of foolish constancy, I were undone; 'tis loitering by daylight in our great journey. Therefore, I declare I'll allow but one year for love, one year for indifference, and one year for hate, and then—go hang yourself—for I profess myself the gay, the kind, and the inconstant—the devil's in't if this won't please you.

WILLMORE   Oh, most damnably—I have a heart with a hole quite through it too, no prison mine to keep a mistress in.

ANGELLICA [*aside*]   Perjured man! How I believe thee now.

HELLENA   Well, I see our business as well as humours are alike; yours to cozen as many maids as will trust you, and I as many men as have faith—see if I have not as desperate a lying look as you can have for the heart of you. [*pulls off her vizard; he starts*]—How do you like it, captain?

WILLMORE   Like it! By heaven, I never saw so much beauty! Oh the charms of those sprightly black eyes! That strangely fair face, full of smiles and dimples! Those soft round melting cherry lips! And small even white teeth! Not to be expressed, but silently adored! [*she replaces her mask*]—

Oh, one look more! And strike me dumb, or I shall repeat nothing else till I am mad.   [*he seems to court her to pull off her vizard: she refuses*]

ANGELLICA   I can endure no more—nor is it fit to interrupt him, for if I do, my jealousy has so destroyed my reason, I shall undo him—therefore I'll retire. [*to one of her* BRAVOES] And you, Sebastian, follow that woman, and learn who 'tis; [*to the other* BRAVO] while you tell the fugitive, I would speak to him instantly.   [*exit*]

[*this while* FLORINDA *is talking to* BELVILE, *who stands sullenly;* FREDERICK *courting* VALERIA]

VALERIA   Prithee, dear stranger, be not so sullen, for though you have lost your love, you see my friend frankly offers you hers to play with in the meantime.

BELVILE   Faith, madam, I am sorry I can't play at her game.

FREDERICK   Pray leave your intercession, and mind your own affair. They'll better agree apart; he's a modest sigher in company, but alone no woman 'scapes him.

FLORINDA   Sure, he does but rally—yet if it should be true—I'll tempt him farther. Believe me, noble stranger, I'm no common mistress—and for a little proof on't—wear this jewel—nay, take it, sir, 'tis right, and bills of exchange may sometimes miscarry.

BELVILE   Madam, why am I chose out of all mankind to be the object of your bounty?

VALERIA   That's another civil question asked.

FREDERICK   Pox of 's modesty, it spoils his own markets, and hinders mine.

FLORINDA   Sir, from my window I have often seen you, and women of quality have so few opportunities for love, that we ought to lose none.

FREDERICK   Aye, this is something! Here's a woman! [*to* VALERIA] When shall I be blest with so much kindness from your fair mouth? [*aside to* BELVILE] Take the jewel, fool.

BELVILE   You tempt me strangely, madam, every way.

FLORINDA [*aside*]   So, if I find him false, my whole repose is gone.

BELVILE   And but for a vow I've made to a very lady, this goodness had subdued me.

FREDERICK   Pox on't, be kind, in pity to me be kind, for I am to thrive here but as you treat her friend.

HELLENA   Tell me what you did in yonder house, and I'll unmask.

WILLMORE   Yonder house?—Oh—I went to—a—to—why, there's a friend of mine lives there.

HELLENA   What a she, or a he friend?

WILLMORE   A man upon honour! A man—A she friend?—No, no, madam, you have done my business, I thank you.

HELLENA   And was't your man friend that had more darts in his eyes than Cupid carries in's whole budget of arrows?

WILLMORE   So—

HELLENA   "Ah, such a *bona roba*! To be in her arms is lying in *fresco*, all perfumed air about me"—was this your man friend too?

WILLMORE   So—

HELLENA   That gave you the he and the she gold, that begets young pleasures?

WILLMORE   Well, well, madam, then you see there are ladies in the world that will not be cruel—there are, madam, there are—

HELLENA   And there be men too, as fine, wild inconstant fellows as yourself, there be, captain, there be, if you go to that now—therefore I'm resolved—

WILLMORE   Oh!

HELLENA   To see your face no more—

WILLMORE   Oh!

HELLENA   Till tomorrow.

WILLMORE   Egad, you frighted me.

HELLENA   Nor then neither, unless you'll swear never to see that lady more.

WILLMORE   See her!—Why, never to think of womankind again.

HELLENA   Kneel—and swear.   [*he kneels, she gives him her hand*]

WILLMORE   I do, never to think—to see—to love—nor lie—with any but thyself.

HELLENA   Kiss the book.

WILLMORE   Oh, most religious.   [*kisses her hand*]

HELLENA   Now, what a wicked creature am I, to damn a proper fellow.

CALLIS [*to* FLORINDA]   Madam, I'll stay no longer, 'tis e'en dark.

FLORINDA   However, sir, I'll leave this with you—that when I'm gone, you may repent the opportunity you have lost by your modesty.

        [*gives him the jewel which is her picture, and exits; he gazes after her*]

WILLMORE   'Twill be an age till tomorrow, and till then I will most impatiently expect you. Adieu, my dear pretty angel.

                                    [*exeunt all the women*]

BELVILE   Ha! Florinda's picture—'twas she herself—what a dull dog was I! I would have given the world for one minute's discourse with her.

FREDERICK   This comes of your modesty! Ah, pox o'your vow, 'twas ten to one, but we had lost the jewel by 't.

BELVILE   Willmore! The blessed'st opportunity lost! Florinda, friends, Florinda!

WILLMORE   Ah, rogue! Such black eyes! Such a face! Such a mouth! Such teeth—and so much wit!

BELVILE   All, all, and a thousand charms besides.

WILLMORE   Why, dost thou know her?

BELVILE   Know her! Aye, aye, and a pox take me with all my heart for being modest.

WILLMORE   But harkee, friend of mine, are you my rival? And have I been only beating the bush all this while?

BELVILE   I understand thee not—I'm mad—see here—

                                                                    [*shows the picture*]

WILLMORE   Ha! Whose picture's this? 'Tis a fine wench!

FREDERICK   The colonel's mistress, sir.

WILLMORE   Oh, oh here—I thought 't had been another prize—come, come, a bottle will set thee right again.   [*gives the picture back*]

BELVILE   I am content to try, and by that time 'twill be late enough for our design.

WILLMORE   Agreed.

    Love does all day the soul's great empire keep,
    But wine at night lulls the soft god asleep.   [*exeunt*]

SCENE II

LUCETTA'S *house*

Enter BLUNT *and* LUCETTA *with a light*

LUCETTA   Now we are safe and free; no fears of the coming home of my old jealous husband, which made me a little thoughtful when you came in first—but now love is all the business of my soul.

BLUNT   I am transported! [*aside*] Pox on't, that I had but some fine things to say to her, such as lovers use—I was a fool not to learn of Fred a little by heart before I came—something I must say—'Sheartlikins, sweet soul! I am not used to compliment, but I'm an honest gentleman, and thy humble servant.

LUCETTA   I have nothing to pay for so great a favour, but such a love as cannot but be great, since at first sight of that sweet face and shape, it made me your absolute captive.

BLUNT [*aside*]   Kind heart! How prettily she talks! Egad, I'll show her husband a Spanish trick; send him out of the world and marry her. She's damnably in love with me, and will ne'er mind settlements, and so there's that saved.

LUCETTA   Well, sir, I'll go and undress me, and be with you instantly.

BLUNT   Make haste then, for 'sheartlikins, dear soul, thou canst not guess at the pain of a longing lover, when his joys are drawn within the compass of a few minutes.

LUCETTA   You speak my sense, and I'll make haste to prove it.   [*exit*]

BLUNT   'Tis a rare girl! And this one night's enjoyment with her will be worth all the days I ever passed in Essex. Would she would go with me into England, though to say truth there's plenty of whores already. But a pox on 'em, they are such mercenary prodigal whores, that they want such a one as this, that's free and generous, to give 'em good examples. Why, what a house she has, how rich and fine!

Enter SANCHO

SANCHO   Sir, my lady has sent me to conduct you to her chamber.

BLUNT   Sir, I shall be proud to follow—here's one of her servants too! 'Sheartlikins, by his garb and gravity he might be a Justice of Peace in Essex, and is but a pimp here.   [*exeunt*]

SCENE III

The scene changes to a chamber with an alcove bed in't, a table, etc.,
LUCETTA *in bed*

Enter SANCHO *and* BLUNT, *who takes the candle of* SANCHO *at the door*

SANCHO   Sir, my commission reaches no farther.

BLUNT   I'll excuse your compliment—what, in bed, my sweet mistress?

LUCETTA   You see, I still outdo you in kindness.

BLUNT   And thou shalt see what haste I'll make to quit scores—oh, the luckiest rogue! [*he undresses himself*]

LUCETTA   Should you be false or cruel now!

BLUNT   False! 'Sheartlikins, what dost thou take me for? A Jew? An insensible heathen? A pox of thy old jealous husband: an he were dead, egad, sweet soul, it should be none of my fault if I did not marry thee.

LUCETTA   It never should be mine.

BLUNT   Good soul! I'm the fortunest dog!

LUCETTA   Are you not undressed yet?

BLUNT   As much as my impatience will permit.
                          [*goes towards the bed in his shirt, drawers, etc.*]

LUCETTA   Hold, sir, put out the light, it may betray us else.

BLUNT   Anything; I need no other light but that of thine eyes! 'Sheartlikins, there I think I had it.
                [*puts out the candle, the bed descends, he gropes about to find it*]
—Why—why—where am I got? What, not yet?—Where are you sweetest? Ah, the rogue's silent now—a pretty love-trick this—How she'll

laugh at me anon! You need not, my dear rogue, you need not! I'm on fire already—come, come, now call me in pity. Sure, I'm enchanted! I have been round the chamber, and can find neither woman, nor bed. I locked the door, I'm sure she cannot go that way—or if she could, the bed could not. Enough, enough, my pretty wanton, do not carry the jest too far—[*lights on a trap, and is let down*] Ha, betrayed! Dogs! Rogues! Pimps!—Help! Help!

ENTER LUCETTA, PHILIPPO, *and* SANCHO *with a light*

PHILIPPO   Ha, ha, ha, he's dispatched finely.

LUCETTA   Now, sir, had I been coy, we had missed of this booty.

PHILIPPO   Nay, when I saw 'twas a substantial fool, I was mollified; but when you dote upon a serenading coxcomb, upon a face, fine clothes, and a lute, it makes me rage.

LUCETTA   You know I never was guilty of that folly, my dear Philippo, but with yourself—but come, let's see what we have got by this.

PHILIPPO   A rich coat! Sword and hat—these breeches, too, are well lined! See here, a gold watch! A purse—Ha, gold! At least two hundred pistoles! A bunch of diamond rings! And one with the family arms! A gold box—with a medal of his king! And his lady mother's picture!— These were sacred relics, believe me! See, the waistband of his breeches have a mine of gold—old Queen Bess's! We have a quarrel to her ever since eighty-eight, and may therefore justify the theft, the Inquisition might have committed it.

LUCETTA   See, a bracelet of bowed gold! These his sister tied about his arm at parting. But well—for all this, I fear his being a stranger may make a noise and hinder our trade with them hereafter.

PHILIPPO   That's our security; he is not only a stranger to us, but to the country too. The common shore into which he is descended, thou knowst conducts him into another street, which this light will hinder him from ever finding again. He knows neither your name, nor that of the street where your house is, nay, nor the way to his own lodgings.

LUCETTA   And art not thou an unmerciful rogue, not to afford him one night for all this? I should not have been such a Jew.

PHILIPPO   Blame me not, Lucetta, to keep as much of thee as I can to myself. Come, that thought makes me wanton! Let's to bed! Sancho, lock up these.

> This is the fleece which fools do bear,
> Designed for witty men to shear.   [*exeunt*]

SCENE IV

The scene changes, and discovers BLUNT *creeping out of a common shore, his face, etc. all dirty*

BLUNT [*climbing up*]   Oh Lord! I am got out at last, and (which is a miracle) without a clue—and now to damning and cursing! But if that would ease me, where shall I begin? With my fortune, myself, or the quean that cozened me? What a dog was I to believe in woman! Oh coxcomb! Ignorant, conceited coxcomb! To fancy she could be enamoured with my person—at first sight enamoured!—Oh, I'm a cursed puppy! 'Tis plain, fool was writ upon my forehead! She perceived it!—Saw the Essex calf there—for what allurements could there be in this countenance, which I can endure, because I'm acquainted with it? Oh, dull silly dog! To be thus soothed into a cozening! Had I been drunk, I might fondly have credited the young quean!—But as I was in my right wits, to be thus cheated confirms it, I am a dull believing English country fop. But my comrades! Death and the devil! There's the worst of all—then a ballad will be sung tomorrow on the Prado, to a lousy tune, of the enchanted 'squire and the annihilated damsel—but Fred, that rogue, and the colonel will abuse me beyond all Christian patience. Had she left me my clothes, I have a bill of exchange at home would have saved my credit, but now all hope is taken from me. Well, I'll home (if I can find the way) with this consolation: that I am not the first kind, believing coxcomb, but there are, gallants, many such good natures amongst ye.

And though you've better arts to hide your follies,
'Adsheartlikins y'are all as arrant cullies.   [*exit*]

SCENE V

The garden in the night

Enter FLORINDA *in an undress, with a key and a little box*

FLORINDA   Well, thus far I'm in my way to happiness: I have got myself free from Callis; my brother too, I find by yonder light, is got into his cabinet, and thinks not of me; I have by good fortune got the key of the garden back door. I'll open it to prevent Belvile's knocking—a little noise will now alarm my brother. Now am I as fearful as a young thief. [*unlocks the door*] Hark, what noise is that? Oh, 'twas the wind that played amongst the boughs—Belvile stays long, methinks—it's time. Stay—for fear of a surprise, I'll hide these jewels in yonder jessamin.

[*she goes to lay down the box*]

Enter WILLMORE *drunk*

WILLMORE   What the devil became of these fellows, Belvile and Frederick? They promised to stay at the next corner for me, but who the devil knows the corner of a full moon—now—whereabouts am I? Hah—what have we here, a garden!—A very convenient place to sleep in. Hah—what has God sent us here?—A female!—By this light, a woman! I'm a dog if it be not a very wench!

FLORINDA   He's come! Ha—who's there?

WILLMORE   Sweet soul! Let me salute thy shoestring.

FLORINDA   'Tis not my Belvile. Good heavens! I know him not.— Who are you, and from whence come you?

WILLMORE   Prithee, prithee, child—not so many hard questions. Let it suffice I am here, child—come, come kiss me.

FLORINDA   Good gods! What luck is mine!

WILLMORE   Only good luck, child, parlous good luck—come hither—'tis a delicate shining wench—by this hand, she's perfumed and smells like any nosegay. Prithee, dear soul, let's not play the fool, and lose time—precious time—for as Gad shall save me, I'm as honest a fellow as breathes, though I'm a little disguised at present. Come, I say—why, thou mayst be free with me, I'll be very secret. I'll not boast who obliged me, not I—for hang me if I know thy name.

FLORINDA   Heavens! What a filthy beast is this?

WILLMORE   I am so, and thou ought'st the sooner to lie with me for that reason—for look you, child, there will be no sin in't, because 'twas neither designed nor premeditated. 'Tis pure accident on both sides— that's a certain thing now. Indeed, should I make love to you, and you vow fidelity—and swear and lie till you believed and yielded—that were to make it wilful fornication—the crying sin of the nation. Thou art therefore (as thou art a good Christian) obliged in conscience to deny me nothing. Now—come, be kind without any more idle prating.

FLORINDA   Oh, I am ruined!—Wicked man, unhand me.

WILLMORE   Wicked! Egad, child, a judge, were he young and vigorous, and saw those eyes of thine, would know 'twas they gave the first blow—the first provocation. Come, prithee, let's lose no time, I say—this is a fine convenient place.

FLORINDA   Sir, let me go, I conjure you, or I'll call out.

WILLMORE   Aye, aye, you were best to call witness to see how finely you treat me—do—

FLORINDA   I'll cry murder! Rape! Or anything, if you do not instantly let me go.

WILLMORE   A rape! Come, come, you lie, you baggage, you lie. What, I'll warrant you would fain have the world believe now that you are not so forward as I. No, not you. Why, at this time of night was your cobweb door set open, dear spider, but to catch flies? Hah! Come—or I shall be damnably angry. Why, what a coil is here—

FLORINDA   Sir, can you think—

WILLMORE   That you would do't for nothing? Oh, oh, I find what you would be at—look here, here's a pistole for you. Here's a work indeed—here—take it I say—

FLORINDA   For heaven's sake, sir, as you're a gentleman—

WILLMORE   So—now—now—she would be wheedling me for more. What, you will not take it then—you are resolved you will not? Come, come take it, or I'll put it up again—for look ye, I never give more. Why how now, mistress, are you so high i'th'mouth a pistole won't down with you? Hah—why, what a work's here?—In good time. Come, no struggling be gone—but an y'are good at a dumb wrestle, I'm for ye—look ye—I'm for ye—   [*she struggles with him*]

Enter BELVILE *and* FREDERICK

BELVILE   The door is open. A pox of this mad fellow, I'm angry that we've lost him, I durst have sworn he had followed us.

FREDERICK   But you were so hasty, colonel, to be gone.

FLORINDA   Help! Help! Murder! Help—oh, I am ruined.

BELVILE   Ha! Sure that's Florinda's voice. [*comes up to them*] A man! Villain, let go that lady!

                    [*a noise;* WILLMORE *turns and draws;* FREDERICK *interposes*]

FLORINDA   Belvile! Heavens! My brother too is coming, and 'twill be impossible to escape. Belvile, I conjure you to walk under my chamber window, from whence I'll give you some instructions what to do—this rude man has undone us.   [*exit*]

WILLMORE   Belvile!

Enter PEDRO, STEPHANO, *and other servants with lights*

PEDRO   I'm betrayed! Run, Stephano, and see if Florinda be safe.
                                        [*exit* STEPHANO]
                    [*they fight, and* PEDRO'S *party beats 'em out*]
So, whoe'er they be, all is not well. I'll to Florinda's chamber.
                                        [*going out, meets* STEPHANO]

STEPHANO   You need not, sir, the poor lady's fast asleep and thinks no harm. I would not wake her, sir, for fear of frightning her with your danger.

PEDRO   I'm glad she's there. Rascals, how came the garden door open?

STEPHANO   That question comes too late, sir; some of my fellow servants masquerading, I'll warrant.

PEDRO   Masquerading! A leud custom to debauch our youth—there's something more in this then I imagine.   [*exeunt*]

SCENE VI

Scene changes to the street

Enter BELVILE *in a rage.* FREDERICK *holding him,*
and WILLMORE *melancholy*

WILLMORE   Why, how the devil should I know Florinda?

BELVILE   A plague of your ignorance! If it had not been Florinda, must you be a beast—a brute—a senseless swine?

WILLMORE   Well, sir, you see I am endured with patience—I can bear—though, egad, y'are very free with me, methinks. I was in good hopes the quarrel would have been on my side, for so uncivilly interrupting me.

BELVILE   Peace, brute, whilst thou'rt safe! Oh, I'm distracted.

WILLMORE   Nay, nay, I'm an unlucky dog, that's certain.

BELVILE   Ah, curse upon the star that ruled my birth! Or whatsoever other influence that makes me still so wretched.

WILLMORE   Thou break'st my heart with these complaints. There is no star in fault, no influence but sack, the cursed sack I drunk.

FREDERICK   Why, how the devil came you so drunk?

WILLMORE   Why, how the devil came you so sober?

BELVILE   A curse upon his thin skull, he was always beforehand that way.

FREDERICK   Prithee, dear colonel, forgive him; he's sorry for his fault.

BELVILE   He's always so after he has done a mischief—a plague on all such brutes.

WILLMORE   By this light, I took her for an arrant harlot.

BELVILE   Damn your debauched opinion! Tell me, sot, hadst thou so much sense and light about thee to distinguish her woman, and couldst not see something about her face and person to strike an awful reverence into thy soul?

WILLMORE   Faith no, I considered her as mere a woman as I could wish.

BELVILE   'Sdeath, I have no patience—draw, or I'll kill you.

WILLMORE   Let that alone till tomorrow, and if I set not all right again, use your pleasure.

BELVILE   Tomorrow! Damn it,
        The spiteful light will lead me to no happiness.
        Tomorrow is Antonio's, and perhaps

Guides him to my undoing. Oh, that I could meet
This rival! This powerful fortunate!

WILLMORE   What then?

BELVILE   Let thy own reason, or my rage, instruct thee.

WILLMORE   I shall be finely informed then, no doubt. Hear me, colonel—hear me—show me the man and I'll do his business.

BELVILE   I know him no more than thou, or if I did I should not need thy aid.

WILLMORE   This you say is Angellica's house; I promised the kind baggage to lie with her tonight.   [*offers to go in*]

Enter ANTONIO *and his* PAGE.
ANTONIO *knocks on the door with the hilt of his sword*

ANTONIO   You paid the thousand crowns I directed?

PAGE   To the lady's old woman, sir, I did.

WILLMORE   Who the devil have we here?

BELVILE   I'll now plant myself under Florinda's window, and if I find no comfort there, I'll die.   [*exeunt* BELVILE *and* FREDERICK]

Enter MORETTA

MORETTA   Page!

PAGE   Here's my lord.

WILLMORE   How is this? A picaroon going to board my frigate? Here's one chase-gun for you.

[*drawing his sword, jostles* ANTONIO,
who turns and draws; they fight, ANTONIO *falls*]

MORETTA   Oh bless us! We're all undone!

[*runs in and shuts the door*]

PAGE   Help! Murder!   [BELVILE *returns at the noise of fighting*]

BELVILE   Ha! The mad rogue's engaged in some unlucky adventure again.

Enter two or three MASQUERADERS

MASQUERADERS   Ha! A man killed!

WILLMORE   How! A man killed! Then I'll go home to sleep.

[*puts up and reels out; exeunt* MASQUERADERS *another way*]

BELVILE   Who should it be? Pray heaven the rogue is safe, for all my quarrel to him.

As BELVILE *is groping about, enter an* OFFICER *and* SIX SOLDIERS

SOLDIER   Who's there?

OFFICER   So, here's one dispatched—secure the murderer.

BELVILE   Do not mistake my charity for murder! I came to his assistance.   [*soldiers seize on* BELVILE]

OFFICER   That shall be tried, sir—St. Jago, swords drawn in the carnival!   [*goes to* ANTONIO]

ANTONIO   Thy hand, prithee.

OFFICER   Ha! Don Antonio! Look well to the villain there. How is
it, sir?

ANTONIO   I'm hurt.

BELVILE   Has my humanity made me a criminal?

OFFICER   Away with him.

BELVILE   What a cursed chance is this!   [*exeunt soldiers with* BELVILE]

ANTONIO [*to the* OFFICER]   This is the man that has set upon me
twice. Carry him to my apartment, till you have farther orders from me.

[*exit* ANTONIO, *led*]

ACT IV

SCENE I

A fine room

Discovers BELVILE *as by dark, alone*

BELVILE   When shall I be weary of railing on Fortune, who is resolved never to turn with smiles upon me? Two such defeats in one night none but the devil, and that mad rogue, could have contrived to have plagued me with. I am here a prisoner, but where, heaven knows—and if there be murder done, I can soon decide the fate of a stranger in a nation without mercy. Yet this is nothing to the torture my soul bows with when I think of losing my fair, my dear Florinda. Hark, my door opens— a light—a man—and seems of quality—armed, too! Now shall I die like a dog, without defence.

Enter ANTONIO *in a night-gown, with a light; his arm in a scarf, and a sword under his arm; he sets the candle on the table*

ANTONIO   Sir, I come to know what injuries I have done you, that could provoke you to so mean an action as to attack me basely, without allowing time for my defence.

BELVILE   Sir, for a man in my circumstances to plead innocence would look like fear. But view me well, and you will find no marks of coward on me, nor anything that betrays that brutality you accuse me with.

ANTONIO   In vain, sir, you impose upon my sense. You are not only he who drew on me last night, but yesterday before the same house, that of Angellica.
   Yet there is something in your face and mien
   That makes me wish I were mistaken.

BELVILE   I own I fought today in the defence of a friend of mine, with whom you (if you're the same) and your party were first engaged.
   Perhaps you think this crime enough to kill me,
   But if you do, I cannot fear you'll do it basely.

ANTONIO   No, sir, I'll make you fit for a defence with this.

[gives him the sword]

BELVILE   This gallantry surprises me—nor know I how to use this
present, sir, against a man so brave.

ANTONIO   You shall not need.

    For know, I come to snatch you from a danger

    That is decreed against you:

    Perhaps your life or long imprisonment;

    And 'twas with so much courage you offended,

    I cannot see you punished.

BELVILE   How shall I pay this generosity?

ANTONIO   It had been safer to have killed another

    Than have attempted me.

    To show your danger, sir, I'll let you know my quality;

    And 'tis the viceroy's son whom you have wounded here.

BELVILE   The viceroy's son!

    [aside] Death and confusion! Was this plague reserved

    To complete all the rest—obliged by him!

    The man of all the world I would destroy.

ANTONIO   You seem disordered, sir.

BELVILE   Yes, trust me, sir, I am, and 'tis with pain

    That man receives such bounties,

    Who wants the power to pay 'em back again.

ANTONIO   To gallant spirits 'tis indeed uneasy;

    But you may quickly overpay me, sir.

BELVILE   Then I am well. *[aside]* Kind heaven, but set us even,

    That I may fight with him, and keep my honour safe.

    —Oh, I'm impatient, sir, to be discounting

    The mighty debt I owe you, command me quickly.

ANTONIO   I have a quarrel with a rival, sir,

    About the maid we love.

BELVILE *[aside]*   Death, 'tis Florinda he means—

    That thought destroys my reason,

    And I shall kill him—

ANTONIO   My rival, sir,

    Is one has all the virtues man can boast of—

BELVILE *[aside]*   Death! Who should this be?

ANTONIO   He challenged me to meet him on the Molo

    As soon as day appeared, but last night's quarrel

    Has made my arm unfit to guide a sword.

BELVILE   I apprehend you, sir, you'd have me kill the man

    That lays a claim to the maid you speak of.

    I'll do't—I'll fly to do't!

ANTONIO   Sir, do you know her?

BELVILE   No, sir, but 'tis enough she is admired by you.

ANTONIO   Sir, I shall rob you of the glory on't,
      For you must fight under my name and dress.

BELVILE   That opinion must be strangely obliging that makes you
think I can personate the brave Antonio, whom I can but strive to imi-
tate.

ANTONIO   You say too much to my advantage.
      Come, sir, the day appears that calls you forth.
      Within, sir, is the habit.   [*exit* ANTONIO]

BELVILE   Fantastic Fortune, thou deceitful light,
      That cheats the wearied traveller by night,
      Though on a precipice each step you tread,
      I am resolved to follow where you lead.   [*exit*]

SCENE II

The Molo

Enter FLORINDA *and* CALLIS *in masks with* STEPHANO

FLORINDA [*aside*]   I'm dying with my fears. Belvile's not coming as I
expected under my window,
      Makes me believe that all those fears were true.
      —Canst thou not tell with whom my brother fights?

STEPHANO   No, madam, they were both in masquerade. I was by
when they challenged one another, and they had decided the question
then, but were prevented by some cavaliers, which made 'em put it off
till now—but I am sure 'tis about you they fight.

FLORINDA [*aside*]   Nay, then, 'tis with Belvile, for what other lover
have I that dares fight for me, except Antonio? And he is too much in
favour with my brother. If it be he, for whom shall I direct my prayers to
heaven?

STEPHANO   Madam, I must leave you, for if my master see me, I shall
be hanged for being your conductor—I escaped narrowly for the excuse
I made for you last night i' th' garden.

FLORINDA   And I'll reward thee for't—prithee, no more.
                                                      [*exit* STEPHANO]

Enter DON PEDRO *in his masquing habit*

PEDRO   Antonio's late today, the place will fill, and we may be
prevented.   [*walks about*]

FLORINDA [*aside*]   Antonio! Sure I heard amiss.

PEDRO   But who will not excuse a happy lover

When soft fair arms confine the yielding neck;
And the kind whisper languishingly breathes,
"Must you be gone so soon?"
Sure, I had dwelt forever on her bosom—
But stay, he's here.

Enter BELVILE *dressed in* ANTONIO'S *clothes*

FLORINDA   'Tis not Belvile, half my fears are vanished.

PEDRO   Antonio!

BELVILE [*aside*]   This must be he.

You're early, sir—I do not use to be outdone this way.

PEDRO   The wretched, sir, are watchful, and 'tis enough
You've the advantage of me in Angellica.

BELVILE [*aside*]   Angellica! Or I've mistook my man, or else Antonio.
Can he forget his interest in Florinda,
And fight for common prize?

PEDRO   Come, sir, you know our terms—

BELVILE [*aside*]   By heaven, not I.

—No talking, I am ready, sir.   [*offers to fight;* FLORINDA *runs in*]

FLORINDA [*to* BELVILE]   O, hold! Whoe'er you be, I do conjure you,
hold!
If you strike here—I die.

PEDRO   Florinda!

BELVILE   Florinda imploring for my rival!

PEDRO   Away, this kindness is unseasonable.
     [*puts her by, they fight; she runs in just as* BELVILE *disarms* PEDRO]

FLORINDA   Who are you, sir, that dares deny my prayers?

BELVILE   Thy prayers destroy him. If thou wouldst preserve him,
Do that thou'rt unacquainted with and curse him.
                                          [*she holds him*]

FLORINDA   By all you hold most dear, by her you love,
I do conjure you, touch him not.

BELVILE   By her I love!
See—I obey—and at your feet resign,
The useless trophy of my victory.   [*lays his sword at her feet*]

PEDRO   Antonio, you've done enough to prove you love Florinda.

BELVILE   Love Florinda!
Does heaven love adoration, prayer, or penitence! Love her! Here,
sir—your sword again. [*snatches up the sword and gives it him*] Upon
this truth, I'll fight my life away.

PEDRO   No, you've redeemed my sister, and my friendship!
          [*he gives him* FLORINDA *and pulls off his vizard to show his face,
                                          and puts it on again*]

BELVILE   Don Pedro!

PEDRO   Can you resign your claims to other women,
  And give your heart entirely to Florinda?

BELVILE   Entire as dying saints' confessions are!
  I can delay my happiness no longer.
  This minute let me make Florinda mine!

PEDRO   This minute let it be—no time so proper,
  This night my father will arrive from Rome,
  And possibly may hinder what we propose!

FLORINDA   Oh heavens! This minute!

    Enter MASQUERADERS *and pass over*

BELVILE   Oh, do not ruin me!

PEDRO   The place begins to fill, and that we may not be observed, do you walk off to St Peter's church, where I will meet you and conclude your happiness.

BELVILE   I'll meet you there.—[*aside*] If there be no more saints' churches in Naples.

FLORINDA   Oh stay, sir, and recall your hasty doom!
  Alas, I have not yet prepared my heart
  To entertain so strange a guest.

PEDRO   Away, this silly modesty is assumed too late.

BELVILE   Heaven, madam! What do you do?

FLORINDA   Do? Despise the man that lays a tyrant's claim
  To what he ought to conquer by submission.

BELVILE   You do not know me—move a little this way.
            [*draws her aside*]

FLORINDA   Yes, you may force me even to the altar,
  But not the holy man that offers there
  Shall force me to be thine. [PEDRO *talks to* CALLIS *this while*]

BELVILE   Oh, do not lose so blest an opportunity!
  See—'tis your Belvile—not Antonio,
  Whom your mistaken scorn and anger ruins. [*pulls off his vizard*]

FLORINDA   Belvile!
  Where was my soul it could not meet thy voice
  And take this knowledge in?

 As they are talking, enter WILLMORE *finely dressed, and* FREDERICK

WILLMORE   No intelligence! No news of Belvile yet—well, I am the most unlucky rascal in nature—ha—am I deceived? Or is it he? Look, Fred—'tis he—my dear Belvile!

    [*runs and embraces him;* BELVILE'S *vizard falls out on's hand*]

BELVILE   Hell and confusion seize thee!

PEDRO   Ha! Belvile! I beg your pardon, sir.

> [*takes* FLORINDA *from him*]

BELVILE   Nay touch her not, she's mine by conquest, sir;
    I won her by my sword.

WILLMORE   Didst thou so? And egad, child, we'll keep her by the
sword.   [*draws on* PEDRO; BELVILE *goes between*]

BELVILE   Stand off!
    Thou'rt so profanely lewd, so cursed by heaven,
    All quarrels thou espousest must be fatal.

WILLMORE   Nay, an you be so hot, my valour's coy,
    And shall be courted when you want it next.   [*puts up his sword*]

BELVILE [*to* PEDRO]   You know I ought to claim a victor's right.
    But you're the brother to divine Florinda,
    To whom I'm such a slave. To purchase her
    I durst not hurt the man she holds so dear.

PEDRO   'Twas by Antonio's, not by Belvile's sword
    This question should have been decided, sir.
    I must confess much to your bravery's due,
    Both now, and when I met you last in arms.
    But I am nicely punctual in my word,
    As men of honour ought, and beg your pardon.
    For this mistake another time shall clear.
    [*aside to* FLORINDA *as they are going out*]
    This was some plot between you and Belvile.
    But I'll prevent you.

> [BELVILE *looks after her and begins to walk up and down in rage*]

WILLMORE   Do not be modest now and lose the woman, but if we
shall fetch her back so—

BELVILE   Do not speak to me—

WILLMORE   Not speak to you! Egad, I'll speak to you, and will be answered too.

BELVILE   Will you, sir—

WILLMORE   I know I've done some mischief, but I'm so dull a puppy,
that I am the son of a whore if I know how, or where—prithee inform
my understanding—

BELVILE   Leave me, I say, and leave me instantly.

WILLMORE   I will not leave you in this humour, nor till I know my
crime.

BELVILE   Death, I'll tell you, sir—

> [*draws and runs at* WILLMORE; *he runs out,*
> BELVILE *after him;* FREDERICK *interposes*]

Enter ANGELLICA, MORETTA *and* SEBASTIAN

ANGELLICA   Ha—Sebastian—
    Is not that Willmore? Haste, haste and bring him back.

FREDERICK   The colonel's mad—I never saw him thus before. I'll
after 'em lest he do some mischief, for I am sure Willmore will not draw
on him.   [*exit*]

ANGELLICA   I am all rage! My first desires defeated!
    For one for aught he knows that has no
    Other merit than her quality—
    Her being Don Pedro's sister. He loves her!
    I know 'tis so—dull, dull, insensible—
    He will not see me now though oft invited;
    And broke his word last night—false, perjured man!
    He that but yesterday fought for my favours,
    And would have made his life a sacrifice
    To've gained one night with me,
    Must now be hired and courted to my arms.

MORETTA   I told you what would come on't, but Moretta's an old
doting fool. Why did you give him five hundred crowns, but to set himself out for other lovers? You should have kept him poor, if you had
meant to have had any good from him.

ANGELLICA   Oh, name not such mean trifles! Had I given
    Him all my youth has earned from sin,
    I had not lost a thought, nor sigh upon't.
    But I have given him my eternal rest,
    My whole repose, my future joys, my heart!
    My virgin heart, Moretta! Oh 'tis gone!

MORETTA   Curse on him, here he comes.
    How fine she has made him too.

  Enter WILLMORE *and* SEBASTIAN; ANGELLICA *turns and walks away*

WILLMORE   How now, turned shadow!
    Fly when I pursue, and follow when I fly!
    [*sings*] Stay, gentle shadow of my dove
    And tell me ere I go,
    Whether the substance may not prove
    A fleeting thing like you.   [*as she turns she looks on him*]
    There's a soft, kind look remaining yet.

ANGELLICA   Well, sir, you may be gay; all happiness,
    All joys pursue you still. Fortune's your slave,
    And gives you every hour choice of new hearts
    And beauties, till you are cloyed with the repeated
    Bliss which others vainly languish for.
    But know, false man, that I shall be revenged. [*turns away in rage*]

WILLMORE   So, gad, there are of those faint-hearted lovers, whom such a sharp lesson next their hearts would make as impotent as fourscore. Pox o'this whining! My business is to laugh and love. A pox on't, I hate your sullen lover: a man shall lose as much time to put you in humour now, as would serve to gain a new woman.

ANGELLICA   I scorn to cool that fire I cannot raise,
    Or do the drudgery of your virtuous mistress.

WILLMORE   A virtuous mistress! Death, what a thing thou hast found out for me! Why, what the devil should I do with a virtuous woman? A sort of ill-natured creatures, that take a pride to torment a lover. Virtue is but an infirmity in woman; a disease that renders even the handsome ungrateful, while the ill-favoured, for want of solicitations and address, only fancy themselves so. I have lain with a woman of quality, who has all the while been railing at whores.

ANGELLICA   I will not answer for your mistress's virtue,
    Though she be young enough to know no guilt;
    And I could wish you would persuade my heart
    'Twas the two hundred thousand crowns you courted.

WILLMORE   Two hundred thousand crowns! What story's this? What trick? What woman?—Ha!

ANGELLICA   How strange you make it; have you forgot the creature you entertained on the piazza last night?

WILLMORE [aside]   Ha! My gypsy worth two hundred thousand crowns! Oh, how I long to be with her—pox, I knew she was of quality.

ANGELLICA   False man! I see my ruin in thy face.
    How many vows you breathed upon my bosom,
    Never to be unjust—have you forgot so soon?

WILLMORE   Faith no, I was just coming to repeat 'em—but here's a humour indeed—would make a man a saint. [aside] Would she would be angry enough to leave me, and command me not to wait on her.

Enter HELLENA *dressed in man's clothes*

HELLENA [aside]   This must be Angellica! I know it by her mumping matron here. Aye, aye, 'tis she! My mad captain's with her too, for all his swearing—how this unconstant humour makes me love him!
    —Pray, good grave gentlewoman, is not this Angellica?

MORETTA   My too young sir, it is—[aside] I hope 'tis one from Don Antonio.   [goes to ANGELLICA]

HELLENA [aside]   Well, something I'll do to vex him for this.

ANGELLICA   I will not speak with him; am I in humour to receive a lover?

WILLMORE   Not speak with him! Why I'll be gone—and wait your idler minutes—can I show less obedience to the thing I love so fondly?
                              [offers to go]

ANGELLICA   A fine excuse this! Stay—

WILLMORE   And hinder your advantage! Should I repay your boun-
ties so ungratefully?

ANGELLICA   Come hither, boy.
      [*to* WILLMORE] That I may let you see
      How much above the advantages you name,
      I prize one minute's joy with you.

WILLMORE   Oh, you destroy me with this endearment. [*impatient to
be gone*] Death! How shall I get away?—Madam, 'twill not be fit I should
be seen with you—besides, it will not be convenient—and I've a
friend—that's dangerously sick.

ANGELLICA   I see you're impatient—yet you shall stay.

WILLMORE [*aside*]   And miss my assignation with my gypsy.
                                        [*walks about impatiently*]
      [MORETTA *brings* HELLENA, *who addresses herself to* ANGELLICA]

HELLENA   Madam,
      You'll hardly pardon my intrusion,
      When you shall know my business!
      And I'm too young to tell my tale with art;
      But there must be a wondrous store of goodness,
      Where so much beauty dwells.

ANGELLICA   A pretty advocate, whoever sent thee.
      Prithee, proceed.—[*to* WILLMORE *who is stealing off*]
      Nay, sir, you shall not go.

WILLMORE [*aside*]   Then I shall lose my dear gypsy forever
      —Pox on't, she stays me out of spite.

HELLENA   I am related to a lady, madam,
      Young, rich, and nobly born, but has the fate
      To be in love with a young English gentleman.
      Strangely she loves him, at first sight she loved him,
      But did adore him when she heard him speak;
      For he, she said, had charms in every word,
      That failed not to surprise, to wound and conquer.

WILLMORE [*aside*]   Ha! Egad, I hope this concerns me.

ANGELLICA [*aside*]   'Tis my false man he means—would he were
gone. This praise will raise his pride, and ruin me—[*to* WILLMORE] Well,
since you are so impatient to be gone I will release you, sir.

WILLMORE [*aside*]   Nay, then, I'm sure 'twas me he spoke of, this cannot be the effects of kindness in her.
      —No, madam, I've considered better on't,
      And will not give you cause of jealousy.

ANGELLICA   But, sir, I've—business, that—

WILLMORE   This shall not do, I know 'tis but to try me.

ANGELLICA   Well, to your story, boy—[*aside*] though 'twill undo me.

HELLENA   With this addition to his other beauties,

     He won her unregarding tender heart.

     He vowed, and sighed, and swore he loved her dearly;

     And she believed the cunning flatterer,

     And thought herself the happiest maid alive.

     Today was the appointed time by both

     To consummate their bliss;

     The virgin, altar, and the priest were dressed,

     And while she languished for th'expected bridegroom,

     She heard he paid his broken vows to you.

WILLMORE [*aside*]   So, this is some dear rogue that's in love with me, and this way lets me know it; or if it be not me, he means someone whose place I may supply.

ANGELLICA   Now I perceive

     The cause of thy impatience to be gone,

     And all the business of this glorious dress.

WILLMORE   Damn the young prater, I know not what he means.

HELLENA   Madam,

     In your fair eyes I read too much concern,

     To tell my farther business.

ANGELLICA   Prithee, sweet youth, talk on, thou mayst perhaps

     Raise here a storm that may undo my passion,

     And then I'll grant thee anything.

HELLENA   Madam, 'tis to entreat you (oh, unreasonable)

     You would not see this stranger;

     For if you do, she vows you are undone,

     Though nature never made a man so excellent,

     And sure he 'ad been a god, but for inconstancy.

WILLMORE [*aside*]   Ah, rogue, how finely he's instructed!—

     'Tis plain; some woman that has seen me *en passant*.

ANGELLICA   Oh, I shall burn with jealousy! Do you know the man you speak of?

HELLENA   Yes, madam, he used to be in buff and scarlet.

ANGELLICA [*to* WILLMORE]   Thou, false as hell, what canst thou say to this?

WILLMORE   By heaven—

ANGELLICA   Hold, do not damn thyself—

HELLENA   Nor hope to be believed.   [*he walks about, they follow*]

ANGELLICA   Oh, perjured man!

     Is't thus you pay my generous passion back?

HELLENA   Why would you, sir, abuse my lady's faith?

ANGELLICA   And use me so inhumanly.

HELLENA   A maid so young, so innocent—

WILLMORE   Ah, young devil!

ANGELLICA   Dost thou not know thy life is in my power?

HELLENA   Or think my lady cannot be revenged?

WILLMORE [aside]   So, so, the storm comes finely on.

ANGELLICA   Now thou art silent, guilt has struck thee dumb.
     Oh, hadst thou still been so, I'd lived in safety.

                                          [she turns away and weeps]

WILLMORE [aside to HELLENA]   Sweetheart, the lady's name and house—quickly, I'm impatient to be with her.

                    [looks towards ANGELLICA to watch her turning,
                            and as she comes towards them he meets her]

HELLENA [aside]   So, now is he for another woman.

WILLMORE   The impudentest young thing in nature; I cannot persuade him out of his error, madam.

ANGELLICA   I know he's in the right—yet thou'st a tongue
     That would persuade him to deny his faith.   [in rage walks away]

WILLMORE [said softly to HELLENA]   Her name, her name, dear boy.

HELLENA   Have you forgot it, sir?

WILLMORE [aside]   Oh, I perceive he's not to know I am a stranger to his lady.

     —Yes, yes, I do know—but—I have forgot the—

                                              [ANGELLICA turns]

     —By heaven, such early confidence I never saw.

ANGELLICA   Did I not charge you with this mistress, sir?
     Which you denied, though I beheld your perjury.
     This little generosity of thine, has rendered back my heart.

                                                  [walks away]

WILLMORE   So, you have made sweet work here, my little mischief. Look your lady be kind and good-natured now, or I shall have but a cursed bargain on't.   [ANGELLICA turns towards them]
     —The rogue's bred up to mischief, art thou so great a fool to credit him?

ANGELLICA   Yes, I do, and you in vain impose upon me.—Come hither, boy—is not this he you speak of?

HELLENA   I think—it is, I cannot swear, but I vow he has just such another lying lover's look.   [HELLENA looks in his face, he gazes on her]

WILLMORE [aside]   Ha! Do not I know that face? By heaven, my little gypsy, what a dull dog was I; had I but looked that way I'd known her. Are all my hopes of a new woman banished?—Egad, if I do not fit thee for this, hang me.

     —Madam, I have found out the plot.

HELLENA [aside]   Oh Lord, what does he say? Am I discovered now?

WILLMORE   Do you see this young spark here?

HELLENA   He'll tell her who I am.

WILLMORE   Who do you think this is?

HELLENA [*aside*]   Aye, aye, he does know me—

Nay, dear captain! I'm undone if you discover me.

WILLMORE   Nay, nay, no cogging; she shall know what a precious mistress I have.

HELLENA   Will you be such a devil?

WILLMORE [*aside*]   Nay, nay, I'll teach you to spoil sport you will not make.

—This small ambassador comes not from a person of quality as you imagine, and he says; but from a very arrant gypsy: the talking'st, prating'st, canting'st little animal thou ever saw'st.

ANGELLICA   What news you tell me, that's the thing I mean.

HELLENA [*aside*]   Would I were well off the place—if ever I go a-captain-hunting again—

WILLMORE   Mean that thing? That gypsy thing? Thou mayst as well be jealous of thy monkey, or parrot, as of her; a German motion were worth a dozen of her, and a dream were a better enjoyment; a creature of constitution fitter for heaven than man.

HELLENA [*aside*]   Though I'm sure he lies, yet this vexes me.

ANGELLICA   You are mistaken, she's a Spanish woman

Made up of no such dull materials.

WILLMORE   Materials! Egad, an she be made of any that will either dispense or admit of love, I'll be bound to continence.

HELLENA [*aside to him*]   Unreasonable man, do you think so?

WILLMORE   You may return, my little brazen head, and tell your lady that till she be handsome enough to be beloved, or I be dull enough to be religious, there will be small hopes of me.

ANGELLICA   Did you not promise then to marry her?

WILLMORE   Not I, by heaven.

ANGELLICA   You cannot undeceive my fears and torments,

Till you have vowed you will not marry her.

HELLENA [*aside*]   If he swears that, he'll be revenged on me indeed for all my rogueries.

ANGELLICA   I know what arguments you'll bring against me—fortune, and honour—

WILLMORE   Honour! I tell you I hate it in your sex; and those that fancy themselves possessed of that foppery are the most impertinently troublesome of all womankind, and will transgress nine commandments to keep one; and to satisfy your jealousy, I swear—

HELLENA [*aside to him*]   Oh, no swearing, dear captain.

WILLMORE   If it were possible I should ever be inclined to marry, it

should be some kind young sinner; one that has generosity enough to
give a favour handsomely to one that can ask it discreetly; one that has
wit enough to manage an intrigue of love—Oh, how civil such a wench
is to a man that does her the honour to marry her.

ANGELLICA   By heaven, there's no faith in anything he says.

Enter SEBASTIAN

SEBASTIAN   Madam, Don Antonio—
ANGELLICA   Come hither.
HELLENA [*aside*]   Ha! Antonio! He may be coming hither, and he'll
certainly discover me. I'll therefore retire without a ceremony.

[*exit* HELLENA]

ANGELLICA   I'll see him, get my coach ready.
SEBASTIAN   It waits you, madam.
WILLMORE [*aside*]   This is lucky.—What, madam, now I may be gone
and leave you to the enjoyment of my rival?
ANGELLICA   Dull man, that canst not see how ill, how poor,
        That false dissimulation looks: be gone,
        And never let me see thy cozening face again,
        Lest I relapse and kill thee.
WILLMORE   Yes, you can spare me now—farewell, till you're in bet-
ter humour. [*aside*] I'm glad of this release—Now for my gypsy:
        For though to worse we change, yet still we find
        New joys, new charms, in a new miss that's kind.

[*exit* WILLMORE]

ANGELLICA   He's gone, and in this ague of my soul
        The shivering fit returns;
        Oh, with what willing haste he took his leave,
        As if the longed-for minute were arrived
        Of some blest assignation.
        In vain I have consulted all my charms,
        In vain this beauty prized, in vain believed
        My eyes could kindle any lasting fires.
        I had forgot my name, my infamy,
        And the reproach that honour lays on those
        That dare pretend a sober passion here.
        Nice reputation, though it leave behind
        More virtues than inhabit where that dwells,
        Yet that once gone, those virtues shine no more.
        —Then since I am not fit to beloved,
        I am resolved to think on a revenge
        On him that soothed me thus to my undoing.   [*exeunt*]

SCENE III

A street

Enter FLORINDA *and* VALERIA *in habits
different from what they have been seen in*

FLORINDA   We're happily escaped, and yet I tremble still.

VALERIA   A lover and fear! Why, I am but half an one, and yet I have courage for any attempt. Would Hellena were here. I would fain have had her as deep in this mischief as we; she'll fare but ill else, I doubt.

FLORINDA   She pretended a visit to the Augustine nuns, but I believe some other design carried her out; pray heaven we light on her. Prithee, what didst do with Callis?

VALERIA   When I saw no reason would do good on her, I followed her into the wardrobe, and as she was looking for something in a great chest, I toppled her in by the heels, snatched the key of the apartment where you were confined, locked her in, and left her bawling for help.

FLORINDA   'Tis well you resolve to follow my fortunes, for thou darest never appear at home again after such an action.

VALERIA   That's according as the young stranger and I shall agree. But to our business—I delivered your note to Belvile when I got out under pretence of going to mass. I found him at his lodging, and believe me it came seasonably, for never was man in so desperate a condition. I told him of your resolution of making your escape today, if your brother would be absent long enough to permit you; if not, to die rather than be Antonio's.

FLORINDA   Thou shouldst have told him I was confined to my chamber upon my brother's suspicion that the business on the Molo was a plot laid between him and I.

VALERIA   I said all this, and told him your brother was now gone to his devotion; and he resolves to visit every church till he find him, and not only undeceive him in that, but caress him so as shall delay his return home.

FLORINDA   Oh heavens! He's here, and Belvile with him too.

[*they put on their vizards*]

Enter DON PEDRO, BELVILE, WILLMORE;
BELVILE *and* DON PEDRO *seeming in serious discourse*

VALERIA   Walk boldly by them, and I'll come at a distance, lest he suspect us.   [*she walks by them, and looks back on them*]

WILLMORE   Ha! A woman, and of an excellent mien.

PEDRO   She throws a kind look back on you.

WILLMORE   Death, 'tis a likely wench, and that kind look shall not be cast away—I'll follow her.

BELVILE   Prithee, do not.

WILLMORE   Do not? By heavens, to the Antipodes, with such an invitation.   [*she goes out, and* WILLMORE *follows her*]

BELVILE   'Tis a mad fellow for a wench.

Enter FREDERICK

FREDERICK   Oh colonel, such news!

BELVILE   Prithee, what?

FREDERICK   News that will make you laugh in spite of fortune.

BELVILE   What, Blunt has had some damned trick put upon him—cheated, banged, or clapped?

FREDERICK   Cheated, sir, rarely cheated of all but his shirt and drawers. The unconscionable whore, too, turned him out before consummation, so that traversing the streets at midnight, the watch found him in this *fresco,* and conducted him home. By heaven, 'tis such a sight, and yet I durst as well been hanged as laugh at him or pity him; he beats all that do but ask him a question, and is in such an humour.

PEDRO   Who is't has met with this ill usage, sir?

BELVILE   A friend of ours whom you must see for mirth's sake. [*aside*] I'll employ him to give Florinda time for an escape.

PEDRO   What is he?

BELVILE   A young countryman of ours, one that has been educated at so plentiful a rate, he yet ne'er knew the want of money, and 'twill be a great jest to see how simply he'll look without it. For my part I'll lend him none, and the rogue know not how to put on a borrowing face and ask first; I'll let him see how good 'tis to play our parts, whilst I play his. Prithee, Fred, do go home and keep him in that posture till we come.

[*exeunt*]

Enter FLORINDA *from the farther end of the scene, looking behind her*

FLORINDA   I am followed still—ha—my brother too, advancing this way. Good heavens, defend me from being seen by him.   [*she goes off*]

Enter WILLMORE, *and after him* VALERIA, *at a little distance*

WILLMORE   Ah! There she sails; she looks back as she were willing to be boarded. I'll warrant her prize.   [*he goes out,* VALERIA *following*]

Enter HELLENA, *just as he goes out, with a Page*

HELLENA   Ha! Is not that my captain that has a woman in chase? 'Tis not Angellica.—Boy, follow those people at a distance, and bring me an account where they go in.   [*exit* PAGE]

I'll find his haunts, and plague him everywhere. Ha, my brother!
  [BELVILE, WILLMORE, PEDRO *cross the stage;* HELLENA *runs off*]

SCENE IV

Scene changes to another street

Enter FLORINDA

FLORINDA   What shall I do? My brother now pursues me. Will no
kind power protect me from his tyranny? Ha! Here's a door open; I'll
venture in, since nothing can be worse than to fall into his hands. My life
and honour are at stake, and my necessity has no choice.   [*she goes in*]

Enter VALERIA *and* HELLENA'S PAGE *peeping after* FLORINDA

PAGE   Here she went in, I shall remember this house.   [*exit* BOY]
VALERIA   This is Belvile's lodgings; she's gone in as readily as if she
knew it. Ha!—here's that mad fellow again, I dare not venture in; I'll
watch my opportunity.   [*goes aside*]

Enter WILLMORE, *gazing about him*

WILLMORE   I have lost her hereabouts. Pox on't, she must not 'scape
me so.   [*goes out*]

SCENE V

Scene changes to BLUNT'S *chamber, discovers him sitting on a couch
in his shirt and drawers, reading*

BLUNT   So, now my mind's a little at peace since I have resolved revenge. A pox on this tailor, though, for not bringing home the clothes I
bespoke. And a pox of all poor cavaliers, a man can never keep a spare
suit for 'em; and I shall have these rogues come in and find me naked,
and then I'm undone. But I'm resolved to arm myself—the rascals shall
not insult over me too much. [*puts on an old rusty sword, and buff belt*] Now,
how like a morris dancer I am equipped. A fine lady-like whore to cheat
me thus, without affording me a kindness for my money. A pox light on
her, I shall never be reconciled to the sex more; she has made me as faithless as a physician, as uncharitable as a churchman, and as ill-natured as a
poet. Oh, how I'll use all womankind hereafter! What would I give to
have one of 'em within my reach now! Any mortal thing in petticoats,
kind Fortune, send me, and I'll forgive thy last night's malice. Here's a
cursed book too—a warning to all young travellers—that can instruct me
how to prevent such mischiefs now 'tis too late. Well, 'tis a rare convenient thing to read a little now and then, as well as hawk and hunt.

[*sits down again and reads; enter to him* FLORINDA]

FLORINDA   This house is haunted, sure; 'tis well furnished and no living thing inhabits it. Ha—a man; heavens, how he's attired! Sure 'tis some rope-dancer, or fencing-master. I tremble now for fear, and yet I must venture now to speak to him.—Sir, if I may not interrupt your meditations—   [*he starts up and gazes*]

BLUNT   Ha, what's here! Are my wishes granted? And is not that a she creature? 'Adsheartlikins, 'tis! What wretched thing art thou, ha?

FLORINDA   Charitable sir, you've told yourself already what I am: a very wretched maid, forced by a strange unlucky accident, to seek a safety here, and must be ruined, if you do not grant it.

BLUNT   Ruined! Is there any ruin so inevitable as that which now threatens thee? Dost thou know, miserable woman, into what den of mischiefs thou art fallen? What abyss of confusion—ha? Dost not see something in my looks that frights thy guilty soul, and makes thee wish to change that shape of woman for any humble animal, or devil? For those were safer for thee, and less mischievous.

FLORINDA   Alas, what mean you, sir? I must confess your looks have something in 'em makes me fear, but I beseech you, as you seem a gentleman, pity a harmless virgin that takes your house for sanctuary.

BLUNT   Talk on, talk on, and weep too, till my faith return. Do, flatter me out of my senses again—a harmless virgin with a pox, as much one as t'other, 'adsheartlikins. Why, what the devil, can I not be safe in my house for you, not in my chamber—nay, even being naked too cannot secure me? This is an impudence greater than has invaded me yet. Come, no resistance.   [*pulls her rudely*]

FLORINDA   Dare you be so cruel?

BLUNT   Cruel, 'adsheartlikins, as a galley slave, or a Spanish whore. Cruel? Yes, I will kiss and beat thee all over, kiss and see thee all over; thou shalt lie with me too, not that I care for the enjoyment, but to let thee see I have ta'en deliberated malice to thee, and will be revenged on one whore for the sins of another. I will smile and deceive thee, flatter thee and beat thee, kiss and swear, and lie to thee, embrace thee and rob thee, as she did me; fawn on thee and strip thee stark naked; then hang thee out at my window by the heels, with a paper of scurvy verses fastened to thy breast, in praise of damnable women. Come, come along.

FLORINDA   Alas, sir, must I be sacrificed for the crimes of the most infamous of my sex? I never understood the sins you name.

BLUNT   Do, persuade the fool you love him, or that one of you can be just or honest; tell me I was not an easy coxcomb, or any strange impossible tale. It will be believed sooner than thy false showers or protestations. A generation of damned hypocrites to flatter my very clothes from my back! Dissembling witches! Are these the returns you make an

honest gentleman that trusts, believes, and loves you? But if I be not even
with you—come along—or I shall—   [*pulls her again; enter* FREDERICK]

FREDERICK   Ha! What's here to do?

BLUNT   'Adsheartlikins, Fred, I am glad thou art come, to be a witness of my dire revenge.

FREDERICK   What's this, a person of quality too, who is upon the
ramble to supply the defects of some grave and impotent husband?

BLUNT   No, this has another pretence; some very unfortunate accident brought her hither, to save a life pursued by I know not who, or
why, and forced to take sanctuary here at Fools' Haven. 'Adsheartlikins,
to me of all mankind for protection! Is the ass to be cajoled again, think
ye? No, young one, no prayers or tears shall mitigate my rage; therefore
prepare for both my pleasures, of enjoyment and revenge, for I am resolved to make up my loss here on thy body; I'll take it out in kindness
and in beating.

FREDERICK   Now, mistress of mine, what do you think of this?

FLORINDA   I think he will not—dares not—be so barbarous.

FREDERICK   Have a care, Blunt, she fetched a deep sigh; she's enamoured with thy shirt and drawers, she'll strip thee even of that. There are
of her calling such unconscionable baggages, and such dexterous thieves,
they'll flay a man, and he shall ne'er miss his skin till he feels the cold.
There was a countryman of ours robbed of a row of teeth whilst he was
a-sleeping, which the jilt made him buy again when he waked—you see,
lady, how little reason we have to trust you.

BLUNT   'Adsheartlikins, why this is most abominable.

FLORINDA   Some such devils there may be; but by all that's holy, I am
none such. I entered here to save a life in danger.

BLUNT   For no goodness, I'll warrant her.

FREDERICK   Faith, damsel, you had e'en confessed the plain truth, for
we are not fellows to be caught twice in the same trap. Look on that
wreck, a tight vessel when he set out of haven, well trimmed and laden;
and see how a female picaroon of this island of rogues has shattered him;
and canst thou hope for any mercy?

BLUNT   No, no, gentlewoman, come along, 'adsheartlikins, we must
be better acquainted. We'll both lie with her, and then let me alone to
bang her.

FREDERICK   I'm ready to serve you in matters of revenge that has a
double pleasure in't.

BLUNT   Well said. You hear, little one, how you are condemned by
public vote to the bed within; there's no resisting your destiny, sweetheart.   [*pulls her*]

FLORINDA   Stay, sir, I have seen you with Belvile, an English cavalier—for his sake use me kindly. You know him, sir.

BLUNT   Belvile? Why, yes, sweeting, we do know Belvile, and wish he were with us now: he's a cormorant at whore and bacon; he'd have a limb or two of thee, my virgin pullet, but 'tis no matter, we'll leave him the bones to pick.

FLORINDA   Sir, if you have any esteem for that Belvile, I conjure you to treat me with more gentleness; he'll thank you for the justice.

FREDERICK   Hark'ee, Blunt, I doubt we are mistaken in this matter.

FLORINDA   Sir, if you find me not worth Belvile's care, use me as you please, and that you may think I merit better treatment than you threaten—pray take this present—   [gives him a ring; he looks on it]

BLUNT   Hum—a diamond! Why, 'tis a wonderful virtue now that lies in this ring, a mollifying virtue. 'Adsheartlikins, there's more persuasive rhetoric in't than all her sex can utter.

FREDERICK   I begin to suspect something; and 'twould anger us vilely to be trussed up for a rape upon a maid of quality, when we only believe we ruffle a harlot.

BLUNT   Thou art a credulous fellow, but 'adsheartlikins, I have no faith yet; why, my saint prattled as parlously as this does, she gave me a bracelet too, a devil on her, but I sent my man to sell it today for necessaries, and it proved as counterfeit as her vows of love.

FREDERICK   However, let it reprieve her till we see Belvile.

BLUNT   That's hard, yet I will grant it.

Enter a SERVANT

SERVANT   Oh, sir, the colonel is just come in with his new friend and a Spaniard of quality, and talks of having you to dinner with 'em.

BLUNT   'Adsheartlikins, I'm undone—I would not see 'em for the world. Harkee, Fred, lock up the wench in your chamber.

FREDERICK   Fear nothing, madam; whate'er he threatens, you are safe whilst in my hands.   [exeunt FREDERICK and FLORINDA]

BLUNT   And, sirrah, upon your life, say I am not at home—or that I am asleep—or—or anything. Away—I'll prevent their coming this way.

            [locks the door and exeunt]

ACT V

SCENE I

BLUNT'S *chamber*

After a great knocking at his chamber door, enter BLUNT,
softly crossing the stage, in his shirt and drawers as before

VOICES [*call within*]   Ned! Ned Blunt! Ned Blunt!

BLUNT   The rogues are up in arms. 'Adsheartlikins, this villainous Frederick has betrayed me, they have heard of my blessed fortune.

VOICES [*and knocking within*]   Ned Blunt! Ned! Ned!—

BELVILE   Why, he's dead, sir, without dispute dead, he has not been seen today. Let's break open the door—here, boy—

BLUNT   Ha, break open the door. 'Adsheartlikins, that mad fellow will be as good as his word.

BELVILE   Boy, bring something to force the door.

[*a great noise within, at the door again*]

BLUNT   So, now must I speak in my own defence, I'll try what rhetoric will do.—Hold—hold, what do you mean, gentlemen, what do you mean?

BELVILE [*within*]   Oh, rogue, art alive? Prithee, open the door and convince us.

BLUNT   Yes, I am alive, gentlemen—but at present a little busy.

BELVILE [*within*]   How! Blunt grown a man of business! Come, come, open and let's see this miracle.

BLUNT   No, no, no, no, gentlemen. 'Tis no great business—but—I am—at—my devotion—'Adsheartlikins, will you not allow a man time to pray?

BELVILE [*within*]   Turned religious! A greater wonder than the first; therefore open quickly, or we shall unhinge, we shall.

BLUNT [*aside*]   This won't do.—Why, hark'ee, colonel, to tell you the plain truth, I am about a necessary affair of life—I have a wench with me—you apprehend me?—The devil's in't if they be so uncivil as to disturb me now.

WILLMORE   How, a wench? Nay then, we must enter and partake, no resistance—unless it be your lady of quality, and then we'll keep our distance.

BLUNT   So, the business is out.

WILLMORE   Come, come, lend's more hands to the door—now, heave all together—so, well done, my boys—   [*breaks open the door*]

Enter BELVILE, WILLMORE, FREDERICK *and* PEDRO;
BLUNT *looks simply; they all laugh at him;*
he lays his hand on his sword, and comes up to WILLMORE

BLUNT   Hark'ee, sir, laugh out your laugh quickly, d'ye hear, and be gone. I shall spoil your sport else, 'adsheartlikins, sir, I shall. The jest has been carried on too long.—[*aside*] A plague upon my tailor.

WILLMORE   'Sdeath, how the whore has dressed him. Faith, sir, I'm sorry.

BLUNT   Are you so, sir? Keep't to yourself then, sir, I advise you, d'ye hear; for I can as little endure your pity as his mirth.
                                    [*lays his hand on's sword*]

BELVILE   Indeed, Willmore, thou wert a little too rough with Ned Blunt's mistress. Call a person of quality whore? And one so young, so handsome, and so eloquent! Ha, ha, he!

BLUNT   Hark'ee, sir, you know me, and know I can be angry. Have a care—for 'adsheartlikins, I can fight, too—I can, sir—do you mark me?—no more.

BELVILE   Why so peevish, good Ned? Some disappointments, I'll warrant. What, did the jealous count, her husband, return just in the nick?

BLUNT   Or the devil, sir—d'ye laugh?—[*they laugh*] Look ye, settle me a good sober countenance, and that quickly too, or you shall know Ned Blunt is not—

BELVILE   Not everybody; we know that.

BLUNT   Not an ass to be laughed at, sir.

WILLMORE   Unconscionable sinner, to bring a lover so near his happiness, a vigorous passionate lover, and then not only cheat him of his moveables, but his very desires too.

BELVILE   Ah, sir, a mistress is a trifle with Blunt. He'll have a dozen the next time he looks abroad. His eyes have charms not to be resisted; there needs no more than to expose that taking person to the view of the fair, and he leads 'em all in triumph.

PEDRO   Sir, though I'm a stranger to you, I'm ashamed at the rudeness of my nation; and could you learn who did it, would assist you to make an example of 'em.

BLUNT   Why aye, there's one speaks sense now, and handsomely, and let me tell you, gentlemen, I should not have showed myself like a jack pudding thus to have made you mirth, but that I have a revenge within my power; for know, I have got into my possession a female who had better have fallen under any curse, than the ruin I design her. 'Adsheartlikins, she assaulted me here in my own lodgings, and had doubtless committed a rape upon me, had not this sword defended me.

FREDERICK   I know not that, but o' my conscience thou had ravished her, had she not redeemed herself with a ring—let's see't, Blunt.

[BLUNT *shows the ring*]

BELVILE   Ha! The ring I gave Florinda, when we exchanged our vows—Hark'ee, Blunt,—   [*goes to whisper to him*]

WILLMORE   No whispering, good colonel, there's a woman in the case, no whispering.

BELVILE [*to* BLUNT]   Hark'ee, fool, be advised and conceal both the ring and the story for your reputation's sake. Do not let people know what despised cullies we English are; to be cheated and abused by one whore, and another rather bribe thee than be kind to thee, is an infamy to our nation.

WILLMORE   Come, come, where's the wench? We'll see her, let her be what she will, we'll see her.

PEDRO   Aye, aye, let us see her. I can soon discover whether she be of quality, or for your diversion.

BLUNT   She's in Fred's custody.

WILLMORE [*to* FREDERICK]   Come, come, the key.

[FREDERICK *gives him the key; they are going*]

BELVILE [*aside*]   Death, what shall I do?—Stay, gentlemen,— [*aside*] Yet if I hinder 'em, I shall discover all.—Hold—let's go one at once; give me the key.

WILLMORE   Nay, hold there, colonel, I'll go first.

FREDERICK   Nay, no dispute, Ned and I have the propriety of her.

WILLMORE   Damn propriety—then we'll draw cuts. [BELVILE *goes to whisper to* WILLMORE]—Nay, no corruption, good colonel; come, the longest sword carries her.

[*they all draw, forgetting* DON PEDRO, *being as a Spaniard, had the longest*]

BLUNT   I yield up my interest to you, gentlemen, and that will be revenge sufficient.

WILLMORE [*to* PEDRO]   The wench is yours. [*aside*] Pox of his Toledo, I had forgot that.

FREDERICK   Come, sir, I'll conduct you to the lady.

[*exeunt* FREDERICK *and* PEDRO]

BELVILE [*aside*]   To hinder him will certainly discover her. [*to* WILLMORE *who is walking up and down out of humour*]—Dost know, dull beast, what mischief thou hast done?

WILLMORE   Aye, aye, to trust our fortune to lots, a devil on't, 'twas madness, that's the truth on't.

BELVILE   Oh, intolerable sot—

Enter FLORINDA *running, masked,* PEDRO *after her;*
WILLMORE *gazing round her*

FLORINDA [*aside*]   Good heaven, defend me from discovery.

PEDRO   'Tis but in vain to fly me, you're fallen to my lot.

BELVILE   Sure she's undiscovered yet, but now I fear there is no way to bring her off.

WILLMORE   Why, what a pox! Is not this my woman, the same I followed but now?

PEDRO [*talking to* FLORINDA, *who walks up and down*]   As if I did not know ye, and your business here.

FLORINDA [*aside*]   Good heaven, I fear he does indeed.

PEDRO   Come, pray be kind, I know you meant to be so when you entered here, for these are proper gentlemen.

WILLMORE   But, sir—perhaps the lady will not be imposed upon, she'll choose her man.

PEDRO   I am better bred than not to leave her choice free.

Enter VALERIA, *and is surprised at the sight of* DON PEDRO

VALERIA [*aside*]   Don Pedro here! There's no avoiding him.

FLORINDA [*aside*]   Valeria! Then I'm undone.

VALERIA [*to* PEDRO, *running to him*]   Oh! Have I found you, sir—the strangest accident—if I had breath—to tell it.

PEDRO   Speak—is Florinda safe? Hellena well?

VALERIA   Aye, aye, sir—Florinda—is safe—[*aside*] from any fears of you.

PEDRO   Why, where's Florinda? Speak.

VALERIA   Aye, where indeed, sir, I wish I could inform you—but to hold you no longer in doubt—

FLORINDA [*aside*]   Oh, what will she say?

VALERIA   She's fled away in the habit—of one of her pages, sir; but Callis thinks you may retrieve her yet, if you make haste away. She'll tell you, sir, the rest—[*aside*] if you can find her out.

PEDRO   Dishonourable girl, she has undone my aim. Sir, you see my necessity in leaving you, and I hope you'll pardon it. My sister, I know, will make her flight to you; and if she do, I shall expect she should be rendered back.

BELVILE   I shall consult my love and honour, sir.   [*exit* PEDRO]

FLORINDA [*to* VALERIA]   My dear preserver, let me embrace thee.

WILLMORE   What the devil's all this?

BLUNT   Mystery, by this light.

VALERIA   Come, come, make haste and get yourselves married quickly, for your brother will return again.

BELVILE   I'm so surprised with fears and joys, so amazed to find you here in safety, I can scarce persuade my heart into a faith of what I see—

WILLMORE   Hark'ee, colonel, is this the mistress who has cost you so many sighs, and me so many quarrels with you?

BELVILE   It is. [*to* FLORINDA]—Pray give him the honour of your hand.

WILLMORE [*kneels and kisses her hand*]   Thus it must be received then. And with it give your pardon too.

FLORINDA   The friend to Belvile may command me anything.

WILLMORE [*aside*]   Death, would I might, 'tis a surprising beauty.

BELVILE   Boy, run and fetch a father instantly.   [*exit* BOY]

FREDERICK   So, now do I stand like a dog, and have not a syllable to plead my own cause with. By this hand, madam, I was never thoroughly confounded before, nor shall I ever more dare look up with confidence, till you are pleased to pardon me.

FLORINDA   Sir, I'll be reconciled to you on one condition: that you'll follow the example of your friend, in marrying a maid that does not hate you, and whose fortune, I believe, will not be unwelcome to you.

FREDERICK   Madam, had I no inclinations that way, I should obey your kind commands.

BELVILE   Who, Fred marry? He has so few inclinations for womankind, that had he been possessed of paradise, he might have continued there to this day, if no crime but love could have disinherited him.

FREDERICK   Oh, I do not use to boast of my intrigues.

BELVILE   Boast? Why, thou dost nothing but boast; and I dare swear wert thou as innocent from the sin of the grape, as thou art from the apple, thou might'st yet claim that right in Eden which our first parents lost by too much loving.

FREDERICK   I wish this lady would think me so modest a man.

VALERIA   She would be sorry then, and not like you half so well, and I should be loath to break my word with you, which was: that if your friend and mine agreed, it should be a match between you and I.

[*she gives him her hand*]

FREDERICK [*kisses her hand*]   Bear witness, colonel, 'tis a bargain.

BLUNT [*to* FLORINDA]   I have a pardon to beg, too. But, 'adsheartlikins, I am so out of countenance that I'm a dog if I can say anything to purpose.

FLORINDA   Sir, I heartily forgive you all.

BLUNT   That's nobly said, sweet lady; Belvile, prithee present her her ring again, for I find I have not courage to approach her myself.

[*gives* BELVILE *the ring, who gives it to* FLORINDA]

Enter BOY

BOY   Sir, I have brought the father that you sent for.

BELVILE   'Tis well, and now my dear Florinda, let's fly to complete that mighty joy we have so long wished and sighed for.—Come, Fred, you'll follow?

FREDERICK   Your example, sir, 'twas ever my ambition in war, and must be so in love.

WILLMORE   And must not I see this juggling knot tied?

BELVILE   No, thou shalt do us better service, and be our guard, lest Don Pedro's sudden return interrupt the ceremony.

WILLMORE   Content; I'll secure this pass.

[*exeunt* BELVILE, FLORINDA, FREDERICK *and* VALERIA]

Enter BOY

BOY [*to* WILLMORE]   Sir, there's a lady without would speak to you.

WILLMORE   Conduct her in, I dare not quit my post.

BOY [*to* BLUNT]   And, sir, your tailor waits you in your chamber.

BLUNT   Some comfort yet, I shall not dance naked at the wedding.

[*exit* BLUNT *and* BOY]

Enter again the BOY, *conducting in* ANGELLICA
in a masquing habit and a vizard; WILLMORE *runs to her*

WILLMORE   This can be none but my pretty gypsy—oh, I see you can follow as well as fly. Come, confess thyself the most malicious devil in nature, you think you have done my business with Angellica.

ANGELLICA   Stand off, base villain—

[*she draws a pistol, and holds it to his breast*]

WILLMORE   Ha, 'tis not she!—Who art thou, and what's thy business?

ANGELLICA   One thou hast injured, and who comes to kill thee for it.

WILLMORE   What the devil canst thou mean?

ANGELLICA   By all my hopes to kill thee—

[*holds still the pistol to his breast, he going back, she following still*]

WILLMORE   Prithee, on what acquaintance? For I know thee not.

ANGELLICA [*pulls off her vizard*]   Behold this face—so lost to thy re-membrance,

And then call all thy sins about thy soul,
And let 'em die with thee.

WILLMORE   Angellica!

ANGELLICA   Yes, traitor,

Does not thy guilty blood run shivering through thy veins?

    Hast thou no horror at this sight, that tells thee
    Thou hast not long to boast thy shameful conquest?

WILLMORE Faith, no, child, my blood keeps its old ebbs and flows still, and that usual heat too, that could oblige thee with a kindness, had I but opportunity.

ANGELLICA Devil! Dost wanton with my pain? Have at thy heart!

WILLMORE Hold, dear virago! Hold thy hand a little, I am not now at leisure to be killed—

    Hold and hear me—[*aside*] Death, I think she's in earnest.

ANGELLICA [*aside, turning from him*] Oh, if I take not heed,
    My coward heart will leave me to his mercy.
    What have you, sir, to say? But should I hear thee,
    Thou'dst talk away all that is brave about me:
        [*follows him with the pistol to his breast*]
    And I have vowed thy death, by all that's sacred.

WILLMORE Why then, there's an end of a proper handsome fellow, that might 'a lived to have done good service yet; that's all I can say to 't.

ANGELLICA [*pausingly*] Yet—I would give thee—time for—penitence.

WILLMORE Faith, child, I thank God, I have ever took care to lead a good sober, hopeful life, and am of a religion that teaches me to believe I shall depart in peace.

ANGELLICA So will the devil! Tell me,
    How many poor believing fools thou hast undone?
    How many hearts thou hast betrayed to ruin?
    Yet these are little mischiefs to the ills
    Thou'st taught mine to commit: thou taught'st it love!

WILLMORE Egad, 'twas shrewdly hurt the while.

ANGELLICA Love, that has robbed it of its unconcern,
    Of all that pride that taught me how to value it.
    And in its room
    A mean submissive passion was conveyed,
    That made me humbly bow, which I ne'er did
    To anything but heaven.
    Thou, perjured man, didst this, and with thy oaths,
    Which on thy knees thou didst devoutly make,
    Softened my yielding heart—and then, I was a slave—
    —Yet still had been content to've worn my chains;
    Worn 'em with vanity and joy for ever,
    Hadst thou not broke those vows that put them on.
    'Twas then I was undone.
      [*all this while follows him with a pistol to his breast*]

WILLMORE Broke my vows! Why, where hast thou lived? Amongst

the gods? For I never heard of mortal man that has not broke a thousand vows.

ANGELLICA   Oh impudence!

WILLMORE   Angellica! That beauty has been too long tempting, not to have made a thousand lovers languish, who in the amorous fever, no doubt have sworn like me: did they all die in that faith? Still adoring? I do not think they did.

ANGELLICA   No, faithless man: had I repaid their vows, as I did thine, I would have killed the ungrateful that had abandoned me.

WILLMORE   This old general has quite spoiled thee; nothing makes a woman so vain as being flattered. Your old lover ever supplies the defects of age with intolerable dotage, vast charge, and that which you call constancy; and attributing all this to your own merits, you domineer, and throw your favours in's teeth, upbraiding him still with the defects of age, and cuckold him as often as he deceives your expectations. But the gay, young, brisk lover, that brings his equal fires, and can give you dart for dart, you'll find will be as nice as you sometimes.

ANGELLICA   All this thou'st made me know, for which I hate thee.
Had I remained in innocent security,
I should have thought all men were born my slaves,
And worn my power like lightning in my eyes,
To have destroyed at pleasure when offended.
But when love held the mirror, the undeceiving glass
Reflected all the weakness of my soul, and made me know
My richest treasure being lost, my honour,
All the remaining spoil could not be worth
The conqueror's care or value.
Oh, how I fell, like a long-worshipped idol,
Discovering all the cheat.
Would not the incense and rich sacrifice,
Which blind devotion offered at my altars,
Have fallen to thee?
Why wouldst thou then destroy my fancied power?

WILLMORE   By heaven, thou'rt brave, and I admire thee strangely.
I wish I were that dull, that constant thing
Which thou wouldst have, and nature never meant me.
I must, like cheerful birds, sing in all groves,
And perch on every bough,
Billing the next kind she that flies to meet me;
Yet after all could build my nest with thee,
Thither repairing when I'd loved my round,
And still reserve a tributary flame.

To gain your credit, I'll pay back your charity,
And be obliged for nothing but for love. [*offers her a purse of gold*]
ANGELLICA   Oh, that thou wert in earnest!
So mean a thought of me
Would turn my rage to scorn, and I should pity thee,
And give thee leave to live;
Which for the public safety of our sex,
And my own private injuries I dare not do,
Prepare—[*follows still, as before*]
—I will no more be tempted with replies.
WILLMORE   Sure—
ANGELLICA   Another word will damn thee! I've heard thee talk too
long.   [*she follows him with the pistol ready to shoot; he retires still amazed*]

   Enter DON ANTONIO, *his arm in a scarf, and lays hold on the pistol*

ANTONIO   Ha! Angellica!
ANGELLICA   Antonio! What devil brought thee hither?
ANTONIO   Love and curiosity, seeing your coach at the door. Let me
disarm you of this unbecoming instrument of death.—[*takes away the pistol*] Amongst the number of your slaves, was there not one worthy the
honour to have fought your quarrel? [*to* WILLMORE] Who are you, sir,
that are so very wretched to merit death from her?
WILLMORE   One, sir, that could have made a better end of an
amorous quarrel without you, than with you.
ANTONIO   Sure 'tis some rival. Ha! The very man took down her picture yesterday—the very same that set on me last night. Blest opportu-
nity!   [*offers to shoot him*]
ANGELLICA   Hold, you're mistaken, sir.
ANTONIO   By heaven, the very same!
   Sir, what pretensions have you to this lady?
WILLMORE   Sir, I do not use to be examined, and am ill at all disputes
but this—   [*draws;* ANTONIO *offers to shoot*]
ANGELLICA [*to* WILLMORE]   Oh hold! You see he's armed with cer-
tain death;
   —And you, Antonio, I command you hold,
By all the passion you've so lately vowed me.

   Enter DON PEDRO, *sees* ANTONIO, *and stays*

PEDRO [*aside*]   Ha, Antonio! And Angellica!
ANTONIO   When I refuse obedience to your will,
May you destroy me with your mortal hate.
By all that's holy I adore you so,
That even my rival, who has charms enough

> To make him fall a victim to my jealousy
> Shall live, nay, and have leave to love on still.

PEDRO [*aside*]   What's this I hear?

ANGELLICA [*pointing to* WILLMORE]
> Ah thus, 'twas thus he talked, and I believed.
> Antonio, yesterday,
> I'd not have sold my interest in his heart
> For all the sword has lost and won in battle.
> [*to* WILLMORE] But now to show my utmost of contempt,
> I give thee life—which, if thou wouldst preserve,
> Live where my eyes may never see thee more,
> Live to undo someone whose soul may prove
> So bravely constant to revenge my love.
>   [*goes out,* ANTONIO *follows, but* PEDRO *pulls back*]

PEDRO   Antonio—stay.

ANTONIO   Don Pedro—

PEDRO   What coward fear was that prevented thee
> From meeting me this morning on the Molo?

ANTONIO   Meet thee?

PEDRO   Yes me; I was the man that dared thee to't.

ANTONIO   Hast thou so often seen me fight in war,
> To find no better case to excuse my absence?
> I sent my sword and one to do thee right,
> Finding myself uncapable to use a sword.

PEDRO   But 'twas Florinda's quarrel that we fought,
> And you to show how little you esteemed her,
> Sent me your rival, giving him your interest.
> But I have found the cause of this affront,
> But when I meet you fit for the dispute,
> I'll tell you my resentment.

ANTONIO   I shall be ready, sir, ere long to do you reason.
>   [*exit* ANTONIO]

PEDRO   If I could find Florinda now, whilst my anger's high, I think I should be kind, and give her to Belvile in revenge.

WILLMORE   Faith, sir, I know not what you would do, but I believe the priest within has been so kind.

PEDRO   How! My sister married?

WILLMORE   I hope by this time she is, and bedded too, or he has not my longings about him.

PEDRO   Dares he do this? Does he not fear my power?

WILLMORE   Faith, not at all. If you will go in and thank him for the favour he has done your sister, so; if not, sir, my power's greater in this house than yours. I have a damned surly crew here that will keep you till the next tide, and then clap you on board for prize. My ship lies but a league off the Molo, and we shall show your donship a damned tramontana rover's trick.

Enter BELVILE

BELVILE   This rogue's in some new mischief. Ha! Pedro returned!
PEDRO   Colonel Belvile, I hear you have married my sister?
BELVILE   You have heard truth then, sir.
PEDRO   Have I so? Then, sir, I wish you joy.
BELVILE   How!
PEDRO   By this embrace I do, and I am glad on't.
BELVILE   Are you in earnest?
PEDRO   By our long friendship and my obligations to thee, I am; the sudden change I'll give you reasons for anon. Come, lead me to my sister, that she may know I now approve her choice.

[*exit* BELVILE *with* PEDRO]

WILLMORE *goes to follow them; enter* HELLENA,
as before in boy's clothes, and pulls him back

WILLMORE   Ha! My gypsy—now a thousand blessings on thee for this kindness. Egad, child, I was e'en in despair of ever seeing thee again; my friends are all provided for within, each man has his kind woman.

HELLENA   Ha! I thought they had served me some such trick!

WILLMORE   And I was e'en resolved to go aboard, condemn myself to my lone cabin, and the thoughts of thee.

HELLENA   And could you have left me behind? Would you have been so ill-natured?

WILLMORE   Why, 'twould have broke my heart, child; but since we are met again, I defy foul weather to part us.

HELLENA   And would you be a faithful friend now, if a maid should trust you?

WILLMORE   For a friend I cannot promise; thou art of a form so excellent, a face and humour too good for cold dull friendship. I am parlously afraid of being in love, child; and you have not forgot how severely you have used me?

HELLENA   That's all one; such usage you must still look for: to find out all your haunts, to rail at you to all that love you, till I have made you love only me in your own defence, because nobody else will love you.

WILLMORE   But hast thou no better quality to recommend thyself by?

HELLENA   Faith, none, captain. Why, 'twill be the greater charity to take me for thy mistress. I am a lone child, a kind of orphan lover; and why I should die a maid, and in a captain's hands too, I do not understand.

WILLMORE   Egad, I was never clawed away with broad-sides from any female before. Thou hast one virtue I adore—good nature. I hate a coy demure mistress, she's as troublesome as a colt; I'll break none. No, give me a mad mistress when mewed, and in flying, one I dare trust upon the wing, that whilst she's kind will come to the lure.

HELLENA   Nay, as kind as you will, good captain, while it lasts, but let's lose no time.

WILLMORE   My time's as precious to me as thine can be. Therefore, dear creature, since we are so well agreed, let's retire to my chamber, and if ever thou wert treated with such savoury love! Come, my bed's prepared for such a guest, all clean and sweet as thy fair self. I love to steal a dish and a bottle with a friend, and hate long graces. Come, let's retire and fall to.

HELLENA   'Tis but getting my consent, and the business is soon done. Let but old gaffer Hymen and his priest say amen to't, and I dare lay my mother's daughter by as proper a fellow as your father's son, without fear or blushing.

WILLMORE   Hold, hold, no bug words child. Priest and Hymen! Prithee add a hangman to 'em to make up the consort. No, no, we'll have no vows but love, child, nor witness but the lover; the kind diety enjoin naught but love and enjoy! Hymen and priest wait still upon portion and jointure; love and beauty have their own ceremonies. Marriage is as certain a bane to love as lending money is to friendship. I'll neither ask nor give a vow, though I could be content to turn gypsy and become a left-handed bridegroom, to have the pleasure of working that great miracle of making a maid a mother, if you durst venture. 'Tis upse gypsy that, and if I miss, I'll lose my labour.

HELLENA   And if you do not lose, what shall I get? A cradle full of noise and mischief, with a pack of repentance at my back? Can you teach me to weave incle to pass my time with? 'Tis upse gypsy that too.

WILLMORE   I can teach thee to weave a true love's knot better.

HELLENA   So can my dog.

WILLMORE   Well, I see we are both upon our guards, and I see there's no way to conquer good nature, but by yielding. Here, give me thy hand—one kiss and I am thine.

HELLENA   One kiss! How like my page he speaks. I am resolved you shall have none, for asking such a sneaking sum. He that will be satisfied with one kiss, will never die of that longing. Good friend single-kiss, is all your talking come to this?—A kiss, a caudle! Farewell, captain single-kiss.   [going out; he stays her]

WILLMORE   Nay, if we part so, let me die like a bird upon a bough, at the sheriff's charge. By heaven, both the Indies shall not buy thee from me. I adore thy humour and will marry thee, and we are so of one humour it must be a bargain. Give me thy hand. [*kisses her hand*] And now let the blind ones, Love and Fortune, do their worst.

HELLENA   Why, God-a-mercy, captain!

WILLMORE   But hark'ee, the bargain is now made: but is it not fit we should know each other's names, that when we have reason to curse one another hereafter (and people ask me who 'tis I give to the devil), I may at least be able to tell what family you came of?

HELLENA   Good reason, captain; and when I have cause (as I doubt not but I shall have plentiful), that I may know at whom to throw my— blessings, I beseech ye your name.

WILLMORE   I am called Robert the Constant.

HELLENA   A very fine name. Pray was it your falconer or butler that christened you? Do they not use to whistle when then call you?

WILLMORE   I hope you have a better, that a man may name without crossing himself, you are so merry with mine.

HELLENA   I am called Hellena the Inconstant.

Enter PEDRO, BELVILE, FLORINDA, FREDERICK, VALERIA

PEDRO   Ha, Hellena!

FLORINDA   Hellena!

HELLENA   The very same. Ha, my brother! Now, captain, show your love and courage; stand to your arms and defend me bravely, or I am lost for ever.

PEDRO   What's this I hear? False girl, how came you hither, and what's your business? Speak.   [*goes roughly to her*]

WILLMORE [*puts himself between*]   Hold off, sir, you have leave to parley only.

HELLENA   I had e'en as good tell it, as you guess it. Faith, brother, my business is the same with all living creatures of my age: to love and be beloved, and here's the man.

PEDRO   Perfidious maid, hast thou deceived me too, deceived thyself and heaven?

HELLENA   'Tis time enough to make my peace with that,
        Be you but kind, let me alone with heaven.

PEDRO   Belvile, I did not expect this false play from you. Was't not enough you'd gain Florinda (which I pardoned), but your lewd friends too must be enriched with the spoils of a noble family?

BELVILE   Faith, sir, I am as much surprised at this as you can be. Yet, sir, my friends are gentlemen, and ought to be esteemed for their misfortunes, since they have the glory to suffer with the best of men and kings. 'Tis true he's a rover of fortune, yet a prince aboard his little wooden world.

PEDRO   What's this to the maintenance of a woman of her birth and quality?

WILLMORE   Faith, sir, I can boast of nothing but a sword which does me right where'er I come, and has defended a worse cause than a woman's; and since I loved her before I knew either her birth or name, I must pursue my resolution and marry her.

PEDRO   And is all your holy intent of becoming a nun debauched into a desire of man?

HELLENA   Why, I have considered the matter, brother, and find the three thousand crowns my uncle left me (and you cannot keep from me), will be better laid out in love than in religion, and turn to as good an account. Let most voices carry it: for heaven, or the captain?

ALL CRY   A captain! A captain!

HELLENA   Look ye, sir, 'tis a clear case.

PEDRO   Oh, I am mad! [aside] If I refuse my life's in danger. —Come, there's one motive induces me. Take her: I shall now be free from the fears of her honour; guard you it now, if you can, I have been a slave to 't long enough.   [gives her to him]

WILLMORE   Faith, sir, I am of a nation that are of opinion a woman's honour is not worth guarding when she has a mind to part with it.

HELLENA   Well said, captain.

PEDRO [to VALERIA]   This was your plot, mistress, but I hope you have married one that will revenge my quarrel to you.

VALERIA   There's no altering destiny, sir.

PEDRO   Sooner than a woman's will; therefore I forgive you all, and wish you may get my father's pardon as easily, which I fear.

Enter BLUNT *dressed in a Spanish habit, looking very ridiculously;*
his man adjusting his band

MAN   'Tis very well, sir.

BLUNT   Well, sir! 'Adsheartlikins, I tell you 'tis damnable ill, sir. A Spanish habit, good Lord! Could the devil and my tailor devise no other punishment for me but the mode of a nation I abominate?

BELVILE   What's the matter, Ned?

BLUNT   Pray view me round, and judge—   [turns round]

BELVILE   I must confess thou art a kind of an odd figure.

BLUNT   In a Spanish habit with a vengeance! I had rather be in the Inquisition for Judaism, than in this doublet and breeches; a pillory were an easy collar to this three handfuls high; and these shoes, too, are worse than the stocks, with the sole an inch shorter than my foot. In fine, gentlemen, methinks I look altogether like a bag of bays stuffed full of fool's flesh.

BELVILE   Methinks 'tis well, and makes thee look *en cavalier*. Come, sir, settle your face, and salute our friends, lady—

BLUNT   Ha, sayst thou so, my little rover! [*to* HELLENA] Lady, if you be one, give me leave to kiss your hand, and tell you, 'adsheartlikins, for all I look so, I am your humble servant. A pox of my Spanish habit!

[*music is heard to play*]

WILLMORE   Hark—what's this?

Enter BOY

BOY   Sir, as the custom is, the gay people in masquerade who make every man's house their own, are coming up.

Enter several men and women in masquing habits with music; they put themselves in order and dance

BLUNT   'Adsheartlikins, would 'twere lawful to pull off their false faces, that I might see if my doxy were not amongst 'em.

BELVILE [*to the masquers*]   Ladies and gentlemen, since you come so apropos, you must take a small collation with us.

WILLMORE   Whilst we'll to the good man within, who stays to give us a cast of his office. [*to* HELLENA] Have you no trembling at the near approach?

HELLENA   No more than you have in an engagement or a tempest.

WILLMORE   Egad, thou 'rt a brave girl, and I admire thy love and courage.

Lead on, no other dangers they can dread,
Who venture in the storms o' th' marriage bed.   [*exeunt*]

EPILOGUE

The banished cavaliers! A roving blade!
A popish carnival! A masquerade!
The devil's in't if this will please the nation,
In these our blessed times of reformation,
When conventicling is so much in fashion.
And yet—
That mutinous tribe less factions do beget
Than your continual differing in wit;
Your judgement's (as your passion's) a disease;
Nor muse nor miss your appetite can please;
You're grown as nice as queasy consciences,
Whose each convulsion, when the spirit moves,

Damns everything that maggot disapproves.
　　With canting rule you would the stage refine,
And to dull method all our sense confine.
With th' insolence of commonwealths you rule,
Where each gay fop, and politic grave fool,
On monarch wit impose, without control.
As for the last, who seldom sees a play,
Unless it be the old Blackfriars way,
Shaking his empty noddle o'er bamboo,
He cries, "Good faith, these plays will never do.
Ah, sir, in my young days, what lofty wit,
What high-strained scenes of fighting there were writ;
These are slight airy toys. But tell me, pray,
What has the House of Commons done today?"
Then shows his politics, to let you see,
Of state affairs he'll judge as notably,
As he can do of wit and poetry.
The younger sparks who hither do resort,
Cry,—
"Pox o'your genteel things, give us more sport;
Damn me, I'm sure 'twill never please the court."
　　Such fops are never pleased, unless the play
Be stuffed with fools as brisk and dull as they.
Such might the half-crown spare, and in a glass
At home, behold a more accomplished ass,
Where they may set their cravats, wigs, and faces,
And practise all their buffoonery grimaces—
See how this huff becomes, this damny,—stare—
Which they at home may act, because they dare,
But must with prudent caution do elsewhere.
Oh, that our Nokes, or Tony Leigh could show
A fop, but half so much to th' life as you.

POSTSCRIPT

This play had been sooner in print, but for a report about the town
(made by some either very malicious or very ignorant) that 'twas
Thomaso altered; which made the booksellers fear some trouble from the
proprietor of that admirable play, which indeed has wit enough to stock
a poet, and is not to be pieced or mended by any but the excellent
author himself. That I have stolen some hints from it, may be a proof that
I valued it more than to pretend to alter it; had I had the dexterity of

some poets, who are not more expert in stealing than in the art of concealing, and who even that way outdo the Spartan boys, I might have appropriated all to myself; but I, vainly proud of my judgement, hang out the sign of Angellica (the only stolen object), to give notice where a great part of the wit dwelt; though if the play of *The Novella* were as well worth remembering as *Thomaso*, they might (bating the name) have as well said I took it from thence. I will only say the plot and business (not to boast on't) is my own. As for the words and characters, I leave the reader to judge and compare with *Thomaso*, to whom I recommend the great entertainment of reading it; though had this succeeded ill, I should have had no need of imploring that justice from the critics, who are naturally so kind to any that pretend to usurp their dominion, especially of our sex, they would doubtless have given me the whole honour on't. Therefore I will only say in English what the famous Virgil does in Latin: I make verses, and others have the fame.

FINIS

The Relapse; or,
Virtue in Danger
Sir John Vanbrugh

Dramatis Personae

SIR NOVELTY FASHION, *newly created* LORD FOPPINGTON
YOUNG FASHION, *his brother*
LOVELESS, *husband to* AMANDA
WORTHY, *a gentleman of the town*
SIR TUNBELLY CLUMSEY, *a country gentleman*
SIR JOHN FRIENDLY, *his neighbour*
COUPLER, *a matchmaker*
BULL, *chaplain to* SIR TUNBELLY
SERRINGE, *a surgeon*
LORY, *servant to* YOUNG FASHION
Shoemaker, Tailor, Periwig-maker, &c.

AMANDA, *wife of* LOVELESS
BERINTHIA, *her cousin, a young widow*
MISS HOYDEN, *a great fortune, daughter to* SIR TUNBELLY
Nurse, her gouvernante
MRS. CALLICOE, *a seamstress*
ABIGAIL, *maid to* BERINTHIA
Maid to AMANDA

THE PREFACE

To go about to excuse half the defects this abortive brat is come into the world with, would be to provoke the town with a long useless preface, when 'tis, I doubt, sufficiently soured already by a tedious play.

I do therefore (with all the humility of a repenting sinner) confess it wants everything—but length; and in that, I hope, the severest critic will be pleased to acknowledge I have not been wanting. But my modesty will sure atone for everything, when the world shall know it is so great I am even to this day insensible of those two shining graces in the play (which some part of the town is pleased to compliment me with) blasphemy and bawdy.

For my part, I cannot find 'em out: if there was any obscene expressions upon the stage, here they are in the print; for I have dealt fairly, I have not sunk a syllable that could (though by racking of mysteries) be ranged under that head; and yet I believe with a steady faith, there is not one woman of a real reputation in town but when she has read it impartially over in her closet will find it so innocent she'll think it no affront to her prayer-book to lay it upon the same shelf. So to them (with all manner of deference) I entirely refer my cause; and I'm confident they'll justify me against those pretenders to good manners, who, at the same time, have so little respect for the ladies they would extract a bawdy jest from an ejaculation, to put 'em out of countenance. But I expect to have these well-bred persons always my enemies, since I'm sure I shall never write anything lewd enough to make 'em my friends.

As for the saints (your thorough-paced ones, I mean, with screwed faces and wry mouths) I despair of them; for they are friends to nobody. They love nothing but their altars and themselves. They have too much zeal to have any charity; they make debauches in piety, as sinners do in wine, and are as quarrelsome in their religion as other people are in their drink: so I hope nobody will mind what they say. But if any man (with flat plod shoes, a little band, greasy hair, and a dirty face, who is wiser than I, at the expense of being forty years older) happens to be offended at a story of a cock and a bull, and a priest and a bulldog, I beg his pardon with all my heart; which, I hope, I shall obtain by eating my words, and making this public recantation. I do therefore, for his satisfaction, acknowledge I lied when I said they never quit their hold; for in that little time I have lived in the world, I thank God I have seen 'em forced to 't more than once; but next time I'll speak with more caution and truth, and only say they have very good teeth.

If I have offended any honest gentleman of the town whose friendship or good word is worth the having, I am very sorry for it; I hope they'll correct me as gently as they can, when they consider I have had no other design, in running a very great risk, than to divert (if possible) some part of their spleen, in spite of their wives and their taxes.

One word more about the bawdy, and I have done. I own, the first night this thing was acted some indecencies had like to have happened; but 'twas not my fault.

The fine gentleman of the play, drinking his mistress's health in Nantes brandy, from six in the morning to the time he waddled on upon the stage in the evening, had toasted himself up to such a pitch of vigour, I confess I once gave Amanda for gone, and I am since (with all due respect to Mrs. Rogers) very sorry she scaped; for I am confident a certain lady (let no one take it to herself that's handsome) who highly blames the play for the barrenness of the conclusion, would then have allowed it a very natural close.

PROLOGUE

Spoken by MISS HOYDEN

Ladies, this play in too much haste was writ
To be o'ercharg'd with either plot or wit;
'Twas got, conceiv'd, and born in six weeks' space,
And wit, you know, 's as slow in growth—as grace.
Sure it can ne'er be ripen'd to your taste;
I doubt 'twill prove our author bred too fast:
For mark 'em well, who with the Muses marry,
They rarely do conceive, but they miscarry.
'Tis the hard fate of those wh'are big with rhyme,
Still to be brought to bed before their time.
Of our late poets, Nature few has made;
The greatest part—are only so by trade.
Still want of something brings the scribbling fit;
For want of money some of 'em have writ,
And others do't, you see—for want of wit.

Honour, they fancy, summons 'em to write,
So out they lug in resty Nature's spite,
As some of you spruce beaux do—when you fight.
Yet let the ebb of wit be ne'er so low,
Some glimpse of it a man may hope to show,
Upon a theme so ample—as a beau.
So, howsoe'er true courage may decay,
Perhaps there's not one smock-face here to-day,
But's bold as Cæsar—to attack a play.
Nay, what's yet more, with an undaunted face,
To do the thing with more heroic grace,
'Tis six to four y'attack the strongest place.
You are such Hotspurs in this kind of venture,
Where there's no breach, just there you needs must enter.
But be advis'd.
E'en give the hero and the critic o'er,
For Nature sent you on another score;
She formed her beau for nothing but her whore.

ACT I

SCENE I

Enter LOVELESS, *reading*

Lov.   How true is that philosophy which says
       Our heaven is seated in our minds!
       Through all the roving pleasures of my youth
       (Where nights and days seem'd all consum'd in joy,
       Where the false face of luxury display'd such charms
       As might have shaken the most holy hermit,
       And made him totter at his altar),
       I never knew one moment's peace like this.
       Here—in this little soft retreat,
       My thoughts unbent from all the cares of life,
       Content with fortune,
       Eas'd from the grating duties of dependence,
       From envy free, ambition under foot,
       The raging flame of wild destructive lust
       Reduc'd to a warm pleasing fire of lawful love,
       My life glides on, and all is well within.

Enter AMANDA

LOV. [*meeting her kindly*]   How does the happy cause of my content,
my dear Amanda?
>   You find me musing on my happy state,
>   And full of grateful thoughts to heaven, and you.

AMAN.   Those grateful offerings heaven can't receive
>   With more delight than I do:
>   Would I could share with it as well
>   The dispensations of its bliss,
>   That I might search its choicest favours out,
>   And shower 'em on your head for ever.

LOV.   The largest boons that heaven thinks fit to grant
>   To things it has decreed shall crawl on earth,
>   Are in the gift of women form'd like you.
>   Perhaps, when time shall be no more,
>   When the aspiring soul shall take its flight,
>   And drop this pond'rous lump of clay behind it,
>   It may have appetites we know not of,
>   And pleasures as refin'd as its desires—
>   But till that day of knowledge shall instruct me,
>   The utmost blessing that my thought can reach,
>   [*taking her in his arms*]
>   Is folded in my arms, and rooted in my heart.

AMAN.   There let it grow for ever.

LOV.   Well said, Amanda—let it be for ever—
>   Would heaven grant that——

AMAN.   'Twere all the heaven I'd ask.
>   But we are clad in black mortality,
>   And the dark curtain of eternal night
>   At last must drop between us.

LOV.   It must: that mournful separation we must see. A bitter pill it is
to all; but doubles its ungrateful taste, when lovers are to swallow it.

AMAN.   Perhaps that pain may only be my lot;
>   You possibly may be exempted from it.
>   Men find out softer ways to quench their fires.

LOV.   Can you then doubt my constancy, Amanda?
>   You'll find 'tis built upon a steady basis—
>   The rock of reason now supports my love,
>   On which it stands so fix'd
>   The rudest hurricane of wild desire
>   Would, like the breath of a soft slumb'ring babe,
>   Pass by, and never shake it.

AMAN.   Yet still 'tis safer to avoid the storm;
>   The strongest vessels, if they put to sea,

May possibly be lost.
Would I could keep you here in this calm port for ever!
Forgive the weakness of a woman,
I am uneasy at your going to stay so long in town;
I know its false insinuating pleasures;
I know the force of its delusions;
I know the strength of its attacks;
I know the weak defence of nature;
I know you are a man—and I—a wife.

Lov.   You know then all that needs to give you rest,
For wife's the strongest claim that you can urge.
When you would plead your title to my heart,
On this you may depend; therefore be calm,
Banish your fears, for they are traitors to your peace;
Beware of 'em: they are insinuating busy things
That gossip to and fro,
And do a world of mischief where they come:
But you shall soon be mistress of 'em all;
I'll aid you with such arms for their destruction
They never shall erect their heads again.
You know the business is indispensable,
That obliges me to go for London,
And you have no reason that I know of
To believe I'm glad of the occasion:
For my honest conscience is my witness,
I have found a due succession of such charms
In my retirement here with you,
I have never thrown one roving thought that way;
But since, against my will, I'm dragg'd once more
To that uneasy theatre of noise,
I am resolv'd to make such use on't,
As shall convince you 'tis an old cast mistress,
Who has been so lavish of her favours
She's now grown bankrupt of her charms,
And has not one allurement left to move me.

Aman.   Her bow, I do believe, is grown so weak,
Her arrows (at this distance) cannot hurt you,
But in approaching 'em you give 'em strength:
The dart that has not far to fly will put
The best of armour to a dangerous trial.

Lov.   That trial past, and y'are at ease for ever;
When you have seen the helmet prov'd,
You'll apprehend no more for him that wears it:

Therefore to put a lasting period to your fears,
I am resolv'd, this once, to launch into temptation.
I'll give you an essay of all my virtues;
My former boon companions of the bottle
Shall fairly try what charms are left in wine:
I'll take my place amongst 'em, they shall hem me in,
Sing praises to their god, and drink his glory;
Turn wild enthusiasts for his sake,
And beasts to do him honour:
Whilst I, a stubborn atheist,
Sullenly look on,
Without one reverend glass to his divinity.
That for my temperance: then for my constancy——

AMAN. Ay, there take heed.

LOV. Indeed the danger's small.

AMAN. And yet my fears are great.

LOV. Why are you so timorous?

AMAN. Because you are so bold.

LOV. My courage should disperse your apprehensions.

AMAN. My apprehensions should alarm your courage.

LOV. Fy, fy, Amanda, it is not kind thus to distrust me.

AMAN. And yet my fears are founded on my love.

LOV. Your love then is not founded as it ought;
For if you can believe 'tis possible
I should again relapse to my past follies,
I must appear to you a thing
Of such an undigested composition,
That but to think of me with inclination
Would be a weakness in your taste
Your virtue scarce could answer.

AMAN. 'Twould be a weakness in my tongue,
My prudence could not answer,
If I should press you farther with my fears;
I'll therefore trouble you no longer with 'em.

LOV. Nor shall they trouble you much longer;
A little time shall show you they were groundless.
This winter shall be the fiery trial of my virtue,
Which, when it once has past,
You'll be convinc'd 'twas of no false alloy;
There all your cares will end.

AMAN. Pray heaven they may!

                                                    [*exeunt hand in hand*]

SCENE II

Whitehall

Enter YOUNG FASHION, LORY, *and Waterman*

Y. FAS.   Come, pay the waterman, and take the portmantle.

LO.   Faith, Sir, I think the waterman had as good take the portmantle and pay himself.

Y. FAS.   Why, sure there's something left in't!

LO.   But a solitary old waistcoat, upon honour, Sir.

Y. FAS.   Why, what's become of the blue coat, Sirrah?

LO.   Sir, 'twas eaten at Gravesend; the reckoning came to thirty shillings, and your privy purse was worth but two half-crowns.

Y. FAS.   'Tis very well.

WAT.   Pray, Master, will you please to dispatch me?

Y. FAS.   Ay, here a—canst thou change me a guinea?

LO. [*aside*]   Good!

WAT.   Change a guinea, Master! Ha, ha, your honour's pleased to compliment.

Y. FAS.   I'gad I don't know how I shall pay thee then, for I have nothing but gold about me.

LO. [*aside*]   Hum, hum.

Y. FAS.   What dost thou expect, friend?

WAT.   Why, Master, so far against wind and tide is richly worth half a piece.

Y. FAS.   Why, faith, I think thou art a good conscionable fellow. I'gad, I begin to have so good an opinion of thy honesty, I care not if I leave my portmantle with thee, till I send thee thy money.

WAT.   Ha! God bless your honour; I should be as willing to trust you, Master, but that you are, as a man may say, a stranger to me, and these are nimble times. There are a great many sharpers stirring. [*taking up the portmantle*] Well, Master, when your worship sends the money, your portmantle shall be forthcoming; my name's Tugg, my wife keeps a brandy-shop in Drab Alley at Wapping.

Y. FAS.   Very well; I'll send for't to-morrow.   [*exit Waterman*]

LO.   So! Now, Sir, I hope you'll own yourself a happy man; you have outlived all your cares.

Y. FAS.   How so, Sir?

LO.   Why you have nothing left to take care of.

Y. FAS.   Yes, Sirrah, I have myself and you to take care of still.

LO.   Sir, if you could but prevail with somebody else to do that for you, I fancy we might both fare the better for't.

Y. FAS.   Why, if thou canst tell me where to apply myself, I have at present so little money, and so much humility about me, I don't know but I may follow a fool's advice.

LO.   Why then, Sir, your fool advises you to lay aside all animosity and apply to Sir Novelty, your elder brother.

Y. FAS.   Damn my elder brother!

LO.   With all my heart; but get him to redeem your annuity, however.

Y. FAS.   My annuity! 'Sdeath, he's such a dog, he would not give his powder-puff to redeem my soul.

LO.   Look you, Sir, you must wheedle him, or you must starve.

Y. FAS.   Look you, Sir, I will neither wheedle him nor starve.

LO.   Why? What will you do then?

Y. FAS.   I'll go into the army.

LO.   You can't take the oaths; you are a Jacobite.

Y. FAS.   Thou may'st as well say I can't take orders because I'm an atheist.

LO.   Sir, I ask your pardon; I find I did not know the strength of your conscience so well as I did the weakness of your purse.

Y. FAS.   Methinks, Sir, a person of your experience should have known that the strength of the conscience proceeds from the weakness of the purse.

LO.   Sir, I am very glad to find you have a conscience able to take care of us, let it proceed from what it will; but I desire you'll please to consider that the army alone will be but a scanty maintenance for a person of your generosity (at least as rents now are paid); I shall see you stand in damnable need of some auxiliary guineas for your *menus plaisirs;* I will therefore turn fool once more for your service, and advise you to go directly to your brother.

Y. FAS.   Art thou then so impregnable a blockhead to believe he'll help me with a farthing?

LO.   Not if you treat him *de haut en bas,* as you use to do.

Y. FAS.   Why, how would'st have me treat him?

LO.   Like a trout—tickle him.

Y. FAS.   I can't flatter.

LO.   Can you starve?

Y. FAS.   Yes.

LO.   I can't; good-by t'ye, Sir——   [*going*]

Y. FAS.   Stay, thou wilt distract me. What would'st thou have me say to him?

LO.   Say nothing to him: apply yourself to his favourites; speak to his periwig, his cravat, his feather, his snuff-box, and when you are well with them—desire him to lend you a thousand pounds. I'll engage you prosper.

Y. Fas.   'Sdeath and Furies! why was that coxcomb thrust into the world before me? O Fortune—Fortune—thou art a bitch, by Gad!

[*exeunt*]

SCENE III

A dressing-room

Enter Lord Foppington *in his night-gown*

L. Fop.   Page!

Enter Page

Page.   Sir.

L. Fop.   "Sir!" Pray, Sir, do me the favour to teach your tongue the title the king has thought fit to honour me with.

Page.   I ask your Lordship's pardon, my Lord.

L. Fop.   Oh, you can pronounce the word, then; I thought it would have choked you. D'ye hear?

Page.   My Lord.

L. Fop.   Call La Vérole; I would dress——   [*exit Page*]

[*solus*] Well, 'tis an unspeakable pleasure to be a man of quality—strike me dumb!—"My Lord!"—"Your Lordship!"—"My Lord Foppington!"—*Ah! c'est quelque chose de beau, que le diable m'emporte.* Why, the ladies were ready to puke at me whilst I had nothing but Sir Navelty to recommend me to 'em. Sure, whilst I was but a knight, I was a very nauseous fellow. Well, 'tis ten thousand pawnd well given—stap my vitals——

Enter La Vérole

L.V.   Me Lord, de shoemaker, de tailor, de hosier, de seamstress, de barber, be all ready, if your Lordship please to be dress.

L. Fop.   'Tis well; admit 'em.

L.V.   *Hey, messieurs, entrez.*

Enter Tailor, etc.

L. Fop.   So, gentlemen, I hope you have all taken pains to show yourselves masters in your professions.

Tai.   I think I may presume to say, Sir——

L.V.   "My Lord"—you clawn, you!

Tai.   Why, is he made a lord?——My Lord, I ask your Lordship's pardon, my Lord; I hope, my Lord, your Lordship will please to own I have brought your Lordship as accomplished a suit of clothes as ever peer of England trod the stage in, my Lord: will your Lordship please to try 'em now?

L. Fop.   Ay, but let my people dispose the glasses so that I may see myself before and behind; for I love to see myself all raund——

Whilst he puts on his clothes, enter YOUNG FASHION *and* LORY

Y. FAS.   Hey-dey, what the devil have we here? Sure my gentleman's grown a favourite at Court, he has got so many people at his levee.

LO.   Sir, these people come in order to make him a favourite at Court; they are to establish him with the ladies.

Y. FAS.   Good God! to what an ebb of taste are women fallen, that it should be in the power of a laced coat to recommend a gallant to 'em.

LO.   Sir, tailors and periwig-makers are now become the bawds of the nation: 'tis they debauch all the women.

Y. FAS.   Thou sayest true; for there's that fop now has not by nature wherewithal to move a cook-maid, and by that time these fellows have done with him, i'gad, he shall melt down a countess.

But now for my reception: I'll engage it shall be as cold a one as a courtier's to his friend, who comes to put him in mind of his promise.

L. Fop. [*to his tailor*]   Death and eternal tartures! Sir, I say the packet's too high by a foot.

TAI.   My Lord, if it had been an inch lower it would not have held your Lordship's pocket-handkerchief.

L. Fop.   Rat my pocket-handkerchief! Have not I a page to carry it? You may make him a packet up to his chin a purpose for it; but I will not have mine come so near my face.

TAI.   'Tis not for me to dispute your Lordship's fancy.

Y. FAS. [*to* LORY]   His Lordship! Lory, did you observe that?

LO.   Yes, Sir; I always thought 'twould end there. Now, I hope, you'll have a little more respect for him.

Y. FAS.   Respect! Damn him for a coxcomb; now has he ruined his estate to buy a title, that he may be a fool of the first rate. But let's accost him. [*to* LORD FOPPINGTON] Brother, I'm your humble servant.

L. Fop.   O Lard, Tam; I did not expect you in England: Brother, I am glad to see you.—[*turning to his tailor*] Look you, Sir, I shall never be reconciled to this nauseous packet; therefore pray get me another suit with all manner of expedition, for this is my eternal aversion. Mrs. Callicoe, are not you of my mind?   [*exit Tailor*]

SEAM.   Oh, directly, my Lord; it can never be too low.

L. Fop.   You are positively in the right on't, for the packet becomes no part of the body but the knee.

SEAM.   I hope your Lordship is pleased with your steenkirk.

L. Fop.   In love with it, stap my vitals. Bring your bill, you shall be paid to-marrow.

SEAM.   I humbly thank your honour.   [*exit Seamstress*]

L. FOP.   Hark thee, shoemaker, these shoes a'n't ugly, but they don't fit me.

SHOE.   My Lord, my thinks they fit you very well.

L. FOP.   They hurt me just below the instep.

SHOE. [*feeling his foot*].   My Lord, they don't hurt you there.

L. FOP.   I tell thee, they pinch me execrably.

SHOE.   My Lord, if they pinch you, I'll be bound to be hanged, that's all.

L. FOP.   Why, wilt thou undertake to persuade me I cannot feel?

SHOE.   Your Lordship may please to feel what you think fit, but that shoe does not hurt you; I think I understand my trade.

L. FOP.   Now by all that's great and powerful, thou art an incomprehensible coxcomb; but thou makest good shoes, and so I'll bear with thee.

SHOE.   My Lord, I have worked for half the people of quality in town these twenty years; and 'twere very hard I should not know when a shoe hurts and when it don't.

L. FOP.   Well, prithee begone about thy business.   [*exit Shoemaker*] [*to the hosier*] Mr. Mend-legs, a word with you; the calves of these stockings are thickened a little too much. They make my legs look like a chairman's.

MEND.   My Lord, my thinks they look mighty well.

L. FOP.   Ay, but you are not so good a judge of these things as I am; I have studied 'em all my life; therefore pray let the next be the thickness of a crawnpiece less.——[*aside*] If the town takes notice my legs are fallen away, 'twill be attributed to the violence of some new intrigue.

                                        [*exit Hosier*]

[*to the Periwig-maker*] Come, Mr. Foretop, let me see what you have done, and then the fatigue of the marning will be over.

FORE.   My Lord, I have done what I defy any prince in Europe t' out-do; I have made you a periwig so long, and so full of hair, it will serve you for hat and cloak in all weathers.

L. FOP.   Then thou hast made me thy friend to eternity: come, comb it out.

Y. FAS.   Well, Lory, what dost think on't? A very friendly reception from a brother after three years' absence!

LO.   Why, Sir, it's your own fault: we seldom care for those that don't love what we love; if you would creep into his heart, you must enter into his pleasures. Here have you stood ever since you came in, and have not commended any one thing that belongs to him.

Y. FAS.   Nor never shall, whilst they belong to a coxcomb.

LO.   Then, Sir, you must be content to pick a hungry bone.

Y. FAS.   No, Sir, I'll crack it, and get to the marrow before I have done.

L. FOP.   Gad's curse! Mr. Foretop, you don't intend to put this upon me for a full periwig?

FORE.   Not a full one, my Lord? I don't know what your Lordship may please to call a full one, but I have crammed twenty ounces of hair into it.

L. FOP.   What it may be by weight, Sir, I shall not dispute; but by tale, there are not nine hairs of a side.

FORE.   O Lord! O Lord! O Lord! Why, as Gad shall judge me, your honour's side-face is reduced to the tip of your nose.

L. FOP.   My side-face may be in eclipse for aught I know; but I'm sure my full-face is like the full moon.

FORE.   [*rubbing his eyes*] Heaven bless my eyesight! Sure I look through the wrong end of the perspective, for by my faith, an't please your honour, the broadest place I see in your face does not seem to me to be two inches diameter.

L. FOP.   If it did, it would be just two inches too broad; far a periwig to a man should be like a mask to a woman: nothing should be seen but his eyes.

FORE.   My Lord, I have done; if you please to have more hair in your wig, I'll put it in.

L. FOP.   Passitively, yes.

FORE.   Shall I take it back now, my Lord?

L. FOP.   No: I'll wear it to-day, though it show such a manstrous pair of cheeks: stap my vitals, I shall be taken for a trumpeter.

[*exit* FORETOP]

Y. FAS.   Now your people of business are gone, Brother, I hope I may obtain a quarter of an hour's audience of you.

L. FOP.   Faith, Tam, I must beg you'll excuse me at this time, for I must away to the House of Lards immediately; my Lady Teaser's case is to come on to-day, and I would not be absent for the salvation of mankind.—— Hey, page! is the coach at the door?

PAGE.   Yes, my Lord.

L. FOP.   You'll excuse me, Brother.   [*going*]

Y. FAS.   Shall you be back at dinner?

L. FOP.   As Gad shall jidge me, I can't tell; for 'tis passible I may dine with some of aur House at Lacket's.

Y. FAS.   Shall I meet you there? for I must needs talk with you.

L. FOP.   That, I'm afraid, mayn't be so praper; far the lards I commonly eat with are people of a nice conversation; and you know, Tam, your education has been a little at large: but if you'll stay here, you'll find a family dinner.—— Hey, fellow! What is there for dinner? There's beef:

I suppose my brother will eat beef.—— Dear Tam, I'm glad to see thee in England, stap my vitals.   [*exit with his equipage*]

Y. FAS.   Hell and Furies, is this to be borne?

LO.   Faith, Sir, I could almost have given him a knock o' th' pate myself.

Y. FAS.   'Tis enough; I will now show thee the excess of my passion by being very calm. Come, Lory, lay your loggerhead to mine, and in cool blood let us contrive his destruction.

LO.   Here comes a head, Sir, would contrive it better than us both, if he would but join in the confederacy.

Enter COUPLER

Y. FAS.   By this light, old Coupler alive still! Why, how now, match-maker, art thou here still to plague the world with matrimony? You old bawd, how have you the impudence to be hobbling out of your grave twenty years after you are rotten!

COUP.   When you begin to rot, Sirrah, you'll go off like a pippin; one winter will send you to the devil. What mischief brings you again? Ha! you young lascivious rogue, you! let me put my hand in your bosom, Sirrah.

Y. FAS.   Stand off, old Sodom.

COUP.   Nay, prithee, now, don't be so coy.

Y. FAS.   Keep your hands to yourself, you old dog you, or I'll wring your nose off.

COUP.   Hast thou then been a year in Italy, and brought home a fool at last? By my conscience, the young fellows of this age profit no more by their going abroad than they do by their going to church. Sirrah, Sirrah, if you are not hanged before you come to my years, you'll know a cock from a hen. But come, I'm still a friend to thy person, though I have a contempt of thy understanding; and therefore I would willingly know thy condition, that I may see whether thou stand'st in need of my assistance; for widows swarm, my boy, the town's infected with 'em.

Y. FAS.   I stand in need of anybody's assistance that will help me to cut my elder brother's throat, without the risk of being hanged for him.

COUP.   I'gad, Sirrah, I could help thee to do him almost as good a turn, without the danger of being burnt in the hand for't.

Y. FAS.   Sayest thou so, old Satan? Show me but that, and my soul is thine.

COUP.   Pox o' thy soul! give me thy warm body, Sirrah; I shall have a substantial title to't when I tell thee my project.

Y. FAS.   Out with it then, dear Dad, and take possession as soon as thou wilt.

Coup. Sayest thou so, my Hephestion? Why, then, thus lies the scene—but hold! who's that? if we are heard we are undone.

Y. Fas. What, have you forgot Lory?

Coup. Who? trusty Lory, is it thee?

Lo. At your service, Sir.

Coup. Give me thy hand, old boy; i'gad, I did not know thee again; but I remember thy honesty, though I did not thy face; I think thou hadst like to have been hanged once or twice for thy master.

Lo. Sir, I was very near once having that honour.

Coup. Well, live and hope; don't be discouraged; eat with him, and drink with him, and do what he bids thee, and it may be thy reward at last as well as another's. [*to* Young Fashion] Well, Sir, you must know I have done you the kindness to make up a match for your brother.

Y. Fas. Sir, I am very much beholding to you, truly.

Coup. You may be, Sirrah, before the wedding-day yet; the lady is a great heiress; fifteen hundred pound a year, and a great bag of money; the match is concluded, the writings are drawn, and the pipkin's to be cracked in a fortnight. Now you must know, stripling (with respect to your mother), your brother's the son of a whore.

Y. Fas. Good!

Coup. He has given me a bond of a thousand pounds for helping him to this fortune, and has promised me as much more in ready money upon the day of marriage, which, I understand by a friend, he ne'er designs to pay me. If therefore you will be a generous young dog, and secure me five thousand pounds, I'll be a covetous old rogue, and help you to the lady.

Y. Fas. I'gad, if thou canst bring this about, I'll have thy statue cast in brass. But don't you dote, you old pander, you, when you talk at this rate?

Coup. That your youthful parts shall judge of. This plump partridge that I tell you of lives in the country, fifty miles off, with her honoured parents, in a lonely old house which nobody comes near; she never goes abroad, nor sees company at home; to prevent all misfortunes, she has her breeding within doors: the parson of the parish teaches her to play upon the bass-viol, the clerk to sing, her nurse to dress, and her father to dance. In short, nobody can give you admittance there but I; nor can I do it any other way than by making you pass for your brother.

Y. Fas. And how the devil wilt thou do that?

Coup. Without the devil's aid, I warrant thee. Thy brother's face not one of the family ever saw; the whole business has been managed by me, and all the letters go through my hands: the last that was writ to Sir Tunbelly Clumsey (for that's the old gentleman's name) was to tell him his Lordship would be down in a fortnight to consummate. Now you shall go away immediately, pretend you writ that letter only to have the romantic pleasure of surprising your mistress, fall desperately in love as soon as you see her; make that your plea of marrying her immediately, and when the fatigue of the wedding-night's over you shall send me a swinging purse of gold, you dog, you.

Y. FAS.   I'gad, old Dad, I'll put my hand in thy bosom now.

COUP.   Ah, you young hot lusty thief, let me muzzle you—[*kissing*]— Sirrah, let me muzzle you.

Y. FAS. [*aside*]   Psha, the old lecher——

COUP.   Well, I'll warrant thou hast not a farthing of money in thy pocket now, no; one may see it in thy face——

Y. FAS.   Not a souse, by Jupiter.

COUP.   Must I advance then. Well, Sirrah, be at my lodgings in half an hour, and I'll see what may be done; we'll sign and seal, and eat a pullet, and when I have given thee some farther instructions, thou shalt hoist sail and be gone. [*kissing*] T'other buss, and so adieu.

Y. FAS.   Um, psha.

COUP.   Ah, you young warm dog, you; what a delicious night will the bride have on't!   [*exit* COUPLER]

Y. FAS.   So, Lory: Providence, thou seest at last, takes care of men of merit: we are in a fair way to be great people.

LO.   Ay, Sir, if the devil don't step between the cup and the lip, as he uses to do.

Y. FAS.   Why, faith, he has played me many a damned trick to spoil my fortune, and, i'gad, I'm almost afraid he's at work about it again now; but if I should tell thee how, thou'dst wonder at me.

LO.   Indeed, Sir, I should not.

Y. FAS.   How dost know?

LO.   Because, Sir, I have wondered at you so often, I can wonder at you no more.

Y. FAS.   No? what wouldst thou say if a qualm of conscience should spoil my design?

LO.   I would eat my words, and wonder more than ever.

Y. FAS.   Why, faith, Lory, though I am a young rake-hell, and have played many a roguish trick, this is so full-grown a cheat, I find I must take pains to come up to't; I have scruples.

LO.   They are strong symptoms of death; if you find they increase, pray, Sir, make your will.

Y. FAS.   No, my conscience shan't starve me, neither. But thus far I will harken to it, before I execute this project. I'll try my brother to the bottom; I'll speak to him with the temper of a philosopher; my reasons (though they press him home) shall yet be clothed with so much modesty, not one of all the truths they urge shall be so naked to offend his sight: if he has yet so much humanity about him as to assist me (though with a moderate aid) I'll drop my project at his feet, and show him I can—do for him much more than what I ask he'd do for me. This one conclusive trial of him I resolve to make.

Succeed or no, still victory's my lot;
If I subdue his heart, 'tis well; if not,
I shall subdue my conscience to my plot.   [*exeunt*]

ACT II

Enter LOVELESS *and* AMANDA

LOV.   How do you like these lodgings, my dear? For my part, I am so well pleased with 'em, I shall hardly remove whilst we stay in town, if you are satisfied.

AMAN.   I am satisfied with everything that pleases you; else I had not come to town at all.

LOV.   Oh, a little of the noise and bustle of the world sweetens the pleasures of retreat: we shall find the charms of our retirement doubled when we return to it.

AMAN.   That pleasing prospect will be my chiefest entertainment, whilst (much against my will) I am obliged to stand surrounded with these empty pleasures which 'tis so much the fashion to be fond of.

LOV.   I own most of 'em are indeed but empty; nay, so empty, that one would wonder by what magic power they act, when they induce us to be vicious for their sakes. Yet some there are we may speak kindlier of: there are delights (of which a private life is destitute) which may divert an honest man, and be a harmless entertainment to a virtuous woman. The conversation of the town is one; and truly (with some small allowances) the plays, I think, may be esteemed another.

AMAN.   The plays, I must confess, have some small charms, and would have more would they restrain that loose, obscene encouragement to vice which shocks, if not the virtue of some women, at least the modesty of all.

LOV.   But till that reformation can be made I would not leave the wholesome corn for some intruding tares that grow amongst it. Doubtless the moral of a well-wrought scene is of prevailing force. Last night there happened one that moved me strangely.

AMAN.   Pray, what was that?

LOV.   Why, 'twas about—but 'tis not worth repeating.

AMAN.   Yes, pray let me know it.

LOV.   No, I think 'tis as well let alone.

AMAN.   Nay, now you make me have a mind to know.

Lov.   'Twas a foolish thing: you'd perhaps grow jealous should I tell it you, though without cause, heaven knows.

Aman.   I shall begin to think I have cause, if you persist in making it a secret.

Lov.   I'll then convince you you have none, by making it no longer so. Know then, I happened in the play to find my very character, only with the addition of a relapse, which struck me so I put a sudden stop to a most harmless entertainment which till then diverted me between the acts. 'Twas to admire the workmanship of Nature in the face of a young lady that sate some distance from me, she was so exquisitely handsome.

Aman.   "So exquisitely handsome!"

Lov.   Why do you repeat my words, my dear?

Aman.   Because you seemed to speak 'em with such pleasure I thought I might oblige you with their echo.

Lov.   Then you are alarmed, Amanda?

Aman.   It is my duty to be so, when you are in danger.

Lov.   You are too quick in apprehending for me; all will be well when you have heard me out. I do confess I gazed upon her, nay, eagerly I gazed upon her.

Aman.   Eagerly? That's with desire.

Lov.   No, I desired her not: I viewed her with a world of admiration, but not one glance of love.

Aman.   Take heed of trusting to such nice distinctions.

Lov.   I did take heed; for, observing in the play that he who seemed to represent me there was, by an accident like this unwarily surprised into a net in which he lay a poor entangled slave, and brought a train of mischiefs on his head, I snatched my eyes away; they pleaded hard for leave to look again, but I grew absolute, and they obeyed.

Aman.   Were they the only things that were inquisitive? Had I been in your place, my tongue, I fancy, had been curious, too: I should have asked her name, and where she lived (yet still without design). Who was she, pray?

Lov.   Indeed I cannot tell.

Aman.   You will not tell.

Lov.   By all that's sacred, then, I did not ask.

Aman.   Nor do you know what company was with her?

Lov.   I do not.

Aman.   Then I am calm again.

Lov.   Why were you disturbed?

Aman.   Had I then no cause?

Lov.   None, certainly.

Aman.   I thought I had.

Lov.   But you thought wrong, Amanda; for turn the case, and let it be your story. Should you come home, and tell me you had seen a handsome man, should I grow jealous because you had eyes?

AMAN.   But should I tell you he were exquisitely so; that I had gazed on him with admiration; that I had looked with eager eyes upon him; should you not think 'twere possible I might go one step farther, and enquire his name?

LOV. [aside]   She has reason on her side: I have talked too much; but I must turn it off another way. [to AMANDA] Will you then make no difference, Amanda, between the language of our sex and yours? There is a modesty restrains your tongues which makes you speak by halves when you commend; but roving flattery gives a loose to ours, which makes us still speak double what we think: you should not therefore in so strict a sense take what I said to her advantage.

AMAN.   Those flights of flattery, Sir, are to our faces only: when women once are out of hearing, you are as modest in your commendations as we are. But I shan't put you to the trouble of farther excuses; if you please, this business shall rest here. Only give me leave to wish, both for your peace and mine, that you may never meet this miracle of beauty more.

LOV.   I am content.

Enter Servant

SERV.   Madam, there's a young lady at the door in a chair, desires to know whether your ladyship sees company. I think her name is Berinthia.

AMAN.   Oh dear! 'tis a relation I have not seen these five years.——
Pray her to walk in.   [exit Servant]
[to LOVELESS] Here's another beauty for you. She was young when I saw her last; but I hear she's grown extremely handsome.

LOV.   Don't you be jealous now, for I shall gaze upon her too.

Enter BERINTHIA

LOV. [aside]   Ha! By heavens, the very woman!

BER. [saluting AMANDA]   Dear Amanda, I did not expect to meet with you in town.

AMAN.   Sweet Cousin, I'm overjoyed to see you. [to LOVELESS] Mr. Loveless, here's a relation and a friend of mine I desire you'll be better acquainted with.

LOV. [saluting BERINTHIA]   If my wife never desires a harder thing, Madam, her request will be easily granted.

BER. [to AMANDA]   I think, Madam, I ought to wish you joy.

AMAN.   Joy! Upon what?

BER.   Upon your marriage: you were a widow when I saw you last.

LOV.   You ought rather, Madam, to wish me joy upon that, since I am the only gainer.

BER.   If she has got so good a husband as the world reports, she has gained enough to expect the compliments of her friends upon it.

LOV.   If the world is so favourable to me, to allow I deserve that title, I hope 'tis so just to my wife to own I derive it from her.

BER.   Sir, it is so just to you both, to own you are, and deserve to be, the happiest pair that live in it.

LOV.   I'm afraid we shall lose that character, Madam, whenever you happen to change your condition.

Enter Servant

SERV.   Sir, my Lord Foppington presents his humble service to you, and desires to know how you do. He but just now heard you were in town. He's at the next door; and if it be not inconvenient, he'll come and wait upon you.

LOV.   Lord Foppington! I know him not.

BER.   Not his dignity, perhaps, but you do his person. 'Tis Sir Novelty; he has bought a barony in order to marry a great fortune: his patent has not been passed eight-and-forty hours, and he has already sent how-do-ye's to all the town, to make 'em acquainted with his title.

LOV.   Give my service to his Lordship, and let him know I am proud of the honour he intends me.   [*exit Servant*]
Sure this addition of quality must have so improved this coxcomb, he can't but be very good company for a quarter of an hour.

AMAN.   Now it moves my pity more than my mirth, to see a man whom nature has made no fool be so very industrious to pass for an ass.

LOV.   No, there you are wrong, Amanda; you should never bestow your pity upon those who take pains for your contempt. Pity those whom nature abuses, but never those who abuse nature.

BER.   Besides, the town would be robbed of one of its chief diversions, if it should become a crime to laugh at a fool.

AMAN.   I could never yet perceive the town inclined to part with any of its diversions for the sake of their being crimes; but I have seen it very fond of some I think had little else to recommend 'em.

BER.   I doubt, Amanda, you are grown its enemy, you speak with so much warmth against it.

AMAN.   I must confess I am not much its friend.

BER.   Then give me leave to make you mine, by not engaging in its quarrel.

AMAN.   You have many stronger claims than that, Berinthia, whenever you think fit to plead your title.

LOV.   You have done well to engage a second, my dear; for here

comes one will be apt to call you to an account for your country principles.

Enter LORD FOPPINGTON

L. FOP. [*to* LOVELESS]   Sir, I am your most humble servant.

LOV.   I wish you joy, my Lord.

L. FOP.   O Lard, Sir!—— Madam, your Ladyship's welcome to tawn.

AMAN.   I wish your Lordship joy.

L. FOP.   O heavens, Madam!

LOV.   My Lord, this young lady is a relation of my wife's.

L. FOP. [*saluting her*]   The beautifullest race of people upon earth, rat
me. Dear Loveless, I am overjoyed to see you have braught your family
to tawn again: I am, stap my vitals—[*aside*] far I design to lie with your
wife. [*to* AMANDA] Far Gad's sake, Madam, haw has your Ladyship been
able to subsist thus long under the fatigue of a country life?

AMAN.   My life has been very far from that, my Lord; it has been a
very quiet one.

L. FOP.   Why, that's the fatigue I speak of, Madam, for 'tis impossible
to be quiet without thinking: now thinking is to me the greatest fatigue
in the world.

AMAN.   Does not your Lordship love reading, then?

L. FOP.   Oh, passionately, Madam—but I never think of what I read.

BER.   Why, can your Lordship read without thinking?

L. FOP.   O Lard—can your Ladyship pray without devotion—
Madam?

AMAN.   Well, I must own I think books the best entertainment in the
world.

L. FOP.   I am so much of your Ladyship's mind, Madam, that I have a
private gallery, where I walk sometimes, is furnished with nothing but
books and looking-glasses. Madam, I have gilded 'em, and ranged 'em so
prettily, before Gad, it is the most entertaining thing in the world to walk
and look upon 'em.

AMAN.   Nay, I love a neat library too; but 'tis, I think, the inside of the
book should recommend it most to us.

L. FOP.   That, I must confess, I am nat altogether so fand of. Far to
mind the inside of a book is to entertain one's self with the forced
product of another man's brain. Naw I think a man of quality and
breeding may be much better diverted with the natural sprauts of his
own. But to say the truth, Madam, let a man love reading never so well,
when once he comes to know this tawn he finds so many better ways
of passing the four-and-twenty hours that 'twere ten thousand pities he
should consume his time in that. Far example, Madam, my life; my life,
Madam, is a perpetual stream of pleasure, that glides through such a va-

riety of entertainments I believe the wisest of our ancestors never had the least conception of any of 'em. I rise, Madam, about ten a'clack. I don't rise sooner, because 'tis the worst thing in the world for the complexion; nat that I pretend to be a beau, but a man must endeavour to look wholesome, lest he make so nauseous a figure in the side-bax, the ladies should be compelled to turn their eyes upon the play. So at ten a'clack, I say, I rise. Naw, if I find 'tis a good day, I resalve to take a turn in the park, and see the fine women; so huddle on my clothes, and get dressed by one. If it be nasty weather, I take a turn in the chocolate-hause, where, as you walk, Madam, you have the prettiest prospect in the world; you have looking-glasses all round you.—— But I'm afraid I tire the company?

BER.   Not at all. Pray go on.

L. FOP.   Why then, ladies, from thence I go to dinner at Lacket's, where you are so nicely and delicately served that, stap my vitals, they shall compose you a dish no bigger than a saucer, shall come to fifty shillings. Between eating my dinner, and washing my mauth, ladies, I spend my time till I go to the play, where, till nine a'clack, I entertain myself with looking upon the company; and usually dispose of one hour more in leading 'em aut. So there's twelve of the four-and-twenty pretty well over. The other twelve, Madam, are disposed of in two articles: in the first four I toast myself drunk, and in t'other eight I sleep myself sober again. Thus, ladies, you see my life is an eternal raund O of delights.

LOV.   'Tis a heavenly one, indeed.

AMAN.   But I thought, my Lord, you beaux spent a great deal of your time in intrigues: you have given us no account of them yet.

L. FOP. [*aside*]   Soh! she would enquire into my amours—that's jealousy—she begins to be in love with me. [*to* AMANDA] Why, Madam—as to time for my intrigues, I usually make detachments of it from my other pleasures, according to the exigency. Far your Ladyship may please to take notice that those who intrigue with women of quality have rarely occasion far above half an hour at a time: people of that rank being under those decorums they can seldom give you a langer view than will just serve to shoot 'em flying. So that the course of my other pleasures is not very much interrupted by my amours.

LOV.   But your Lordship now is become a pillar of the state; you must attend the weighty affairs of the nation.

L. FOP.   Sir—as to weighty affairs—I leave them to weighty heads. I never intend mine shall be a burthen to my body.

LOV.   Oh, but you'll find the House will expect your attendance.

L. FOP.   Sir, you'll find the House will compound for my appearance.

LOV.   But your friends will take it ill if you don't attend their particular causes.

L. Fop.   Not, Sir, if I come time enough to give 'em my particular vote.

Ber.   But pray, my Lord, how do you dispose of yourself on Sundays? for that, methinks, is a day should hang wretchedly upon your hands.

L. Fop.   Why, faith, Madam—Sunday—is a vile day, I must confess. I intend to move for leave to bring in a bill that the players may work upon it, as well as the hackney coaches. Though this I must say for the Government, it leaves us the churches to entertain us—but then again, they begin so abominably early, a man must rise by candle-light to get dressed by the psalm.

Ber.   Pray, which church does your Lordship most oblige with your presence?

L. Fop.   Oh, St. James's, Madam—there's much the best company.

Aman.   Is there good preaching too?

L. Fop.   Why, faith, Madam—I can't tell. A man must have very little to do there, that can give an account of the sermon.

Ber.   You can give us an account of the ladies, at least?

L. Fop.   Or I deserve to be excommunicated. There is my Lady Tattle, my Lady Prate, my Lady Titter, my Lady Leer, my Lady Giggle, and my Lady Grin. These sit in the front of the boxes, and all church-time are the prettiest company in the world, stap my vitals. [to Amanda] Mayn't we hope for the honour to see your Ladyship added to our society, Madam?

Aman.   Alas, my Lord, I am the worst company in the world at church: I'm apt to mind the prayers, or the sermon, or——

L. Fop.   One is indeed strangely apt at church to mind what one should not do. But I hope, Madam, at one time or other, I shall have the honour to lead your Ladyship to your coach there. [aside] Methinks she seems strangely pleased with everything I say to her. 'Tis a vast pleasure to receive encouragement from a woman before her husband's face—I have a good mind to pursue my conquest, and speak the thing plainly to her at once. I'gad, I'll do 't, and that in so cavalier a manner she shall be surprised at it.—— Ladies, I'll take my leave; I'm afraid I begin to grow troublesome with the length of my visit.

Aman.   Your Lordship's too entertaining to grow troublesome anywhere.

L. Fop. [aside]   That now was as much as if she had said "Pray lie with me." I'll let her see I'm quick of apprehension. [to Amanda] O Lard, Madam, I had like to have forgot a secret I must needs tell your ladyship. [to Loveless] Ned, you must not be so jealous now as to listen.

Lov.   Not I, my Lord; I am too fashionable a husband to pry into the secrets of my wife.

L. Fop. [to Amanda, squeezing her hand]   I am in love with you to desperation, strike me speechless.

AMAN. [*giving him a box o' th' ear*]   Then thus I return your passion—an impudent fool!

L. FOP.   Gad's curse, Madam, I'm a peer of the realm.

LOV.   Hey; what the devil! do you affront my wife, Sir? Nay, then——

[*they draw and fight; the women run shrieking for help*]

AMAN.   Ah! What has my folly done? Help! Murder, help! Part 'em, for heaven's sake!

L. FOP. [*falling back, and leaning upon his sword*]   Ah—quite through the body—stap my vitals.

Enter Servants

LOV. [*running to him*]   I hope I han't killed the fool, however.—— Bare him up!—— Where's your wound?

L. FOP.   Just through the guts.

LOV.   Call a surgeon there: unbutton him quickly.

L. FOP.   Ay, pray make haste.   [*exit Servant*]

LOV.   This mischief you may thank yourself for.

L. FOP.   I may so—love's the devil indeed, Ned.

Enter SERRINGE *and Servant*

SERV.   Here's Mr. Serringe, Sir, was just going by the door.

L. FOP.   He's the welcom'st man alive.

SER.   Stand by, stand by, stand by. Pray, gentlemen, stand by. Lord have mercy upon us! did you never see a man run through the body before? Pray stand by.

L. FOP.   Ah, Mr. Serringe—I'm a dead man.

SER.   A dead man, and I by—I should laugh to see that, i'gad.

LOV.   Prithee don't stand prating, but look upon his wound.

SER.   Why, what if I won't look upon his wound this hour, Sir?

LOV.   Why, then he'll bleed to death, Sir.

SER.   Why, then I'll fetch him to life again, Sir.

LOV.   'Slife, he's run through the guts, I tell thee.

SER.   Would he were run through the heart: I should get the more credit by his cure. Now I hope you're satisfied?—— Come, now let me come at him; now let me come at him. [*viewing his wound*] Oons, what a gash is here!—— Why, Sir, a man may drive a coach and six horses into your body.

L. FOP.   Ho!——

SER.   Why, what the devil! have you run the gentleman through with a scythe?—— [*aside*] A little prick between the skin and the ribs, that's all.

LOV.   Let me see his wound.

SER. Then you shall dress it, Sir; for if anybody looks upon it, I won't.

LOV. Why, thou art the veriest coxcomb I ever saw.

SER. Sir, I am not master of my trade for nothing.

L. FOP. Surgeon!

SER. Well, Sir?

L. FOP. Is there any hopes?

SER. Hopes? I can't tell. What are you willing to give for your cure?

L. FOP. Five hundred paunds with pleasure.

SER. Why, then perhaps there may be hopes. But we must avoid farther delay. Here, help the gentleman into a chair, and carry him to my house presently: that's the properest place—[aside] to bubble him out of his money.—— Come, a chair, a chair quickly—there, in with him.

[they put him into a chair]

L. FOP. Dear Loveless—adieu. If I die—I forgive thee; and if I live— I hope thou'lt do as much by me. I'm very sorry you and I should quarrel; but I hope here's an end on't, for if you are satisfied—I am.

LOV. I shall hardly think it worth my prosecuting any farther, so you may be at rest, Sir.

L. FOP. Thou art a generous fellow, strike me dumb. [aside] But thou hast an impertinent wife, stap my vitals.

SER. So, carry him off, carry him off; we shall have him prate himself into a fever by and by; carry him off.

[exit SERRINGE with LORD FOPPINGTON]

AMAN. Now on my knees, my dear, let me ask your pardon for my indiscretion: my own I never shall obtain.

LOV. Oh! there's no harm done: you served him well.

AMAN. He did indeed deserve it. But I tremble to think how dear my indiscreet resentment might have cost you.

LOV. Oh, no matter; never trouble yourself about that.

BER. For heaven's sake, what was't he did to you?

AMAN. Oh, nothing; he only squeezed me kindly by the hand and frankly offered me a coxcomb's heart. I know I was to blame to resent it as I did, since nothing but a quarrel could ensue. But the fool so surprised me with his insolence I was not mistress of my fingers.

BER. Now I dare swear he thinks you had 'em at great command, they obeyed you so readily.

Enter WORTHY

WOR. Save you, save you, good people; I'm glad to find you all alive; I met a wounded peer carrying off. For heaven's sake, what was the matter?

LOV. Oh, a trifle: he would have lain with my wife before my face, so she obliged him with a box o' the ear, and I run him through the body: that was all.

WOR.   Bagatelle on all sides. But, pray, Madam, how long has this noble lord been an humble servant of yours?

AMAN.   This is the first I have heard on't. So I suppose 'tis his quality, more than his love, has brought him into this adventure. He thinks his title an authentic passport to every woman's heart, below the degree of a peeress.

WOR.   He's coxcomb enough to think anything. But I would not have you brought into trouble for him: I hope there's no danger of his life?

LOV.   None at all: he's fallen into the hands of a roguish surgeon I perceive designs to frighten a little money out of him. But I saw his wound—'tis nothing; he may go to the play to-night if he pleases.

WOR.   I am glad you have corrected him without farther mischief. And now, Sir, if these ladies have no farther service for you, you'll oblige me if you can go to the place I spoke to you of t'other day.

LOV.   With all my heart. [*aside*] Though I could wish, methinks, to stay and gaze a little longer on that creature. Good gods! how beautiful she is!—but what have I to do with beauty? I have already had my portion, and must not covet more. [*to* WORTHY] Come, Sir, when you please.

WOR.   Ladies, your servant.

AMAN.   Mr. Loveless, pray one word with you before you go.

LOV. [*to* WORTHY]   I'll overtake you, Sir.   [*exit* WORTHY]
——What would my dear?

AMAN.   Only a woman's foolish question; how do you like my cousin here?

LOV.   Jealous already, Amanda?

AMAN.   Not at all; I ask you for another reason.

LOV. [*aside*]   Whate'er her reason be, I must not tell her true. [*to* AMANDA] Why, I confess she's handsome. But you must not think I slight your kinswoman if I own to you, of all the women who may claim that character she is the last would triumph in my heart.

AMAN.   I'm satisfied.

LOV.   Now tell me why you asked.

AMAN.   At night I will. Adieu.

LOV. [*kissing her*]   I'm yours.   [*exit* LOVELESS]

AMAN. [*aside*]   I'm glad to find he does not like her; for I have a great mind to persuade her to come and live with me. [*to* BERINTHIA] Now, dear Berinthia, let me enquire a little into your affairs: for I do assure you I am enough your friend to interest myself in everything that concerns you.

BER.   You formerly have given me such proofs on't I should be very much to blame to doubt it. I am sorry I have no secrets to trust you with, that I might convince you how entire a confidence I durst repose in you.

AMAN. Why, is it possible that one so young and beautiful as you should live and have no secrets?

BER. What secrets do you mean?

AMAN. Lovers.

BER. Oh, twenty; but not one secret one amongst 'em. Lovers in this age have too much honour to do anything underhand; they do all above-board.

AMAN. That, now, methinks, would make me hate a man.

BER. But the women of the town are of another mind: for by this means a lady may, with the expense of a few coquet glances, lead twenty fools about in a string for two or three years together. Whereas, if she should allow 'em greater favours, and oblige 'em to secrecy, she would not keep one of 'em a fortnight.

AMAN. There's something indeed in that to satisfy the vanity of a woman, but I can't comprehend how the men find their account in it.

BER. Their entertainment, I must confess, is a riddle to me. For there's very few of 'em ever get farther than a bow and an ogle. I have half a score for my share, who follow me all over the town; and at the play, the park, and the church do (with their eyes) say the violent'st things to me—but I never hear any more of 'em.

AMAN. What can be the reason of that?

BER. One reason is they don't know how to go farther. They have had so little practice they don't understand the trade. But besides their ignorance, you must know there is not one of my half-score lovers but what follows half a score mistresses. Now their affections, being divided amongst so many, are not strong enough for any one to make 'em pursue her to the purpose. Like a young puppy in a warren, they have a flirt at all, and catch none.

AMAN. Yet they seem to have a torrent of love to dispose of.

BER. They have so: but 'tis like the rivers of a modern philosopher (whose works, though a woman, I have read): it sets out with a violent stream, splits in a thousand branches, and is all lost in the sands.

AMAN. But do you think this river of love runs all its course without doing any mischief? Do you think it overflows nothing?

BER. Oh yes; 'tis true, it never breaks into anybody's ground that has the least fence about it; but it overflows all the commons that lie in its way. And this is the utmost achievement of those dreadful champions in the field of love—the beaux.

AMAN. But prithee, Berinthia, instruct me a little farther, for I'm so great a novice, I am almost ashamed on't. My husband's leaving me whilst I was young and fond threw me into that depth of discontent that ever since I have led so private and recluse a life my ignorance is scarce conceivable. I therefore fain would be instructed; not, heaven knows, that what you call intrigues have any charms for me: my love and principles are too well fixed. The practic part of all unlawful love is——

BER. Oh, 'tis abominable: but for the speculative—that we must all confess is entertaining. The conversation of all the virtuous women in the town turns upon that and new clothes.

AMAN. Pray be so just then to me to believe 'tis with a world of innocency I would enquire whether you think those women we call women of reputation do really 'scape all other men, as they do those shadows of 'em, the beaux.

BER. Oh no, Amanda; there are a sort of men make dreadful work amongst 'em: men that may be called the beaux' antipathy, for they agree in nothing but walking upon two legs.

These have brains: the beau has none.

These are in love with their mistress: the beau with himself.

They take care of her reputation: he's industrious to destroy it.

They are decent: he's a fop.

They are sound: he's rotten.

They are men: he's an ass.

AMAN. If this be their character, I fancy we had here e'en now a pattern of 'em both.

BER. His Lordship and Mr. Worthy?

AMAN. The same.

BER. As for the lord, he's eminently so: and for the other, I can assure you there's not a man in town who has a better interest with the women that are worth having an interest with. But 'tis all private: he's like a back-stair minister at Court, who, whilst the reputed favourites are sauntering in the bed-chamber, is ruling the roast in the closet.

AMAN. He answers then the opinion I had ever of him. Heavens! what a difference there is between a man like him and that vain, nauseous fop, Sir Novelty! [*taking her hand*] I must acquaint you with a secret, Cousin. 'Tis not that fool alone has talked to me of love: Worthy has been tampering too. 'Tis true, he has done't in vain: not all his charms or art have power to shake me. My love, my duty, and my virtue are such faithful guards, I need not fear my heart should e'er betray me. But what I wonder at is this: I find I did not start at his proposal, as when it came from one whom I contemned. I therefore mention his attempt that I may learn from you whence it proceeds that vice, which cannot change its nature, should so far .change at least its shape as that the self-same crime proposed from one shall seem a monster gaping at your ruin, when from another it shall look so kind as though it were your friend, and never meant to harm you.

Whence, think you, can this difference proceed? For 'tis not love, heaven knows.

BER.   Oh, no. I would not for the world believe it were. But possibly, should there a dreadful sentence pass upon you to undergo the rage of both their passions, the pain you'd apprehend from one might seem so trivial to the other, the danger would not quite so much alarm you.

AMAN.   Fy, fy, Berinthia! You would indeed alarm me, could you incline me to a thought that all the merit of mankind combined could shake that tender love I bear my husband. No, he sits triumphant in my heart, and nothing can dethrone him.

BER.   But should he abdicate again, do you think you should preserve the vacant throne ten tedious winters more, in hopes of his return?

AMAN.   Indeed I think I should. Though I confess, after those obligations he has to me, should he abandon me once more, my heart would grow extremely urgent with me to root him thence, and cast him out forever.

BER.   Were I that thing they call a slighted wife, somebody should run the risk of being that thing they call—a husband.

AMAN.   Oh fy, Berinthia! No revenge should ever be taken against a husband: but to wrong his bed is a vengeance, which of all vengeance——

BER.   Is the sweetest—ha, ha, ha! Don't I talk madly?

AMAN.   Madly indeed.

BER.   Yet I'm very innocent.

AMAN.   That I dare swear you are. I know how to make allowances for your humour: you were always very entertaining company; but I find since marriage and widowhood have shown you the world a little, you are very much improved.

BER. [aside]   Alack-a-day, there has gone more than that to improve me, if she knew all.

AMAN.   For heaven's sake, Berinthia, tell me what way I shall take to persuade you to come and live with me.

BER.   Why, one way in the world there is—and but one.

AMAN.   Pray which is that?

BER.   It is to assure me—I shall be very welcome.

AMAN.   If that be all, you shall e'en lie here to-night.

BER.   To-night?

AMAN.   Yes, to-night.

BER.   Why, the people where I lodge will think me mad.

AMAN.   Let 'em think what they please.

BER.   Say you so, Amanda? Why then they shall think what they please: for I'm a young widow, and I care not what anybody thinks. Ah, Amanda, it's a delicious thing to be a young widow.

AMAN.   You'll hardly make me think so.

BER.   Phu, because you are in love with your husband: but that is not every woman's case.

AMAN.   I hope 'twas yours, at least.

BER.   Mine, say ye? Now have I a great mind to tell you a lie, but I should do it so awkwardly you'd find me out.

AMAN.   Then e'en speak the truth.

BER.   Shall I? Then after all, I did love him, Amanda—as a nun does penance.

AMAN.   Why did not you refuse to marry him, then?

BER.   Because my mother would have whipped me.

AMAN.   How did you live together?

BER.   Like man and wife—asunder;
He loved the country, I the town:
He hawks and hounds, I coaches and equipage:
He eating and drinking, I carding and playing:
He the sound of a horn, I the squeak of a fiddle.
We were dull company at table, worse abed.
Whenever we met, we gave one another the spleen.
And never agreed but once, which was about lying alone.

AMAN.   But tell me one thing truly and sincerely.

BER.   What's that?

AMAN.   Notwithstanding all these jars, did not his death at last—extremely trouble you?

BER.   Oh, yes: not that my present pangs were so very violent, but the after-pains were intolerable. I was forced to wear a beastly widow's band a twelve-month for't.

AMAN.   Women, I find, have different inclinations.

BER.   Women, I find, keep different company. When your husband ran away from you, if you had fallen into some of my acquaintance, 'twould have saved you many a tear. But you go and live with a grandmother, a bishop, and an old nurse, which was enough to make any woman break her heart for her husband. Pray, Amanda, if ever you are a widow again, keep yourself so as I do.

AMAN.   Why, do you then resolve you'll never marry?

BER.   Oh, no; I resolve I will.

AMAN.   How so?

BER.   That I never may.

AMAN.   You banter me.

BER.   Indeed I don't. But I consider I'm a woman, and form my resolutions accordingly.

AMAN.   Well, my opinion is, form what resolution you will matrimony will be the end on't.

BER.   Faith it won't.

AMAN.   How do you know?

BER.   I'm sure on't.

AMAN.   Why, do you think 'tis impossible for you to fall in love?

BER.   No.

AMAN.   Nay, but to grow so passionately fond that nothing but the man you love can give you rest?

BER.   Well, what then?

AMAN.   Why, then you'll marry him.

BER.   How do you know that?

AMAN.   Why, what can you do else?

BER.   Nothing—but sit and cry.

AMAN.   Psha!

BER.   Ah, poor Amanda, you have led a country life: but if you'll consult the widows of this town, they'll tell you you should never take a lease of a house you can hire for a quarter's warning.   [*exeunt*]

ACT III

SCENE I

Enter LORD FOPPINGTON *and Servant*

L. FOP.   Hey, fellow, let the coach come to the door.

SERV.   Will your Lordship venture so soon to expose yourself to the weather?

L. FOP.   Sir, I will venture as soon as I can to expose myself to the ladies: though give me my cloak, however, for in that side-box, what between the air that comes in at the door on one side, and the intolerable warmth of the masks on t'other, a man gets so many heats and colds, 'twould destroy the canstitution of a harse.

SERV. [*putting on his cloak*]   I wish your Lordship would please to keep house a little longer; I'm afraid your honour does not well consider your wound.

L. FOP.   My wound?—I would not be in eclipse another day, though I had as many wounds in my guts as I have had in my heart.

Enter YOUNG FASHION

Y. FAS.   Brother, your servant: how do you find yourself to-day?

L. FOP.   So well that I have ardered my coach to the door: so there's no great danger of death this baut, Tam.

Y. FAS.   I'm very glad of it.

L. FOP. [*aside*]   That I believe's a lie.—— Prithee, Tam, tell me one thing: did nat your heart cut a caper up to your mauth, when you heard I was run through the bady?

Y. FAS.   Why do you think it should?

L. FOP.   Because I remember mine did so, when I heard my father was shat through the head.

Y. FAS.   It then did very ill.

L. FOP.   Prithee, why so?

Y. FAS.   Because he used you very well.

L. FOP.   Well?—naw strike me dumb, he starved me. He has let me want a thausand women for want of a thausand paund.

Y. FAS.   Then he hindered you from making a great many ill bargains, for I think no woman is worth money that will take money.

L. FOP.   If I were a younger brother, I should think so too.

Y. FAS.   Why, is it possible you can value a woman that's to be bought?

L. FOP.   Prithee, why not as well as a pad-nag?

Y. FAS.   Because a woman has a heart to dispose of; a horse has none.

L. FOP.   Look you, Tam, of all things that belang to a woman, I have an aversion to her heart; far when once a woman has given you her heart—you can never get rid of the rest of her bady.

Y. FAS.   This is strange doctrine. But pray, in your amours how is it with your own heart?

L. FOP.   Why, my heart in my amours—is like my heart aut of my amours: *à la glace.*

My bady, Tam, is a watch, and my heart is the pendulum to it; whilst the finger runs raund to every hour in the circle, that still beats the same time.

Y. FAS.   Then you are seldom much in love?

L. FOP.   Never, stap my vitals.

Y. FAS.   Why then did you make all this bustle about Amanda?

L. FOP.   Because she was a woman of an insolent virtue, and I thought myself picked in honour to debauch her.

Y. FAS.   Very well. [*aside*] Here's a rare fellow for you, to have the spending of five thousand pounds a year. But now for my business with him. [*to* LORD FOPPINGTON]—Brother, though I know to talk to you of business (especially of money) is a theme not quite so entertaining to you as that of the ladies, my necessities are such I hope you'll have patience to hear me.

L. FOP.   The greatness of your necessities, Tam, is the worst argument in the world far your being patiently heard. I do believe you are going to make me a very good speech, but, strike me dumb, it has the worst beginning of any speech I have heard this twelvemonth.

Y. FAS.   I'm very sorry you think so.

L. FOP.   I do believe thau art. But come, let's know thy affair quickly; far 'tis a new play, and I shall be so rumpled and squeezed with pressing through the crawd to get to my servant the women will think I have lain all night in my clothes.

Y. FAS.   Why then (that I may not be the author of so great a misfortune) my case in a word is this: the necessary expenses of my travels have so much exceeded the wretched income of my annuity that I have been forced to mortgage it for five hundred pounds, which is spent; so that unless you are so kind to assist me in redeeming it, I know no remedy but to go take a purse.

L. Fop.   Why, faith, Tam—to give you my sense of the thing, I do think taking a purse the best remedy in the world; for if you succeed, you are relieved that way; if you are taken—you are relieved t'other.

Y. Fas.   I'm glad to see you are in so pleasant a humour; I hope I shall find the effects on't.

L. Fop.   Why, do you then really think it a reasonable thing I should give you five hundred paunds?

Y. Fas.   I do not ask it as a due, Brother; I am willing to receive it as a favour.

L. Fop.   Thau art willing to receive it any haw, strike me speechless. But these are damned times to give money in: taxes are so great, repairs so exorbitant, tenants such rogues, and periwigs so dear, that the devil take me, I am reduced to that extremity in my cash I have been forced to retrench in that one article of sweet pawder, till I have braught it dawn to five guineas a manth. Naw judge, Tam, whether I can spare you five hundred paunds?

Y. Fas.   If you can't, I must starve, that's all. [*aside*] Damn him!

L. Fop.   All I can say is, you should have been a better husband.

Y. Fas.   'Oons, if you can't live upon five thousand a year, how do you think I should do't upon two hundred?

L. Fop.   Don't be in a passion, Tam, far passion is the most unbecoming thing in the world—to the face. Look you, I don't love to say anything to you to make you melancholy; but upon this occasion I must take leave to put you in mind that a running horse does require more attendance than a coach-horse. Nature has made some difference 'twixt you and I.

Y. Fas.   Yes, she has made you older. [*aside*] Pox take her!

L. Fop.   That is nat all, Tam.

Y. Fas.   Why, what is there else?

L. Fop. [*looking first upon himself, then upon his brother*]   Ask the ladies.

Y. Fas.   Why, thou essence bottle, thou musk-cat, dost thou then think thou hast any advantage over me but what fortune has given thee?

L. Fop.   I do—stap my vitals.

Y. Fas.   Now, by all that's great and powerful, thou art the prince of coxcombs.

L. Fop.   Sir—I am praud of being at the head of so prevailing a party.

Y. Fas.   Will nothing then provoke thee?—— Draw, coward!

L. Fop.   Look you, Tam, you know I have always taken you for a mighty dull fellow, and here is one of the foolishest plats broke out that I have seen a long time. Your paverty makes your life so burthensome to you you would provoke me to a quarrel, in hopes either to slip through my lungs into my estate, or to get yourself run through the guts, to put an end to your pain. But I will disappoint you in both your designs; far

with the temper of a philasapher, and the discretion of a statesman—I
will go to the play with my sword in my scabbard.

[*exit* LORD FOPPINGTON]

Y. FAS.   So! Farewell, snuff-box. And now, conscience, I defy thee.
Lory!

Enter LORY

LO.   Sir.

Y. FAS.   Here's rare news, Lory; his Lordship has given me a pill has
purged off all my scruples.

LO.   Then my heart's at ease again: for I have been in a lamentable
fright, Sir, ever since your conscience had the impudence to intrude into
your company.

Y. FAS.   Be at peace, it will come there no more: my brother has given
it a wring by the nose, and I have kicked it down stairs. So run away to
the inn; get the horses ready quickly, and bring 'em to old Coupler's,
without a moment's delay.

LO.   Then, Sir, you are going straight about the fortune?

Y. FAS.   I am: away! fly, Lory!

LO.   The happiest day I ever saw. I'm upon the wing already.

[*exeunt several ways*]

SCENE II

A garden

Enter LOVELESS *and Servant*

LOV.   Is my wife within?

SERV.   No, Sir, she has been gone out this half hour.

LOV.   'Tis well; leave me.
   [*solus*] Sure, fate has yet some business to be done,
   Before Amanda's heart and mine must rest;
   Else why, amongst those legions of her sex,
   Which throng the world,
   Should she pick out for her companion
   The only one on earth
   Whom nature has endow'd for her undoing?
   "Undoing" was't I said?—Who shall undo her?
   Is not her empire fix'd? Am I not hers?
   Did she not rescue me, a grov'ling slave?
   When, chain'd and bound by that black tyrant, Vice,
   I labour'd in his vilest drudgery,
   Did she not ransom me, and set me free?

Nay, more:
When by my follies sunk
To a poor tatter'd, despicable beggar,
Did she not lift me up to envy'd fortune?
Give me herself, and all that she possessed?
Without a thought of more return,
Than what a poor repenting heart might make her.
Han't she done this? And if she has,
Am I not strongly bound to love her for it?
To love her!—Why, do I not love her then?
By earth and heaven, I do!
Nay, I have demonstration that I do:
For I would sacrifice my life to serve her.
Yet hold:—if laying down my life
Be demonstration of my love,
What is't I feel in favour of Berinthia?
For should she be in danger, methinks, I could incline
To risk it for her service too; and yet I do not love her.
How then subsists my proof?—
—Oh, I have found it out.
What I would do for one is demonstration of my love;
And if I'd do as much for t'other,
If there is demonstration of my friendship—
Ay—It must be so.
I find I'm very much her friend.
—Yet let me ask myself one puzzling question more:
Whence springs this mighty friendship all at once?
For our acquaintance is of later date.
Now friendship's said to be a plant of tedious growth,
Its root compos'd of tender fibres,
Nice in their taste, cautious in spreading,
Check'd with the least corruption in the soil;
Long ere it take, and longer still ere it appear to do so.
Whilst mine is in a moment shot so high,
And fix'd so fast, it seems beyond the power
Of storms to shake it. I doubt it thrives too fast.   [*musing*]

Enter BERINTHIA

Ha! she here! Nay, then,
Take heed, my heart, for there are dangers towards.

BER.   What makes you look so thoughtful, Sir? I hope you are not
ill?

LOV.   I was debating, Madam, whether I was so or not; and that was it which made me look so thoughtful.

BER.   Is it then so hard a matter to decide? I thought all people had been acquainted with their own bodies, though few people know their own minds.

LOV.   What if the distemper I suspect be in the mind?

BER.   Why, then I'll undertake to prescribe you a cure.

LOV.   Alas, you undertake you know not what.

BER.   So far at least then allow me to be a physician.

LOV.   Nay, I'll allow you so yet farther: for I have reason to believe should I put myself into your hands you would increase my distemper.

BER.   Perhaps I might have reasons from the college not to be too quick in your cure; but 'tis possible I might find ways to give you often ease, Sir.

LOV.   Were I but sure of that, I'd quickly lay my case before you.

BER.   Whether you are sure of it or no, what risk do you run in trying?

LOV.   Oh, a very great one.

BER.   How?

LOV.   You might betray my distemper to my wife.

BER.   And so lose all my practice.

LOV.   Will you then keep my secret?

BER.   I will, if it don't burst me.

LOV.   Swear.

BER.   I do.

LOV.   By what?

BER.   By woman.

LOV.   That's swearing by my deity. Do it by your own, or I shan't believe you.

BER.   By man, then.

LOV.   I'm satisfied. Now hear my symptoms,
     And give me your advice. The first were these:
     When 'twas my chance to see you at the play,
     A random glance you threw, at first alarm'd me;
     I could not turn my eyes from whence the danger came:
     I gaz'd upon you, till you shot again,
     And then my fears came on me.
     My heart began to pant, my limbs to tremble,
     My blood grew thin, my pulse beat quick,
     My eyes grew hot and dim, and all the frame of nature
     Shook with apprehension.
     'Tis true, some small recruits of resolution
     My manhood brought to my assistance,

And by their help I made a stand a while,
But found at last your arrows flew so thick,
They could not fail to pierce me;
So left the field,
And fled for shelter to Amanda's arms.
What think you of these symptoms, pray?

BER.   Feverish, every one of 'em.
But what relief, pray, did your wife afford you?

LOV.   Why, instantly she let me blood,
Which for the present much assuag'd my flame.
But when I saw you, out it burst again,
And rag'd with greater fury than before.
Nay, since you now appear, 'tis so encreas'd
That in a moment, if you do not help me,
I shall, whilst you look on, consume to ashes.

[*taking hold of her hand*]

BER. [*breaking from him*]   O Lard, let me go:
'Tis the plague, and we shall all be infected.

LOV. [*catching her in his arms, and kissing her*]
Then we'll die together, my charming angel.

BER.   O Ged—the devil's in you.
Lord, let me go, here's somebody coming.

Enter Servant

SERV.   Sir, my lady's come home, and desires to speak with you: she's in her chamber.

LOV.   Tell her I'm coming.   [*exit Servant*]
[*to* BERINTHIA] But before I go, one glass of nectar more to drink her health.

BER.   Stand off, or I shall hate you, by heavens.

LOV. [*kissing her*]   In matters of love, a woman's oath is no more to be minded than a man's.

BER.   Um——

Enter WORTHY

WOR. [*aside*]   Ha! What's here? my old mistress, and so close, i'faith? I would not spoil her sport for the universe.   [*he retires*]

BER.   O Ged—— Now do I pray to heaven, [*exit* LOVELESS *running*] with all my heart and soul, that the devil in hell may take me, if ever—I was better pleased in my life—this man has bewitch'd me, that's certain. [*sighing*] Well, I am condemn'd, but, thanks to heaven, I feel myself each moment more and more prepar'd for my execution—nay, to that degree, I don't perceive I have the least fear of dying. No, I find, let the—executioner be but a man, and there's nothing will suffer with more resolution than a woman. Well, I never had but one intrigue yet: but I confess I long to have another. Pray heaven it end as the first did, though, that we may both grow weary at a time; for 'tis a melancholy thing for lovers to out-live one another.

Enter WORTHY

WOR. [*aside*]   This discovery's a lucky one; I hope to make a happy use on't. That gentlewoman there is no fool, so I shall be able to make her understand her interest.—[*to* BERINTHIA] Your servant, Madam; I need not ask you how you do, you have got so good a colour.

BER.   No better than I used to have, I suppose?

WOR.   A little more blood in your cheeks.

BER.   The weather's hot.

WOR.   If it were not, a woman may have a colour.

BER.   What do you mean by that?

WOR.   Nothing.

BER.   Why do you smile then?

WOR.   Because the weather's hot.

BER.   You'll never leave roguing, I see that.

WOR. [*putting his finger to his nose*]   You'll never leave—— I see that.

BER.   Well, I can't imagine what you drive at. Pray tell me what you mean?

WOR.   Do you tell me; it's the same thing.

BER.   I can't.

WOR.   Guess!

BER.   I shall guess wrong.

WOR.   Indeed you won't.

BER.   Psha! either tell, or let it alone.

WOR.   Nay, rather than let it alone, I will tell. But first I must put you in mind that, after what has past 'twixt you and I, very few things ought to be secrets between us.

BER.   Why, what secrets do we hide? I know of none.

WOR.   Yes, there are two; one I have hid from you, and t'other you would hide from me. You are fond of Loveless, which I have discovered; and I am fond of his wife——

BER.   Which I have discovered.

WOR.   Very well, now I confess your discovery to be true: what do you say to mine?

BER.   Why, I confess—I would swear 'twere false, if I thought you were fool enough to believe me.

WOR.   Now am I almost in love with you again. Nay, I don't know but I might be quite so, had I made one short campaign with Amanda.

Therefore, if you find 'twould tickle your vanity to bring me down once more to your lure, e'en help me quickly to dispatch her business, that I may have nothing else to do but to apply myself to yours.

BER.   Do you then think, Sir, I am old enough to be a bawd?

WOR.   No, but I think you are wise enough to——

BER.   To do what?

WOR.   To hoodwink Amanda with a gallant, that she mayn't see who is her husband's mistress.

BER. [*aside*]   He has reason: the hint's a good one.

WOR.   Well, Madam, what think you on't?

BER.   I think you are so much a deeper politician in these affairs than I am, that I ought to have a very great regard to your advice.

WOR.   Then give me leave to put you in mind that the most easy, safe, and pleasant situation for your own amour is the house in which you now are, provided you keep Amanda from any sort of suspicion: that the way to do that is to engage her in an intrigue of her own, making yourself her confidante: and the way to bring her to intrigue, is to make her jealous of her husband in a wrong place; which the more you foment, the less you'll be suspected.

This is my scheme, in short; which if you follow as you should do (my dear Berinthia) we may all four pass the winter very pleasantly.

BER.   Well, I could be glad to have nobody's sins to answer for but my own. But where there is a necessity——

WOR.   Right as you say; where there is a necessity, a Christian is bound to help his neighbour. So, good Berinthia, lose no time, but let us begin the dance as fast as we can.

BER.   Not till the fiddles are in tune, pray, Sir. Your lady's strings will be very apt to fly, I can tell you that, if they are wound up too hastily. But if you'll have patience to screw 'em to their pitch by degrees, I don't doubt but she may endure to be played upon.

WOR.   Ay, and will make admirable music, too, or I'm mistaken. But have you had no private closet discourse with her yet about males and females, and so forth, which may give you hopes in her constitution? for I know her morals are the devil against us.

BER.   I have had so much discourse with her that I believe were she once cured of her fondness to her husband, the fortress of her virtue would not be so impregnable as she fancies.

WOR.   What? she runs, I'll warrant you, into that common mistake of fond wives, who conclude themselves virtuous because they can refuse a man they don't like when they have got one they do.

BER.   True, and therefore I think 'tis a presumptuous thing in a woman to assume the name of virtuous till she has heartily hated her husband and been soundly in love with somebody else, whom if she has withstood—then—much good may it do her!

WOR.   Well, so much for her virtue. Now, one word of her inclinations, and everyone to their post. What opinion do you find she has of me?

BER.   What you could wish; she thinks you handsome and discreet.

WOR.   Good! that's thinking half-seas over. One tide more brings us into port.

BER.   Perhaps it may, though still remember there's a difficult bar to pass.

WOR.   I know there is, but I don't question I shall get well over it, by the help of such a pilot.

BER.   You may depend upon your pilot, she'll do the best she can; so weigh anchor, and be gone as soon as you please.

WOR.   I'm under sail already. Adieu.   [exit WORTHY]

BER.   *Bon voyage.* [*sola*] So, here's fine work. What a business have I undertaken! I'm a very pretty gentlewoman, truly; but there was no avoiding it: he'd have ruined me if I had refused him. Besides, faith, I begin to fancy there may be as much pleasure in carrying on another body's intrigue as one's own. This at least is certain, it exercises almost all the entertaining faculties of a woman: for there's employment for hypocrisy, invention, deceit, flattery, mischief, and lying.

Enter AMANDA, *her Woman following her*

WOM.   If you please, Madam, only to say, whether you'll have me buy 'em or not.

AMAN.   Yes, no, go fiddle! I care not what you do. Prithee leave me.

WOM.   I have done.   [exit Woman]

BER.   What in the name of Jove's the matter with you?

AMAN.   The matter, Berinthia! I'm almost mad, I'm plagued to death.

BER.   Who is it that plagues you?

AMAN.   Who do you think should plague a wife but her husband?

BER.   O ho, is it come to that? We shall have you wish yourself a widow by and by.

AMAN.   Would I were anything but what I am! A base ungrateful man, after what I have done for him, to use me thus!

BER.   What! he has been ogling now, I'll warrant you?

AMAN.   Yes, he has been ogling.

BER.   And so you are jealous? Is that all?

AMAN.   That all! Is jealousy then nothing?

BER.   It should be nothing, if I were in your case.

AMAN.   Why, what would you do?

BER.   I'd cure myself.

AMAN.   How?

BER.   Let blood in the fond vein: care as little for my husband as he did for me.

AMAN.   That would not stop his course.

BER.   Nor nothing else, when the wind's in the warm corner. Look you, Amanda, you may build castles in the air, and fume, and fret, and grow thin and lean and pale and ugly, if you please. But I tell you, no man worth having is true to his wife, or can be true to his wife, or ever was, or ever will be so.

AMAN.   Do you then really think he's false to me? for I did but suspect him.

BER.   Think so? I know he's so.

AMAN.   Is it possible? Pray tell me what you know.

BER.   Don't press me then to name names, for that I have sworn I won't do.

AMAN.   Well, I won't; but let me know all you can without perjury.

BER.   I'll let you know enough to prevent any wise woman's dying of the pip; and I hope you'll pluck up your spirits, and show, upon occasion, you can be as good a wife as the best of 'em.

AMAN.   Well, what a woman can do I'll endeavour.

BER.   Oh, a woman can do a great deal, if once she sets her mind to it. Therefore pray don't stand trifling any longer, and teasing yourself with this and that, and your love and your virtue, and I know not what. But resolve to hold up your head, get a-tiptoe, and look over 'em all; for to my certain knowledge your husband is a-pickering elsewhere.

AMAN.   You are sure on't?

BER.   Positively; he fell in love at the play.

AMAN.   Right, the very same; do you know the ugly thing?

BER.   Yes, I know her well enough; but she's no such an ugly thing, neither.

AMAN.   Is she very handsome?

BER.   Truly, I think so.

AMAN.   Hey ho!

BER.   What do you sigh for now?

AMAN.   Oh, my heart!

BER. [*aside*]   Only the pangs of nature! she's in labour of her love; heaven send her a quick delivery; I'm sure she has a good midwife.

AMAN.   I'm very ill, I must go to my chamber. Dear Berinthia, don't leave me a moment.

BER.   No, don't fear. [*aside*] I'll see you safe brought to bed, I'll warrant you.   [*exeunt,* AMANDA *leaning upon* BERINTHIA]

SCENE III

A country house

Enter YOUNG FASHION *and* LORY

Y. FAS.   So, here's our inheritance, Lory, if we can but get into possession. But methinks the seat of our family looks like Noah's ark, as if the chief part on't were designed for the fowls of the air and the beasts of the field.

LO.   Pray, Sir, don't let your head run upon the orders of building here; get but the heiress, let the devil take the house.

Y. FAS.   Get but the house, let the devil take the heiress, I say; at least if she be as old Coupler describes her. But come, we have no time to squander. Knock at the door. [LORY *knocks two or three times*] What the devil, have they got no ears in this house? Knock harder.

LO.   I'gad, Sir, this will prove some enchanted castle; we shall have the giant come out by and by with his club, and beat our brains out.

[*knocks again*]

Y. FAS.   Hush! they come.

[*from within*] Who is there?

LO.   Open the door and see: is that your country breeding?

[*within*] Ay, but two words to a bargain: Tummas, is the blunderbuss primed?

Y. FAS.   Oons, give 'em good words, Lory; we shall be shot here a fortune-catching.

LO.   I'gad, Sir, I think y'are in the right on't.—— Ho, Mr. What d'ye-call-um.   [*Servant appears at the window with a blunderbuss*]

SERV.   Weall naw what's yare business?

Y. FAS.   Nothing, Sir, but to wait upon Sir Tunbelly, with your leave.

SERV.   To weat upon Sir Tunbelly? Why, you'll find that's just as Sir Tunbelly pleases.

Y. FAS.   But will you do me the favour, Sir, to know whether Sir Tunbelly pleases or not?

SERV.   Why, look you, do you see, with good words much may be done.—— Ralph, go thy weas, and ask Sir Tunbelly if he pleases to be waited upon. And, dost hear? call to nurse, that she may lock up Miss Hoyden before the geats open.

Y. FAS.   D'ye hear that, Lory?

LO.   Ay, sir, I'm afraid we shall find a difficult job on't. Pray heaven that old rogue Coupler han't sent us to fetch milk out of the gunroom!

Y. FAS.   I'll warrant thee all will go well: see, the door opens.

Enter SIR TUNBELLY, *with his Servants armed with
guns, clubs, pitchforks, scythes, etc.*

LO. [*running behind his master*]   O Lord, O Lord, O Lord, we are both dead men!

Y. FAS.   Take heed, fool; thy fear will ruin us.

LO.   My fear, Sir—'sdeath, Sir, I fear nothing. [*aside*] Would I were well up to the chin in a horse-pond!

SIR TUN.   Who is it here has any business with me?

Y. FAS.   Sir, 'tis I, if your name be Sir Tunbelly Clumsey.

SIR TUN.   Sir, my name is Sir Tunbelly Clumsey, whether you have any business with me or not. So you see I am not ashamed of my name— nor my face, neither.

Y. FAS.   Sir, you have no cause that I know of.

SIR TUN.   Sir, if you have no cause neither, I desire to know who you are; for till I know your name, I shall not ask you to come into my house; and when I know your name—'tis six to four I don't ask you neither.

Y. FAS. [*giving him a letter*]   Sir, I hope you'll find this letter an authentic passport.

SIR TUN.   Cod's my life, I ask your Lordship's pardon ten thousand times. [*to his Servants*] Here, run in a-doors quickly: get a Scotch coal fire in the great parlour; set all the Turkey-work chairs in their places; get the great brass candlesticks out, and be sure stick the sockets full of laurel; run! [*turning to* YOUNG FASHION] My Lord, I ask your Lordship's pardon. [*to other Servants*] And do you hear, run away to nurse, bid her let Miss Hoyden loose again, and if it was not shifting-day, let her put on a clean tucker—quick! [*exeunt Servants confusedly*] [*to* YOUNG FASHION] I hope your honour will excuse the disorder of my family; we are not used to receive men of your Lordship's great quality every day; pray, where are your coaches and servants, my Lord?

Y. FAS.   Sir, that I might give you and your fair daughter a proof how impatient I am to be nearer akin to you, I left my equipage to follow me, and came away post with only one servant.

SIR TUN.   Your Lordship does me too much honour; it was exposing your person to too much fatigue and danger, I protest it was; but my daughter shall endeavour to make you what amends she can; and though I say it, that should not say it—Hoyden has charms.

Y. FAS.   Sir, I am not a stranger to them, though I am to her; common fame has done her justice.

SIR TUN.   My Lord, I am common fame's very grateful humble servant. My Lord—my girl's young: Hoyden is young, my Lord; but this I must say for her, what she wants in art, she has by nature; what she wants in experience, she has in breeding; and what's wanting in her age is made good in her constitution. So pray, my Lord, walk in; pray, my Lord, walk in.

Y. FAS.   Sir, I wait upon you.   [*exeunt*]

SCENE IV

MISS HOYDEN, *sola*

Sure, never nobody was used as I am. I know well enough what other girls do, for all they think to make a fool of me: it's well I have a husband a-coming, or i'cod, I'd marry the baker, I would so. Nobody can knock at the gate, but presently I must be locked up; and here's the young grey-hound bitch can run loose about the house all day long, she can; 'tis very well.

NURSE [*without opening the door*]   Miss Hoyden! Miss, Miss, Miss; Miss Hoyden!

Enter Nurse

MISS   Well, what do you make such a noise for, ha? What do you din a body's ears for? Can't one be at quiet for you!

NURSE   What do I din your ears for? Here's one come will din your ears for you.

MISS   What care I who's come? I care not a fig who comes, nor who goes, as long as I must be locked up like the ale-cellar.

NURSE   That, Miss, is for fear you should be drank before you are ripe.

MISS   Oh, don't you trouble your head about that: I'm as ripe as you, though not so mellow.

NURSE   Very well; now have I a good mind to lock you up again, and not let you see my Lord to-night.

MISS   My Lord? Why, is my husband come?

NURSE   Yes, marry is he, and a goodly person too.

MISS [*hugging Nurse*]   O my dear nurse, forgive me this once, and I'll never misuse you again; no, if I do, you shall give me three thumps on the back, and a great pinch by the cheek.

NURSE   Ah, the poor thing, see how it melts; it's as full of good-nature as an egg's full of meat.

MISS   But, my dear nurse, don't lie now; is he come, by your troth?

NURSE   Yes, by my truly, is he.

MISS   O Lord! I'll go put on my laced smock, though I'm whipped till the blood run down my heels for't.   [*exit running*]

NURSE   Eh—the Lord succour thee, how thou art delighted!

[*exit after her*]

SCENE V

Enter SIR TUNBELLY *and* YOUNG FASHION; *a Servant with wine*

SIR TUN.   My Lord, I am proud of the honour to see your Lordship within my doors, and I humbly crave leave to bid you welcome in a cup of sack wine.

Y. FAS.   Sir, to your daughter's health.   [*drinks*]

SIR TUN.   Ah, poor girl, she'll be scared out of her wits on her wedding night; for, honestly speaking, she does not know a man from a woman, but by his beard and his britches.

Y. FAS.   Sir, I don't doubt but she has a virtuous education, which, with the rest of her merit, makes me long to see her mine. I wish you would dispense with the canonical hour, and let it be this very night.

SIR TUN.   Oh, not so soon, neither; that's shooting my girl before you bid her stand. No, give her fair warning: we'll sign and seal to-night if you please, and this day seven-night—let the jade look to her quarters.

Y. FAS.   This day sennight?—Why, what! do you take me for a ghost, Sir? 'Slife, Sir, I'm made of flesh and blood, and bones and sinews, and can no more live a week without your daughter—[*aside*] than I can live a month with her.

SIR TUN.   Oh, I'll warrant you, my hero; young men are hot, I know, but they don't boil over at that rate, neither; besides, my wench's wedding gown is not come home yet.

Y. FAS.   Oh, no matter, Sir; I'll take her in her shift. [*aside*] A pox of this old fellow; he'll delay the business till my damned star finds me out, and discovers me. [*to* SIR TUNBELLY] Pray, Sir, let it be done without ceremony; 'twill save money.

SIR TUN.   Money?—save money when Hoyden's to be married? Udswoons, I'll give my wench a wedding dinner, though I go to grass with the King of Assyria for't; and such a dinner it shall be, as is not to be cooked in the poaching of an egg. Therefore, my noble Lord, have a little patience; we'll go and look over our deeds and settlements immediately; and as for your bride, though you may be sharp set before she's quite ready, I'll engage for my girl she stays your stomach at last.

[*exeunt*]

ACT IV

SCENE I

Enter MISS HOYDEN *and Nurse*

NURSE   Well, Miss, how do you like your husband that is to be?

MISS   O Lord, nurse, I'm so overjoyed, I can scarce contain myself.

NURSE   Oh, but you must have a care of being too fond, for men nowadays hate a woman that loves 'em.

MISS   Love him? Why, do you think I love him, nurse? I'cod, I would not care if he were hanged, so I were but once married to him. No—that which pleases me is to think what work I'll make when I get to London; for when I am a wife and a lady both, nurse, i'cod, I'll flaunt it with the best of 'em.

NURSE   Look, look, if his honour be not coming again to you; now if I were sure you would behave yourself handsomely, and not disgrace me that have brought you up, I'd leave you alone together.

MISS   That's my best nurse: do as you would be done by; trust us together this once, and if I don't show my breeding from the head to the foot of me, may I be twice married, and die a maid!

NURSE   Well, this once I'll venture you; but if you disparage me——

MISS   Never fear; I'll show him my parts, I'll warrant him.

[exit Nurse]

[*sola*] These old women are so wise when they get a poor girl in their clutches, but ere it be long I shall know what's what, as well as the best of 'em.

Enter YOUNG FASHION

Y. FAS.   Your servant, Madam: I'm glad to find you alone, for I have something of importance to speak to you about.

MISS   Sir (my Lord, I meant) you may speak to me about what you please; I shall give you a civil answer.

Y. FAS.   You give me so obliging a one, it encourages me to tell you in few words what I think both for your interest and mine. Your father,

I suppose you know, has resolved to make me happy in being your husband, and I hope I may depend upon your consent to perform what he desires.

MISS   Sir, I never disobey my father in anything but eating of green gooseberries.

Y. FAS.   So good a daughter must needs make an admirable wife; I am therefore impatient till you are mine, and hope you will so far consider the violence of my love that you won't have the cruelty to defer my happiness so long as your father designs it.

MISS   Pray, my Lord, how long is that?

Y. FAS.   Madam, a thousand year—a whole week.

MISS   A week!—why, I shall be an old woman by that time.

Y. FAS.   And I an old man, which you'll find a greater misfortune than t'other.

MISS   Why, I thought 'twas to be to-morrow morning, as soon as I was up; I'm sure nurse told me so.

Y. FAS.   And it shall be to-morrow morning still, if you'll consent.

MISS   If I'll consent? Why, I thought I was to obey you as my husband.

Y. FAS.   That's when we are married; till then I am to obey you.

MISS   Why then, if we are to take it by turns, it's the same thing: I'll obey you now, and when we are married, you shall obey me.

Y. FAS.   With all my heart; but I doubt we must get nurse on our side, or we shall hardly prevail with the chaplain.

MISS   No more we shan't, indeed, for he loves her better than he loves his pulpit, and would always be a-preaching to her, by his good will.

Y. FAS.   Why then, my dear little bedfellow, if you'll call her hither, we'll try to persuade her presently.

MISS   O Lord, I can tell you a way how to persuade her to anything.

Y. FAS.   How's that?

MISS   Why, tell her she's a wholesome, comely woman—and give her half a crown.

Y. FAS.   Nay, if that will do, she shall have half a score of 'em.

MISS   O Gemini! for half that she'd marry you herself: I'll run and call her.   [*exit* MISS HOYDEN]

Y. FAS. [*solus*]   So, matters go swimmingly; this is a rare girl, i'faith; I shall have a fine time on't with her at London. I'm much mistaken if she don't prove a March hare all the year round. What a scamp'ring chase will she make on't, when she finds the whole kennel of beaux at her tail! hey to the park, and the play, and the church, and the devil; she'll show 'em sport, I'll warrant 'em. But no matter: she brings an estate will afford me a separate maintenance.

Enter MISS HOYDEN *and Nurse*

Y. FAS.   How do you do, good Mistress Nurse; I desired your young lady would give me leave to see you, that I might thank you for your extraordinary care and conduct in her education; pray accept of this small acknowledgment for it at present, and depend upon my farther kindness when I shall be that happy thing, her husband.

NURSE [*aside*]   Gold, by makings!——Your honour's goodness is too great: alas! all I can boast of is, I gave her pure good milk, and so your honour would have said, an you had seen how the poor thing sucked it—Eh, God's blessing on the sweet face on't! how it used to hang at this poor tett, and suck and squeeze, and kick and sprawl it would, till the belly on't was so full it would drop off like a leech.

MISS [*to Nurse, taking her angrily aside*]   Pray one word with you; prithee, nurse, don't stand ripping up old stories, to make one ashamed before one's love: do you think such a fine proper gentleman as he cares for a fiddlecome tale of a draggle-tailed girl? if you have a mind to make him have a good opinion of a woman, don't tell him what one did then: tell him what one can do now. [*to* YOUNG FASHION] I hope your honour will excuse my mismanners to whisper before you; it was only to give some orders about the family.

Y. FAS.   Oh, everything, Madam, is to give way to business; besides, good housewifery is a very commendable quality in a young lady.

MISS   Pray, Sir, are the young ladies good housewives at London town? do they darn their own linen?

Y. FAS.   Oh, no; they study how to spend money, not to save it.

MISS   I'cod, I don't know but that may be better sport than t'other; ha, nurse?

Y. FAS.   Well, you shall have your choice when you come there.

MISS   Shall I?—then by my troth I'll get there as fast as I can. [*to Nurse*] His honour desires you'll be so kind as to let us be married to-morrow.

NURSE   To-morrow, my dear Madam?

Y. FAS.   Yes, to-morrow, sweet nurse, privately; young folks, you know, are impatient, and Sir Tunbelly would make us stay a week for a wedding-dinner. Now all things being signed and sealed and agreed, I fancy there could be no great harm in practising a scene or two of matrimony in private, if it were only to give us the better assurance when we come to play it in public.

NURSE   Nay, I must confess stol'n pleasures are sweet; but if you should be married now, what will you do when Sir Tunbelly calls for you to be wed?

MISS   Why, then we'll be married again.

NURSE   What, twice, my child?

MISS   I'cod, I don't care how often I'm married, not I.

Y. FAS.   Pray, nurse, don't you be against your young lady's good; for by this means she'll have the pleasure of two wedding-days.

MISS [*to Nurse softly*]   And of two wedding-nights, too, nurse.

NURSE   Well, I'm such a tender-hearted fool, I find I can refuse nothing; so you shall e'en follow your own inventions.

MISS   Shall I? [*aside*] O Lord, I could leap over the moon.

Y. FAS.   Dear nurse, this goodness of yours shan't go unrewarded; but now you must employ your power with Mr. Bull, the chaplain, that he may do us his friendly office too, and then we shall all be happy; do you think you can prevail with him?

NURSE   Prevail with him?—or he shall never prevail with me, I can tell him that.

MISS   My Lord, she has had him upon the hip this seven year.

Y. FAS.   I'm glad to hear it; however, to strengthen your interest with him, you may let him know I have several fat livings in my gift, and that the first that falls shall be in your disposal.

NURSE   Nay, then I'll make him marry more folks than one, I'll promise him.

MISS   Faith, do nurse, make him marry you too; I'm sure he'll do't for a fat living; for he loves eating more than he loves his Bible; and I have often heard him say a fat living was the best meat in the world.

NURSE   Ay, and I'll make him commend the sauce too, or I'll bring his gown to a cassock, I will so.

Y. FAS.   Well, nurse, whilst you go and settle matters with him, then your lady and I will go take a walk in the garden.

NURSE   I'll do your honour's business in the catching up of a garter.
                                                                    [*exit Nurse*]

Y. FAS. [*giving her his hand*]   Come, Madam, dare you venture yourself alone with me?

MISS   Oh dear, yes, Sir; I don't think you'll do anything to me I need be afraid on.   [*exeunt*]

SCENE II

Enter AMANDA *and* BERINTHIA

A SONG

I

"I smile at love, and all its arts,"
    The charming Cynthia cried;

"Take heed, for Love has piercing darts,"
   A wounded swain replied.
"Once free and blest as you are now,
   I trifled with his charms;
I pointed at his little bow,
   And sported with his arms:
Till urg'd too far, 'Revenge!' he cries,
   A fatal shaft he drew;
It took its passage through your eyes,
   And to my heart it flew.

II

"To tear it thence I tried in vain;
   To strive, I quickly found,
Was only to encrease the pain,
   And to enlarge the wound.
Ah! much too well I fear you know
   What pain I'm to endure,
Since what your eyes alone could do,
   Your heart alone can cure.
And that (grant heaven I may mistake)
   I doubt is doom'd to bear
A burthen for another's sake,
   Who ill rewards its care."

AMAN.   Well, now, Berinthia, I'm at leisure to hear what 'twas you had to say to me.

BER.   What I had to say was only to echo the sighs and groans of a dying lover.

AMAN.   Phu, will you never learn to talk in earnest of anything?

BER.   Why, this shall be in earnest, if you please; for my part, I only tell you matter of fact—you may take it which way you like best, but if you'll follow the women of the town, you'll take it both ways; for when a man offers himself to one of them, first she takes him in jest, and then she takes him in earnest.

AMAN.   I'm sure there's so much jest and earnest in what you say to me, I scarce know how to take it; but I think you have bewitched me, for I don't find it possible to be angry with you, say what you will.

BER.   I'm very glad to hear it, for I have no mind to quarrel with you, for more reasons than I'll brag of; but quarrel or not, smile or frown, I must tell you what I have suffered upon your account.

AMAN.   Upon my account?

BER.   Yes, upon yours; I have been forced to sit still and hear you commended for two hours together, without one compliment to myself; now don't you think a woman had a blessed time of that?

AMAN.   Alas! I should have been unconcerned at it; I never knew where the pleasure lay of being praised by the men: but pray who was this that commended me so?

BER.   One you have a mortal aversion to—Mr. Worthy; he used you like a text, he took you all to pieces, but spoke so learnedly upon every point, one might see the spirit of the church was in him: if you are a woman, you'd have been in an ecstasy to have heard how feelingly he handled your hair, your eyes, your nose, your mouth, your teeth, your tongue, your chin, your neck, and so forth. Thus he preached for an hour, but when he came to use an application, he observed that all these, without a gallant, were nothing. Now consider of what has been said, and heaven give you grace to put it in practice!

AMAN.   Alas! Berinthia, did I incline to a gallant (which you know I do not), do you think a man so nice as he could have the least concern for such a plain unpolished thing as I am? It is impossible!

BER.   Now have you a great mind to put me upon commending you.

AMAN.   Indeed that was not my design.

BER.   Nay, if it were, it's all one, for I won't do't; I'll leave that to your looking-glass. But to show you I have some good-nature left, I'll commend him, and maybe that may do as well.

AMAN.   You have a great mind to persuade me I am in love with him.

BER.   I have a great mind to persuade you you don't know what you are in love with.

AMAN.   I am sure I am not in love with him, nor never shall be; so let that pass: but you were saying something you would commend him for.

BER.   Oh, you'd be glad to hear a good character of him, however.

AMAN.   Psha!

BER.   "Psha!"—Well, 'tis a foolish undertaking for women, in these kind of matters, to pretend to deceive one another—have not I been bred a woman as well as you?

AMAN.   What then?

BER.   Why, then I understand my trade so well, that whenever I am told of a man I like, I cry, "Psha!" But that I may spare you the pains of putting me a second time in mind to commend him, I'll proceed, and give you this account of him: that though 'tis possible he may have had women with as good faces as your Ladyship's (no discredit to it neither), yet you must know your cautious behaviour, with that reserve in your humour, has given him his death's wound; he mortally hates a coquette; he says 'tis impossible to love where we cannot esteem; and that no woman can be esteemed by a man who has sense if she makes herself cheap in the eye of a fool. That pride to a woman is as necessary as humility to a divine; and that far-fetched and dear bought is meat for gentlemen as well as for ladies—in short, that every woman who has beauty may set a price upon herself, and that by underselling the market they ruin the trade. This is his doctrine: how do you like it?

AMAN.   So well that, since I never intend to have a gallant for myself, if I were to recommend one to a friend, he should be the man.

Enter WORTHY

Bless me, he's here! pray heaven he did not hear me!

BER.   If he did, it won't hurt your reputation; your thoughts are as safe in his heart as in your own.

WOR.   I venture in at an unseasonable time of night, ladies; I hope if I'm troublesome you'll use the same freedom in turning me out again.

AMAN.   I believe it can't be late, for Mr. Loveless is not come home yet, and he usually keeps good hours.

WOR.   Madam, I'm afraid he'll transgress a little to-night; for he told me about half an hour ago he was going to sup with some company he doubted would keep him out till three or four o'clock in the morning, and desired I would let my servant acquaint you with it, that you might not expect him: but my fellow's a blunder-head, so, lest he should make some mistake, I thought it my duty to deliver the message myself.

AMAN.   I'm very sorry he should give you that trouble, Sir: but——

BER.   But since he has, will you give me leave, Madam, to keep him to play at ombre with us?

AMAN.   Cousin, you know you command my house.

WOR. [*to* BERINTHIA]   And, Madam, you know you command me, though I'm a very wretched gamester.

BER.   Oh, you play well enough to lose your money, and that's all the ladies require; so without any more ceremony let us go into the next room and call for the cards.

AMAN.   With all my heart.   [*exit* WORTHY *leading* AMANDA]

BER. [*sola*]   Well, how this business will end, heaven knows; but she seems to me to be in as fair a way—as a boy is to be a rogue, when he's put clerk to an attorney.   [*exit* BERINTHIA]

SCENE III

BERINTHIA'S *chamber*

Enter LOVELESS *cautiously in the dark*

LOV.   So, thus far all's well. I'm got into her bed-chamber, and I think nobody has perceived me steal into the house; my wife don't expect me home till four o'clock; so if Berinthia comes to bed by eleven, I shall have a chase of five hours. Let me see, where shall I hide myself? under her bed? No; we shall have her maid searching there for something or other; her closet's a better place, and I have a master key will open it: I'll e'en in there, and attack her just when she comes to her prayers: that's the most likely to prove her critical minute, for then the devil will be there to assist me.   [*he opens the closet, goes in, and shuts the door after him*]

Enter BERINTHIA *with a candle in her hand*

BER.   Well, sure I am the best-natured woman in the world. I that love cards so well (there is but one thing upon earth I love better) have pretended letters to write, to give my friends—a *tête-à-tête;* however, I'm innocent, for picquet is the game I set 'em to: at her own peril be it, if she ventures to play with him at any other. But now what shall I do with myself? I don't know how in the world to pass my time; would Loveless were here to *badiner* a little. Well, he's a charming fellow; I don't wonder his wife's so fond of him. What if I should sit down and think of him till I fall asleep, and dream of the Lord knows what? Oh, but then if I should dream we were married, I should be frightened out of my wits. [*seeing a book*] What's this book? I think I had best go read. Oh, *splénétique!* it's a sermon. Well, I'll go into my closet, and read *The Plotting Sisters*. [*she opens the closet, sees LOVELESS, and shrieks out*] O Lord, a ghost, a ghost, a ghost, a ghost!

Enter LOVELESS, *running to her*

LOV.   Peace, my dear; it's no ghost; take it in your arms, you'll find 'tis worth a hundred of 'em.
BER.   Run in again; here's somebody coming.   [*exit LOVELESS*]

Enter her Maid

MAID   Lord, Madam, what's the matter?
BER.   O heavens! I'm almost frighted out of my wits: I thought verily I had seen a ghost, and 'twas nothing but the white curtain, with a black hood pinned up against it; you may be gone again, I am the fearfullest fool.   [*exit Maid*]

Re-enter LOVELESS

LOV.   Is the coast clear?
BER.   The coast clear! I suppose you are clear, you'd never play such a trick as this else.

Lov.   I am very well pleased with my trick thus far, and shall be so till I have played it out, if it ben't your fault: where's my wife?

Ber.   At cards.

Lov.   With whom?

Ber.   With Worthy.

Lov.   Then we are safe enough.

Ber.   Are you so? Some husbands would be of another mind, if he were at cards with their wives.

Lov.   And they'd be in the right on't too. But I dare trust mine. Besides, I know he's in love in another place, and he's not one of those who court half a dozen at a time.

Ber.   Nay, the truth on't is you'd pity him if you saw how uneasy he is at being engaged with us; but 'twas my malice: I fancied he was to meet his mistress somewhere else, so did it to have the pleasure of seeing him fret.

Lov.   What says Amanda to my staying abroad so late?

Ber.   Why, she's as much out of humour as he; I believe they wish one another at the devil.

Lov.   Then I'm afraid they'll quarrel at play, and soon throw up the cards; [*offering to pull her into the closet*] therefore, my dear charming angel, let us make a good use of our time.

Ber.   Heavens, what do you mean?

Lov.   Pray, what do you think I mean?

Ber.   I don't know.

Lov.   I'll show you.

Ber.   You may as well tell me.

Lov.   No, that would make you blush worse than t'other.

Ber.   Why, do you intend to make me blush?

Lov.   Faith, I can't tell that; but if I do, it shall be in the dark.

                                                 [*pulling her*]

Ber.   O, heavens! I would not be in the dark with you for all the world.

Lov.   I'll try that.   [*puts out the candle*]

Ber.   O Lord! are you mad? What shall I do for light?

Lov.   You'll do as well without it.

Ber.   Why, one can't find a chair to sit down!

Lov.   Come into the closet, Madam: there's moonshine upon the couch.

Ber.   Nay, never pull, for I will not go.

Lov.   Then you must be carried.   [*carrying her*]

Ber. [*very softly*]   Help, help, I'm ravished, ruined, undone! O Lord, I shall never be able to bear it.   [*exeunt*]

SCENE IV

Sir Tunbelly's *house*

Enter Miss Hoyden, *Nurse,* Young Fashion, *and* Bull

Y. Fas.   This quick dispatch of yours, Mr. Bull, I take so kindly, it shall give you a claim to my favour as long as I live, I do assure you.

Miss   And to mine too, I promise you.

Bull   I must humbly thank your honours, and I hope, since it has been my lot to join you in the holy bands of wedlock, you will so well cultivate the soil which I have craved a blessing on that your children may swarm about you like bees about a honeycomb.

Miss   I'cod, with all my heart: the more the merrier, I say; ha, nurse?

Enter Lory, *taking his master hastily aside*

Lo.   One word with you, for heaven's sake.

Y. Fas.   What the devil's the matter?

Lo.   Sir, your fortune's ruined, and I don't think your life's worth a quarter of an hour's purchase: yonder's your brother arrived with two coaches and six horses, twenty footmen and pages, a coat worth fourscore pound, and a periwig down to his knees: so judge what will become of your lady's heart.

Y. Fas.   Death and Furies! 'tis impossible.

Lo.   Fiends and spectres, Sir! 'tis true.

Y. Fas.   Is he in the house yet?

Lo.   No, they are capitulating with him at the gate; the porter tells him he's come to run away with Miss Hoyden, and has cocked the blunderbuss at him; your brother swears, Gad damme, they are a parcel of clowns, and he has a good mind to break off the match; but they have given the word for Sir Tunbelly, so I doubt all will come out presently. Pray, Sir, resolve what you'll do this moment, for i'gad they'll maul you.

Y. Fas.   Stay a little.—— [*to* Miss Hoyden] My dear, here's a troublesome business my man tells me of; but don't be frightened, we shall be too hard for the rogue. Here's an impudent fellow at the gate (not knowing I was come hither *incognito*) has taken my name upon him, in hopes to run away with you.

Miss   Oh, the brazen-faced varlet! it's well we are married, or maybe we might never a been so.

Y. Fas. [*aside*]   I'gad, like enough!—— Prithee, dear Doctor, run to Sir Tunbelly and stop him from going to the gate before I speak with him.

Bull   I fly, my good Lord——   [*exit* Bull]

Nurse   An't please your honour, my lady and I had best lock ourselves up till the danger be over.

Y. FAS.   Ay, by all means.

MISS   Not so fast: I won't be locked up any more. I'm married.

Y. FAS.   Yes, pray, my dear, do, till we have seized this rascal.

MISS   Nay, if you pray me, I'll do any thing.

[*exeunt* MISS HOYDEN *and Nurse*]

Y. FAS.   Oh! here's Sir Tunbelly coming. [*to* LORY] Hark you, Sirrah, things are better than you imagine: the wedding's over.

LO.   The devil it is, Sir.

Y. FAS.   Not a word, all's safe: but Sir Tunbelly don't know it, nor must not yet; so I am resolved to brazen the business out, and have the pleasure of turning the imposter upon his Lordship, which I believe may easily be done.

Enter SIR TUNBELLY, *Chaplain and Servants armed*

Y. FAS.   Did you ever hear, Sir, of so impudent an undertaking?

SIR TUN.   Never, by the mass; but we'll tickle him, I'll warrant him.

Y. FAS.   They tell me, Sir, he has a great many people with him disguised like servants.

SIR TUN.   Ay, ay, rogues enough; but I'll soon raise the posse upon 'em.

Y. FAS.   Sir, if you'll take my advice, we'll go a shorter way to work; I find, whoever this spark is, he knows nothing of my being privately here; so if you pretend to receive him civilly, he'll enter without suspicion; and as soon as he is within the gate we'll whip up the drawbridge upon his back, let fly the blunderbuss to disperse his crew, and so commit him to gaol.

SIR TUN.   I'gad, your Lordship is an ingenious person, and a very great general; but shall we kill any of 'em, or not?

Y. FAS.   No, no, fire over their heads only to fright 'em; I'll warrant the regiment scours when the colonel's a prisoner.

SIR TUN.   Then come along, my boys, and let your courage be great—for your danger is but small.   [*exeunt*]

SCENE V

The gate

Enter LORD FOPPINGTON *and Followers*

LORD FOP.   A pax of these bumpkinly people!—will they open the gate, or do they desire I should grow at their moat-side like a willow? [*to the Porter*] Hey, fellow—prithee do me the favour, in as few words as thou canst find to express thyself, to tell me whether thy master will admit me or not, that I may turn about my coach and be gone.

POR.   Here's my master himself now at hand; he's of age, he'll give you his answer.

Enter SIR TUNBELLY *and Servants*

SIR TUN.   My most noble Lord, I crave your pardon for making your honour wait so long; but my orders to my servants have been to admit nobody without my knowledge for fear of some attempt upon my daughter, the times being full of plots and roguery.

LORD FOP.   Much caution, I must confess, is a sign of great wisdom: but, stap my vitals, I have got a cold enough to destroy a porter—he, hem——

SIR TUN.   I am very sorry for't, indeed, my Lord; but if your Lordship please to walk in, we'll help you to some brown sugar-candy. My Lord, I'll show you the way.

LORD FOP.   Sir, I follow you with pleasure.   [*exeunt*]
                    [*as* LORD FOPPINGTON'S *Servants go to follow him in,
                    they clap the door against* LA VÉROLE]

SERVANTS [*within*]   Nay, hold you me there, Sir.
LA VÉR.   *Jernie die, qu'est ce que veut dire ça?*
SIR TUN. [*within*]   ——Fire, porter.
PORT. [*fires*]   Have among ye, my masters!
LA VÉR.   *Ah, je suis mort*——   [*the Servants all run off*]
PORT.   Not one soldier left, by the mass.

SCENE VI

Scene changes to the hall

Enter SIR TUNBELLY, *the Chaplain and Servants,
with* LORD FOPPINGTON *disarmed*

SIR TUN.   Come, bring him along, bring him along.

LORD FOP.   What the pax do you mean, gentlemen? is it fair time, that you are all drunk before dinner?

SIR TUN.   Drunk, Sirrah? Here's an impudent rogue for you! Drunk or sober, bully, I'm a justice of the peace, and know how to deal with strollers.

LORD FOP.   Strollers!

SIR TUN.   Ay, strollers; come, give an account of yourself; what's your name? where do you live? Do you pay scot and lot? Are you a Williamite, or a Jacobite? Come.

LORD FOP.   And why dost thou ask me so many impertinent questions?

SIR TUN.   Because I'll make you answer 'em before I have done with you, you rascal you.

LORD FOP.   Before Gad, all the answer I can make thee to 'em, is, that thou art a very extraordinary old fellow; stap my vitals——

SIR TUN.   Nay, if you are for joking with deputy-lieutenants, we'st know how to deal with you.—Here, draw a warrant for him immediately.

LORD FOP.   A warrant—what the devil is't thou wouldst be at, old gentleman?

SIR TUN.   I would be at you, Sirrah (if my hands were not tied as a magistrate), and with these two double fists beat your teeth down your throat, you dog you.

LORD FOP.   And why would'st thou spoil my face at that rate?

SIR TUN.   For your design to rob me of my daughter, villain.

LORD FOP.   Rab thee of thy daughter!—[aside] Now do I begin to believe I am abed and asleep, and that all this is but a dream. If it be, 'twill be an agreeable surprise enough to waken by and by and instead of the impertinent company of a nasty country justice, find myself, perhaps, in the arms of a woman of quality. [to SIR TUNBELLY] Prithee, old father, wilt thou give me leave to ask thee one question?

SIR TUN.   I can't tell whether I will or not, till I know what it is.

LORD FOP.   Why, then, it is whether thou didst not write to my Lord Foppington to come down and marry thy daughter.

SIR TUN.   Yes, marry did I, and my Lord Foppington is come down, and shall marry my daughter before she's a day older.

LORD FOP.   Now give me thy hand, dear Dad: I thought we should understand one another at last.

SIR TUN.   This fellow's mad—here, bind him hand and foot.

[they bind him down]

LORD FOP.   Nay, prithee, knight, leave fooling: thy jest begins to grow dull.

SIR TUN.   Bind him, I say, he's mad—bread and water, a dark room, and a whip, may bring him to his senses again.

LORD FOP. [aside]   I'gad, if I don't waken quickly, by all I can see, this is like to prove one of the most impertinent dreams that ever I dreamt in my life.

Enter MISS HOYDEN and Nurse

MISS [going up to him]   Is this he that would have run away with me? Fough, how he stinks of sweets! Pray, Father, let him be dragged through the horse-pond.

LORD FOP. [aside]   This must be my wife, by her natural inclination to her husband.

MISS   Pray, Father, what do you intend to do with him? hang him?

SIR TUN.   That at least, child.

NURSE   Ay, and it's e'en too good for him too.

LORD FOP. [*aside*]   *Madame la gouvernante,* I presume: hitherto this appears to me to be one of the most extraordinary families that ever man of quality matched into.

SIR TUN.   What's become of my Lord, daughter?

MISS   He's just coming, Sir.

LORD FOP. [*aside*]   "My Lord!"—what does he mean by that, now?

Enter YOUNG FASHION *and* LORY

[*seeing him*] Stap my vitals—Tam! Now the dream's out.

Y. FAS.   Is this the fellow, Sir, that designed to trick me of your daughter?

SIR TUN.   This is he, my Lord: how do you like him? Is not he a pretty fellow to get a fortune?

Y. FAS.   I find by his dress, he thought your daughter might be taken with a beau.

MISS   O Gemini! Is this a beau? let me see him again—ha! I find a beau is no such ugly thing, neither.

Y. FAS.   I'gad, she'll be in love with him presently; I'll e'en have him sent away to gaol. [*to* LORD FOPPINGTON] Sir, though your undertaking shows you are a person of no extraordinary modesty, I suppose you han't confidence enough to expect much favour from me?

LORD FOP.   Strike me dumb, Tam, thou art a very impudent fellow.

NURSE   Look if the varlet has not the frontery to call his Lordship plain Thomas.

BULL   The business is, he would feign himself mad, to avoid going to gaol.

LORD FOP. [*aside*]   That must be the chaplain, by his unfolding of mysteries.

SIR TUN.   Come, is the warrant writ?

CLERK   Yes, Sir.

SIR TUN.   Give me the pen, I'll sign it—so!—now, Constable, away with him.

LORD FOP.   Hold one moment—pray, gentlemen! My Lord Foppington, shall I beg one word with your Lordship?

NURSE   O ho, it's "my Lord" with him now; see how afflictions will humble folks.

MISS   Pray, my Lord, don't let him whisper too close, lest he bite your ear off.

LORD FOP.   I am not altogether so hungry as your Ladyship is pleased to imagine. [*to* YOUNG FASHION] Look you, Tam, I am sensible I have not been so kind to you as I ought, but I hope you'll forget what's past, and accept of the five thousand pounds I offer; thou may'st live in extreme splendour with it, stap my vitals.

Y. FAS.   It's a much easier matter to prevent a disease than to cure it; a quarter of that sum would be secured your mistress; twice as much won't redeem her.   [*leaving him*]

SIR TUN.   Well, what says he?

Y. FAS.   Only the rascal offered me a bribe to let him go.

SIR TUN.   Ay, he shall go, with a pox to him.—— Lead on, Constable.

LORD FOP.   One word more, and I have done.

SIR TUN.   Before Gad, thou art an impudent fellow to trouble the court at this rate, after thou art condemned; but speak once for all.

LORD FOP.   Why then once for all, I have at last luckily called to mind that there is a gentleman of this country, who I believe cannot live far from this place, if he were here would satisfy you I am Navelty, Baron of Foppington, with five thousand pounds a year, and that fellow there a rascal not worth a groat.

SIR TUN.   Very well; now who is this honest gentleman you are so well acquainted with? [*to* YOUNG FASHION] Come, Sir, we shall hamper him.

LORD FOP.   'Tis Sir John Friendly.

SIR TUN.   So: he lives within half a mile, and came down into the country but last night; this bold-faced fellow thought he had been at London still, and so quoted him; now we shall display him in his colours: I'll send for Sir John immediately.—— Here, fellow, away presently, and desire my neighbour he'll do me the favour to step over, upon an extraordinary occasion; [*exit Servant*]—and in the meanwhile you had best secure this sharper in the gate-house.

CONST.   An't please your Worship, he may chance to give us the slip thence: if I were worthy to advise, I think the dog-kennel's a surer place.

SIR TUN.   With all my heart, anywhere.

LORD FOP.   Nay, for heaven's sake, Sir, do me the favour to put me in a clean room, that I mayn't daub my clothes.

SIR TUN.   Oh, when you have married my daughter, her estate will afford you new ones.—— Away with him.

LORD FOP.   A dirty country justice is a barbarous magistrate, stap my vitals!   [*exit Constable with* LORD FOPPINGTON]

Y. FAS. [*aside*]   I'gad, I must prevent this knight's coming, or the house will grow soon too hot to hold me. [*to* SIR TUNBELLY] Sir, I fancy 'tis not worth while to trouble Sir John upon this impertinent fellow's desire: I'll send and call the messenger back——

SIR TUN.   Nay, with all my heart; for to be sure he thought he was far enough off, or the rogue would never have named him.

Enter Servant

SERV. Sir, I met Sir John just lighting at the gate; he's come to wait upon you.

SIR TUN. Nay, then it happens as one could wish.

Y. FAS. [*aside*] The devil it does!——— Lory, you see how things are: here will be a discovery presently, and we shall have our brains beat out, for my brother will be sure to swear he don't know me: therefore run into the stable, take the two first horses you can light on: I'll slip out at the back door, and we'll away immediately.

LO. What, and leave your lady, Sir?

Y. FAS. There's no danger in that, as long as I have taken possession; I shall know how to treat with 'em well enough, if once I am out of their reach: away, I'll steal after thee.

[*exit* LORY: *his master follows him out at one door,*
as SIR JOHN *enters at t'other*]

Enter SIR JOHN

SIR TUN. Sir John, you are the welcom'st man alive; I had just sent a messenger to desire you'd step over, upon a very extraordinary occasion—we are all in arms here.

SIR JOHN How so?

SIR TUN. Why, you must know—a finical sort of a tawdry fellow here (I don't know who the devil he is, not I) hearing, I suppose, that the match was concluded between my Lord Foppington and my girl Hoyden, comes impudently to the gate, with a whole pack of rogues in liveries, and would have passed upon me for his Lordship: but what does I? I comes up to him boldly at the head of his guards, takes him by the throat, strikes up his heels, binds him hand and foot, dispatches a warrant, and commits him prisoner to the dog-kennel.

SIR JOHN So, but how do you know but this was my Lord? for I was told he set out from London the day before me, with a very fine retinue, and intended to come directly hither.

SIR TUN. Why now to show you how many lies people raise in that damned town, he came two nights ago post, with only one servant, and is now in the house with me. But you don't know the cream of the jest yet; this same rogue (that lies yonder neck and heels among the hounds) thinking you were out of the country, quotes you for his acquaintance, and said if you were here you'd justify him to be Lord Foppington, and I know not what.

SIR JOHN Pray will you let me see him?

SIR TUN. Ay, that you shall presently.——— Here, fetch the prisoner.

[*exit Servant*]

SIR JOHN   I wish there ben't some mistake in this business; where's my Lord? I know him very well.

SIR TUN.   He was here just now—— see for him, Doctor, tell him Sir John is here to wait upon him.   [*exit Chaplain*]

SIR JOHN   I hope, Sir Tunbelly, the young lady is not married yet.

SIR TUN.   No, things won't be ready this week; but why do you say you hope she is not married?

SIR JOHN   Some foolish fancies only; perhaps I'm mistaken.

Re-enter Chaplain

BULL   Sir, his Lordship is just rid out to take the air.

SIR TUN.   To take the air! is that his London breeding, to go take the air when gentlemen come to visit him?

SIR JOHN   'Tis possible he might want it: he might not be well, some sudden qualm perhaps.

Enter Constable, etc., with LORD FOPPINGTON

LORD FOP.   Stap my vitals, I'll have satisfaction.

SIR JOHN [*running to him*]   My dear Lord Foppington!

LORD FOP.   Dear Friendly, thou art come in the critical minute, strike me dumb.

SIR JOHN   Why, I little thought I should have found you in fetters.

LORD FOP.   Why truly, the world must do me the justice to confess I do use to appear a little more *dégagé:* but this old gentleman, not liking the freedom of my air, has been pleased to skewer down my arms like a rabbit.

SIR TUN.   Is it then possible that this should be the true Lord Foppington at last?

LORD FOP.   Why, what do you see in his face to make you doubt of it? Sir, without presuming to have any extraordinary opinion of my fig-ure, give me leave to tell you, if you had seen as many lords as I have done, you would not think it impossible a person of a worse *taille* than mine might be a modern man of quality.

SIR TUN.   Unbind him, slaves.—— My Lord, I'm struck dumb: I can only beg pardon by signs; but if a sacrifice will appease you, you shall have it.—— Here, pursue this Tartar, bring him back—away, I say!—a dog, oons!—I'll cut off his ears and his tail, I'll draw out all his teeth, pull his skin over his head—and—and what shall I do more?

SIR JOHN   He does indeed deserve to be made an example of.

LORD FOP.   He does deserve to be *châtré,* stap my vitals.

SIR TUN.   May I then hope I have your honour's pardon?

LORD FOP.   Sir, we courtiers do nothing without a bribe; that fair young lady might do miracles.

SIR TUN.   Hoyden, come hither, Hoyden.

LORD FOP.   Hoyden is her name, Sir?

SIR TUN.   Yes, my Lord.

LORD FOP.   The prettiest name for a song I ever heard.

SIR TUN.   My Lord—here's my girl, she's yours; she has a wholesome
body and a virtuous mind; she's a woman complete, both in flesh and in
spirit; she has a bag of milled crowns, as scarce as they are, and fifteen
hundred a year stitched fast to her tail: so go thy ways, Hoyden.

LORD FOP.   Sir, I do receive her like a gentleman.

SIR TUN.   Then I'm a happy man, I bless heaven, and if your Lordship
will give me leave, I will, like a good Christian at Christmas, be very
drunk by way of thanksgiving. Come, my noble peer, I believe dinner's
ready; if your honour pleases to follow me, I'll lead you on to the attack
of a venison pasty.   [*exit* SIR TUNBELLY]

LORD FOP.   Sir, I wait upon you.—— Will your Ladyship do me the
favour of your little finger, Madam?

MISS   My Lord, I'll follow you presently: I have a little business with
my nurse.

LORD FOP.   Your Ladyship's most humble servant.—— Come, Sir
John, the ladies have *des affaires.*

[*exeunt* LORD FOPPINGTON *and* SIR JOHN]

MISS   So, nurse, we are finely brought to bed! What shall we do now?

NURSE   Ah, dear miss, we are all undone! Mr. Bull, you were used to
help a woman to a remedy.   [*crying*]

BULL   Alack-a-day, but it's past my skill now; I can do nothing.

NURSE   Who would have thought that ever your invention should
have been drained so dry?

MISS   Well, I have often thought old folks fools, and now I'm sure
they are so; I have found a way myself to secure us all.

NURSE   Dear lady, what's that?

MISS   Why, if you two will be sure to hold your tongues, and not say
a word of what's past, I'll e'en marry this lord too.

NURSE   What! two husbands, my dear?

MISS   Why you have had three, good nurse; you may hold your
tongue.

NURSE   Ay, but not all together, sweet child.

MISS   Psha, if you had, you'd ne'er a thought much on't.

NURSE   Oh, but 'tis a sin—sweeting.

BULL   Nay, that's my business to speak to, nurse: I do confess, to take
two husbands for the satisfaction of the flesh is to commit the sin of ex-
orbitancy, but to do it for the peace of the spirit is no more than to be
drunk by way of physic: besides, to prevent a parent's wrath is to avoid
the sin of disobedience; for when the parent's angry the child is froward.

So that upon the whole matter, I do think, though Miss should marry again, she may be saved.

MISS   I'cod, and I will marry again then, and so there's an end of the story.   [*exeunt*]

ACT V

SCENE I

London

Enter COUPLER, YOUNG FASHION, *and* LORY

COUP.   Well, and so Sir John coming in——?

Y. FAS.   And so Sir John coming in, I thought it might be manners in me to go out, which I did, and getting on horseback as fast as I could, rid away as if the devil had been at the rear of me; what has happened since, heav'n knows.

COUP.   I'gad, Sirrah, I know as well as heaven.

Y. FAS.   What do you know?

COUP.   That you are a cuckold.

Y. FAS.   The devil I am! by who?

COUP.   By your brother.

Y. FAS.   My brother! which way?

COUP.   The old way—he has lain with your wife.

Y. FAS.   Hell and Furies, what dost thou mean?

COUP.   I mean plainly; I speak no parable.

Y. FAS.   Plainly! Thou dost not speak common sense; I cannot understand one word thou say'st.

COUP.   You will do soon, youngster. In short, you left your wife a widow, and she married again.

Y. FAS.   It's a lie.

COUP.   ——I'cod, if I were a young fellow, I'd break your head, Sirrah.

Y. FAS.   Dear Dad, don't be angry, for I'm as mad as Tom of Bedlam.

COUP.   Then I had fitted you with a wife, you should have kept her.

Y. FAS.   But is it possible the young strumpet could play me such a trick?

COUP.   A young strumpet, Sir—can play twenty tricks.

Y. FAS.   But prithee instruct me a little farther; whence comes thy intelligence!

COUP.   From your brother, in this letter: there you may read it.

Y. FAS. [*reads*]   "DEAR COUPLER, [*pulling off his hat*] I have only time to tell thee in three lines, or thereabouts, that here has been the devil: that rascal Tam, having stole the letter thou hadst formerly writ for me to bring to Sir Tunbelly, formed a damnable design upon my mistress, and was in a fair way of success when I arrived. But after having suffered some indignities (in which I have all daubed my embroidered coat) I put him to flight. I sent out a party of horse after him, in hopes to have made him my prisoner, which if I had done, I would have qualified him for the seraglio, stap my vitals.

"The danger I have thus narrowly 'scaped has made me fortify myself against further attempts by entering immediately into an association with the young lady, by which we engage to stand by one another as long as we both shall live.

"In short, the papers are sealed and the contract is signed, so the business of the lawyer is *achevé;* but I defer the divine part of the thing till I arrive at London, not being willing to consummate in any other bed but my own.

"POSTSCRIPT. 'Tis passible I may be in tawn as soon as this letter, for I find the lady is so violently in love with me, I have determined to make her happy with all the dispatch that is practicable, without disardering my coach harses."

So, here's rare work, i'faith!

LO.   I'gad, Miss Hoyden has laid about her bravely.

COUP.   I think my country girl has played her part as well as if she had been born and bred in St. James's parish.

Y. FAS.   ——That rogue the chaplain!

LO.   And then that jade the nurse, Sir.

Y. FAS.   And then that drunken sot, Lory, Sir, that could not keep himself sober to be a witness to the marriage.

LO.   Sir—with respect—I know very few drunken sots that do keep themselves sober.

Y. FAS.   Hold your prating, Sirrah, or I'll break your head. Dear Coupler, what's to be done?

COUP.   Nothing's to be done till the bride and bridegroom come to town.

Y. FAS.   Bride and bridegroom? Death and Furies, I can't bear that thou shouldst call 'em so.

COUP.   Why, what shall I call 'em, dog and cat?

Y. FAS.   Not for the world; that sounds more like man and wife than t'other.

COUP.   Well, if you'll hear of 'em in no language, we'll leave 'em for the nurse and the chaplain.

Y. Fas.   The devil and the witch.

Coup.   When they come to town——

Lo.   We shall have stormy weather.

Coup.   Will you hold your tongues, gentlemen, or not?

Lo.   Mum.

Coup.   I say, when they come we must find what stuff they are made of—whether the churchman be chiefly composed of the flesh or the spirit; I presume the former, for as chaplains now go, 'tis probable he eats three pounds of beef to the reading of one chapter; this gives him carnal desires: he wants money, preferment, wine, a whore; therefore we must invite him to supper, give him fat capons, sack and sugar, a purse of gold, and a plump sister. Let this be done, and I'll warrant thee, my boy, he speaks truth like an oracle.

Y. Fas.   Thou art a profound statesman, I allow it; but how shall we gain the nurse?

Coup.   Oh, never fear the nurse, if once you have got the priest, for the devil always rides the hag.

Well, there's nothing more to be said of the matter at this time, that I know of; so let us go and enquire if there's any news of our people yet; perhaps they may be come.

But let me tell you one thing by the way, Sirrah: I doubt you have been an idle fellow; if thou hadst behaved thyself as thou shouldst have done, the girl would never have left thee.   [*exeunt*]

SCENE II

Berinthia's *apartment*

Enter her Maid, passing the stage, followed by Worthy

Wor.   Hem, Mrs. Abigail, is your mistress to be spoken with?

Ab.   By you, Sir, I believe she may.

Wor.   Why 'tis by me I would have her spoken with.

Ab.   I'll acquaint her, Sir.   [*exit* Abigail]

Wor. [*solus*]   One lift more I must persuade her to give me, and then I'm mounted. Well, a young bawd and a handsome one for my money: 'tis they do the execution; I'll never go to an old one, but when I have occasion for a witch.

Lewdness looks heavenly to a woman when an angel appears in its cause, but when a hag is advocate, she thinks it comes from the devil.

An old woman has something so terrible in her looks, that whilst she is persuading your mistress to forget she has a soul, she stares hell and damnation full in her face.

Enter Berinthia

BER.   Well, Sir, what news bring you?

WOR.   No news, Madam: there's a woman going to cuckold her husband.

BER.   Amanda?

WOR.   I hope so.

BER.   Speed her well.

WOR.   Ay, but there must be more than a Godspeed, or your charity won't be worth a farthing.

BER.   Why, han't I done enough already?

WOR.   Not quite.

BER.   What's the matter?

WOR.   The lady has a scruple still, which you must remove.

BER.   What's that?

WOR.   Her virtue—she says.

BER.   And do you believe her?

WOR.   No, but I believe it's what she takes for her virtue; it's some relics of lawful love: she is not yet fully satisfied her husband has got another mistress, which unless I can convince her of, I have opened the trenches in vain, for the breach must be wider before I dare storm the town.

BER.   And so I'm to be your engineer?

WOR.   I'm sure you know best how to manage the battery.

BER.   What think you of springing a mine? I have a thought just now come into my head, how to blow her up at once.

WOR.   That would be a thought, indeed!

BER.   ——Faith, I'll do't, and thus the execution of it shall be. We are all invited to my Lord Foppington's to-night to supper; he's come to town with his bride, and makes a ball, with an entertainment of music. Now you must know, my undoer here, Loveless, says he must needs meet me about some private business (I don't know what 'tis) before we go to the company. To which end he has told his wife one lie, and I have told her another. But to make her amends, I'll go immediately and tell her a solemn truth.

WOR.   What's that?

BER.   Why, I'll tell her that to my certain knowledge her husband has a rendezvous with his mistress this afternoon; and that if she'll give me her word she'll be satisfied with the discovery without making any violent inquiry after the woman, I'll direct her to a place where she shall see 'em meet. Now, friend, this I fancy may help you to a critical minute. For home she must go again to dress. You, with your good breeding, come to wait upon us to the ball, find her all alone, her spirit enflamed against her husband for his treason, and her flesh in a heat from some contemplations upon the treachery; her blood on a fire, her con-

science in ice; a lover to draw, and the devil to drive—— Ah, poor
Amanda!

WOR. [*kneeling*]　Thou angel of light, let me fall down and adore
thee!

BER.　Thou minister of darkness, get up again, for I hate to see the
devil at his devotions.

WOR.　Well, my incomparable Berinthia—how shall I requite you?

BER.　Oh, ne'er trouble yourself about that: Virtue is its own reward:
there's a pleasure in doing good, which sufficiently pays itself. Adieu.

WOR.　Farewell, thou best of women.　　　　　[*exeunt several ways*]

Enter AMANDA, *meeting* BERINTHIA

AMAN.　Who was that went from you?

BER.　A friend of yours.

AMAN.　What does he want?

BER.　Something you might spare him, and be ne'er the poorer.

AMAN.　I can spare him nothing but my friendship; my love already's
all disposed of: though, I confess, to one ungrateful to my bounty.

BER.　Why, there's the mystery: you have been so bountiful you have
cloyed him. Fond wives do by their husbands as barren wives do by their
lap-dogs: cram 'em with sweetmeats till they spoil their stomachs.

AMAN.　Alas! Had you but seen how passionately fond he has been
since our last reconciliation, you would have thought it were impossible
he ever should have breathed an hour without me.

BER.　Ay, but there you thought wrong again, Amanda; you should
consider that in matters of love men's eyes are always bigger than their
bellies. They have violent appetites, 'tis true, but they have soon dined.

AMAN.　Well; there's nothing upon earth astonishes me more than
men's inconstancy.

BER.　Now there's nothing upon earth astonishes me less, when I
consider what they and we are composed of. For nature has made them
children, and us babies. Now, Amanda, how we used our babies, you may
remember. We were mad to have 'em as soon as we saw 'em; kissed 'em
to pieces as soon as we got 'em; then pulled off their clothes, saw 'em
naked, and so threw 'em away.

AMAN.　But do you think all men are of this temper?

BER.　All but one.

AMAN.　Who is that?

BER.　Worthy.

AMAN.　Why, he's weary of his wife too, you see.

BER.　Ay, that's no proof.

AMAN.　What can be a greater?

BER.　Being weary of his mistress.

AMAN.   Don't you think 'twere possible he might give you that too?

BER.   Perhaps he might, if he were my gallant; not if he were yours.

AMAN.   Why do you think he should be more constant to me than he would to you? I'm sure I'm not so handsome.

BER.   Kissing goes by favour; he likes you best.

AMAN.   Suppose he does: that's no demonstration he would be constant to me.

BER.   No, that I'll grant you: but there are other reasons to expect it; for you must know after all, Amanda, the inconstancy we commonly see in men of brains does not so much proceed from the uncertainty of their temper as from the misfortunes of their love. A man sees perhaps a hundred women he likes well enough for an intrigue and away, but possibly, through the whole course of his life, does not find above one who is exactly what he could wish her: now her, 'tis a thousand to one, he never gets. Either she is not to be had at all (though that seldom happens, you'll say) or he wants those opportunities that are necessary to gain her. Either she likes somebody else much better than him or uses him like a dog because he likes nobody so well as her. Still something or other fate claps in the way between them and the woman they are capable of being fond of: and this makes them wander about from mistress to mistress, like a pilgrim from town to town, who every night must have a fresh lodging, and 's in haste to be gone in the morning.

AMAN.   'Tis possible there may be something in what you say; but what do you infer from it, as to the man we were talking of?

BER.   Why, I infer that you being the woman in the world the most to his humour, 'tis not likely he would quit you for one that is less.

AMAN.   That is not to be depended upon, for you see Mr. Loveless does so.

BER.   What does Mr. Loveless do?

AMAN.   Why, he runs after something for variety, I'm sure he does not like so well as he does me.

BER.   That's more than you know, Madam.

AMAN.   No, I'm sure on't: I'm not very vain, Berinthia, and yet I'd lay my life, if I could look into his heart, he thinks I deserve to be preferred to a thousand of her.

BER.   Don't be too positive in that, neither: a million to one, but she has the same opinion of you. What would you give to see her?

AMAN.   Hang her, dirty trull! though I really believe she's so ugly she'd cure me of my jealousy.

BER.   All the men of sense about town say she's handsome.

AMAN.   They are as often out in those things as any people.

BER.   Then I'll give you farther proof—all the women about town say she's a fool: now I hope you're convinced?

AMAN.   Whate'er she be, I'm satisfied he does not like her well enough to bestow anything more than a little outward gallantry upon her.

BER.   Outward gallantry?—— [*aside*] I can't bear this. [*to* AMANDA] Don't you think she's a woman to be fobbed off so. Come, I'm too much your friend to suffer you should be thus grossly imposed upon by a man who does not deserve the least part about you, unless he knew how to set a greater value upon it. Therefore, in one word, to my certain knowledge he is to meet her, now, within a quarter of an hour, somewhere about that Babylon of wickedness, Whitehall. And if you'll give me your word that you'll be content with seeing her masked in his hand, without pulling her headclothes off, I'll step immediately to the person from whom I have my intelligence, and send you word whereabouts you may stand to see 'em meet. My friend and I'll watch 'em from another place, and dodge 'em to their private lodging: but don't you offer to follow 'em, lest you do it awkwardly, and spoil all. I'll come home to you again, as soon as I have earthed 'em, and give you an account in what corner of the house the scene of their lewdness lies.

AMAN.   If you can do this, Berinthia, he's a villain.

BER.   I can't help that: men will be so.

AMAN.   Well! I'll follow your directions, for I shall never rest till I know the worst of this matter.

BER.   Pray, go immediately, and get yourself ready, then. Put on some of your woman's clothes, a great scarf and a mask, and you shall presently receive orders. [*calls within*] Here, who's there? get me a chair quickly.

Enter Servant

SERV.   There are chairs at the door, Madam.

BER.   'Tis well; I'm coming.   [*exit Servant*]

AMAN.   But pray, Berinthia, before you go, tell me how I may know this filthy thing, if she should be so forward (as I suppose she will) to come to the rendezvous first; for methinks I would fain view her a little.

BER.   Why, she's about my height, and very well shaped.

AMAN.   I thought she had been a little crooked?

BER.   Oh no, she's as straight as I am. But we lose time: come away.
                                                        [*exeunt*]

SCENE III

Enter YOUNG FASHION, *meeting* LORY

Y. FAS.   Well, will the doctor come?

LO.   Sir, I sent a porter to him as you ordered me. He found him with a pipe of tobacco and a great tankard of ale, which he said he would dispatch while I could tell three, and be here.

Y. FAS.   He does not suspect 'twas I that sent for him?

LO.   Not a jot, Sir; he divines as little for himself as he does for other folks.

Y. FAS.   Will he bring nurse with him?

LO.   Yes.

Y. FAS.   That's well; where's Coupler?

LO.   He's half way up the stairs taking breath; he must play his bellows a little before he can get to the top.

Enter COUPLER

Y. FAS.   Oh, here he is. Well, old phthisic? The doctor's coming.

COUP.   Would the pox had the doctor—I'm quite out of wind. [*to* LORY] Set me a chair, Sirrah. Ah! [*sits down; to* YOUNG FASHION] Why the plague canst not thou lodge upon the ground floor?

Y. FAS.   Because I love to lie as near heaven as I can.

COUP.   Prithee let heaven alone; ne'er affect tending that way: thy centre's downwards.

Y. FAS.   That's impossible. I have too much ill luck in this world to be damned in the next.

COUP.   Thou art out in thy logic. Thy major is true, but thy minor is false; for thou art the luckiest fellow in the universe.

Y. FAS.   Make out that.

COUP.   I'll do't: last night the devil ran away with the parson of Fatgoose living.

Y. FAS.   If he had run away with the parish too, what's that to me?

COUP.   I'll tell thee what it's to thee. This living is worth five hundred pound a year, and the presentation of it is thine, if thou canst prove thyself a lawful husband to Miss Hoyden.

Y. FAS.   Say'st thou so, my protector? then i'cad I shall have a brace of evidences here presently.

COUP.   The nurse and the doctor?

Y. FAS.   The same: the devil himself won't have interest enough to make 'em withstand it.

COUP.   That we shall see presently: here they come.

Enter Nurse and Chaplain; they start back, seeing YOUNG FASHION

NURSE   Ah goodness, Roger, we are betrayed.

Y. FAS. [*laying hold on 'em*]   Nay, nay, ne'er flinch for the matter, for I have you safe. Come, to your trials immediately: I have no time to give you copies of your indictment. There sits your judge.

BOTH. [*kneeling*]   Pray, Sir, have compassion on us.

NURSE   I hope, Sir, my years will move your pity: I am an aged woman.

COUP.   That is a moving argument, indeed.

BULL   I hope, Sir, my character will be considered; I am heaven's ambassador.

COUP. [*to* BULL]   Are not you a rogue of sanctity?

BULL   Sir, with respect to my function, I do wear a gown.

COUP.   Did not you marry this vigorous young fellow to a plump young buxom wench?

NURSE [*to* BULL]   Don't confess, Roger, unless you are hard put to it, indeed.

COUP.   Come, out with't!—— Now is he chewing the cud of his roguery, and grinding a lie between his teeth.

BULL   Sir—I cannot positively say—I say, Sir—positively I cannot say——

COUP.   Come, no equivocations, no Roman turns upon us. Consider thou standest upon Protestant ground, which will slip from under thee like a Tyburn cart; for in this country we have always ten hangmen for one Jesuit.

BULL [*to* YOUNG FASHION]   Pray, Sir, then will you but permit me to speak one word in private with nurse?

Y. FAS.   Thou art always for doing something in private with nurse.

COUP.   But pray let his betters be served before him for once. I would do something in private with her myself. Lory, take care of this reverend gownman in the next room a little. Retire, priest. [*exit* LORY *with* BULL] ——Now, virgin, I must put the matter home to you a little: do you think it might not be possible to make you speak truth?

NURSE   Alas! Sir, I don't know what you mean by truth.

COUP.   Nay, 'tis possible thou may'st be a stranger to it.

Y. FAS.   Come, nurse, you and I were better friends when we saw one another last and I still believe you are a very good woman in the bottom. I did deceive you and your young lady, 'tis true, but I always designed to make a very good husband to her, and to be a very good friend to you. And 'tis possible, in the end she might have found herself happier and you richer than ever my brother will make you.

NURSE   Brother! Why, is your Worship then his Lordship's brother?

Y. FAS.   I am; which you should have known, if I durst have stayed to have told you; but I was forced to take horse a little in haste, you know.

NURSE   You were, indeed, Sir: poor young man, how he was bound to scour for't. Now won't your Worship be angry if I confess the truth to you: when I found you were a cheat (with respect be it spoken) I verily believed Miss had got some pitiful skip-jack varlet or other to her hus-band, or I had ne'er let her think of marrying again.

COUP.   But where was your conscience all this while, woman? Did not that stare in your face with huge saucer-eyes, and a great horn upon the forehead? Did not you think you should be damned for such a sin? Ha?

Y. FAS.   Well said, divinity: pass that home upon her.

NURSE   Why, in good truly, Sir. I had some fearful thoughts on't, and could never be brought to consent, till Mr. Bull said it was a *peckadilla,* and he'd secure my soul for a tithe-pig.

Y. FAS.   There was a rogue for you!

COUP.   And he shall thrive accordingly: he shall have a good living. Come, honest nurse, I see you have butter in your compound: you can melt. Some compassion you can have of this handsome young fellow.

NURSE   I have, indeed, Sir.

Y. FAS.   Why, then, I'll tell you what you shall do for me. You know what a warm living here is fallen, and that it must be in the disposal of him who has the disposal of Miss. Now if you and the doctor will agree to prove my marriage, I'll present him to it, upon condition he makes you his bride.

NURSE   Naw the blessing of the Lord follow your good Worship both by night and by day! Let him be fetched in by the ears; I'll soon bring his nose to the grindstone.

COUP. [*aside*]   Well said, old white-leather.—— Hey; bring in the prisoner there.

Enter LORY *with* BULL

COUP.   Come, advance, holy man! Here's your duck, does not think fit to retire with you into the chancel at this time; but she has a proposal to make to you in the face of the congregation. Come, nurse, speak for yourself; you are of age.

NURSE   Roger, are not you a wicked man, Roger, to set your strength against a weak woman, and persuade her it was no sin to conceal Miss's nuptials? My conscience flies in my face for it, thou priest of Baal; and I find by woful experience, thy absolution is not worth an old cassock. Therefore I am resolved to confess the truth to the whole world, though I die a beggar for it. But his worship overflows with his mercy and his bounty: he is not only pleased to forgive us our sins, but designs thou shalt squat thee down in Fatgoose living; and, which is more than all, has prevailed with me to become the wife of thy bosom.

Y. FAS.   All this I intend for you, Doctor. What you are to do for me, I need not tell you.

BULL   Your Worship's goodness is unspeakable. Yet there is one thing seems a point of conscience, and conscience is a tender babe. If I should bind myself, for the sake of this living, to marry nurse, and maintain her afterwards, I doubt it might be looked on as a kind of simony.

COUP. [*rising up*]   If it were sacrilege, the living's worth it: therefore no more words, good Doctor, but with the parish—here [*giving Nurse to him*]—take the parsonage-house. 'Tis true, 'tis a little out of repair; some dilapidations there are to be made good; the windows are broke, the wainscot is warped, the ceilings are peeled, and the walls are cracked; but a little glazing, painting, whitewash, and plaster will make it last thy time.

BULL   Well, Sir, if it must be so, I shan't contend: what Providence orders, I submit to.

NURSE   And so do I, with all humility.

COUP.   Why, that now was spoke like good people: come, my turtle-doves, let us go help this poor pigeon to his wandering mate again; and after institution and induction you shall all go a-cooing together.

[*exeunt*]

SCENE IV

Enter AMANDA, *in a scarf, etc., as just returned, her Woman following her*

AMAN.   Prithee, what care I who has been here?

WOM.   Madam, 'twas my Lady Bridle and my Lady Tiptoe.

AMAN.   My Lady Fiddle and my Lady Faddle. What dost stand troubling me with the visits of a parcel of impertinent women? when they are well seamed with the small-pox they won't be so fond of showing their faces. There are more coquettes about this town——

WOM.   Madam, I suppose they only came to return your Ladyship's visit, according to the custom of the world.

AMAN.   Would the world were on fire, and you in the middle on't! Begone: leave me.   [*exit Woman*]

AMAN. [*sola*]   At last I am convinc'd. My eyes are testimonies of his falsehood.

The base, ungrateful, perjur'd villain——
Good gods—what slippery stuff are men compos'd of?
Sure the account of their creation's false,
And 'twas the woman's rib that they were form'd of.
But why am I thus angry?
This poor relapse should only move my scorn.
'Tis true, the roving flights of his unfinish'd youth
Had strong excuse from the plea of Nature:
Reason had thrown the reins loose on his neck,
And slipt him to unlimited desire.
If therefore he went wrong, he had a claim
To my forgiveness, and I did him right.

But since the years of manhood rein him in,
And reason, well digested into thought,
Has pointed out the course he ought to run;
If now he strays?
'Twould be as weak and mean in me to pardon,
As it has been in him t'offend. But hold:
'Tis an ill cause indeed, where nothing's to be said for't.
My beauty possibly is in the wane:
Perhaps sixteen has greater charms for him:
Yes, there's the secret. But let him know,
My quiver's not entirely empty'd yet,
I still have darts, and I can shoot 'em too;
They're not so blunt, but they can enter still;
The want's not in my power, but in my will.
Virtue's his friend; or, through another's heart,
I yet could find the way to make his smart.

                          [*going off, she meets* WORTHY]

Ha! He here?
Protect me, heaven, for this looks ominous.

WOR.   You seem disorder'd, Madam;
  I hope there's no misfortune happen'd to you?

AMAN.   None that will long disorder me, I hope.

WOR.   Whate'er it be disturbs you,
  I would to heaven 'twere in my power
  To bear the pain till I were able to remove the cause.

AMAN.   I hope ere long it will remove itself.
  At least, I have given it warning to be gone.

WOR.   Would I durst ask, where 'tis the thorn torments you?
  Forgive me if I grow inquisitive;
  'Tis only with desire to give you ease.

AMAN.   Alas! 'tis in a tender part.
  It can't be drawn without a world of pain:
  Yet out it must;
  For it begins to fester in my heart.

WOR.   If 'tis the sting of unrequited love, remove it instantly:
  I have a balm will quickly heal the wound.

AMAN.   You'll find the undertaking difficult:
  The surgeon who already has attempted it
  Has much tormented me.

WOR.   I'll aid him with a gentler hand
  —If you will give me leave.

AMAN.   How soft soe'er the hand may be,
  There still is terror in the operation.

WOR. Some few preparatives would make it easy,
　　Could I persuade you to apply 'em.
　　Make home reflections, Madam, on your slighted love.
　　Weigh well the strength and beauty of your charms:
　　Rouse up that spirit women ought to bear,
　　And slight your god, if he neglects his angel.
　　With arms of ice receive his cold embraces,
　　And keep your fire for those who come in flames.
　　Behold a burning lover at your feet,
　　His fever raging in his veins.
　　See how he trembles, how he pants!
　　See how he glows, how he consumes!
　　Extend the arms of mercy to his aid;
　　His zeal may give him title to your pity,
　　Although his merit cannot claim your love.

AMAN. Of all my feeble sex,
　　Sure I must be the weakest,
　　Should I again presume to think on love.
　　[*sighing*] Alas! my heart has been too roughly treated.

WOR. 'Twill find the greater bliss in softer usage.

AMAN. But where's that usage to be found?

WOR.　　　　　　　　　　　　　'Tis here,
　　Within this faithful breast; which, if you doubt,
　　I'll rip it up before your eyes,
　　Lay all its secrets open to your view,
　　And then you'll see 'twas sound.

AMAN. With just such honest words as these
　　The worst of men deceiv'd me.

WOR.　　　　　　　　　　He therefore merits
　　All revenge can do; his fault is such,
　　The extent and stretch of vengeance cannot reach it.
　　Oh, make me but your instrument of justice;
　　You'll find me execute it with such zeal
　　As shall convince you I abhor the crime.

AMAN. The rigour of an executioner
　　Has more the face of cruelty than justice,
　　And he who puts the cord about the wretch's neck
　　Is seldom known to exceed him in his morals.

WOR. What proof then can I give you of my truth?

AMAN. There is on earth but one.

WOR.　　　　　　　　　And is that in my power?

AMAN.　　　　　　　　　　　　　　　It is.
　　And one that would so thoroughly convince me,

I should be apt to rate your heart so high,
I possibly might purchas't with a part of mine.

WOR.   Then, heav'n, thou art my friend, and I am blest;
For if 'tis in my power, my will, I'm sure,
Will reach it. No matter what the terms may be,
When such a recompense is offer'd.
Oh, tell me quickly what this proof must be.
What is it will convince you of my love?

AMAN.   I shall believe you love me as you ought
If from this moment you forbear to ask
Whatever is unfit for me to grant.
——You pause upon it, Sir—I doubt, on such hard terms
A woman's heart is scarcely worth the having.

WOR.   A heart like yours on any terms is worth it;
'Twas not on that I paus'd. But I was thinking [*drawing nearer to her*]
Whether some things there may not be
Which women cannot grant without a blush,
And yet which men may take without offense.
[*taking her hand*] Your hand, I fancy, may be of the number:
Oh, pardon me, if I commit a rape
Upon it [*kissing it eagerly*] and thus devour it with my kisses.

AMAN.   O heavens! let me go!

WOR.   Never, whilst I have strength to hold you here.
[*forcing her to sit down on a couch*] My life, my soul, my goddess—
     Oh, forgive me!

AMAN.   Oh, whither am I going? Help, heaven, or I am lost.

WOR.   Stand neuter, gods, this once I do invoke you.

AMAN.   Then save me, virtue, and the glory's thine.

WOR.   Nay, never strive!

AMAN.   I will, and conquer, too.
My forces rally bravely to my aid, [*breaking from him*]
And thus I gain the day.

WOR.   Then mine as bravely double their attack, [*seizing her again*]
And thus I wrest it from you. Nay, struggle not,
For all's in vain: or death or victory,
I am determined.

AMAN.   And so am I. [*rushing from him*]
Now keep your distance, or we part forever.

WOR. [*offering again*]   For heaven's sake——

AMAN. [*going*]   Nay, then farewell.

WOR. [*kneeling and holding by her clothes*]   Oh, stay, and see the magic
force of love:
     Behold this raging lion at your feet,

    Struck dead with fear, and tame as charms can make him.
    What must I do to be forgiven by you?
AMAN.   Repent, and never more offend.
WOR.   Repentance for past crimes is just and easy;
    But sin no more's a task too hard for mortals.
AMAN.   Yet those who hope for heaven
    Must use their best endeavours to perform it.
WOR.   Endeavours we may use; but flesh and blood
    Are got in t'other scale,
    And they are pond'rous things.
AMAN.   Whate'er they are,
    There is a weight in resolution
    Sufficient for their balance. The soul, I do confess,
    Is usually so careless of its charge,
    So soft, and so indulgent to desire,
    It leaves the reins in the wild hand of Nature,
    Who, like a Phaeton, drives the fiery chariot,
    And sets the world on flame.
    Yet still the sovereignty is in the mind,
    Whene'er it pleases to exert its force.
    Perhaps you may not think it worth your while
    To take such mighty pains for my esteem;
    But that I leave to you.
    You see the price I set upon my heart;
    Perhaps 'tis dear: but spite of all your art,
    You'll find on cheaper terms we ne'er shall part.   [*exit* AMANDA]
WOR. [*solus*]   Sure there's divinity about her;
    And sh'as dispens'd some portion on't to me.
    For what but now was the wild flame of love,
    Or (to dissect that specious term)
    The vile, the gross desires of flesh and blood,
    Is in a moment turned to adoration.
    The coarser appetite of nature's gone,
    And 'tis, methinks, the food of angels I require:
    How long this influence may last, heaven knows.
    But in this moment of my purity
    I could on her own terms accept her heart.
    Yes, lovely woman, I can accept it,
    For now 'tis doubly worth my care.
    Your charms are much encreas'd, since thus adorn'd.
    When truth's extorted from us, then we own
    The robe of virtue is a graceful habit.
    Could women but our secret counsels scan,

Could they but reach the deep reserves of man,
They'd wear it on, that that of love might last;
For when they throw off one, we soon the other cast.
Their sympathy is such——
The fate of one the other scarce can fly;
They live together, and together die.   [*exit*]

SCENE V

Enter MISS HOYDEN *and Nurse*

MISS   But is it sure and certain, say you, he's my Lord's own brother?

NURSE   As sure as he's your lawful husband.

MISS   I'cod, if I had known that in time, I don't know but I might have kept him; for between you and I, nurse, he'd have made a husband worth two of this I have. But which do you think you should fancy most, nurse?

NURSE   Why, truly, in my poor fancy, Madam, your first husband is the prettier gentleman.

MISS   I don't like my Lord's shapes, nurse.

NURSE   Why, in good truly, as a body may say, he is but a slam.

MISS   What do you think now he puts me in mind of? Don't you remember a long, loose, shambling sort of a horse my father called Washy?

NURSE   As like as two twin brothers.

MISS   I'cod, I have thought so a hundred times: 'faith, I'm tired of him.

NURSE   Indeed, Madam, I think you had e'en as good stand to your first bargain.

MISS   Oh, but, nurse, we han't considered the main thing yet. If I leave my Lord, I must leave "my Lady" too: and when I rattle about the streets in my coach, they'll only say, There goes Mistress—Mistress—Mistress what? What's this man's name I have married, nurse?

NURSE   Squire Fashion.

MISS   Squire Fashion, is it?—— Well, Squire, that's better than nothing: do you think one could not get him made a knight, nurse?

NURSE   I don't know but one might, Madam, when the king's in a good humour.

MISS   I'cod, that would do rarely. For then he'd be as good a man as my father, you know.

NURSE   By'r Lady, and that's as good as the best of 'em.

MISS   So 'tis, faith; for then I shall be "my Lady" and "your Ladyship" at every word, and that's all I have to care for. Ha, nurse! but hark you me, one thing more, and then I have done. I'm afraid, if I change my husband again, I shan't have so much money to throw about, nurse.

NURSE   Oh, enough's as good as a feast: besides, Madam, one don't know but as much may fall to your share with the younger brother as with the elder. For though these lords have a power of wealth, indeed, yet as I have heard say, they give it all to their sluts and their trulls, who joggle it about in their coaches, with a murrain to 'em, whilst poor madam sits sighing and wishing, and knotting and crying, and has not a spare half-crown to buy her a *Practice of Piety*.

MISS   Oh, but for that, don't deceive yourself, nurse. For this I must say for my Lord, and a—— [*snapping her fingers*] for him: he's as free as an open house at Christmas. For this very morning he told me I should have two hundred a year to buy pins. Now, nurse, if he gives me two hundred a year to buy pins, what do you think he'll give me to buy fine petti- coats?

NURSE   Ah, my dearest, he deceives thee faully, and he's no better than a rogue for his pains. These Londoners have got a gibberidge with 'em, would confound a gypsy. That which they call pin-money is to buy their wives everything in the varsal world, dawn to their very shoe-ties: nay, I have heard folks say that some ladies, if they will have gallants, as they call 'em, are forced to find them out of their pin-money too.

MISS   Has he served me so, say ye?—then I'll be his wife no longer, so that's fixed. Look, here he comes, with all the fine folk at 's heels. I'cod, nurse, these London ladies will laugh till they crack again, to see me slip my collar, and run away from my husband. But, d'ye hear? pray take care of one thing: when the business comes to break out, be sure you get be- tween me and my father, for you know his tricks; he'll knock me down.

NURSE   I'll mind him, ne'er fear, Madam.

Enter LORD FOPPINGTON, LOVELESS, WORTHY, AMANDA, *and* BERINTHIA

LORD FOP.   Ladies and gentlemen, you are all welcome. [*to* LOVELESS] Loveless—that's my wife; prithee do me the favour to salute her: and dost hear, [*aside to him*] if thou hast a mind to try thy fartune, to be revenged of me, I won't take it ill, stap my vitals.

LOV.   You need not fear, Sir: I'm too fond of my own wife to have the least inclination to yours.   [*all salute* MISS HOYDEN]

LORD FOP. [*aside*]   I'd give a thausand paund he would make love to her, that he may see she has sense enough to prefer me to him, though his own wife has not: [*viewing him*]—he's a very beastly fellow, in my opinion.

MISS [*aside*]   What a power of fine men there are in this London! He that kissed me first is a goodly gentleman, I promise you: sure those wives have a rare time on't, that live here always!

Enter SIR TUNBELLY, *with Musicians, Dancers, etc.*

SIR TUN.   Come; come in, good people, come in; come, tune your
fiddles, tune your fiddles. [*to the Hautboys*] Bag-pipes, make ready there.
Come, strike up! [*sings*]

> For this is Hoyden's wedding-day;
> And therefore we keep holy-day,
> And come to be merry.

Ha! there's my wench, i'faith: touch and take, I'll warrant her; she'll breed
like a tame rabbit.

MISS [*aside*]   I'cod, I think my father's gotten drunk before supper.

SIR TUN. [*to* LOVELESS *and* WORTHY]   Gentlemen, you are welcome.
[*saluting* AMANDA *and* BERINTHIA] Ladies, by your leave.—— Ha—they
bill like turtles. Udsookers, they set my old blood afire; I shall cuckold
somebody before morning.

LORD FOP. [*to* SIR TUNBELLY]   Sir, you being master of the entertainment, will you desire the company to sit?

SIR TUN.   Oons, Sir—I'm the happiest man on this side the Ganges.

LORD FOP. [*aside*]   This is a mighty unaccountable old fellow. [*to* SIR
TUNBELLY] I said, Sir, it would be convenient to ask the company to sit.

SIR TUN.   Sit?—with all my heart.—— Come, take your places,
ladies; take your places, gentlemen: come, sit down, sit down; a pox of
ceremony, take your places.   [*they sit, and the masque begins*]

DIALOGUE BETWEEN CUPID AND HYMEN

1

CUPID.   Thou bane to my empire, thou spring of contest,
   Thou source of all discord, thou period to rest;
   Instruct me what wretches in bondage can see,
   That the aim of their life is still pointed to thee.

2

HYMEN.   Instruct me, thou little impertinent god,
   From whence all thy subjects have taken the mode
   To grow fond of a change, to whatever it be,
   And I'll tell thee why those would be bound, who are free.

Chorus

> For change, w'are for change, to whatever it be,
> We are neither contented with freedom nor thee.
> Constancy's an empty sound.
> Heaven and earth and all go round;
> All the works of nature move,

And the joys of life and love
    Are in variety.

3

CUPID.   Were love the reward of a painstaking life,
    Had a husband the art to be fond of his wife,
    Were virtue so plenty, a wife could afford,
    These very hard times, to be true to her lord;
    Some specious account might be given of those
    Who are tied by the tail, to be led by the nose.

4

But since 'tis the fate of a man and his wife
To consume all their days in contention and strife:
Since whatever the bounty of heaven may create her,
He's morally sure he shall heartily hate her;
I think 'twere much wiser to ramble at large,
And the volleys of love on the herd to discharge.

5

HYMEN.   Some colour of reason thy counsel might bear,
    Could a man have no more than his wife to his share:
    Or were I a monarch so cruelly just,
    To oblige a poor wife to be true to her trust;
    But I have not pretended, for many years past,
    By marrying of people, to make 'em grow chaste.

6

I therefore advise thee to let me go on,
Thou'lt find I'm the strength and support of thy throne;
For hadst thou but eyes, thou would'st quickly perceive it,
    How smoothly thy dart
    Slips into the heart
    Of a woman that's wed;
    Whilst the shivering maid
Stands trembling, and wishing, but dare not receive it.

Chorus

For change, *etc.*

The masque ended, enter YOUNG FASHION, COUPLER, *and* BULL

SIR TUN.   So, very fine, very fine, i'faith; this is something like a wedding; now if supper were but ready, I'd say a short grace; and if I had such

a bedfellow as Hoyden to-night—I'd say as short prayers. [*seeing* YOUNG
FASHION] How now—what have we got here? a ghost? Nay, it must be
so, for his flesh and his blood could never have dared to appear before
me. [*to him*] Ah, rogue——!

LORD FOP.   Stap my vitals, Tam again.

SIR TUN.   My Lord, will you cut his throat? or shall I?

LORD FOP.   Leave him to me, Sir, if you please.—— Prithee, Tam, be
so ingenuous, now, as to tell me what thy business is here?

Y. FAS.   'Tis with your bride.

LORD FOP.   Thau art the impudent'st fellow that nature has yet
spawned into the warld, strike me speechless.

Y. FAS.   Why, you know my modesty would have starved me; I sent it
a-begging to you, and you would not give it a groat.

LORD FOP.   And dost thau expect by an excess of assurance to extart
a maintenance fram me?

Y. FAS. [*taking* MISS HOYDEN *by the hand*]   I do intend to extort your
mistress from you, and that I hope will prove one.

LORD FOP.   I ever thaught Newgate or Bedlam would be his fartune,
and naw his fate's decided. Prithee, Loveless, dost know of ever a mad-
doctor hard by?

Y. FAS.   There's one at your elbow will cure you presently. [*to* BULL]
Prithee, Doctor, take him in hand quickly.

LORD FOP.   Shall I beg the favour of you, Sir, to pull your fingers out
of my wife's hand?

Y. FAS.   His wife! Look you there; now I hope you are all satisfied he's
mad?

LORD FOP.   Naw is it nat possible far me to penetrate what species of
fally it is thau art driving at.

SIR TUN.   Here, here, here, let me beat out his brains, and that will
decide all.

LORD FOP.   No, pray, Sir, hold: we'll destray him presently accarding
to law.

Y. FAS. [*to* BULL]   Nay, then advance, Doctor; come, you are a man of
conscience; answer boldly to the questions I shall ask: Did not you marry
me to this young lady, before ever that gentleman there saw her face?

BULL   Since the truth must out, I did.

Y. FAS.   Nurse, sweet nurse, were not you a witness to it?

NURSE   Since my conscience bids me speak—I was.

Y. FAS. [*to* MISS HOYDEN]   Madam, am not I your lawful husband?

MISS   Truly I can't tell, but you married me first.

Y. FAS.   Now I hope you are all satisfied?

SIR TUN. [*offering to strike him, is held by* LOVELESS *and* WORTHY]
Oons and thunder, you lie.

LORD FOP.   Pray, Sir, be calm: the battle is in disorder, but requires more conduct than courage to rally our forces.—— Pray, Dactar, one word with you. [*to* BULL *aside*] Look you, Sir, though I will not presume to calculate your notions of damnation fram the description you give us of hell, yet since there is at least a passibility you may have a pitchfark thrust in your backside, methinks it should not be worth your while to risk your saul in the next warld far the sake of a beggarly yaunger brather who is nat able to make your bady happy in this.

BULL   Alas! my Lord, I have no worldly ends; I speak the truth, heaven knows.

LORD FOP.   Nay, prithee, never engage heaven in the matter, far, by all I can see, 'tis like to prove a business for the devil.

Y. FAS.   Come, pray, Sir, all above-board: no corrupting of evidences, if you please; this young lady is my lawful wife, and I'll justify it in all the courts of England; so your Lordship (who always had a passion for variety) may go seek a new mistress, if you think fit.

LORD FOP.   I am struck dumb with his impudence, and cannot passitively tell whether ever I shall speak again or nat.

SIR TUN.   Then let me come and examine the business a little: I'll jerk the truth out of 'em presently; here, give me my dog-whip.

Y. FAS.   Look you, old gentleman, 'tis in vain to make a noise; if you grow mutinous, I have some friends within call have swords by their sides above four foot long; therefore be calm, hear the evidence patiently, and when the jury have given their verdict, pass sentence according to law: here's honest Coupler shall be foreman, and ask as many questions as he pleases.

COUP.   All I have to ask is whether nurse persists in her evidence? The parson, I dare swear, will never flinch from his.

NURSE [*to* SIR TUNBELLY, *kneeling*]   I hope in heaven your Worship will pardon me; I have served you long and faithfully, but in this thing I was overreached; your Worship, however, was deceived as well as I, and if the wedding-dinner had been ready, you had put Madam to bed to him with your own hands.

SIR TUN.   But how durst you do this, without acquainting of me?

NURSE   Alas! if your Worship had seen how the poor thing begged, and prayed, and clung, and twined about me, like ivy to an old wall, you would say I, who had suckled it, and swaddled it, and nursed it both wet and dry, must have had a heart of adamant to refuse it.

SIR TUN.   Very well!

Y. FAS.   Foreman, I expect your verdict.

COUP.   Ladies and gentlemen, what's your opinions?

ALL.   A clear case, a clear case.

COUP.   Then, my young folks, I wish you joy.

SIR TUN. [*to* YOUNG FASHION]   Come hither, stripling; if it be true, then, that thou hast married my daughter, prithee tell me who thou art?

Y. FAS.   Sir, the best of my condition is, I am your son-in-law; and the worst of it is, I am brother to that noble peer there.

SIR TUN.   Art thou brother to that noble peer? Why then, that noble peer, and thee, and thy wife, and the nurse, and the priest—may all go and be damned together.   [*exit* SIR TUNBELLY]

LORD FOP. [*aside*]   Now, for my part, I think the wisest thing a man can do with an aching heart, is to put on a serene countenance, for a philosophical air is the most becoming thing in the world to the face of a person of quality; I will therefore bear my disgrace like a great man, and let the people see I am above an affront. [*to* YOUNG FASHION] Dear Tam, since things are thus fallen aut, prithee give me leave to wish thee jay: I do it *de bon cœur,* strike me dumb: you have married a woman beautiful in her person, charming in her airs, prudent in her conduct, canstant in her inclinations, and of a nice marality, split my windpipe.

Y. FAS.   Your Lordship may keep up your spirits with your grimace, if you please; I shall support mine with this lady and two thousand pound a year.

[*taking* MISS HOYDEN] Come, Madam:
We once again, you see, are man and wife,
And now, perhaps, the bargain's struck for life;
If I mistake, and we should part again,
At least you see you may have choice of men:
Nay, should the war at length such havoc make
That lovers should grow scarce, yet for your sake,
Kind heaven always will preserve a beau:
                                        [*pointing to* LORD FOPPINGTON]
You'll find his Lordship ready to come to.

LORD FOP.   Her ladyship shall stap my vitals if I do.

EPILOGUE

Spoken by LORD FOPPINGTON

Gentlemen and ladies,
These people have regal'd you here to-day
(In my opinion) with a saucy play,
In which the author does presume to show
That coxcomb, *ab origine*—was beau.
Truly I think the thing of so much weight,
That if some smart chastisement ben't his fate,

Gad's curse, it may in time destroy the state.
I hold no one its friend, I must confess,
Who would discauntenance your men of dress.
Far, give me leave t'asberve, good clothes are things
Have ever been of great support to kings:
All treasons come fram slovens; it is nat
Within the reach of gentle beaux to plat.
They have no gall, no spleen, no teeth, no stings,
Of all Gad's creatures, the most harmless things.
Through all recard, no prince was ever slain
By one who had a feather in his brain.
They're men of too refin'd an education,
To squabble with a court—for a vile dirty nation.
I'm very passitive, you never saw
A through republican a finish'd beau.
Nor truly shall you very often see
A Jacobite much better dress'd than he;
In shart, through all the courts that I have been in,
Your men of mischief—still are in faul linen.
Did ever one yet dance the Tyburn jig
With a free air, ar a well pawdered wig?
Did ever highway-man yet bid you stand
With a sweet bawdy snuff-bax in his hand;
Ar do you ever find they ask your purse
As men of breeding do?—Ladies, Gad's curse,
This author is a dag, and 'tis not fit
You should allow him ev'n one grain of wit.
To which, that his pretence may ne'er be nam'd,
My humble motion is—he may be damn'd.

DOVER · THRIFT · EDITIONS

POETRY

LA VITA NUOVA, Dante Alighieri. 56pp. 41915-0

101 GREAT AMERICAN POEMS, The American Poetry & Literacy Project (ed.). (Available in U.S. only.) 96pp. 40158-8

ENGLISH ROMANTIC POETRY: An Anthology, Stanley Appelbaum (ed.). 256pp. 29282-7

DOVER BEACH AND OTHER POEMS, Matthew Arnold. 112pp. 28037-3

SELECTED POEMS FROM "FLOWERS OF EVIL," Charles Baudelaire. 64pp. 28450-6

BHAGAVADGITA, Bhagavadgita. 112pp. 27782-8

THE BOOK OF PSALMS, King James Bible. 128pp. 27541-8

IMAGIST POETRY: AN ANTHOLOGY, Bob Blaisdell (ed.). 176pp. (Available in U.S. only.) 40875-2

BLAKE'S SELECTED POEMS, William Blake. 96pp. 28517-0

SONGS OF INNOCENCE AND SONGS OF EXPERIENCE, William Blake. 64pp. 27051-3

THE CLASSIC TRADITION OF HAIKU: An Anthology, Faubion Bowers (ed.). 96pp. 29274-6

BEST POEMS OF THE BRONTË SISTERS (ed. by Candace Ward), Emily, Anne, and Charlotte Brontë. 64pp. 29529-X

SONNETS FROM THE PORTUGUESE AND OTHER POEMS, Elizabeth Barrett Browning. 64pp. 27052-1

MY LAST DUCHESS AND OTHER POEMS, Robert Browning. 128pp. 27783-6

POEMS AND SONGS, Robert Burns. 96pp. 26863-2

SELECTED POEMS, George Gordon, Lord Byron. 112pp. 27784-4

SELECTED CANTERBURY TALES, Geoffrey Chaucer. 144pp. 28241-4

THE RIME OF THE ANCIENT MARINER AND OTHER POEMS, Samuel Taylor Coleridge. 80pp. 27266-4

WAR IS KIND AND OTHER POEMS, Stephen Crane. 64pp. 40424-2

THE CAVALIER POETS: An Anthology, Thomas Crofts (ed.). 80pp. 28766-1

SELECTED POEMS, Emily Dickinson. 64pp. 26466-1

SELECTED POEMS, John Donne. 96pp. 27788-7

SELECTED POEMS, Paul Laurence Dunbar. 80pp. 29980-5

"THE WASTE LAND" AND OTHER POEMS, T. S. Eliot. 64pp. (Available in U.S. only.) 40061-1

THE CONCORD HYMN AND OTHER POEMS, Ralph Waldo Emerson. 64pp. 29059-X

THE RUBÁIYÁT OF OMAR KHAYYÁM: FIRST AND FIFTH EDITIONS, Edward FitzGerald. 64pp. 26467-X

A BOY'S WILL AND NORTH OF BOSTON, Robert Frost. 112pp. (Available in U.S. only.) 26866-7

THE ROAD NOT TAKEN AND OTHER POEMS, Robert Frost. 64pp. (Available in U.S. only.) 27550-7

HARDY'S SELECTED POEMS, Thomas Hardy. 80pp. 28753-X

"GOD'S GRANDEUR" AND OTHER POEMS, Gerard Manley Hopkins. 80pp. 28729-7

A SHROPSHIRE LAD, A. E. Housman. 64pp. 26468-8

LYRIC POEMS, John Keats. 80pp. 26871-3

GUNGA DIN AND OTHER FAVORITE POEMS, Rudyard Kipling. 80pp. 26471-8

SNAKE AND OTHER POEMS, D. H. Lawrence. 64pp. 40647-4

DOVER·THRIFT·EDITIONS

FICTION

A JOURNAL OF THE PLAGUE YEAR, Daniel Defoe. 192pp. 41919-3

SIX GREAT SHERLOCK HOLMES STORIES, Sir Arthur Conan Doyle. 112pp. 27055-6

SHORT STORIES, Theodore Dreiser. 112pp. 28215-5

SILAS MARNER, George Eliot. 160pp. 29246-0

JOSEPH ANDREWS, Henry Fielding. 288pp. 41588-0

THIS SIDE OF PARADISE, F. Scott Fitzgerald. 208pp. 28999-0

"THE DIAMOND AS BIG AS THE RITZ" AND OTHER STORIES, F. Scott Fitzgerald. 29991-0

MADAME BOVARY, Gustave Flaubert. 256pp. 29257-6

THE REVOLT OF "MOTHER" AND OTHER STORIES, Mary E. Wilkins Freeman. 128pp. 40428-5

A ROOM WITH A VIEW, E. M. Forster. 176pp. (Available in U.S. only.) 28467-0

WHERE ANGELS FEAR TO TREAD, E. M. Forster. 128pp. (Available in U.S. only.) 27791-7

THE IMMORALIST, André Gide. 112pp. (Available in U.S. only.) 29237-1

HERLAND, Charlotte Perkins Gilman. 128pp. 40429-3

"THE YELLOW WALLPAPER" AND OTHER STORIES, Charlotte Perkins Gilman. 80pp. 29857-4

THE OVERCOAT AND OTHER STORIES, Nikolai Gogol. 112pp. 27057-2

CHELKASH AND OTHER STORIES, Maxim Gorky. 64pp. 40652-0

GREAT GHOST STORIES, John Grafton (ed.). 112pp. 27270-2

DETECTION BY GASLIGHT, Douglas G. Greene (ed.). 272pp. 29928-7

THE MABINOGION, Lady Charlotte E. Guest. 192pp. 29541-9

"THE FIDDLER OF THE REELS" AND OTHER SHORT STORIES, Thomas Hardy. 80pp. 29960-0

THE LUCK OF ROARING CAMP AND OTHER STORIES, Bret Harte. 96pp. 27271-0

THE HOUSE OF THE SEVEN GABLES, Nathaniel Hawthorne. 272pp. 40882-5

THE SCARLET LETTER, Nathaniel Hawthorne. 192pp. 28048-9

YOUNG GOODMAN BROWN AND OTHER STORIES, Nathaniel Hawthorne. 128pp. 27060-2

THE GIFT OF THE MAGI AND OTHER SHORT STORIES, O. Henry. 96pp. 27061-0

THE NUTCRACKER AND THE GOLDEN POT, E. T. A. Hoffmann. 128pp. 27806-9

THE ASPERN PAPERS, Henry James. 112pp. 41922-3

THE BEAST IN THE JUNGLE AND OTHER STORIES, Henry James. 128pp. 27552-3

DAISY MILLER, Henry James. 64pp. 28773-4

THE TURN OF THE SCREW, Henry James. 96pp. 26684-2

WASHINGTON SQUARE, Henry James. 176pp. 40431-5

THE COUNTRY OF THE POINTED FIRS, Sarah Orne Jewett. 96pp. 28196-5

THE AUTOBIOGRAPHY OF AN EX-COLORED MAN, James Weldon Johnson. 112pp. 28512-X

DUBLINERS, James Joyce. 160pp. 26870-5

A PORTRAIT OF THE ARTIST AS A YOUNG MAN, James Joyce. 192pp. 28050-0

THE METAMORPHOSIS AND OTHER STORIES, Franz Kafka. 96pp. 29030-1

THE MAN WHO WOULD BE KING AND OTHER STORIES, Rudyard Kipling. 128pp. 28051-9

YOU KNOW ME AL, Ring Lardner. 128pp. 28513-8

SELECTED SHORT STORIES, D. H. Lawrence. 128pp. 27794-1

GREEN TEA AND OTHER GHOST STORIES, J. Sheridan LeFanu. 96pp. 27795-X

THE CALL OF THE WILD, Jack London. 64pp. 26472-6

FIVE GREAT SHORT STORIES, Jack London. 96pp. 27063-7

THE SEA-WOLF, Jack London. 248pp. 41108-7

WHITE FANG, Jack London. 160pp. 26968-X

DEATH IN VENICE, Thomas Mann. 96pp. (Available in U.S. only.) 28714-9

IN A GERMAN PENSION: 13 Stories, Katherine Mansfield. 112pp. 28719-X

THE NECKLACE AND OTHER SHORT STORIES, Guy de Maupassant. 128pp. 27064-5

BARTLEBY AND BENITO CERENO, Herman Melville. 112pp. 26473-4

THE OIL JAR AND OTHER STORIES, Luigi Pirandello. 96pp. 28459-X

THE GOLD-BUG AND OTHER TALES, Edgar Allan Poe. 128pp. 26875-6

TALES OF TERROR AND DETECTION, Edgar Allan Poe. 96pp. 28744-0

DOVER · THRIFT · EDITIONS

NONFICTION

NARRATIVE OF THE LIFE OF FREDERICK DOUGLASS, Frederick Douglass. 96pp. 28499-9
SELF-RELIANCE AND OTHER ESSAYS, Ralph Waldo Emerson. 128pp. 27790-9
THE LIFE OF OLAUDAH EQUIANO, OR GUSTAVUS VASSA, THE AFRICAN, Olaudah Equiano. 192pp. 40661-X
THE AUTOBIOGRAPHY OF BENJAMIN FRANKLIN, Benjamin Franklin. 144pp. 29073-5
TOTEM AND TABOO, Sigmund Freud. 176pp. (Not available in Europe or United Kingdom.) 40434-X
LOVE: A Book of Quotations, Herb Galewitz (ed.). 64pp. 40004-2
PRAGMATISM, William James. 128pp. 28270-8
THE STORY OF MY LIFE, Helen Keller. 80pp. 29249-5
TAO TE CHING, Lao Tze. 112pp. 29792-6
GREAT SPEECHES, Abraham Lincoln. 112pp. 26872-1
THE PRINCE, Niccolò Machiavelli. 80pp. 27274-5
THE SUBJECTION OF WOMEN, John Stuart Mill. 112pp. 29601-6
SELECTED ESSAYS, Michel de Montaigne. 96pp. 29109-X
UTOPIA, Sir Thomas More. 96pp. 29583-4
BEYOND GOOD AND EVIL: Prelude to a Philosophy of the Future, Friedrich Nietzsche. 176pp. 29868-X
THE BIRTH OF TRAGEDY, Friedrich Nietzsche. 96pp. 28515-4
COMMON SENSE, Thomas Paine. 64pp. 29602-4
SYMPOSIUM AND PHAEDRUS, Plato. 96pp. 27798-4
THE TRIAL AND DEATH OF SOCRATES: Four Dialogues, Plato. 128pp. 27066-1
A MODEST PROPOSAL AND OTHER SATIRICAL WORKS, Jonathan Swift. 64pp. 28759-9
CIVIL DISOBEDIENCE AND OTHER ESSAYS, Henry David Thoreau. 96pp. 27563-9
SELECTIONS FROM THE JOURNALS (Edited by Walter Harding), Henry David Thoreau. 96pp. 28760-2
WALDEN; OR, LIFE IN THE WOODS, Henry David Thoreau. 224pp. 28495-6
NARRATIVE OF SOJOURNER TRUTH, Sojourner Truth. 80pp. 29899-X
THE THEORY OF THE LEISURE CLASS, Thorstein Veblen. 256pp. 28062-4
DE PROFUNDIS, Oscar Wilde. 64pp. 29308-4
OSCAR WILDE'S WIT AND WISDOM: A Book of Quotations, Oscar Wilde. 64pp. 40146-4
UP FROM SLAVERY, Booker T. Washington. 160pp. 28738-6
A VINDICATION OF THE RIGHTS OF WOMAN, Mary Wollstonecraft. 224pp. 29036-0

PLAYS

PROMETHEUS BOUND, Aeschylus. 64pp. 28762-9
THE ORESTEIA TRILOGY: Agamemnon, The Libation-Bearers and The Furies, Aeschylus. 160pp. 29242-8
LYSISTRATA, Aristophanes. 64pp. 28225-2
WHAT EVERY WOMAN KNOWS, James Barrie. 80pp. (Not available in Europe or United Kingdom.) 29578-8
THE CHERRY ORCHARD, Anton Chekhov. 64pp. 26682-6
THE SEA GULL, Anton Chekhov. 64pp. 40656-3
THE THREE SISTERS, Anton Chekhov. 64pp. 27544-2
UNCLE VANYA, Anton Chekhov. 64pp. 40159-6
THE WAY OF THE WORLD, William Congreve. 80pp. 27787-9
BACCHAE, Euripides. 64pp. 29580-X
MEDEA, Euripides. 64pp. 27548-5

DOVER · THRIFT · EDITIONS

PLAYS

THE MIKADO, William Schwenck Gilbert. 64pp. 27268-0

FAUST, PART ONE, Johann Wolfgang von Goethe. 192pp. 28046-2

THE INSPECTOR GENERAL, Nikolai Gogol. 80pp. 28500-6

SHE STOOPS TO CONQUER, Oliver Goldsmith. 80pp. 26867-5

A DOLL'S HOUSE, Henrik Ibsen. 80pp. 27062-9

GHOSTS, Henrik Ibsen. 64pp. 29852-3

HEDDA GABLER, Henrik Ibsen. 80pp. 26469-6

THE WILD DUCK, Henrik Ibsen. 96pp. 41116-8

VOLPONE, Ben Jonson. 112pp. 28049-7

DR. FAUSTUS, Christopher Marlowe. 64pp. 28208-2

THE MISANTHROPE, Molière. 64pp. 27065-3

ANNA CHRISTIE, Eugene O'Neill. 80pp. 29985-6

BEYOND THE HORIZON, Eugene O'Neill. 96pp. 29085-9

THE EMPEROR JONES, Eugene O'Neill. 64pp. 29268-1

THE LONG VOYAGE HOME AND OTHER PLAYS, Eugene O'Neill. 80pp. 28755-6

RIGHT YOU ARE, IF YOU THINK YOU ARE, Luigi Pirandello. 64pp. (Not available in Europe or United Kingdom.) 29576-1

SIX CHARACTERS IN SEARCH OF AN AUTHOR, Luigi Pirandello. 64pp. (Not available in Europe or United Kingdom.) 29992-9

PHÈDRE, Jean Racine. 64pp. 41927-4

HANDS AROUND, Arthur Schnitzler. 64pp. 28724-6

ANTONY AND CLEOPATRA, William Shakespeare. 128pp. 40062-X

AS YOU LIKE IT, William Shakespeare. 80pp. 40432-3

HAMLET, William Shakespeare. 128pp. 27278-8

HENRY IV, William Shakespeare. 96pp. 29584-2

JULIUS CAESAR, William Shakespeare. 80pp. 26876-4

KING LEAR, William Shakespeare. 112pp. 28058-6

LOVE'S LABOUR'S LOST, William Shakespeare. 64pp. 41929-0

MACBETH, William Shakespeare. 96pp. 27802-6

MEASURE FOR MEASURE, William Shakespeare. 96pp. 40889-2

THE MERCHANT OF VENICE, William Shakespeare. 96pp. 28492-1

A MIDSUMMER NIGHT'S DREAM, William Shakespeare. 80pp. 27067-X

MUCH ADO ABOUT NOTHING, William Shakespeare. 80pp. 28272-4

OTHELLO, William Shakespeare. 112pp. 29097-2

RICHARD III, William Shakespeare. 112pp. 28747-5

ROMEO AND JULIET, William Shakespeare. 96pp. 27557-4

THE TAMING OF THE SHREW, William Shakespeare. 96pp. 29765-9

THE TEMPEST, William Shakespeare. 96pp. 40658-X

TWELFTH NIGHT; OR, WHAT YOU WILL, William Shakespeare. 80pp. 29290-8

ARMS AND THE MAN, George Bernard Shaw. 80pp. (Not available in Europe or United Kingdom.) 26476-9

HEARTBREAK HOUSE, George Bernard Shaw. 128pp. (Not available in Europe or United Kingdom.) 29291-6

PYGMALION, George Bernard Shaw. 96pp. (Available in U.S. only.) 28222-8

THE RIVALS, Richard Brinsley Sheridan. 96pp. 40433-1

THE SCHOOL FOR SCANDAL, Richard Brinsley Sheridan. 96pp. 26687-7

ANTIGONE, Sophocles. 64pp. 27804-2

OEDIPUS AT COLONUS, Sophocles. 64pp. 40659-8

OEDIPUS REX, Sophocles. 64pp. 26877-2

DOVER·THRIFT·EDITIONS

PLAYS

ELECTRA, Sophocles. 64pp. 28482-4

MISS JULIE, August Strindberg. 64pp. 27281-8

THE PLAYBOY OF THE WESTERN WORLD AND RIDERS TO THE SEA, J. M. Synge. 80pp. 27562-0

THE DUCHESS OF MALFI, John Webster. 96pp. 40660-1

THE IMPORTANCE OF BEING EARNEST, Oscar Wilde. 64pp. 26478-5

LADY WINDERMERE'S FAN, Oscar Wilde. 64pp. 40078-6

BOXED SETS

FAVORITE JANE AUSTEN NOVELS: *Pride and Prejudice*, *Sense and Sensibility* and *Persuasion* (Complete and Unabridged), Jane Austen. 800pp. 29748-9

BEST WORKS OF MARK TWAIN: Four Books, Dover. 624pp. 40226-6

EIGHT GREAT GREEK TRAGEDIES: Six Books, Dover. 480pp. 40203-7

FIVE GREAT ENGLISH ROMANTIC POETS, Dover. 496pp. 27893-X

FIVE GREAT PLAYS, Dover. 368pp. 27179-X

FIVE GREAT POETS: Poems by Shakespeare, Keats, Poe, Dickinson, and Whitman, Dover. 416pp. 26942-6

47 GREAT SHORT STORIES: Stories by Poe, Chekhov, Maupassant, Gogol, O. Henry, and Twain, Dover. 688pp. 27178-1

GREAT AFRICAN-AMERICAN WRITERS: Seven Books, Dover. 704pp. 29995-3

GREAT AMERICAN NOVELS, Dover. 720pp. 28665-7

GREAT ENGLISH NOVELS, Dover. 704pp. 28666-5

GREAT IRISH WRITERS: Five Books, Dover. 672pp. 29996-1

GREAT MODERN WRITERS: Five Books, Dover. 720pp. (Available in U.S. only.) 29458-7

GREAT WOMEN POETS: 4 Complete Books, Dover. 256pp. (Available in U.S. only.) 28388-7

MASTERPIECES OF RUSSIAN LITERATURE: Seven Books, Dover. 880pp. 40665-2

SEVEN GREAT ENGLISH VICTORIAN POETS: Seven Volumes, Dover. 592pp. 40204-5

SIX GREAT AMERICAN POETS: Poems by Poe, Dickinson, Whitman, Longfellow, Frost, and Millay, Dover. 512pp. (Available in U.S. only.) 27425-X

38 SHORT STORIES BY AMERICAN WOMEN WRITERS: Five Books, Dover. 512pp. 29459-5

26 GREAT TALES OF TERROR AND THE SUPERNATURAL, Dover. 608pp. (Available in U.S. only.) 27891-3